Workplace Romance:

Prescription of Love

AMY ANDREWS

CAROL MARINELLI

TINA BECKETT

MILLS & BOON

First Published in Great Britain 2024
by Mills & Boon, an imprint of HarperCollins*Publishers* Ltd,
1 London Bridge Street, London, SE1 9GF

www.harpercollins.co.uk

HarperCollins*Publishers*
Macken House, 39/40 Mayor Street Upper,
Dublin 1, D01 C9W8, Ireland

Workplace Romance: Prescription of Love © 2024 Harlequin Enterprises ULC.

Tempted by Mr Off-Limits © 2018 Amy Andrews
Seduced by the Sheikh Surgeon © 2016 Carol Marinelli
One Hot Night with Dr Cardoza © 2020 Tina Beckett

ISBN: 978-0-263-32310-8

This book contains FSC™ certified paper and other controlled sources to ensure responsible forest management.

For more information visit: www.harpercollins.co.uk/green

Printed and Bound in the UK using 100% Renewable Electricity at CPI Group (UK) Ltd, Croydon, CR0 4YY

TEMPTED BY MR OFF-LIMITS

AMY ANDREWS

I dedicate this book to my brother-in-law
Ron MacMaster,

a great husband and father who was taken too young.

You are greatly missed.

CHAPTER ONE

LOLA FRASER NEEDED a drink in the worse way. Thank God for Billi's, the bar across the road from the Kirribilli General Hospital. The ice-blue neon of the welcome sign filled her with relief—she didn't think she could wait until she got home to Manly and it was less than a thirty-minute drive at nine-thirty on a Sunday night.

The place was jumping. There was some music playing on the old-fashioned jukebox but it wasn't too loud. Most of the noise was coming from a large group of people Lola recognised as belonging to the Herd Across the Harbour event. It had taken place earlier today and they were all clearly celebrating the success of the fundraising venture.

Grace, Lola's bestie and flatmate, was the renal transplant co-ordinator for the hospital and had been one of the organisers. In fact, her entire family had been heavily involved. Lola had also been roped in to help out this morning before her afternoon shift, and although she'd gratefully escaped horses, cows and, well…anything country a long time ago, there had been something magnificent about all those cattle walking over the Sydney Harbour Bridge.

Talk about a contrast—one of the world's most iconic architectural landmarks overrun by large, hooved beasts.

It had certainly made a splash on news services all around the world. Not to mention the pile of money it had raised for dialysis machines for rural and remote hospitals. And then there was the exposure it had given to the Australian Organ Donor Register and the importance of talking with family about your wishes.

A conversation Lola wished her patient tonight had taken the time to have with his family. Maybe, out of his tragic death, some other families could have started living again.

And she was back to needing a drink.

She moved down the bar, away from the happy crowd. Their noise was good—celebratory and distracting—but she couldn't really relate to that right now.

Gary, a big bear of a man, took one look at her and said, 'You okay?'

Lola shook her head, a sudden rush of emotion thickening her throat. Gary had been running the bar over the road for a lot of years now and knew all the Kirribilli staff who frequented his establishment. He also knew, in that freaky bartender way, if a shift hadn't gone so well.

'Whaddya need?'

'Big, *big* glass of wine.'

He didn't bat an eyelid at her request. 'Your car in the multi-storey?'

Lola nodded. 'I'll get a cab home.' She had another afternoon shift tomorrow so she'd get a cab to work and drive her car home tomorrow night.

Within thirty seconds, Gary placed a chilled glass of white wine in front of her. It was over the standard drink line clearly marked on the glass. *Well* over.

'Let me know when you want a refill.'

Lola gave him a grateful smile. She loved it that Gary

already knew this was a more-than-one-glass-of-wine night. 'Thanks.'

Raising the glass to her lips, Lola took three huge swallows and shut her eyes, trying to clear her mind of the last few hours. Working in Intensive Care was the most rewarding work she'd done in the thirty years of her life. People came to them *desperately* ill and mostly they got better and went home. And that was such an *incredible* process to be a part of.

But not everyone was so lucky.

For the most part, Lola coped with the flip side. She'd learned how to compartmentalise the tragedies and knew the importance of debriefing with colleagues. She also knew that sometimes you weren't ready to talk about it. And for that there was booze, really loud music and streaming movies.

Sometimes sex.

And she had no problems with using any of them for their temporary amnesiac qualities.

Lola took another gulp of her wine but limited it to just the one this time.

'Now, what's a gorgeous woman like you doing sitting at a bar all by yourself?'

Lola smiled at the low voice behind her, and the fine blonde hairs at her nape that had escaped the loose low plait stood to attention. 'Hamish.'

Hamish Gibson laughed softly and easily as he plonked himself down on the chair beside her. Her heart fluttered a little as it has this morning when she'd first met him on the Harbour Bridge. He was tall and broad and good looking. And he knew it.

Patently up for some recreational sex.

But he was also Grace's brother and staying at their

apartment for the night. So it would be wrong to jump his bones.

Right?

She *could* have a drink with him, though, and he wasn't exactly hard on the eyes. 'Let me buy you a drink,' she said.

He grinned that lovely easy grin she'd been so taken with this morning. She'd bet he *killed* the ladies back home with that grin. *That mouth.*

'Isn't that supposed to be my line?'

'You're in the big smoke now,' she teased. 'We Sydney women tend to be kinda forthright. Got a problem with that?'

'Absolutely none. I love forthright women.' He gestured to Gary and ordered a beer. 'And for you?'

Lola lifted her still quite full glass. 'I'm good.' She took another big swig.

Hamish's keen blue eyes narrowed a little. 'Bad shift?'

'I've had better.'

He nodded. Hamish was a paramedic so Lola was certain she didn't have to explain her current state of mind. 'You wanna talk about it?'

'Nope.' Another gulp of her wine.

'You wanna get drunk?'

'Nope. Just a little distracted.'

He grinned again and things a little lower than Lola's heart fluttered this time. 'I give good distraction.'

Lola laughed. 'You *are* good distraction.'

'And you are good for my ego, Lola Fraser.'

'Yeah. I can tell your ego is badly in need of resuscitation.'

He threw back his head and laughed and Lola followed the very masculine line of his throat etched with five o'clock shadow to a jaw so square he could have been a cartoon superhero. Was it wrong she wanted to lick him there?

Gary placed Hamish's beer on the bar in front of him and he picked it up. 'What shall we drink to?'

Lola smiled. 'Crappy shifts?'

'Here's to crappy shifts.' He tapped his glass against the rim of hers. 'And distractions.'

They were home by eleven. Lola had drunk another—standard—glass of wine and Hamish had sat on his beer. They'd chatted about the Herd Across the Harbour event and cattle and he'd made her laugh about his hometown of Toowoomba and some of the incidents he'd gone to as a paramedic. He *was* a great distraction in every sense of the word but when she'd started to yawn he'd insisted on driving them home and she'd directed.

But now they were here, Lola wasn't feeling tired. In fact, she dreaded going to bed. She wasn't drunk enough to switch off her brain—only pleasantly buzzed—and sex with Hamish was out of the question.

Completely off-limits.

'You fancy another drink?' She headed through to the kitchen and made a beeline for the fridge. She ignored the three postcards attached with magnets to the door. They were from her Aunty May's most recent travels—India, Vietnam and South Korea. Normally they made her smile but tonight they made her feel restless.

She was off to Zimbabwe for a month next April. It couldn't come soon enough.

'Ah…sure. Okay.'

He didn't sound very sure. 'Past your bedtime?' she teased as she pulled a bottle of wine and a beer out of the fridge.

He smiled as he took the beer. His thick, wavy, nutmeg

hair flopped down over his forehead and made her want to furrow her fingers in it. There were red-gold highlights in it that shone in the downlights and reminded Lola of Grace's gorgeous red hair.

'I'd have thought Grace would still be up.'

Lola snorted. 'I'm sure she is. Just not here. Did you forget she got engaged to Marcus today?'

'No.' He grinned. 'I didn't forget.'

'Yes well…' Lola poured her wine. 'I'm pretty sure they're probably *celebrating*. If you get my drift.'

The way his gaze strayed to her mouth left Lola in no doubt he did.

'He's a good guy, yeah?'

'Oh, yeah.' Lola nodded. 'They're both hopelessly in love.'

Lola was surprised at the little pang that hit her square in the chest. She'd never yearned for a happily ever after—she liked being footloose and fancy-free. Why on earth would she suddenly feel like she was missing something?

She shook it away. It was just *this* night. This awful, awful night. 'Let's go out to the balcony.'

She didn't wait for him to follow her or even check to see if he was—she could *feel* the weight of his gaze on her back. On her ass, actually, and she wished she was in something more glamorous than her navy work trousers and the pale blue pinstriped blouse with the hospital logo on the left pocket.

Lola leaned against the railing when she reached her destination, looking out over the parkland opposite, the night breeze cool as befitting August in Sydney. She could just detect the faint trace of the ocean—salt and sand—despite being miles from Manly Beach.

She loved that smell and inhaled it deeply, pulling it

into her lungs, savouring it, grateful for nights like this. Grateful to be alive. And suddenly the view was blurring before her eyes and the faint echo of a thirteen-year-old girl's cries wrapped fingers around Lola's heart and squeezed.

Her patient tonight would never feel the sea breeze on his face again. His wife and two kids would probably never appreciate something as simple ever again.

'Hey.'

She hadn't heard Hamish approach and she quickly shut her eyes to stop the moisture becoming tears. But he lifted her chin with his finger and she opened them. She was conscious of the dampness on her lashes as she was drawn into his compelling blue gaze. 'Are you sure you don't want to talk about it?'

His voice was low and Lola couldn't stop staring at him. He was wearing one of those checked flannel shirts that was open at the throat and blue jeans, soft and faded from years of wear and tear. They fitted him in all the right places. He radiated warmth and smelled like beer and the salt and vinegar chips they'd eaten at the bar, and she *wanted* to talk about it.

Who knew, maybe it would help? Maybe talking with a guy who'd probably seen his fair share of his own crappy shifts would be a relief. Lola turned back to the view across the darkened park. His hand fell away, but she was conscious of his nearness, of the way his arm brushed hers.

'My patient… He was pronounced brain dead tonight. We switched him off. He had teenage kids and…' She shrugged, shivering as the echo of grief played through her mind again. 'It was…hard to watch.'

Her voice had turned husky and tears pricked again at the backs of her eyes. She blinked them away once more as he turned to his side, his hip against the railing, watching her.

'Sorry...' She dashed away a tear that had refused to be quelled. 'I'm being melodramatic.'

He shrugged. 'Some get to you more than others.'

The sentiment was simple but the level of understanding was anything but and something gave a little inside Lola at his response. There were no meaningless platitudes about *tomorrow being another day* or empty compliments about what an *angel* she must be. Hamish understood that sometimes a patient sneaked past the armour.

'True but... Just ignore me.' She shot him a watery smile.

'I'm being stupid.'

He shook his head. 'No, you're not.'

Lola gave a half laugh, half snort. 'Yes. I am. My tears aren't important.' This wasn't about her. It was about a family who'd just lost everything. 'This man's death shouldn't be about my grief. I don't know what's wrong with me tonight.'

'I think it's called being human.'

He smiled at her with such gentleness and insight she really, really wanted to cry. But she didn't, she turned blind eyes back to the view, her arm brushing his. Neither said anything for long moments as they sipped at their drinks.

'Was it trauma?' Hamish asked.

'Car accident.' Lola was glad to be switching from the *emotion* of the death to the more practical facts of it.

'Did he donate his organs?'

Hamish and Grace's sister-in-law, Merridy, had undergone a kidney transplant four years ago, so Lola knew the issue meant a lot to the Gibson family.

She shook her head. 'No.'

'Was he not a candidate?'

Lola could hear the frown in Hamish's voice as she shook her head, a lump thickening her throat. What the hell was *wrong* with her tonight? She was usually excellent at shaking this stuff off.

'He wasn't on the register?'

The lump blossomed and pressed against Lola's vocal cords. She cleared her throat. 'He was but…'

Her sentence trailed off and she could see Hamish nod in her peripheral vision as realisation dawned. It was a relief not to have to say it. That Hamish knew the cold hard facts and she didn't have to go into them or try and explain something that made no sense to most people.

'I hate when that happens.' Hamish's knuckles turned white as he gripped the railing.

'Me too.'

'It's wrong that family can override the patient in situations like that.'

She couldn't agree more but the fact of the matter was that family always had the final say in these matters, regardless of the patient's wishes.

'Why can't doctors just say, too bad, this was clearly your loved one's intention when they put their name down on the donation register?'

Lola gave a half-smile, understanding the frustration but knowing it was never as simple as that. 'Because we don't believe in further traumatising people who are already in the middle of their worst nightmare.'

It was difficult to explain how her role as a nurse changed in situations of impending death. How her duty of care shifted—mentally anyway—from her patient to the family. In a weird way they became her responsibility too and trying to help ease them through such a terrible time in their lives—even just a little—became paramount.

They were going to have to live on, after all, and how the hospital process was managed had a significant bearing on how they coped with their grief.

'Loved ones don't say no out of spite or grief or even personal belief, Hamish. They say no because they've *never* had a conversation with that person about it. And if they've never *specifically* heard that person say they want their organs donated in the event of their death. They...' Lola shrugged '...err on the side of caution.'

It was such a terrible time to have to make that kind of decision when people were grappling with so much already.

'I know, I know.' He sighed and he sounded as heavy-hearted as she'd felt when her patient's wife had tearfully declined to give consent for organ donation.

'Which is why things like Herd Across the Harbour are so important.' Lola made an effort to drag them back from the dark abyss she'd been trying to step back from all night, turning slightly to face him, the railing almost at her waist. 'Raising awareness about people having those kinds of conversations is vital. So they know and support the wishes of their nearest and dearest if it ever comes to an end-of-life situation.'

She raised her glass towards him and Hamish smiled and tapped his beer bottle against it. 'Amen.'

They didn't drink, though, they just stared at each other, the blue of his eyes as mesmerising in the night as the perfect symmetry of his jaw and cheekbones and the fullness of his mouth. They were close, their thighs almost brushing, their hands a whisper apart on the railing.

Lola was conscious of his heat and his solidness and

the urge to put her head on his chest and just be held was surprisingly strong.

When was the last time she'd wanted to be just held by a man?

The need echoed in the sudden thickness of her blood and the stirring deep inside her belly, although neither of them felt particularly platonic. Confused by her feelings, she pushed up onto her tippy-toes and kissed him, trapping their drinks between them.

She shouldn't have. *She really shouldn't have.*

But, oh…it was lovely. The feel of his arms coming around her, the heat of his mouth, the swipe of his tongue. The quick rush of warmth to her breasts and belly and thighs. The funny bump of her heart in her chest.

The way he groaned her name against her mouth.

But she had to stop. 'I'm sorry.' She broke away and took a reluctant step back. 'I shouldn't have done that.'

His fingers on the railing covered hers. 'Yeah,' he whispered. 'You absolutely should have.'

Lola gave him a half-smile, touched by his certainty but knowing it couldn't go anywhere. She slipped her hand out from under his, smiled again then turned away, heading straight to her room and shutting out temptation.

CHAPTER TWO

BUT LOLA COULDN'T SLEEP. Not after finishing her glass of wine in bed or taking a bath or one of those all-natural sleeping tablets that usually did the trick. She lay awake staring at the ceiling, the events of the shift playing over and over in her head.

Her patient's wife saying, *'But there's not a scratch on him...'* and his daughter crying, *'No, Daddy!'* and his teenage son being all stoic and brave and looking so damn *stricken* it still clawed at her gut. The faces and the words turned around and around, a noisy wrenching jumble inside her head, while the oppressive weight of silence in the house practically deafened her.

She felt...alone...she realised. Damn it, she *never* felt alone. She was often here by herself overnight if Grace was at work or at Marcus's and it had never bothered her before. She'd *never* felt alone in a city. But tonight she did.

It was because Hamish was out there. She knew that. Human company—*male company*—was lying on the couch and she was in here, staring at the shadows on the ceiling. And because it wouldn't be the first time she'd turned to a man to forget a bad shift, her body was restless with confusion.

Was it healthy to *sex* away her worries? No. But it wasn't a regular habit and it sure as hell helped from time to time.

Lola had no doubt Hamish would be up for it. He'd been flirting with her from the beginning and he'd certainly been all in when she'd kissed him on the balcony. The message in his eyes when she'd pulled away had been loud and clear.

If you want to take this to the bedroom, I'm your guy.

And if he hadn't been Grace's brother, she would have followed through. And not just because she needed the distraction but because there was something about Hamish Gibson that tugged at her. She'd felt it on the bridge this morning *and* at the bar.

It was no doubt to do with his empathy, with his innate understanding of what she'd witnessed tonight. She didn't usually go for men who came from her world, particularly in these situations. Someone outside it—who didn't know or care what she'd been through—was usually a much better distraction.

Someone who only cared about getting her naked.

Who knew familiarity and empathy could be so damn sexy? Who knew they could stroke right between your legs as well as clutch at your heart?

Lola rolled on her side and stuffed her hands between her thighs to quell the heat and annoying buzz of desire. *Wasn't going to happen.* Hamish was Grace's brother. And she *couldn't* go there. No matter how much she needed the distraction. No matter how well he kissed. No matter the fire licking through her veins and roaring at the juncture of her legs.

Lola shut her eyes—tight.

Go to sleep, damn it.

* * *

At two o'clock in the morning, Lola gave up trying to fight it. Grace wasn't here—she'd texted an hour ago to say she was staying at Marcus's—and Hamish would be gone in the morning.

What could it hurt? As long as he knew it was a one-off?

Decision made, she kicked off the sheet and stood. She paused as she contemplated her attire, her underwear and a tank top. Should she dress in something else? Slip on one of her satiny scraps of lingerie that covered more but left absolutely nothing to the imagination? She'd been surprised to learn over the years that some guys preferred subtlety.

Or should she go out there buck naked?

What kind of guy was Hamish—satin and lace or bare flesh?

Oh, bloody hell. What was wrong with her? *Had she lost her freaking mind?* Hamish was probably just going to be grateful for her giving it up for him at two in the morning and smart enough to take it any way it was offered. She was going to be naked soon enough anyway.

Just get out there, Lola!

Quickly snatching a condom out of the box in her bedside drawer, she headed for her door, opened it and tiptoed down the darkened hallway. Ambient light from a variety of electrical appliances cast a faint glow into the living room and she could make out a large form on the couch. She came closer, stepping around the coffee table to avoid a collision with her shins, and the form became more defined.

He'd kicked off the sheet, which meant Lola could see a lot of bare skin—abs, legs, chest—and she looked her fill. A pair of black boxer briefs stopped her from seeing *everything* and his face was hidden by one bare arm thrown up over it. The roundness of his biceps as it pushed against his jaw was distracting as all giddy up.

As was the long stretch of his neck.

It was tempting to do something really crazy like run her fingers along that exposed, whiskery skin. Possibly her tongue.

But she needed to wake him first. She couldn't just jump on him, no matter how temptingly he was lying there.

Lola clenched her fists, the sharp foil edges of the condom cutting into her palm as she took a step towards him. Her foot landed on the only squeaky floorboard in the entire room and he was awake in an instant. She froze as his abs tensed and his body furled upwards, his legs swinging over the edge of the couch. His feet had found the floor before she had a chance to take another breath.

He blinked up at her, running his palms absently up and down the length of his bare thighs. 'Lola?'

Lola let out a shaky breath as she took a step back. 'I guess it's true what they say about country guys, then.'

'Hung like horses?' He shot her a sleepy smile. His voice was low and rumbly but alert.

She laughed and it was loud in the night. 'Light sleepers.'

'Oh, that.' He rubbed his palm along his jawline and the scratchy noise went straight to her belly button. 'Are you okay?'

Lola shook her head, her heart suddenly racing as she contemplated the width of his shoulders and the proposition she was about to lay on him. 'I...can't sleep.'

'So you came out for...a cup of warm milk?'

The smile on his face matched the one in his voice, all playful and teasing, and Lola blushed. Her cheeks actually heated! What the hell?

Since when did she start blushing?

Most nurses she knew, including herself, were generally immune to embarrassment. She'd seen far too much stuff in her job to be embarrassed by *anything*.

'No.' She held up the condom, her fingers trembling slightly, grateful for the cover of night. 'I was thinking of something more…physical.'

His gaze slid to the condom and Lola's belly clenched as he contemplated the foil packet like it was the best damn thing he'd seen all night. 'I have read,' he said after a beat or two, refocusing on her face, 'that *physical activity* is very good for promoting sleep.'

Lola's nipples puckered at the slight emphasis on 'physical activity' and she swallowed against a mouth suddenly dry as the couch fabric. 'Yeah.' She smiled. 'I read that too.'

He held out his hand. 'Come here.'

Lola's heart leapt in her chest but she ground her feet into the floor. They had to establish some ground rules. 'This can only be a one-time thing.'

'I know.'

His assurance grazed Lola's body like a physical force, rubbing against all the *good* spots, but she needed to make certain he was absolutely on the same page. 'You're leaving tomorrow,' she continued. 'We'll probably never see each other again.' This was the first time she'd met Hamish after all, despite having lived with Grace for almost all the last two years. 'And I'm good with that.'

'Me too.'

'I don't do relationships. Especially not long-distance relationships.'

He nodded again. 'I understand. We're one and done. I *am* good with it, Lola.'

'Also… I don't think we should tell Grace about this.'

He sat back a little, clearly startled at the suggestion,

looking slightly askance. 'Do I look like I took a stupid pill to you?'

Lola laughed. He looked like he'd taken an up-for-it pill and heat wound through her abdomen. Hamish leaned forward at the hips and crooked his finger, a small smile playing on his wicked mouth.

'Come here, *Lola*.'

The way he said her name when he was mostly naked was like fingers stroking down her belly. Lola took a small step forward, her entire body trembling with anticipation. She took another and then she was standing in front of him, the outsides of her thighs just skimming the insides of his knees.

He held his hand out and she placed the condom in his palm. He promptly shoved it under a cushion before sliding his hands onto the sides of her thighs. Lola's breath hitched as they slid all the way up and the muscles in her stomach jumped as they slid under the hem of her T-shirt, pushing it up a little.

Leaning closer, he brushed his mouth against the bare skin, his lips touching down just under her belly button. Lola's mouth parted on a soft gasp and her hands found his shoulders as their gazes locked. One hand kept travelling, pushing into the thick wavy locks of his hair, holding him there as they stared at each other, their breathing low and rough.

Then he fell back against the couch, pulling her with him, urging her legs apart so she was straddling him, the heat and pulse at her heart settling over the heat and hardness of him.

His hands slid into her hair, pulling her head down, his mouth seeking hers.

Her pulse thundered through her ears and throbbed

between her legs and she moaned as their lips met. She couldn't have stopped it even had she wanted to.

And she didn't.

He swallowed it up, his mouth opening over hers, a faint trace of his toothpaste a cool undercurrent to all the heat. He kissed her slow but deep, wet and thorough, and Lola's entire body tingled and yearned as she clutched at his shoulders from her dominant position, moaning and gasping against his mouth.

He was all she could think about. His mouth and his heat and the hardness between his legs. No work, no death, no stricken children, no disbelieving wives. Just Hamish, good and hard and hot and *hers*, filling her senses and her palms and the space between her thighs.

Lola barely registered falling or the softness of landing as his hands guided her backwards. But she did register the long naked stretch of him against her. The way his hips settled into the cradle of her pelvis, the way his erection notched along the seam of her sex, the way his body pressed her hard and good into the cushions.

He was dominating her now and she loved it. Wanted more. *Needed* more. His skin sliding over hers. His body sliding *into* hers. It was as if he could read her mind. His hands pushing her shirt up, gliding over her stomach and ribs and breasts, pulling it off over her head before returning to her breasts, squeezing and kneading, pinching her nipples, his mouth coming back hard and hot on hers, kissing and kissing and kissing until she was dizzy with the magic of his mouth, clawing at his back and gasping her pleasure.

He kissed down her neck and traced the lines of her collar bones with the tip of his tongue before lapping it over her sternum and circling her nipples, sucking each one into his mouth making her cry out, making her mutter, *'Yes, yes, yes,'* in some kind of incoherent jumble. And he kept doing it, licking and sucking as his hands pushed at her underwear and hers pushed at his until they were both free of barriers.

He broke away, tearing the foil open and rolling the condom on, then he was back and she almost lost her breath at the thickness of his erection sliding between her legs. He was big and hard, gliding through her slickness, finding her entrance and settling briefly.

'You feel so good,' he muttered, before easing inside her, slowly at first then pushing home on a groan that stirred the cells in her marrow and lit the wick on her arousal.

She flared like a torch in the night, insane with wanting him, wanting him more than she'd ever wanted anybody before, panting her need straight into his ear, *'God yes*, like that,' revelling in the thickness of him, the way he stretched her, the way he filled her. 'Just like that…'

And he gave it to her like *that* and more, rocking and pounding, kissing her again, swallowing her moans and her cries and her pants, smothering them with his own as he thrust in and pulled out, a slow steady stroke, the rhythm of his hips setting the rhythm in her blood and the sizzle in her cells. Electricity buzzed from the base of her spine to the arch of her neck.

Her mind was blank of everything but the heat and the thrust and the feel of him. The prison of his strong, rounded biceps either side of her and the broad, naked cage of his chest pinning her to the couch and the piston of his hard, narrow hips nailing her into the cushions. And the smell of him, hot and male and aroused, filling up her head, making her nostrils flare with the wild mix of toothpaste and testosterone.

Lola gasped, tearing her mouth from his as her orgasm

burst around her, starting in her toes, curling them tight before rolling north, undulating through her calves and her knees and her thighs, exploding between her legs and imploding inside her belly, breaking over her in waves of ever-increasing intensity until all she could do was hold on and cry out *'Hamish!'* as it took her.

'I know.' He panted into her neck, his breathing hot and heavy, his body trembling like hers. 'I know.' He reared above her, thrusting hard one last time, his back bowed, his fists ground into the cushions either side of her head. *'Lola-a-a...'*

He came hard, his release bellowing out of him as his hips took over again and he rocked and rocked and rocked her, pushing her orgasm higher and higher and higher, taking her with him all the way to top until they were both spent, panting and clinging and falling back to earth in a messy heap of limbs and satisfaction.

Lola hadn't even realised she'd drifted off to sleep when Hamish moved away and she muttered something in protest. He hushed her as she drifted again. Somewhere in the drunken quagmire of her brain she thought she should get up and leave, but it was nice here in the afterglow.

Too nice to move.

Hell, a normal woman would have dragged him back to her bed. It was bigger with a lot more potential for further nocturnal activity of the carnal kind. But then he was back and he was shuffling in behind her, his heavy arm dragging her close as he spooned her and she could barely open her eyes let alone co-ordinate her brain and limbs to make a move.

She was finally in a place where there was *nothing* on her mind and she liked it there.

She liked it very, very much.

CHAPTER THREE

Three months later...

HAMISH WASN'T SURE how he was going to be greeted by Lola as he stood in front of her door. Sure, they'd *spoken* in the last few weeks since Grace had arranged for him to live with Lola for the next two months while he did his urban intensive care rotation, but they hadn't *seen* each other since that night.

And he still wasn't sure this was the wisest idea.

He'd assured Lola that he could find somewhere else. Had stressed that she shouldn't let Grace steamroller her into sharing her home with him because his sister felt guilty about her snap decision to finally move in with Marcus. It was true, someone paying the rent for the next eight weeks would give Lola time and breathing space to find the *right* roomie rather than just *a* roomie, but Grace wasn't aware of their history.

Unless Lola had told Grace. But he didn't think his sister would be so keen on this proposed temporary arrangement if that had been the case. Neither did he think for a single second that he wouldn't have heard from her about it if she did know.

Lola had assured him she hadn't felt backed into a corner and it made perfect sense for him to live with her temporarily. It would help her out and their apartment was conveniently located for him.

Perfect sense.

Except for their chemistry. And for the number of times he'd thought about her these past three months. He'd told her it had been unforgettable and that had proved to be frustratingly true. How often had he thought about ringing her? Or sending her flirty texts? Not to mention how often he'd dreamed about her.

About what they'd done. And the things he still wanted to do.

Things that woke him in the middle of the night with her scent in his nostrils and a raging erection that never seemed satisfied with his hand. He shut his eyes against the movie reel of images.

Just roomies.

That's what she'd insisted on when they'd spoken about the possibility of this. Insisted that what had happened between them was in the past and they weren't going to speak of it again. They definitely weren't going to *act* on it again.

Just roomies. That was the deal-breaker, she'd said.

And he'd agreed. After all, it hadn't seemed *too* difficult over a thousand kilometres away. But standing in front of her door like this, the *reality* of her looming, was an entirely different prospect. He felt like a nervous teenager, which was utterly idiotic.

Where was the country guy who could rope a cow, ride a horse, mend a fence and fix just about any engine? Where was the paramedic who could do CPR for an hour, stabilise a trauma victim in the middle of nowhere in the pouring rain, smash a window or rip off a door and insert an IV practically hanging upside down like a bat in the shell of car crashed halfway down a mountain?

That's who he was. So he *could* share a home, in a purely platonic way, with a woman he was hot for.

Because he was a grown man, damn it!

Hamish knocked quickly before he stood any longer staring at the door like he'd lost his mind. His hand shook and his pulse spiked as the sound of her footsteps drew nearer.

The door opened abruptly and Lola stood there in her uniform. He wondered absently if she was going *to* or coming *from* work as his body registered more basic details. Like her gorgeous green eyes and the blonde curls pulled back into a loose plait at her nape, just as it had been that night at Billi's.

Suddenly he was back there again, remembering how much she'd *touched* him that night. *Emotionally.* How much he'd wanted to comfort her. To ease the burden so clearly weighing heavily on her shoulders.

To make her smile.

She smiled at him now and he blinked and came back to the present. It was the kind of smile she'd given him when she'd first met him on the harbour bridge that morning—friendly and open. The kind of smile reserved for a best friend's brother or a new roomie. Like they were buddies. *Mates.*

Like he'd never been inside her body.

She'd obviously put what had happened between them behind her. Way, *way* behind her.

'Hey, you.' She leaned forward, rising on tiptoe to kiss him on the cheek.

Like a sister.

It was such an exaggeratedly platonic kiss but his body tensed in recognition anyway. She was soft and warm and smelled exactly like he remembered, and he fought the urge to turn his head and kiss her properly.

She pulled back and smiled another friendly smile and he forced himself to relax. Forced himself to lounge lazily in the doorway and pretend he didn't want to be inside her again. *Right now.* Because he really, really did.

This is what you agreed to, *dumbass.*

'That all you got?' She tipped her chin at his battered-looking duffel bag.

Hamish glanced down, pleased to have some other direction to look. 'Should I have more?' She didn't seem impressed by his ninja packing skills.

She tutted and shook her head. 'After two months in the city you'll need that for your skin products alone.'

Laughter danced in her eyes and Hamish was impressed with her ability to act like nothing had happened between them while he felt stripped bare. Lola Fraser was as cool as a cucumber.

'I'll have you all metrosexual before you know it.'

Hamish laughed. Was that what she liked in a man? A guy who spent more time in front of the mirror than she did? Who used skin care products and waxed places that he wouldn't let hot wax anywhere near? 'Thanks. I'm happy with the way I am.'

And so were you. He suppressed the urge to give voice to the thought. He wasn't naive enough to think he'd been anything other than a port in a storm for Lola. A convenient distraction. He'd known full well what he'd been agreeing to that night.

Hell, he'd been *more* than happy to be used.

'Ah I see. You can take the boy out of the country—'

'But not the country out of the boy.' He laughed again as he finished the saying.

She grinned and said, 'We'll see,' then stood aside. 'Come on in.'

Hamish picked up his duffel bag and followed her inside. Lola gave him a quick tour even though he was familiar with the layout from that night three months ago and nothing appeared to have changed.

The couch was *definitely* the same. He had no idea how he was going to sit on it with her without some seriously sexy flashbacks.

'And this is Grace's room.' Lola walked past a shut door on the opposite side of the short hallway, which Hamish assumed was Lola's room. 'She moved out a couple of days ago.'

Hamish hadn't been in his sister's bedroom when he'd last been here. He hadn't been in Lola's either. Not that that had stopped them…

'Make yourself at home.' She swept her arm around to indicate the space. 'It's a good size with big built-in cupboards and several power points if you want a TV or something in here.'

Hamish looked around. Grace had left her bed for him and the bedside tables. Everything was ruthlessly clean as per his sister's ways. They could have taken an appendix out on the stripped mattress. Although now they were both in the room together with a massive bed dominating the space, other things they could do on the mattress came to mind.

Lola was staring at it too as if she was just realising the level of temptation it represented. 'There are sheets, pillows, blankets, etcetera in the linen cupboard in the hallway.'

'Thanks.' Hamish threw his bag on the bed to fill up the acres of space staring back at them. And to stop himself from throwing her on it instead.

The action seemed to snap Lola out of her fixation. 'And that's it.' She turned. 'Tour over.'

Once again Hamish followed her down the hallway

and into the kitchen, where she grabbed her bag and keys off the counter top. 'I'm sorry, I have to run now or I'll be late for work. I couldn't swap the shift.'

She didn't sound that sorry. In fact, she was jingling the keys like she couldn't wait to get out of there.

'It's fine.'

A part of him had assumed she'd be home this weekend to help him get settled. *Which was ridiculous*. He was a thirty-year-old man living in one of the world's most exciting cities—he didn't need to have his hand held.

And Lola was a shift worker, just like him. With bills to pay and a twenty-four-hour roster she helped to fill, including Saturdays. She had her own life that didn't involve pandering to her friend's brother.

'I'm sure I can occupy myself. What time do you finish?'

She fished in her bag and pulled out her sunglasses, opening the arms and perching them on the top of her head. 'I'm on till nine-thirty tonight. I should be home by ten, providing everything is calm at work.'

'Cool.'

'Help yourself to whatever's in the fridge. There's a supermarket three blocks away, if you're looking for something in particular. Grace and I usually shopped together and split the bill but we can discuss those details tomorrow.'

Hamish nodded. 'I'm having dinner with Grace and Marcus tonight actually. At their new apartment. So we'll probably be getting in around the same time.'

'Oh…right.' She glanced away and Hamish wondered if she was remembering the last time they'd been here together at night. She had some colour in her cheeks when her gaze met his again. 'Don't feel like you have to be home for me. If you want to have a few drinks and end up crashing at theirs, that's fine. I'm often here by myself, it doesn't bother me.'

Hamish didn't think anything much bothered Lola. There was a streak of independence about her that grabbed him by his country-boy balls. But *he* knew that under all that Independent Woman of the World crust was someone who could break like a little girl and he really hoped she didn't feel the need to pretend to be tough all the time to compensate for how vulnerable she'd been the last time they'd met.

That would be an exhausting eight weeks for her.

And he just wanted Lola to be Lola. He could handle whatever she threw at him.

'And miss my first night in my new home?' He smiled at her to keep it light. 'No way.'

'Okay, well…' She nodded. 'I'll…see you later.'

She turned and walked away, choosing the longer route rather than brush past him—*interesting*—and within seconds he was listening to the quiet click of the front door as it shut.

Well…that was an anti-climax. He'd been building this meeting up in his head for weeks. None of the scenarios had involved Lola bolting within twenty minutes of his arrival. Still, it *had* been good, seeing her again. And she had *definitely* avoided any chance that they might come into contact as she'd left.

That had to mean something, right?

Hamish rolled his eyes as he realised where his brain was heading. *Get a grip,* idiot. *Not going to happen.*

And he went to unpack and make up his bed.

It was a relief to get to work. A relief to stop thinking about Hamish. It was crazy but Lola hadn't expected to feel what she'd felt when she'd opened the door to him.

She'd actually been looking forward to seeing Hamish again. Quite aside from the sex, he was a nice guy and a fun to be around. Even a few months later she still caught herself smiling at the memory of the note she'd found the morning after they'd had sex on the couch.

> *You looked so beautiful sleeping I didn't want to disturb you.*
> *I'm heading home now.*
> *Thank you for an unforgettable night.*
> *Hamish*

He'd drawn a smiley face beside his name and Lola had laughed and hugged it to her chest, secretly thrilled to be *unforgettable*.

Sure, she'd known their first meeting after that night would be awkward to begin with but had expected it to dissipate quickly.

She'd been dead wrong about that.

His presence on her doorstep—big and solid, more jaw than any man had a right to—had been like a shockwave breaking over her. She'd felt like she was having some kind of out-of-body experience, where she was above herself, looking down, the universe whispering *He's the one* in her ear.

She'd panicked. Hell, she was *still* panicking.

Firstly, she didn't believe in *the one*. Sure, she knew people stayed together for ever. Her parents had been married for thirty-two years. But to her it was absurd to think there was only *one* person out there for everyone. It was more statistically believable, given the entire population of the world, that there were many *ones* out there.

People just didn't know it because they were too busy with their current *one*.

Secondly, she honestly believed finding *the one* didn't apply to every person on the planet. Lola believed some people were destined to never settle down, that they were too content with the company of many and being children of the world to ground themselves.

And that was the category into which Lola fell. Into which Great-Aunt May fell. A spinster at seventy-five, May hadn't needed *the one* to be fulfilled. Lola had never known a person more accomplished, more well travelled or more Zen with her life.

And, thirdly, if Lola fell and smacked her head and had a complete personality change and suddenly *did* believe in such nonsense, her *one* would never be a guy from a small town.

Never.

She'd run from a small town for a reason. She hadn't wanted to be with a guy who was content to stay put, whose whole life was his patch of dirt or his business, or the place he'd grown up. Which was why her reaction to Hamish was so disconcerting.

Hamish Gibson *couldn't* be the one for her.

No. She was just really…sexually attracted to him. Hell, she'd thought about him so much these past three months it was only natural to have had a reaction to him when she'd opened the door and seen him standing right in front of her.

But she wasn't going there again.

Which was why work was such a blessing. Something else to occupy her brain. And, *yowsers*, did she need it today to deal with her critical patient.

Emma Green was twenty-three years old and in acute cardiac failure. She'd been born with a complex cardiac disorder and had endured several operations and bucketloads of medication already in her young life. But a mild illness had pushed her system to the limit and her enlarged heart muscle into the danger zone.

She'd gone into cardiac arrest at the start of the shift down in the emergency department and had been brought to ICU in a critical condition. Which meant it was a whirlwind of a shift. There were a lot of drugs to give, bloods to take, tests to run. Medication and ventilation settings were constantly tweaked and adjusted as the intensive care team responded to Emma's condition minute by minute.

As well as that, there was a veritable royal flush of specialists and their entourages constantly in and out, needing extra things, sucking up time she didn't have, all wanting their orders prioritised. There were cardiac and respiratory teams as well as radiologists and pharmacists, physiotherapists and social workers.

And there was Emma's family to deal with. Her parents, who had already been through so much with Emma over the years. Her mother teary, her father stoic—both old hands at the jargon and the solemn medical faces. And Emma's boyfriend, Barry, who was not. He was an emotional wreck, swinging from sad to angry, from positive to despondent.

Not that she could blame him. Emma looked awful. There was barely a spare inch of skin that wasn't crisscrossed by some kind of tubing or wires. She had a huge tube in her nose where the life support was connected and securing it obscured half of her face, which was puffy— as was the rest of her body—from days of retained fluid due to her worsening cardiac condition.

Lola was used to this environment, to how terrible critical patients could look. She was immune to it. But she understood full well how hard it was for people to see someone they loved in this condition. She'd witnessed the shocked gasps too many times, the audible sobs as the sucker-punch landed.

The gravity of the situation always landed with a blow. The sudden knowledge that their loved one was really, *really* sick, that they could die, was a terrible whammy. So Emma's boyfriend's reactions were perfectly normal, as far as Lola was concerned.

And all just part of her job.

'It really is okay to talk to her,' Lola assured Barry as he sat rigidly in a chair by the window, repeatedly finger-combing his hair. It was the first time he'd been alone with Emma since she'd been admitted. Her mother and father were taking it in turns to sit with Barry at the bedside but they'd both ducked out for a much-needed cup of coffee and a bite to eat.

Barry glanced at Emma and shook his head. 'I don't want to get in the way or bump anything.'

Lola smiled. 'It's okay, I'll be right here keeping an eye on you.' She kept it light because she could tell that Barry was petrified of the high-tech environment, which was quite common. 'And I promise I'll push you out the way if I need to, okay?'

He gave a worried laugh, still obviously doubtful, and Lola nodded encouragingly and smiled again. 'I'm sure she'd love to hear your voice.'

His eyes flew to Lola's in alarm. 'I thought she was sedated.'

'She is,' Lola replied calmly. 'But even unconscious patients can still hear things. There have been plenty of people who've woken from comas or sedation and been able to recite bedside conversations word for word.'

Barry chewed on his bottom lip. 'I…don't know what to say to her.'

The despair in his voice hit Lola in every way. Barry

was clearly overwhelmed by everything. She gestured him over to the seat Emma's mother had vacated not that long ago. He came reluctantly.

'Just tell her you're here,' Lola said, as he sat. 'Tell her you love her. Tell her she's in safe hands.'

'Okay.' Barry's voice trembled a little.

Lola turned to her patient. 'Emma,' she said quietly, placing a gentle hand on Emma's forearm, 'Barry's here. He's going to sit with you for a while.'

There wasn't any response from Emma—Lola didn't expect there would be—just the steady rise and fall of her chest and the rapid blipping of her monitor. Lola smiled at Barry as she withdrew her hand. 'Just put your hand where I had mine, okay? There's nothing you can bump there.' Barry tentatively slid his hand into place and Lola nodded. 'That's good. Now just talk to her.'

Lola moved away but not very far, hovering until Barry became more confident. He didn't say anything for a moment or two and when he started his voice was shaky but he *started*. 'Hey, Emsy.' His voice cracked and he cleared it. 'I'm here and… I'm not going anywhere. You're in good hands and everything's going to be okay.'

Lola wasn't entirely sure that was true. She knew how fragile Emma's condition was and part of her was truly worried her patient wasn't going to make it through the shift. But humans needed hope to go on, to *endure*, and she'd certainly been proved wrong before by patients.

Barry was doing the right thing. For him *and* for Emma.

CHAPTER FOUR

'So? When *are* you going to settle down?'

Hamish sighed at his sister, who was slightly tipsy after a few glasses of champagne. They were sitting on the balcony of their new apartment, which was also in Manly but at the more exclusive end, with harbour views. Marcus had moved out of his apartment near Kirribilli General when he and Grace had decided to move in together because they'd wanted an apartment that was *theirs*.

'God, you're like a reformed smoker. You're in love so you want everyone else to be as well.'

Grace smiled at Marcus, who smiled back as he slid his hand onto her nape. Hamish rolled his eyes at them but it was obvious his sister was in love and he was happy for her. She'd had a tough time in her first serious relationship so it was good to see her like this.

'You're thirty, Hamish. You're not getting any younger. Surely there has to be some girl in Toowoomba who takes your fancy.'

'There's no point getting into a relationship when I'm hoping to spend a few years doing rural service after the course is done.'

Hamish had recently been passed over for a transfer to a station in the far west of the state because he didn't have an official intensive care paramedic qualification, even though he had the skills. It had spurred him to apply for a position on the course.

'It's hardly fair to get involved with someone knowing I could be off to the back of beyond at a moment's notice,' he added.

Grace sighed in exasperation. 'Maybe she'd want to go with you.'

Unbidden, an image of Lola slipped into his mind. He couldn't begin to imagine her in a small country town. She'd cornered the market in exotic city girl. She was like a hothouse flower—temperamental, high maintenance— and the outback was no place for hothouse flowers.

Women had to be more like forage sorghum. Durable and tough. And although Lola *was* tough and independent in many ways, there was something indefinably *urban* about her.

'I don't know whether you know this or not, but you're a bit of catch, Hamish Gibson. Good looking even, though it pains me to admit it. Don't you think so, Marcus?'

Grace smiled at her fiancé, a teasing light in her eyes. 'Absolutely,' he agreed, his expression totally deadpan. 'I was just saying that very thing to Lola the other day.'

Lola.

It seemed the universe was doing its best to keep her on his mind. 'And did she agree?' Hamish was pretty sure Marcus was just making it up to indulge his sister but, hell, if they'd had a conversation about him, then Hamish wanted to know!

'Of course she'd agree,' Grace said immediately. 'Lola can pick good looking out of a Sydney New Year's Eve crowd blindfolded.'

Hamish grinned at his sister. 'I'll have to remember that this New Year.'

Something in Hamish's voice must have pinged on his sister's radar. Apparently she wasn't tipsy *enough* to dull that sucker. Her eyes narrowed as her gaze zeroed in on him. '*No*, Hamish.'

'What?' Hamish spread his hands in an innocent gesture.

'You and Lola would *not* be good for each other.'

Hamish grabbed his chest as if she'd wounded him. 'Why not?'

'Because you're too alike. You're both flirts. You like the conquest but suck at any follow-through. You have to *live together* for two months, Hamish. That's a lot of awkward breakfasts. And I don't want to be caught in the middle between you two or have my friendship with Lola jeopardised because you couldn't keep it in your pants.'

Hamish didn't think Lola would be the one who'd get burned in a relationship between the two of them. He at least was open to the idea of relationships—she, on the other hand, was not. He glanced at his soon-to-be brother-in-law. 'Help me out here, man.'

Marcus laughed and shook his head. 'You're on your own, buddy.'

'C'mon, dude. Solidarity.'

Grace shook her head at her brother. 'In an hour I'm going to take my fiancé to bed and do bad things to him. You think he's going to side with you?'

Hamish glanced at a clearly besotted Marcus, who was smiling at Grace like the sun rose and set with her, and a wave of hot green jealousy swamped his chest. He wanted that. What his sister had found with Marcus.

Contrary to *apparent* popular opinion, he'd never been opposed to settling down. He just hadn't found the right woman. For ever was, after all, a *long* time! But watching these two together...

They were the perfect advertisement for happily ever after.

Once upon a time the idea of eternal monogamy would have sent him running for the hills but these two sure knew how to sell it.

'Okay. Well, that was TMI.' He gave the lovebirds an exaggerated grimace. 'And is definitely my cue to go.'

He stood, but his sister wasn't done with him yet. 'I mean it, Hamish. I wouldn't have suggested you move in with Lola if I thought you'd make a move on her.'

'I'm not going to,' he protested.

Clearly, Grace didn't believe him. 'She's off-limits, okay?'

He was much too much of a gentleman to suggest Grace have this conversation with her bestie who had all but jumped him three months ago. But it did annoy him that somehow he was the bad guy here. 'I think Lola can take care of herself.'

Grace shook her head at his statement, thankfully a little too tipsy to read anything into his terseness. 'She comes across that way, I know. Brash and tough and in control. But she feels things as deeply as the next woman.'

A memory of Lola's glistening eyelashes flashed on his retinas, the weight of her sadness about her patient as tangible now as it had been that night. Hamish sighed. Yeah. He knew how deeply Lola felt.

'Lola and I are roomies *only*.' He moved around to his sister and kissed her on the top of her head. 'Thank you for dinner.' She went to stand but he placed a hand on her shoulder. 'You guys stay there. I can let myself out.'

Grace squeezed the hand on her shoulder. 'Good luck on Monday. Ring me and let me know how your first shift went.'

'I will.' Hamish shook Marcus's hand. 'Goodnight.'

He left them to it, happy that his sister had found love but pleased to be away from their enviable public displays of affection.

Lola enjoyed about five seconds of contentment when she woke on Sunday morning before she remembered who was sleeping in the room across the hallway.

The feeling evaporated immediately.

She rolled her head to the side. Nine thirty. Normally she'd stretch and sigh happily and contemplate a lazy Sunday morning. No work to get to. No place to be. Her time her own.

Normally she'd walk down to one of the cafés that lined the Manly esplanade to eat smashed avocado and feta on rye bread while she watched people amble past. Maybe even stay in bed, read a good book. Or sloth around in front of the television, watching rom coms and eating Vegemite toast.

But she wasn't going to be able to sloth around for the next two months. Because Hamish was here.

Lola stared at the ceiling fan turning lazy circles above her. It was dark and cool in her room as it was on the western side of the apartment but the prediction was for a warm day. She strained her ears to hear any movement from outside.

Was he up?

Lola shut her eyes as that led to completely inappropriate thoughts and a strange dropping sensation in the pit of her stomach.

Do not think about Hamish being *up,* Lola.

Was he out of bed? That was more appropriate. She couldn't hear any noises but she'd bet her last cent he was.

He was a country boy after all. And she'd known enough of them in her life to know they liked their sunrises.

Ugh. Give her a sunset any day.

Gathering her courage, she sat up and swung her legs out of bed. She had to face him some time. She couldn't spend the next two months avoiding him like she had yesterday, running out on him about twenty minutes after he'd arrived and nodding a quick hello to him last night before heading to her room with the excuse of being tired.

So just get out there, already, and face him!

Dressing quickly in a simple floral sundress with shoestring straps, Lola pulled the band on her plait and fluffed out her hair a little. She'd left it in overnight to help with knot control and to tame the curls to a crinkly wave instead of a springy mess.

But that was it—she refused to make herself pretty for Hamish. Normally when meeting a guy she'd put on some make-up, spray on her favourite perfume and wear her best lingerie. Today she was wearing no make-up, she smelled only of the washing powder she used on her clothes and she deliberately chose mismatched, *comfortable* underwear.

Not that he was in the kitchen or the living room when she made an appearance and, for a second, a ribbon of hope wound through her belly before she flicked her gaze to the balcony to find him sitting at the table. Resigned, Lola poured two glasses of juice, slamming most of hers down before topping it up and wondering if it was too early for a slug of vodka.

Pulling in a steadying breath, she picked up the glasses and went out to make polite conversation. He turned as she slid the screen door open. Her heart was practically in her mouth as she prepared herself for her body to go crazy again but the incredibly visceral reaction from yesterday didn't reappear and Lola smiled in relief.

It had clearly been an anomaly.

He smiled back and her belly swooped but it was still an improvement on yesterday. Plus, he *was* sitting there shirtless. A damp pair of running shorts clinging to his thighs was the only thing keeping him decent and that was up for debate.

'You've been for a run?' Lola gave herself full marks for how normal she sounded as she slid his glass across the tabletop. She was going to need to channel a lot of that if he was planning on walking around here shirtless very often.

'Yep.' He lifted the glass as if he was toasting her and swallowed the whole thing in several long gulps. Gulps that drew her gaze to the stretch of his neck and those gingery whiskers. 'Thanks.' He put the glass on the table. 'I needed that.'

She noticed he had an empty water bottle by his elbow.

'I can get you some more.' Lola stood. She needed a moment after that display of manliness. Escaping to the fridge seemed the perfect excuse.

He waved her back down. 'Nah. I'm good.'

'So you…run every morning.'

'Not every morning. But regularly enough. I figured it was a good way to get to know the neighbourhood.'

'Did you make it to the beach?'

'Yep. Ran along the esplanade. It's very different to the scenery I'm used to.'

It was about five kilometres to the beach so he'd already run ten kilometres this morning. *While she was sleeping.* She'd have felt like a sloth if she was capable of feeling anything other than lust.

'A lot more beach, I'd imagine.' Toowoomba was a

regional inland city, well over a hundred kilometres to the nearest beach.

'Yes.' He laughed. 'Are you a runner?'

It was Lola's turn to laugh. 'I'm more of a hit-and-miss yoga in the park kinda gal.' If she was going to get hot, sweaty and breathless, she could think of much more satisfying ways to do it. Preferably naked.

'I saw a group doing that.'

'Yeah, there's a regular morning and afternoon class not far from the beach.'

Lola hadn't been in a while. Who knew, maybe living with Mr Exercise would guilt her into being more energetic herself and she was clearly going to need to put her sexual energy somewhere. Just sitting opposite him was hell on her libido.

'What are your plans for the day?' Time to move the conversation to safer territory.

He shrugged those big bare shoulders and Lola resisted the urge to stare. 'Thought I'd do a bit of sightseeing. It's pretty full on for the next couple of weeks. Might take me a while to get out again.'

'That's a great idea. It's not your first time to Sydney, though?'

'No. I've been a few times but until recently not for almost ten years.'

Lola only just stopped herself from gaping at Hamish. Ten years? Had he been *anywhere* in a decade? 'So you'll be doing the usual, then? You saw the bridge a few months ago, probably more intimately than anyone in the city, actually. You should definitely climb it while you're here.'

Lola had climbed the Sydney Harbour Bridge several times. She loved the rush of adrenaline that heights gave her. That any kind of precarious situation gave her—from white-water rafting to bungee jumping to zip lining.

The thrill. The buzz. It was better than sex.

It was also why she was such a good ICU nurse. She knew how to ride the adrenaline in critical situations. She appreciated how it honed her reactions and sharpened her focus. She thrived on how well she anticipated orders, knowing what was going to be asked for even before it was, putting her hand to something a second before the doctor wanted it.

'I'd love to climb it. It's on my to-do list. Today I was just going to get a ferry across to Circular Quay and check out the Opera House and Darling Harbour.'

Lola glanced at the layers of blue sky crowning the ancient trees in the park opposite, pleased for the distraction from his body. 'It's a good day for it. And an easy walk into the city from there.'

Especially for someone who'd just run ten kilometres. And had those legs. And those abs. And that chest. *Bloody hell.*

'Grace's favourite haunt is the Rocks area; you'll find a lot of old convict-era stuff there. You can walk it or jump on one of those hop-on, hop-off buses.'

'And what's *your* favourite haunt?'

Lola's breath caught at the tease in his tone and the flirt in his smile. 'Sydney's such a beautiful city, it's hard to choose.'

'Oh, come on.' He rolled his eyes at her. 'You must have a place you love more than any other.'

She did. But... 'My favourite place is not a tourist spot.'

'Ah. It's a secret? Even better.'

Lola smiled at him—she couldn't not. He was hard

to resist when he was teasing, so endearingly boyish. He must have broken some hearts in high school.

'Not a secret. It's just a street I really love.'

'Does this street have a name? Spill, woman.'

Lola laughed. This was better. If she could hide behind some friendly teasing and banter the next couple of months might not be so awkward. 'I find these things are more meaningful if you stumble across them yourself.'

He snorted. 'I'm here for two months. How long did it take you to find it?'

She smiled. 'About two years.'

'Well, then.' He stood and Lola's pulse fluttered. 'I insist you take me there. Today. And I solemnly swear...' he slapped a clenched fist against his sternum, which was dizzily distracting '...to keep it a secret, on pain of death.'

Lola hadn't shown anyone her spot. Well, she'd told Grace and May about it but neither of them had seen it yet and she'd never really wanted to share it with a guy. She couldn't have borne it if he'd been dismissive of something that was essentially girly.

But, surprisingly, she *wanted* to show Hamish. Maybe she was being influenced by the whole country-boy thing but she had a feeling he appreciated nature and that he'd understand why she loved it so much.

And she hadn't checked it out this season yet so what better way to visit than playing tour guide? Plus it would occupy the day and give them a chance to establish a rapport that wasn't sexual. After today they'd probably pass like ships in the night—the hazards of shift work— so starting as she meant them to go on was a good idea.

'Okay.' She nodded. 'But only because this is actually the most perfect time of year to see it.'

'Well, that sounds even more intriguing. I'll just have a quick shower. Give me fifteen minutes.'

Lola's gaze followed him into the apartment. Broad shoulders swept down to a pair of fascinating dimples just above the waistband of his shorts. Two tight ass cheeks filling out said shorts in a way that almost made Lola believe in miracles.

And possibilities.

She tried really hard not to imagine him stripping off and stepping into the shower, water clinging to his body, running *everywhere*, wet and soapy and slippery.

She failed dramatically.

CHAPTER FIVE

WITHIN HALF AN hour Hamish was following Lola onto one of the harbour's iconic yellow and green ferries, enjoying the way her sundress fluttered around mid-thigh and the way she kept scooping up her right shoulder strap as it slipped off repeatedly.

He was pleased but surprised she'd agreed to this outing. He'd been expecting to be rebuffed, for her to keep putting him firmly at a distance. But then she'd invited him to her secret spot as if she'd made some kind of decision to accept him and their situation and wild horses couldn't have dragged him away.

He liked Lola and, who knew, maybe they could even become friends? He doubted they were the only two people in the world who'd fallen into bed and wound up as friends.

'So, we're taking the ferry?' Hamish said as Lola led him to the bow and lowered herself into one of the open-air seats. She looked very city chic in her big sunglasses, short and cute and curvy, her hair blowing around her shoulders, her cutesy dress riding up high on her thighs.

Hamish felt very *country* next to her.

'Yep. Have you been on the harbour before?'

He nodded. 'When I was in high school. Mum and Dad took us on the ferry to Taronga Zoo.'

The engines rumbled out of idle and the boat pulled away from the wharf. She breathed in deeply and sighed. 'I love taking the ferry. We're so lucky here, the harbour is gorgeous. The best in the world.'

Hamish laughed. 'Biased much?' It *was* a beautiful day, though. The sky was a stark blue dome unblemished by clouds, the sun a glorious shining bauble, refracting its golden-white light across the surface of the water like a glitter ball.

'Nope.' She shook her head and her curls, already fluttering in the breeze, swung some more. 'Trust me, I've been to a lot of harbours but Sydney wins the prize.'

'Well travelled, huh?'

Hamish realised he didn't know much about Lola at all. And the only person he could ask was his sister, who would have been highly suspicious of his interest.

'I've done quite a bit of travelling, yes.'

'What's quite a bit?'

She crossed one leg over the other and Hamish tried not to look at the dress hem riding up a little more. 'I lived in the UK for several years after I finished my degree. I did a lot of agency nursing to support my travel obsession. I've been back here for four years but go travelling again at least once a year. I've backpacked extensively through Asia, Europe and America and seen a little of Africa.'

Hamish whistled. 'Intrepid. I like it. Got any favourites?'

She didn't hesitate. 'India. It's such a land of contrasts. And Iceland. So majestic.' She glanced at him and he could just make out her eyes behind those dark brown lenses. 'It's my goal to go to every country in the world before I die.'

'A worthy goal.'

'I'm off to Zimbabwe next April.'

'On a safari thing?'

She smiled. 'For some of it. What about you? Ever had a hankering to see the world or are you one of those people who think living in the country is the be all and end all?'

Hamish blinked at the fine seam of bitterness entrenched in her words. 'Hey,' he protested, keeping it light. 'What have you got against living in the country? Don't knock it till you've tried it.'

She snorted and even that was cute. 'No, thanks. I spent seventeen years in the middle of bloody nowhere. I've paid my dues.'

Hamish stared at her. Lola Fraser had come from the sticks? He'd never met a female more *urban* in his life. 'Whereabouts?'

'You won't have heard of it.'

Hamish folded his arms. 'Try me.'

He was pretty sure she was rolling her eyes at him behind those shades.

'Doongabi.'

Yeah…she was right. He hadn't heard of it. 'Nope.'

'Imagine my surprise.' He could *hear* the eye-roll now. 'It's a rural community way past west of Dubbo, population two thousand.'

'And you couldn't wait to get out?'

'You can say that again.'

'Was it that bad?' Hamish was intrigued now.

She sighed. 'No.' Her strap slipped down giving him a peek at the slope of her breast before she pulled it back into place. 'It's a nice enough town, if that's your thing, I suppose. But it's hard to be put in a small-town straitjacket when you were born a free spirit.'

'So you're a gypsy, huh?'

Physically she was far from the traditional gypsy

type—she was blonde and busty rather than exotic and reedy—but he supposed *gypsy* was a state of mind.

'Yes. I am.' The ferry horn tooted almost directly above their heads. 'Always have been. I'm a living-in-the-moment kinda woman, although I suspect...' A smile touched her mouth. 'You probably already know that.'

Hamish acknowledged her reference with a slight smile of his own and she continued, 'I've always craved adventure. I wanted to bungee jump and climb mountains and parasail and deep sea dive and jump out of planes.'

He nodded. 'And you can't do any of that in Doongabi.'

She laughed and Hamish felt it all the way down to his toes before the breeze snatched it away. 'No.'

'Have you ever gone back?'

'I've been back a few times. For Christmas.'

'Are your parents still alive? Don't you miss them?'

'Yes. They're both still on the farm.'

The farm? Try as he might, Hamish couldn't believe Lola had come from a farming background. She was as at home in Sydney as the sails of the Opera House.

'And, yes, I do miss them in the way you miss people you love when you haven't seen them for a long time. But they don't really *get* me and I think it's honestly as much a relief for them as it is for me when I head back to Sydney.'

'Why don't they *get* you?' Hamish felt sorry for Lola. Sure, his family had their disagreements and their differences but he'd always felt like he belonged. Like his parents *got* him.

She glanced away, the back of her head resting on the wall behind. 'Doongabi's the kind of place that people tie themselves to. Generations of families, including my father's and my mother's, have come from the district. And that's fine.' She rolled her head to look at him, the frown crinkling her forehead speaking of her turmoil. 'It's their lives and it's their choice. But…how can it be a choice?'

Her eyebrows raised in question but Hamish was sure the question was rhetorical.

'They don't *know* anything else. Women…tie themselves there to Doongabi men and have Doongabi babies, without ever venturing out into the world to see what else is on offer. They're so stuck in their ways. Unwilling to change a century of this-is-the-way-we-do-it-here.'

She sighed heavily and, once again, Hamish felt for Lola. She obviously grappled with her mixed feelings.

'And I…wanted to fly. So…' She shrugged. 'My mother blames her aunt.'

'Her aunt?'

'My Great-Aunt May.'

'Oh…the postcards on the fridge.' She smiled at him then and it was so big and genuine it almost stole Hamish's breath.

'Yes. She's the family black sheep. Hitchhiked out of Doongabi when she was eighteen. Never married, never settled in one place. She's lived all over the world, seen all kinds of things and can swear in a dozen different languages. I have a postcard from every place she's ever been. I was five when I received my first one.'

Hamish nodded. 'And you knew you wanted to be just like her.'

'No.' Lola shook her head, her curls bounced. 'I knew I *was* just like her.' She gave a half-laugh. 'Poor Mum. I don't think she's ever forgiven May.'

'She sounds fabulous.'

'She is.' Lola's gaze fixed on the foam spraying over the bow and Hamish studied her profile, as gorgeous as the rest of her. 'I can see the bridge.' She pointed at the arch just coming into view and sighed. 'I never get tired of that sight.'

Hamish dragged his gaze off her face, following the line of her finger. But he didn't want to. He could look at Lola Fraser all damn day and never get tired of *that* sight either.

They alighted from the ferry at the North Sydney Wharf about fifteen minutes later. 'It's a few minutes' walk from here.'

Hamish fell in beside her as they sauntered down what looked very much like a suburban street. 'What suburb is this?'

'It's Kirribilli.'

'So the hospital's not far, then?'

'Um, yes. Up that way...somewhere.' She waved her hand vaguely in the general direction they were heading. 'At the dodgy end.'

Hamish laughed as they passed beautifully restored terraced houses, big gnarly trees that looked as if they'd been in the ground for a century and cars with expensive price tags. It was hard to believe this harbourside sub-urb—*any* harbourside suburb—had a dodgy end.

She turned right at an intersection. 'So, are you going to tell me what's so special about this street?'

'Nope.' Lola shook her head. 'You'll see soon enough.'

'Mystery woman, huh?'

She just shrugged and kept walking but there was a bounce to her step. Like she couldn't wait to get there. Like *maybe* she couldn't wait to show him? It was intrigu-ing that a woman who'd just confessed to having itchy feet and being a bit of a daredevil would choose a place so quiet and unassuming to take him.

They passed a park and Hamish could see down to

the harbour again, glittering like a jewel and the massive motor boats moored at what looked like a marina. A personal trainer was putting a group of people through a session and a large gathering of people were picnicking under the shade of a tree.

'This,' she said as she turned left at another street, 'is my favourite place to visit in Sydney.'

Hamish turned the corner to discover an avenue of massive Jacaranda trees alive with colour. The dry, gnarly branches knotted and tangled together overhead to form a lilac canopy down the entire length of the street. A carpet of dropped, purple-blue flowers covered the road.

It was stunning. Toowoomba had plenty of Jacarandas as well but this avenue was something else, the trees all lined up together to create an accidental work of art. A sight so *purple* it was almost blinding.

The kind of purple usually only found on coral reefs or in magic forests.

He glanced at Lola. She'd taken her sunglasses off and was staring down the street with rapt attention, like she'd discovered it all over again. Like she was seeing it for the first time.

She switched her attention to him and caught Hamish staring at her, but she didn't seem to mind. 'Isn't it the most beautiful thing you've ever seen?'

It was. *She* was. Looking down the street like a kid staring at an avenue of Christmas trees just lit up for the season, giddy with the magic shimmering in the air.

And she'd shared it with him. This beautiful place she loved so much.

'Yes. It's stunning.' *Just like you.*

She smiled at him and for a crazy second he wanted to pull her close and kiss her. Kiss her in this place she'd taken nobody else, so every time she came here she'd remember that she'd taken *him*.

But he didn't. He just said, 'Shall we walk up and down a few times?'

She gave a half-laugh, a girly edge of excitement to it as he offered her his arm and she looped hers through it. 'I thought you'd never ask.'

They didn't speak for a while, just strolled along, admiring the scenery as lilac flowers floated down all around them, quiet as snowfall. It was like walking in a purple wonderland. He turned to tell her that as two almost luminescent blue-purple flowers drifting in the gentle harbour breeze landed in Lola's hair.

It couldn't have been more perfect. 'You have flowers in your hair.'

'So do you.' She stood on tippytoes and plucked out the trumpet-shaped blooms. Their eyes locked for a moment and Hamish's pulse spiked before she dragged her gaze to the flowers in her palm. 'Only in nature could you get this colour.'

She blew them both off her hand, her gaze tracking them as they fluttered to the ground. 'Where are mine?' she asked, fixing him with a gaze that was all business now.

Hamish lifted his hand to remove them then decided against it. 'Wait.' He pulled his phone out of his pocket. 'I think this needs a picture first.'

She rolled her eyes but acquiesced. 'I get to veto it if it's terrible.'

He took the pic, zooming in tight on her face but conscious of snapping the background blaze of purple too, of framing this woman just right. He took several in quick succession then handed over his phone for Lola to approve what he'd taken.

'They're all pretty good,' she said, her thumb swiping back and forth between them. 'Hard to screw up with that background, I guess.'

Hard to screw up with the *foreground* too.

'This one.' She handed the phone over. 'Can you send it to me?'

Hamish glanced at it. She'd chosen one he'd zoomed out on a little but she was smiling a big, crazy smile that went all the way to her eyes and squished her full cheeks into chipmunk cuteness. The flowers in her hair drew attention to its blonde bounciness and the way it brushed her shoulders drew attention to her fallen-down strap.

'Sure.' His fingers got busy as they walked on again.

'So, Grace's big brother…' She smiled at him. 'Have *you* travelled?'

'Sure. I'm afraid it's kinda tame compared to you.'

She rolled her eyes. 'It's not a competition.'

Hamish thought back to that first trip, a smile spreading across his face. 'I did a tour of the Greek Islands with some mates when I was nineteen. Got a snowglobe from every place we stopped.'

Lola blinked. 'A snowglobe?' *In Greece?*

'Yeah. You know, those terrible, tacky things they sell in tourist traps everywhere.'

Lola laughed. 'I know.'

'Had to get something to remember the best damn trip of my life.'

'The Greek islands are beautiful, aren't they? And the people are wonderful. So generous.'

His smile became a grin. 'You have no idea.'

'Oh, *really*?' She cocked an eyebrow at him. 'I take it you were a recipient of some generosity? Of the female kind maybe?'

He laughed. 'I lost my virginity in Mykonos.'

'Ah. Was she a local or one of the women on the tour?'

Hamish shook his head. 'She was Greek. The daughter of the innkeeper. She couldn't speak much English and all I could say was please, thank you, good morning and can I have some ouzo.'

She laughed. 'What else do you need?'

'Nothing, as it turned out.' Hamish laughed too. 'A little ouzo and good manners go a long way.'

'That's a great life motto,' she said as they crossed to the other side of the street, trampling a sea of fallen purple flowers. 'I don't suppose there was an *I lost my virginity in Mykonos* snowglobe?'

'No, sadly… I would have bought the hell out of that.'

Lola shook her head as they headed back the other way. 'Where else?'

'I did a tour of Europe the following year. Fifteen countries in twenty-five days.'

'Oh, God,' Lola groaned. 'This isn't where you tell me that you could only ever get laid on a tour so that's all you've ever done?'

'No.' He grinned. 'But it is surprising how…accommodating being on holiday makes a woman.'

'I would say that is most definitely true.'

Hamish didn't really want to think about how much travelling Lola had done and how much adrenaline she must have had to burn off after all her death-defying adventures. But he was jealous as hell of whoever had been in the right place at the right time to be the recipient of all that excess energy.

He knew how mind-blowing she was in grief. He could only begin to imagine how amazing she'd be pumped with devil-may-care.

'Since then I've been to LA and New York for brief visits. And to New Zealand for a ski trip last year.'

'Let me guess, you have snowglobes from all of them?'

'Absolutely. It's worth, like, fifty bucks, that collection.'

She laughed. 'And where's your favourite place out of everywhere you've been?'

'Well, Mykonos, obviously.'

He smiled and she rolled her eyes. '*Obviously*. What about your second favourite place?'

'London. I was only there for three days and I need to go back because I loved it. What about you? What's your number one pick of all the places you've been?'

She sucked in air through her teeth. 'That's a hard call.'

'I bet. But there must be something that just grabbed you by the gut?'

'Last year I went on a tandem hangglider flight over an Austrian lake. It was…magical. We hovered for so long, riding the air currents I actually felt like I was flying and the Alps in the distance were all snow-capped. It was almost…spiritual, you know?'

'It does sound spiritual but I'd rather get my thrills with both feet planted firmly on the ground.'

'Afraid of heights?'

Hamish's breath caught at the amusement in her voice. She was something else when she teased him. She wasn't flirting exactly but it felt good to have her green eyes dancing at him.

'Afraid of plunging to my death attached to some dude I don't know is more like it.'

She shrugged. 'Life's too short to worry about the what-ifs.'

'Maybe. But I tend to see all the disastrous things that go wrong for people indulging in high-risk ventures. I think it skews my view somewhat.'

'Hey, there are plenty of ICU patients who were doing risky things that didn't work out. But you could trip over your feet tomorrow, smack your head on the ground and die. Just getting out of bed each day is a risk.'

'Exactly.' Hamish grinned. 'Which is why I plan on dying in my bed at the grand old age of ninety-six after having sex with a beautiful woman.'

A smile played on her mouth as she stopped and looked up at him. 'Sex, huh? Wow, you do like to push the envelope.'

'Hey, sex at ninety-six *is* pushing the envelope.'

She laughed. 'Come on. Let's walk down again and keep going. There's a great little café that overlooks the harbour. We might not be able to get a seat but you don't know if you don't try, right?'

Hamish cocked an eyebrow. 'You even like to take risks with tables.'

'You really need to take a walk on the wild side, Hamish Gibson.'

Hamish grinned. He'd grown up around horses and cattle and farm machinery. He'd done his fair share of wild *and* stupid. He didn't feel like he had anything to prove. But Lola could probably persuade him to do anything. 'I'm starting to see the attraction.'

CHAPTER SIX

LOLA TRIED NOT to make too much noise the next morning as she crept down the hall of the silent apartment, tightening the knot on her short gown. Hamish was on a couple of days of orientation so he didn't start till nine but she didn't want to disturb him at five thirty in the morning with her fridge opening and toast popping and teaspoon clinking.

Grace had always been a light sleeper and Lola figured it probably ran in the Gibson family. Her parents were the same so she knew it was a *country* thing. She needn't have worried, though. Her toast had just popped when she heard the front door open and a sweaty Hamish appeared a few moments later, his damp shorts and shirt clinging to him.

'Is that coffee?'

Lola nodded, lost for words both at his appearance and the fact he was not only out of bed but had already been for a *run.*

Who was he?

'Is there enough for two?'

Lola nodded again, still finding it difficult to locate adequate speech. His pheromones wafted to her on a wave of healthy sweat and she leaned against the kitchen bench as her legs weakened in an exceedingly unhelpful way. She ground her feet into the floor to stop herself launching at him.

'Can you pour me one? I'll just have a quick shower.'

And then she was looking at empty space, the tang of salt in the air a tangible reminder he *had* been here, an image in her head of Hamish in the shower a reminder of where he *was* right now.

Lola hoped like hell these shower fantasies weren't going to be a regular thing.

Determined to think of something else, her mind drifted to Hamish's confession about his virginity. The fact he still enjoyed the memory in a sexily smug way over ten years later was either testament to the greatness of the event or the depth of his gratitude. Both were endearing as all giddy-up.

Was it crazy to feel a tiny bit jealous of the woman on Mykonos?

She'd lost her virginity travelling too. She'd been eighteen and in Phuket where she'd met a backpacker called Jeremy. He'd been exotically handsome—Eurasian with a sexy Brit accent—and had known it. But she hadn't cared. She'd wanted to show her parents and everyone in Doongabi she was sophisticated and worldly. Plus there'd been cheap beer and a little too much sun earlier in the day.

Lola didn't remember a lot of it. Unlike Hamish, who appeared to remember his first time in great detail. She wondered if Jeremy still thought about that night with the same mix of pleasure and reminiscence that Hamish obviously did. How awesome would it be, knowing there was a guy out there in the world who got a secret, goofy grin every time he thought about his first time with you?

Knowing that you'd rocked his world?

She thought about that note again, the one Hamish

had left for her the morning after, with its goofy smiley face. Did he smile like that whenever he thought about what *they'd* done together?

Had she been as *unforgettable* as he'd claimed?

Hamish reappeared fifteen minutes later as she sat in front of the TV, listening to the morning news, And, hell, he looked seriously hot in his uniform. Like a freaking action man in his multi-pocketed lightweight overalls with a utility belt crammed with all the bits and bobs a paramedic needed on the road.

He looked strong and capable. Wide shoulders, wavy cinnamon hair with a sprinkle of ginger, powerful thighs. He looked like he could fix anything—*anyone*—and Lola's heart fluttered just looking at him. When he plonked himself down next to her on the couch—the same couch where they'd done *it*—any hope of following the news reports was dashed.

Lola took a sip of her coffee. 'Are you nervous? About your first day?'

He seemed to consider the question for a beat or two. 'Not of the work. I know Toowoomba may seem like a country backwater compared to the size and population of Sydney, but it's a decent-sized regional city and I've seen a lot on the job. I *am* nervous about the people I'm going to be working with. I don't know anyone so I'm not sure who knows what and who to be wary of.'

Lola nodded. Finding out colleagues' levels of experience and their limitations always took a little time. Sometimes that could be detrimental, especially in emergency situations.

'Well, if it helps, I know quite a few of the paramedics stationed at Kirribilli. They all seem professional and they all get along, work as a team. A lot of them go to

Billi's after their shift. Make sure you go along. It's a great place to de-stress.'

It was also a great place to pick up women—as he would know. The sudden thought was like a hot knife sliding between her ribs as she thought about him hooking up at Billi's, bringing her back here. Which was crazy. He could sleep with every woman in Sydney if he wanted to—it wasn't any of her business or her concern.

'Right. Well…' She stood. 'I'd better get ready.'

She didn't wait for his reply, scooping her plate off the coffee table and heading to the kitchen. She was going to be late if she didn't hustle.

Lola had another busy morning with Emma. The condition of her heart was worsening. Her body was becoming more oedematous which was putting pressure on other organs. Even the conjunctivas of her eyes bulged with oedema, requiring frequent ointment to prevent them drying.

The specialists were now at the stage where they were talking about a transplant. The question, though, was whether they could stabilise Emma enough to survive the rigors of such a massive operation and if they could, how long could they keep her heart going in its current state while they waited for another to become available?

Sadly, they didn't grow on trees. Even an emergency listing could still sometimes take weeks. And nobody was confident Emma's heart could last that long.

Her family were beside themselves with worry and Lola spent a lot of the morning trying to meet their growing need for comfort, assurance and answers. Lola could give the first and she did, she just wished she could give the other two as well.

At least Barry was more comfortable about being near

Emma now. He'd grown more confident and had taken to reading out all the supportive messages that family and friends had left for Emma on social media. There were hundreds every day and Lola knew the outpouring was not only good for Emma to hear but for Barry and her parents as well.

'I think she *can* hear me,' Barry said.

Lola smiled and nodded. 'I do too.' She'd noticed how Emma's heart rate settled a little every time Barry or her parents touched and talked to her. 'Keep it up.'

By the time Lola was heading to lunch she felt like she'd been working for a week. Seeing Grace in the kitchen alcove of the deserted staffroom was a fabulous rejuvenator.

'Hey, you here with the team?' Lola asked as she threw a tea bag into her mug and filled it with hot water from the boiler attached to the wall. Although she was the renal transplant co-ordinator, Grace often stepped in when a co-ordinator from a different department was on annual leave.

Grace nodded, following Lola's lead and also filling her mug. 'Just finished the Emma Green meeting. You're looking after her?'

Lola settled her butt against the edge of the kitchen counter. 'Yep.'

Grace settled hers beside Lola's. 'She's not doing very well, is she?'

Lola shook her head as she blew on her hot tea. 'No. She's going backwards at the moment, which is a worry.' Emma's chances of survival decreased every minute they couldn't stabilise her condition. 'She's just about reached maximum drug support.'

'Do you think she'll stabilise?'

It wasn't an unusual question to ask. Experienced

nurses often had gut feelings about patients. 'Well, her body's been pummelled over the years so… But she's got this far. She's obviously a fighter. I just…don't know.' Lola took a sip of her tea. 'Are they going to list her?'

Lola knew they didn't list people just on the gut feeling of the nurses. But she also knew that if Emma pulled through, if she stabilised, she was going to need a transplant because she couldn't stay on life support for ever and she couldn't survive without it. Unless she had a new heart.

Grace sipped her tea. 'The team is discussing it now.'

'Good.' Relief flowed through Lola's core and she smiled. 'Fingers crossed.'

They sipped at their tea for a moment or two. 'Hamish tells me you took him to see the jacarandas yesterday.'

Lola was instantly on guard, not fooled by Grace's casual slouch against the bench. 'Yes.'

One elegantly arched eyebrow lifted. 'I thought that was a state secret?'

'I told you about it,' Lola protested, dropping her gaze to the surface of her tea.

Grace regarded her over the rim of her cup, speculation coming off her in waves, even though Lola was finding the depths of her tea utterly fascinating.

'He's going back to Toowoomba, Lola.'

'I know.'

'And then he's moving to a rural post.'

'I know.'

'And you're not interested in settling down, remember?'

'I know.'

She wasn't. There were still places to go and people she hadn't met yet. And she couldn't do that being with Hamish in some rural outpost somewhere.

'Lola?'

Lola almost cringed at *that* note in her friend's voice—
that mix of suspicion and dawning knowledge were a
deadly accurate cocktail. She girded her loins to look
directly at Grace as if she and Hamish hadn't got naked
and done the wild thing already and this conversation
wasn't too late.

'I said I know, Grace. Take a chill pill.' Lola plastered
a smile on her face. 'He wanted to know my favourite
spot in Sydney and I figured a country boy would probably appreciate some nature.'

Grace studied her closely. 'But *you* went with him.'

Lola shifted uncomfortably under her friend's all-
seeing gaze. 'I haven't seen it yet this year. Plus, he's your
brother. I thought it might be...polite to play tour guide.'

The expression on Grace's face finally cleared and she
nodded slowly, as if she'd reached her conclusion. She
glanced around to make sure no one had slipped into the
room unnoticed while they'd been deep in conversation.
'You two have *slept* together.'

It wasn't a question and it took all Lola's willpower
not to glance away, to hold her friend's gaze and brazen
it out. 'Don't be ridiculous. He's been here two nights
during which we have *not* slept together.'

Which was the truth.

'No.' Grace slowly shook her head. 'Not this time.
Last time.'

Oh, hell. Grace had missed her calling as a PI. 'As
if I would sleep with Hamish.' Lola lowered her voice.
'He's your *brother*.'

Grace waved a hand. 'I don't care about that.'

Lola blinked at Grace's easy dismissal. She'd thought

her friend would care but it ultimately didn't matter—
Lola cared.

That was what mattered.

'I care about the fact that while you two are exactly alike in a lot of ways, you want completely different things, which means that you're both going to get hurt and that I'm going to be in the middle of it all.'

Lola had to admire how well Grace could summarise things. 'There's nothing going on, Grace.'

Another *almost* truth. There *was* an undercurrent between them but they weren't acting on it. And that was the most important thing.

'Lola?'

For a brief second, the sudden appearance of one of the shift runners was a welcome relief until concern spiked Lola's pulse. 'Emma?'

'No, sorry, she's okay. Just thought you'd like to know Dr Wright is heading in to talk to the family now.'

'Is he?' She plonked the mostly untouched mug on the bench. 'Sorry,' she said to Grace. 'I've gotta go.'

'Isn't this your lunch break?'

Lola nodded. 'But I have to sit in on it.'

She hated it when the doctors had a family conference without the nurse present. Invariably a patient's loved ones only heard some of the conversation or misheard it or didn't understand it but nodded along anyway because they were too overwhelmed by everything. When they had questions later—and they always had questions later—Lola could answer them, could reiterate what the doctor had said exactly, could interpret *and* correct any misperceptions.

But only *if* she was privy to what had been discussed.

Grace nodded. 'That's fine. Go. I'll pop around later

this afternoon after I have some ducks in a row and introduce myself to the family.'

'Okay. Thanks.' Lola scuttled off to the conference room.

Lola was on her second glass of wine on the balcony when she heard the front door open. Her pulse spiked followed by a quick stab of annoyance. She had to stop this stupid behaviour around him, for crying out loud.

Why couldn't she just look at him and think, *Oh, a guy I once slept with*, and act normal. Instead of, *Holy cow, a guy I once slept with. Danger! Danger! Danger!* Why was having to deal with him again after they'd got naked and done the wild thing *such* a problem?

She usually handled the ex-lover stuff really well.

It was probably just the newness of the situation. It'd only been a few days since Hamish had come to stay after all. She probably just needed time to get used to their living arrangements.

Of course, Grace's speculation about them hadn't helped. Lola hadn't had much of a chance to think about the implications of that during the remainder of her shift but she'd been thinking about it plenty since. She should have known Grace would guess something was going on. They may not have been besties since kindergarten, but they had known each other for several years and had lived together for the last two.

Of course Grace could read her like a book.

Which meant she was going to have to give Hamish a heads-up, because Lola had no doubt Grace would soon be seeking an explanation from her brother.

And she needed to get ahead of that.

Despite the inner uproar at the thought and Hamish's tread getting closer and closer, Lola forced herself to stay right where she was, her feet casually up on the railing of the balcony. They at least weren't throbbing any more after her long, busy day with Emma. A good soak in a bath had helped.

So had the wine.

'Hey.'

'Hey.' Lola plastered a smile on her face as she half turned in her seat.

He stepped onto the balcony, returning her smile, his gaze shifting to her legs before quickly shifting back again.

'How was orientation?'

He gave a half-laugh as he undid his utility belt and discarded it on the table with a dull thud. 'Let's just say I can't wait to get out on the road.'

Lola nodded. Orientation days were generally tedious. They were a necessary evil and HR boffins loved them, but staring at a bunch of policy and procedure manuals all day was not fun for most people.

He pulled up the chair beside her, turned it around and plonked himself in it, raising his feet to the railing also, his legs outstretched. Fabric pulled taut across power-ful thighs as he crossed his feet at the ankles. Lola fixed her gaze on the darkening outline of the Norfolk pine in the park opposite.

'Met my partner, though. A woman called Jenny Bell. She seems good. Know her?'

Lola nodded. 'Yeah. She's an excellent intensive care paramedic. One of the best.'

'Good.' He dropped his head from side to side to stretch out his traps. 'How was your shift?'

'Long.' She took a sip of her wine, resolutely pushing worry for Emma out of her mind. 'One of those shifts where you're on your toes every second.'

'Well, I've been sitting on my ass all day, so I can cook us something to eat if you like.'

Lola blinked at the unexpected offer. 'You can cook?'

'Well...' He smiled. 'Nothing too gourmet but I manage.'

'Good to know. But—' Lola grabbed a menu off the table she'd been studying earlier. 'Let's just order something gourmet and get it delivered for tonight.'

He took the menu and opened it. 'Delivered, huh?'

Lola laughed. 'Yeah, *Country*, it's a city thing. Choose something from the extensive menu then I order it through an app and a nice person delivers it right to the door.'

'I like the sound of that.'

They chose some pasta and garlic bread and Lola ordered it online. 'Should be here in thirty.'

'Good.' He stood and reached for his utility belt. 'I'll take a shower.'

Lola shut her eyes against a sudden welling of images in her head. *Enough with the shower already.*

At least she knew something that could combat the seduction of those images this time. 'Before you go...'

He paused, belt in hand, his gaze meeting hers. 'What?'

Lola sighed. Damn Grace's observation skills for putting her in this position. 'Look, I know I said we weren't to speak of this again but...'

'But?' Two cinnamon eyebrows rose in query.

She let out a breath. *Just say it!* 'Your sister knows we slept together.'

His face went blank for a second before his eyebrows lifted in surprise this time. 'You told Grace we slept together?'

'No.' Lola shook her head. 'Not exactly. She kinda guessed.'

'Ah. Yeah...she's like a bulldog when she scents blood.'

'I denied it. Told her there wasn't anything going on but... I'm sure you'll be hearing from her so I thought you might like some prior notice.'

'I have a missed call from her actually. I was going to ring her soon.'

'Well...that's probably why.'

He gave a soft snort. 'She always was one of those pain-in-the-ass, know-it-all little sisters.'

Lola laughed. 'Well, like I said, I did deny it. I just don't think she believed me so...sorry if you cop some flak from her.'

'Don't worry.' He grinned. 'I know how to handle Gracie.'

In Lola's experience men tended to underestimate a woman's tenacity when her mind was made up but that was between him and his sister and, to be honest, it was good to be able to pass that hot potato on to someone else.

'All right. I'll hit the shower.'

She didn't watch him go. She stared straight ahead at the trees silhouetted against a velvety purple sky. Did he *have* to constantly announce his intention to take a shower? Couldn't he just go and do it without informing her all the time?

Planting images in her head. Naked images. Wet images.

It was going to be a very long two months.

CHAPTER SEVEN

A FEW WEEKS later Hamish was sitting in the work vehicle, eating lunch under a shady tree. It was exceptionally hot today and they were between jobs. He was flicking through images on his phone to show Jenny some pictures of the feed lot his family ran back in Toowoomba. He came across the one he'd taken of Lola that day with jacaranda flowers in her hair and smiled.

Things had been a little weird to start with between them but they seemed to have settled down into an easy kind of co-existence. It wasn't the flirty banter of their relationship a few months ago, or sex on the couch, which he probably wouldn't say no to, but it was something he could walk away from when his time in Sydney was up.

Because the more he got to know Lola, the more he knew, she was city right down to her bootstraps. And it didn't matter how *wicked* his thoughts got alone in his room each night, Lola wasn't going country for anyone.

Just then a call came over the radio and Jenny threw the last of her sandwich down her neck. 'Buckle up,' she said as they climbed into the vehicle and she flicked on the siren.

Hamish turned his phone off, shutting down thoughts of Lola as adrenaline flushed into his system and he concentrated on that as they screamed through the Sydney streets.

They arrived at the home of a fifty-six-year-old man called Robert twelve minutes later. He'd had a probable MI—myocardial infarction or heart attack. He had no pulse and wasn't breathing.

It was Hamish and Jenny's second of the day. The heat wave they were experiencing was no doubt contributing to that.

Two advanced care paramedics were already on scene. They'd arrived six minutes previously and were administering CPR, having taken over from the patient's wife and a neighbour who was a nurse.

The fact that Robert had had lifesaving measures carried out immediately on collapsing could probably mean the difference between him dying today and living.

Jenny quickly intubated the patient and stayed at the head, delivering puffs of oxygen into Robert's lungs via the breathing tube, while one of the advanced care paramedics, another woman, continued to do compressions. The other was busy inserting a couple of intravenous lines and Hamish was managing the emergency drugs and the defibrillator, which had already been connected when they'd arrived.

'Recommends another shock,' he said, as he flipped the lids on another mini-jet of adrenaline and wiped his brow with his forearm. It was stiflingly hot in the little, inner-suburban shoebox house.

Jenny gave a few quick hyper-inflating puffs of oxygen before she joined the others, who had shuffled out of contact with the body. 'All clear,' Hamish called, double checking everyone was away before he pushed the button and delivered the recommended shock.

The patient's body jerked slightly—not quite like the dramatic arch seen on TV shows—and all eyes watched the heart trace on the monitor.

A hot flood of relief washed over Hamish as the previous frenetic, squiggly line suddenly flipped into an organised pattern. 'Sinus tachy,' he announced, although he didn't need to. Everyone there knew how to read an ECG trace.

Jenny and the other female paramedic high-fived before she said, 'Okay, let's get him locked and loaded.'

They'd revived the patient, brought Robert back from the brink, but heart-attack patients were notoriously unstable in the hours immediately after the heart muscle dying, which meant Robert needed a tertiary care facility pronto. Somewhere with a cath lab, a cardiac surgeon and an intensive care unit.

'We'll take him to Kirribilli General,' Jenny said.

They unloaded the patient in the emergency department twenty minutes later. Hamish listened to Jenny's rapid-fire handover to the team. Lola was right, she was an excellent paramedic.

'I wonder where the third one's going to be,' Hamish said as they headed back to the ambulance.

Because these things tended to come in threes.

'Somewhere with air-con, I hope,' Jenny quipped.

Hamish laughed. It was nice working with someone who was not only good at their job but also knew how to make light of a situation.

It was the kind of job that needed it.

A call came over the radio as soon as they were seated. Another suspected MI. 'No rest for the wicked,' Jenny said, flicking the sirens on.

And Hamish's thoughts went straight to Lola.

* * *

Hamish sighed as he entered the apartment later that evening. It was good to be home. It was still warm outside but their apartment was getting a nice breeze from the direction of the beach and Lola had all the doors and windows open to catch it.

The sheer curtain at the sliding door to the balcony was billowing with it and Lola was shimmying in the kitchen to some music she was obviously listening to via her ear buds. She had her back to him as she stood at the counter, a bottle of beer in one hand and a fork in the other, attacking a container of leftover Chinese takeaway.

She'd obviously had a shower. Her hair was wet and she was wearing her short gown that brushed her legs at mid-thigh. He didn't know for sure what she wore underneath it but he had spent a lot of time speculating over it.

Tank top and lacy thong were his current picks.

She looked cool and relaxed and was a sight for sore eyes after a long day. Something he wouldn't mind coming home to every day, in fact...

He shoved his shoulder against the doorframe. 'You're chipper today.'

She startled and whipped around. 'Bloody hell, Hamish. You scared the living daylights out of me.'

She brought the hand holding her beer to her chest and Hamish's temperature kicked up a notch as the action pulled the gown taut across her cleavage and the tight buds of two erect nipples.

He dragged his gaze upwards. 'Is your patient improving?'

Lola had told him about the woman waiting for a heart transplant. Not any particulars of her identity, just her situation, and he could tell by how fondly she talked about the family and how often she seemed to be assigned to the case that this particular patient had slipped under Lola's barriers.

A hazard of the job. He'd been there himself.

'Yeah.' She grinned as she pulled her ear buds out and her face lit up. His breath hitched. 'She's really turned a corner. She's coming along in leaps and bounds now. Still needs a heart, of course, but...'

Hamish nodded. The imminent threat to her life had passed but she needed a transplant to survive going forward. He hoped she got one and that the family got something extra-special to celebrate as the festive season approached. Even if it meant some other family would have the worst Christmas of their life.

He remembered when his sister-in-law, Merridy, had got her kidney. In her case, his brother Lachlan had fortunately been a tissue match for her and had been able to donate one of his. What a joy, a relief, it had been, knowing they hadn't had to wait for somebody to die to give Merridy that gift. But also how sobering it had been for everyone, knowing that others weren't so lucky.

'You're drinking beer?' He'd only ever seen her drinking wine.

Why was there something hot about a chick drinking beer?

'That's because it's *Die Hard* marathon night.'

Hamish laughed. 'And that requires beer?'

She rolled her eyes. 'You think John MacClane drinks Sauvignon Blanc?'

'I wouldn't think so.' They both smiled and Hamish ground his feet into the floor as the urge to walk over and kiss her almost overwhelmed him. 'I thought we were out of beer? I meant to get some on my way home.'

'I picked some up from the liquor warehouse on my way home.'

Hamish grimaced. That place gave him the willies. A football stadium of booze was mind-boggling. 'Rather you than me.'

'It's okay, *Country*.' A smile hovered on her mouth. 'I know you don't get shops that big where you come from. I've got your back.'

Hamish laughed. Her teasing set a warm glow in the centre of his chest. 'Toowoomba isn't exactly a two-horse town. It's a fairly decent size.'

'You're going to be moving to a two-horse town, though, right? Once your course is done?'

'Hopefully. Those jobs don't come up very often. People don't tend to leave them once they're in.' Hamish laughed at her visible shudder. 'Newsflash, *City*, some people like living in small towns.'

'If you say so.'

'Plus, it's a professional challenge. Out there, it'll be just me on shift, no back-up. The next ambulance service could be a couple of hundred kilometres away.'

'Sounds terrifying.'

'Nah. There'll be a doctor and Flying Doctor back-up but the autonomy…the skills I'll acquire can only make me a better paramedic.'

'I think that would drive me nuts. I like working with a team. I thrive on being a small part in a well-oiled machine. I like the people I work with. I enjoy their company. I wouldn't want to work in isolation.'

Hamish shrugged. 'I don't want to do it for ever necessarily. But I'd like to do it for a while.' Clearly, though, she didn't. And it bothered him more than it should have.

'Well…' She looked at him like he was a little crazy. 'Each to their own, I guess.' She took a slug of her beer. 'Are you joining me tonight?'

'*Die Hard* marathon?' He grinned, shaking off the

urban-rural divide between them. 'Absolutely! I'll just have a shower.'

She nodded. 'I'll pop the corn.'

Lola watched him go. Good Lord! The man took more showers than a teenage boy who'd just discovered the Victoria's Secret catalogue. Which led her down a whole other path she did not want to go...

She got busy in the kitchen instead, putting the popcorn bag in the microwave and grabbing two frosty longnecked bottles out of the fridge. When her mind started to wander to his shower, she distracted herself by rereading the latest postcard from May stuck on the fridge. She was in Mongolia, the usual *Wish you were here* in her lovely loopy handwriting making Lola smile.

By the time the popcorn had popped and been decanted into a bowl, Lola had cracked the lids off the beers, and the first movie was queued, Hamish was out of the shower. He reappeared in a T-shirt and loose basketball shorts that fell to just above his knee but clung a little due to the humidity.

It was what he usually wore after his shower—just a little more indecent tonight.

But that wasn't a particularly helpful thought right now as he stood there, temptation incarnate, his hair damp and curling against his neck. She had to remind herself that this *thing* she felt could go nowhere.

That they lived very different lives. Wanted very different things.

Still, the lights were out and the glow from the television caught the ginger highlights of his stubbly jawline and he smelled like coconut and the deodorant he used that reminded her of fresh Alpine air, heavy with the scent of pine.

How could a man smell like the beach and the Alps all at once?

'Beer?' Lola thrust a long-necked bottle at him.

'You read my mind.'

He took it from her and they clinked. He took a pull of his as he sat beside her, the popcorn bowl between them. It was a large bowl but it still put him closer than was good for her sanity. Of course, if he thought about what they'd done on this couch half as much as she did, no amount of space was adequate.

'Okay, roll it,' he said.

Lola laughed and pressed 'play', taking a long cool swallow of her beer as the credits did their thing. She could do this. She could sit here on this couch with Hamish, where they'd done the wild thing a few months ago, and watch one of her favourite movies as if they'd never laid hands on each other.

A sudden thought occurred to her and she turned to face him slightly. 'You *are* a *Die Hard* fan, right?'

He smiled and her heart skipped a beat as he raised his bottle to her. 'Yippie-ki-yay.' He tapped it against hers again and settled back against the couch, grabbing a handful of popcorn.

Lola was so damn happy she actually sighed.

After two of the most entertaining hours of her life, Lola was sad to see the end of the movie. Normally she and Grace just sat and watched it, gobbling it up like they gobbled the popcorn. But Hamish was a much more active consumer. He kept up a running commentary of interesting asides about the films or the actors and mimicked his favourite lines, even adlibbing better ones.

They'd also had a serious discussion about it being a

rom-com. He'd been horrified in an endearingly masculine way when Lola had dared to suggest it.

'Well…thank you very much for your insights into the
movie,' he said, as Lola hit 'stop' on the DVD remote.
'They're wrong, of course…' his lips quirked '…but it's
given me a whole different perspective on it.'

Lola laughed and threw a kernel of popcorn at him.
It was a spontaneous thing that fitted the mood of the
moment but one she regretted immediately as the glitter
of laughter in his eyes changed to a competitive gleam.

'Oh, it's going to be like that, is it?' He dug into their
second bowl of popcorn and grabbed a handful of kernels.

'Hamish.'

If he heard the warning note in her voice he chose
to ignore it as he slowly lifted his hand above her head.

'Don't you *dare*.'

He just smiled and opened it. Popcorn fell around
her like snow. When they settled he plucked one out of
her hair and ate it, his eyes goading her to do something
about it.

'Right.' She grinned at him, plunging both hands into
the frothing bowl and coming out with two fistfuls. 'You
asked for it.'

He laughed, which only encouraged her further. He
was prepared to swerve and duck, obviously, but not prepared for her to grab his T-shirt and dump the popcorn
down his front.

'Well, now,' Hamish muttered, 'this is war.'

He reached for the front of her gown with one hand
and the popcorn with the other. Lola half laughed, half
squealed, flinging herself back, trying to twist away, but
Hamish was bigger and stronger and more determined,
laughing as he followed her down, sending the popcorn
bowl flying as he anchored her squirming body to the

couch and stuffed a handful of kernels down the front of her gown.

Lola joined him in laughter as the popcorn scratched against her skin. She tried to remove it but he just shook his head and said, 'Nuh-uh,' as he grabbed her hands.

They were both panting and laughing hard from their playful struggle so it took a moment to register that he had her well and truly pinned, his hips over hers, one big thigh shoved between her legs, his hands entwined in hers above their heads.

He seemed to realise at the same time, the glitter in his eyes different now—not light or teasing.

Darker. Hotter.

Their gazes locked and Lola's heart punched against her rib cage, nothing but the sounds of their breathing between them now. Panting had turned into something rougher, more needy as she stared at him looming over her. An ache roared to life between her legs, right where his knee was shoved, and she couldn't fight the urge to squirm against the pressure to relieve the ache.

His eyes widened at the action and he pressed his knee against her harder. She gasped at the heat and friction building between her legs and he pushed again.

'Lola,' he muttered, his breathing as rough as sandpaper, his gaze boring into hers. Then, as if something had snapped, he swooped down and kissed her.

Lola flared like a lit match beneath the onslaught, moaning his name. Her hands, suddenly free from his, slid into the back of his hair, holding him there. His hands found her hips, gripping them tight as he ground his knee against her over and over.

Lights popped and flared behind Lola's eyes, her whole world melting down as his mouth and his body worked hers. She was hot, too hot, and her heart was beating too fast. There were too many clothes. She wanted them gone. Wanted them off. Wanted him naked and inside her, pounding away, calling her name.

She reached down between them for his shorts, needing them gone while she could still think, while his kisses hadn't quite stolen her capacity to participate. Her hand connected with his erection and she made a triumphant noise at the back of her throat as she grabbed it and fondled him through his shorts. He groaned, breaking off the kiss, dropping his forehead to her neck, his lips warm against the frantic beat of her pulse at the base of her throat.

He was big and hard and solid in her hand. She squeezed him and he swore into her neck, his voice like gravel, his breath a hot caress.

This. She wanted this. Him. Inside her. Right where his knee was pressed tight and hard.

Lola moved her hand to his waistband, sliding her fingers beneath it, her pulse so loud in her ears it was like Niagara Falls inside her head. But before she hit her objective, his big hand clamped around her wrist.

'Wait.'

He panted into her neck for a few more moments, his body a dead weight on top of hers. Lola also panted, blinking into the dark room, grappling with the sudden cessation of endorphins, confused yet still craving at the same time.

He eased himself up a little, his hand still shackling her wrist. 'Are you sure about this, Lola?'

His gaze bored into hers once again and she could see he was struggling with this as much as she was. His arousal was as obvious in his eyes as it had been in her hand. But there was conflict there as well.

'Because if we keep going like this we'll end up hav-

ing sex on this couch again, and I'm telling you now I
don't think I can go back to being just roomies again if
we do.'

The implication of his words slowly sank in, the sexual buzz fizzling as Lola's brain started to kick in. It was
like a cold bucket of water.

But it was the cold bucket of water she needed.

'Right.' She nodded and pulled her hand out of his,
her breathing erratic. What the hell had she been thinking? 'Of course. Sorry… I…' She trailed off because she
didn't have any kind of adequate explanation for what
the hell had just happened.

'Don't worry about it. It's fine.' He rolled off her, his
butt sliding to the floor, his back against the couch.

'No…it's not,' she said breathily, her hands shaking a
little. He was right, they'd overstepped their boundary.
And they probably needed to re-establish it. 'I think we
need to talk about it.'

'Okay.'

He didn't turn and perversely Lola wanted him to turn
and look at her. And, *Lordy*, she wanted to touch him.

She didn't.

'It wouldn't work out between you and me. No matter
how good the sex is. We have different jobs and different lives and different *goals*.'

He nodded. 'I know.'

'I'm sorry that we got carried away but I think we both
need to agree that if this living arrangement is to work
out, we just can't go there.'

He nodded again before rising to his feet. He was looking down at her but his eyes were too hooded in the semi-
darkness to really see what he was feeling. He shoved a
hand through his hair. 'You're right.'

Lola reached for his hand but he pulled back slightly

and it felt like a slap to the face. 'I'm sorry,' she whispered once more.

'Me too,' he whispered back then stepped away, feet crunching over popcorn as he headed to his room.

CHAPTER EIGHT

NOVEMBER MORPHED INTO DECEMBER. The weather got hotter, the days longer. The Christmas tree had gone up in the apartment. Hamish had been in Sydney for five weeks and was working his first run of night shifts. He didn't mind working nights usually, he was a good sleeper and night shift in Sydney was a hell of a lot busier than back home. Which was great—there was nothing more tiring than trying to fill in twelve empty hours.

But Lola was also working nights, which meant they were home together during the day. *Sleeping.* A much bigger psychological temptation than being at home together and sleeping during the night.

Because the night was for sleeping. And being in bed during the day felt decadent. Like flying first class or a good bottle of cognac. Or daytime sex.

Totally and utterly *decadent.*

They weren't having daytime sex, of course. They weren't having *any* sex, thanks to their conversation after things had got out of hand on movie night. She was right, their lives were going in different directions and he respected that.

But it didn't help him sleep any better.

Having Lola just across the hallway from him was far too distracting. Sure as hell *not* conducive to sleep. Not conducive to night shifts. Not conducive to being a safe practitioner when he was so damn tired when he was on shift he couldn't think straight.

Consequently, Hamish wasn't looking forward to heading home in a few hours to repeat the whole not-sleeping process again. But it was his third night. Maybe if he was tired enough he could sleep despite the temptation of Lola in the next room.

Hamish's thoughts were interrupted by a squawk from his radio. 'Damn,' Jenny grumbled. It was almost two in the morning, they'd been going since they'd clocked on at eight and they'd only just left the hospital from their last emergency room drop-off. 'Are we ever going to get a chance for a cup of coffee tonight?'

But her grumbles quickly ceased when the seriousness of the call became evident. Some kind of explosion had happened in a night club in Kings Cross. It was a Saturday night in one of the city's oldest club districts. 'We have a mass casualty incident. Repeat mass casualty. Multiple fatalities, multiple victims. Code one please.'

Code one. Lights and sirens.

Neither Hamish nor Jenny needed to be told that. As intensive care paramedics, all their jobs were lights and sirens, but the urgency in the voice on the other end of the radio painted a pretty grim picture.

Jenny flicked on the siren. 'Hold onto your hat.'

Hamish had never seen anything like what greeted them when they arrived on scene twelve minutes later. A cacophony of sirens from a cavalcade of arriving emergency services vehicles—police, fire and ambulance, including several intensive care cars—*whooped* into the warm night air. The area had been cordoned off and over

AMY ANDREWS   89

two dozen firemen were battling the blaze that currently
forked out of the windows on the upper storey.

Others were running in and out of the lower floor,
evacuating victims, masks in place to protect them from
the smoke that billowed from the blown-out windows.
It hung in the air, clogging Hamish's nose and stinging
his eyes.

He and Jenny, their fully loaded packs in hand, re-
ported to the scene controller. 'Some kind of incendiary
device, although we won't know for sure until afterwards.
Blast killed several people instantly and started a fire on
the first floor, panic caused a stampede and the upper
balcony collapsed under the weight of people trying to
get out. The night club was packed to the gills, so we're
talking at least a couple of hundred people.'

Hamish glanced around the scene as evacuated victims huddled in groups across the road from the night
club. Some stood and some sat as they stared dazedly at
the building, their faces bloodied, their clothes ripped.
A lot of them were crying, some quietly in a kind of despair, others loudly in shock and rage and disbelief, railing against the police who had been tasked to question
them and stop them from running back into the building
to find their mates.

An incendiary device?

Someone had done this deliberately?

'Go to the triage station. There are several red tags
there and more coming out all the time. The collapse has
trapped quite a few people and the rescue squad are digging them out.'

'Red tag' referred to the colour system employed in
mass casualty events to prioritise treatment. Everyone in
the triage section would be tagged with a colour. Green
for the walking wounded, yellow for stable but requir-

ing observation, white for minor injury not requiring medical assistance.

And black. For the deceased.

Red identified patients who couldn't survive without immediate attention but still had survivable injuries.

Hamish followed Jenny down the street, adrenaline pumping through his system at the job ahead. He slowed as he passed an area that was obviously being used as a temporary morgue, a tarp being erected to shield the scene from the television cameras already vying for the most grisly footage. He didn't need to see them to know the dozen or so bodies lying under the sheets would be wearing black tags.

He glanced away, concentrating on what was ahead of them, not behind. On the people he could help, not the ones he couldn't. If he went there now, if he started thinking about such a senseless waste of life, about the horror of it, he'd get too angry to be of any use. He needed to channel his adrenaline, harness it for the hours ahead, not burn it all up in his rage.

A dozen paramedics, their reflective stripes glowing in the flare of emergency sirens, were working their way through the victims when they pulled up at triage. Jenny introduced both of them to the senior paramedic in charge. She calmly and efficiently pointed them to a section where two other intensive care paramedics were currently working among half a dozen casualties. 'Over there, please.'

Jenny shook her head in dismay as they made their way over. 'Who would do this?'

Hamish didn't have an answer, he was still grappling with it himself.

They got to work, steadily treating the red cards—establishing airways, treating haemorrhages and burns, getting access for fluids and drugs. In two hours Hamish had intubated four patients who hadn't looked much older than twenty and dispatched them for transport to one of the many hospitals around the city that had already activated their mass casualty protocols.

He'd hadn't been able to save two people and they'd died despite his attempts to treat their life-threatening injuries.

One, a girl wearing an 'Eighteen today' sash across her purple dress, was going to haunt his dreams, he just knew it. The dress was the colour of Lola's jacarandas, with the exception of the bright crimson blood spray across the front.

'Help me.' That's what she'd said to him, her eyes large and frightened, just before blood had welled up her throat and she'd coughed and spluttered and the light had drained from her eyes as she'd lost consciousness.

Hamish had worked frantically on her to staunch the bleeding, to stabilise her enough to get her to hospital, but he hadn't been able to save her.

He hadn't even known her name.

In all probability the chunk of whatever the hell had hit her chest had probably ruptured something major. What she'd needed had been a cardiothoracic surgeon and an operating theatre. What she'd got had been him.

And he hadn't been enough.

'This is the last of them,' a female voice said.

Hamish looked up from the chest tube he was taping into place, surprised to realise that dawn had broken. He hadn't noticed. Just as he hadn't noticed the stench of smoke in the air any more or the constant background wail of sirens as they came and went from the scene.

He'd shut everything out as he'd lurched from one person to the next, concentrating only on the one in front of him.

Two rescue squad officers, a male and the female who'd spoken, placed a stretcher bearing a long, lanky male on the ground. He was sporting an oxygen mask and there was a hard collar around his neck. A small portable monitor blipped away next to his head.

Hamish nodded at a crew who were waiting to whisk his current patient away. 'Thanks,' he said as they snapped up the rails of the gurney and pushed the patient briskly towards the waiting ambulance.

He turned his attention to the new patient. 'He's breathing,' the female officer continued as if she hadn't stopped. 'His pulse is fifty-eight but he's unconscious, sats are good.'

Hamish didn't like the pulse being that low—it should be rattling along, working overtime to compensate for the trauma his body had sustained.

'He was right at the bottom of the collapsed balcony debris.'

The guy looked remarkably untouched, considering, but Hamish had been doing this long enough to know that sometimes it was the way of things. That internal injuries weren't visible from the outside.

He pulled off his gloves and grabbed a new pair from the box in his bag and snapped them on. The bag was somewhat depleted now. He crouched then knelt against the rough bitumen yet again. His knees protested the move but Hamish ignored the pain. Gravel rash was a minor inconvenience compared to burns, blast injuries and the other trauma he'd seen in the last few hours.

'Do you know his name?' So many of the victims hadn't had an ID on them but Hamish always liked to know who he was treating.

'Wesley, according to the driver's licence in the wallet we found in his pocket.'

Hamish nodded. 'Thanks.' The rescue squad officers turned to go. 'How many fatalities?' His voice was quiet but enough to stop the woman in her tracks. He'd been trying not to notice the line of bodies beneath the sheets growing but every time he lifted his head they were in his line of sight.

'Twenty-six.'

He shut his eyes briefly, the image of a purple dress fluttering through his mind like the sails of a kite. It was going to be a really terrible Christmas for a lot of families across the city.

'Wesley.' Hamish turned to his patient, his voice deep and authoritative as he delivered a brisk sternal rub.

Nothing.

'Wesley,' he said again, deeper and a little louder as he shone his penlight into the patient's eyes. Both were fixed and dilated. Neither responded to light.

Oh, no. Crap.

Jenny crouched beside him. 'Bad?'

Hamish nodded. 'Non-responsive. Pupils fixed, dilated. GCS of three.'

'Okay, then.' Jenny grabbed her bag. 'Let's intubate, get some lines in and get him to hospital. This guy has a date with a neurosurgeon's drill.'

Hamish didn't think Jenny really believed performing a burr hole was going to result in a positive outcome. They had no idea how long Wesley had been in this condition. If he'd had surgery performed immediately post-injury, it *might* have helped, but it was probably way too late by now.

More likely the sustained pressure in his head from a bleed, which had probably occurred when his skull had crashed into the ground, had caused diffuse injury. If he came though this, the likelihood of a severe neurological deficit was strong.

But one thing he knew for sure was that sometimes people surprised you and it wasn't their job to make ethical decisions. It was their job to save who could be saved and Wesley had made it thus far. And, hell, Hamish wanted to believe that a guy who was still breathing, despite the trauma he'd received, could pull through this.

God knew, they needed a Christmas miracle after everything tonight.

Lola wasn't surprised to see Hamish pushing through the swing doors of her intensive care unit. Normally paramedics dropped patients in the emergency department and Emergency brought them to ICU if warranted. But when a patient was already intubated it saved time and handling for paramedics to bring the patient directly to ICU. They'd had two admissions like this already tonight from the night club bombing.

She was pleased it was him accompanying the patient this time, though. She'd figured he'd be there on scene somewhere and she hadn't realised how tense she'd been about it until she'd spotted him and the grimness of his mouth had kicked up into a familiar smile.

It wasn't that she thought Hamish might be in some kind of danger, it was more professional empathy. Lola could only guess at the kind of carnage he must have witnessed from what had already come in here and from the news reports they were hearing. Dozens of crushed, broken and burned bodies. Bright young things just out having fun. And so close to Christmas.

Things like that could do a number on your head.

'Bed twelve,' she said.

As one of the shifts runners, it had been Lola's job to get the bed space ready for their new admission. They'd been alerted to this arrival about fifteen minutes ago so she'd had time to customise the set-up for a patient with a head injury. And now it was action stations as two more nurses—the one assigned to look after Wesley and the nurse in charge—and two doctors—the ICU and the neuro registrar—descended on bed twelve.

They worked as a team, listening to Hamish's methodical handover as they got Wesley on the bed, hooked him up to the ventilator, plugged him into the monitors, started up some fluids and commenced some sedation.

The ICU registrar was inserting an arterial line as Hamish's handover drew to a close. By the time he'd answered all the questions that had been thrown at him, the arterial line was in, they had a red blood-pressure trace on the screen with an alarmingly wide pulse pressure and the registrar had thrust a full arterial blood gas syringe at Lola and she filled some lab tubes with blood from another syringe.

'Go and get some coffee,' she threw over her shoulder to Hamish and Jenny as she headed for the blood gas machine out back. Jenny knew where the staffroom was and they looked like they could do with some bolstering.

Lola was inserting the blood-filled syringe into the machine when Hamish appeared and said, 'Hey.'

He reeked of smoke and looked like hell. 'Hey.' She smiled at him for a beat or two, her heart squeezing, before she returned her attention to entering Wesley's details into the computer.

He didn't say anything, just watched her, and she waited for the machine to beep at her to remove the syringe before she said anything. 'Are you okay?' she asked.

It would take a couple of minutes for the machine to print out the results so she had the time to check up on him.

'Yep.' His smile warmed his eyes and was immensely reassuring. 'Just tired.'

She nodded. 'How was it out there?'

He didn't say anything for a moment then shook his head. 'Awful.'

Lola didn't have any reply to that. No easy words to soothe the terrible memories no doubt still fresh in his mind. So she did the only thing she knew how to do, what nurses always did—she touched him. She reached across and squeezed his arm.

'Go.' She squeezed his arm again. 'Get coffee. I think there's still some choc-chip biscuits someone brought in earlier too. You look like you need a sugar hit.'

He gave a half-laugh that sounded so weary she wanted to tuck him into bed herself. 'You look tired too.'

That was an understatement. It was almost six and Lola hadn't even had a break yet. Not even to go to the bathroom. She wasn't tired mentally, but physically she was exhausted. Her feet throbbed, her lower back twinged, her stomach growled and she had a dull ache behind her eyes.

Being a runner usually meant a busy shift but some shifts were crazily busy. Like tonight with their third critical admission as well as several existing patients who'd decided tonight was the night to destabilise.

Emma was one of them.

Her blood pressure had shot up at the start of the shift and it'd taken them several worrying hours to get it down to a much safer reading. She was fine again now but it was just further evidence of the instability of her failing heart. A transplant couldn't happen soon enough.

Lola shrugged off her weariness. It was just the way

it went sometimes. 'It's almost knock-off time.' That was the one consolation. In an hour and a half her shift would be over—so would his—and they could both get some well-earned sleep.

The blood-gas machine spewed out a strip of paper, which Lola tore off and studied. 'How is it?' Hamish asked.

'Not great.' She handed it to him. 'His carbon dioxide level's too high.' Which would increase his intracranial pressure—not the thing Wesley's brain needed.

'I've got to get this back to the reg.' He nodded and handed the slip over, stepping away from the doorway so she could pass. He fell in beside her as she walked briskly to the bed space. 'I'll probably be late home,' she said. 'This place is a mess and we're not going to get a chance to play catch-up until the morning staff come on.'

There was a roomful of discarded equipment out back that needed attention and things were in desperate need of a restock.

'I don't think I'm going to be home early either. Jenny mentioned something about the boss probably wanting to do a bit of an informal debrief with her before we leave so...'

Lola nodded. 'Good idea.' She pulled up beside the registrar and handed over the blood-gas printout. 'Now go get coffee.'

He smiled. 'Yes ma'am.'

CHAPTER NINE

LOLA HAD NOT long succumbed to sleep on the couch when the door opened and her eyelids pinged open. Between the hurricane-like roar of the fan overhead and the fact that she'd dropped like a stone into the deepest depths of unconsciousness, she was amazed she'd heard a thing.

She must have really been attuned to the key in the lock!

Squinting at the time on the television display—it was almost ten—she swung her legs to the floor. 'Hamish?'

'Sorry,' he said from somewhere behind her. 'I didn't mean to wake you. I thought you'd be in bed. What are you doing out here?'

Lola's thoughts floated in a thick soup of disorientation. What *was* she doing out here? 'I'm…waiting for you to come home.'

'Sorry, I didn't realise. Debrief went on for ever.'

He appeared in front of her, lowering himself down on the end of the coffee table and setting his backpack on the floor. There were a few feet separating them but, as always, she felt the tug of him.

'You didn't have to wait up.'

Lola shrugged. Did he think she'd just go to bed after the things he'd seen last night without checking in with him first? Just because she didn't think they should get intimately involved, it didn't mean they still couldn't care for each other, have empathy for each other.

'It's fine,' she dismissed, suddenly realising that he was in shorts and T-shirt instead of his uniform and that his russet hair was damp and curling at his nape. 'You had a shower at work?' He didn't usually.

'Yeah. Everything stank of smoke, even my hair.'

He ran his palms down his thighs, drawing her gaze to the gold-blond hairs on his legs and the state of his knees. They were criss-crossed with tiny livid cuts and areas that had been rubbed raw.

'Do they hurt?'

'A little.' He shrugged as if it was just a mild inconvenience. 'How's Wesley?'

Lola had been waiting for the question, knowing it would come. She wished she had better news to tell Hamish, even though she knew *he* knew full well the severity of Wesley's injuries. 'He'd not long come back from CT when I left.'

He nodded slowly. 'Bad?'

'Diffuse brain injury with severe cerebral swelling. They were prepping him for Theatre.'

'Right.' He nodded and rose from the table, heading to the kitchen. She heard the fridge door open and he called, 'You want a beer?'

'No.' Lola didn't think twice at Hamish consuming a beer at ten in the morning. Quite a few of her colleagues had a drink or two before going to sleep after night duty. They swore it was better than sleeping tablets, which many shift workers resorted to.

He reappeared in the kitchen doorway, leaning against the jamb as he took a few deep swallows. The hem of his T-shirt lifted slightly, flashing a strip of tanned abs.

'They're saying on television that the bomb was set off by some guy who's a disgruntled ex-employee,' she said.

'Yeah, I heard. Death toll's risen to thirty-four too.' He wandered closer as if he was going to resume his seat on the table but changed course, heading for the balcony, stopping short to just stare out the door she'd opened earlier.

Lola didn't say anything, waiting for him to say more. If he wanted to. When he didn't, she filled the silence. 'You want to talk about it?'

He shook his head. 'Nope.' But within a few seconds he was turning around, his eyes seeking hers, searching hers. 'I've been trying to wrap my head around how that guy justified this to himself.' He took a swig of his beer. 'I mean, you got sacked, dude. I get it. That sucks.' He shrugged. 'Rant at your boss or your wife, go home and kick the wall. But *why* would anyone think it's okay to seek revenge like this? To kill so many innocent people?'

Lola shook her head. 'I…don't know.' She wished she did. She wished she had the answers he sought.

He was obviously still in the thick of the action inside his head. Probably second-guessing his every move, wishing he'd done something differently. That stuff took time to fully tease out. Took a lot of reflection before a person came to the conclusion that they'd done the best they could.

'I don't know why some people do terrible things, Hamish, but thank goodness for people like you.' She smiled at him because he looked so lonely all the way over there by himself. 'For those who charge in to help when everyone else is running away. There'd be a lot more fatalities from last night without people like you around.'

He nodded. 'Yeah.' Tipping his head back, he drained

his beer, staring at the bottle in his hands for a moment or two before he glanced at her and said, 'Think I'll hit the sack now.'

'You should. You look dead on your feet.' He was swaying and his eyes were bloodshot. She'd bet her last cent they were as gritty as hers. There were tiny lines around his eyes that she'd never noticed before and his impossibly square jaw was as tight as a steel trap.

'Says the woman with a cushion mark on her face and scary hair.'

Lola gaped for a moment before his lips spread into a smile and a low chuckle slipped from his mouth. She pushed her hands through her fuzzy mane to tame the knotty, blonde ringlets but there was no nope for them. She probably looked like she'd been pulled through a hedge backwards, while he looked good enough to eat.

Even exhausted, the man wore sexy better than any man had a right to.

'Your sense of humour's pretty tired too, I see.'

'Yep.' He grinned. 'We're both kinda beat.'

'At least you only have one more night. I have three.' Lola didn't mind night shift but when the unit was busy for a sustained period of time like it had been, a run of night shifts could really take it out of her.

'Some days off would be good,' Hamish said, cutting into her thoughts.

Yeah. He could no doubt use some mental time-out after last night. But, more than anything, right now he needed to sleep.

They both did.

'Okay, well, I'm taking my scary hair to bed.' It didn't seem like he was going to make the first move towards the bedrooms so she did it for him. 'Night-night.'

She didn't look at him as she turned away in case she

did something crazy like offer to rock him to sleep. She just kept walking until she pulled her door shut, placing temptation firmly on the other side.

Hamish woke at two in the afternoon for about the tenth time. His room was on the side of the apartment that copped full sunlight for most of the day, and the curtains at the big window wouldn't block out candlelight, let alone the December sun in Sydney. It hadn't ever bothered him before and he could usually sleep like the dead after night shift.

But he hadn't just been through a normal night shift.

He was coming off an adrenaline high that had left him wrung out and edgy, his brain grappling with the images of the kids he'd helped and all those bodies under sheets. When he did manage to drift off, his dreams were haunted by a woman in a purple dress.

Just like he'd known they would be.

And now he was awake again. Exhausted, but too chicken to close his eyes, plus it was too hot to fall asleep, anyway. There was sweat on his chest and in the small of his back. The fan going at full speed did nothing but push the stifling air around.

He *had* to sleep. He *needed* to sleep. He had to operate a vehicle in six hours *and* be thinking clearly. He wouldn't be any help to anyone if he went to work even more exhausted than he'd left it.

Hamish rolled on his side, forced himself to shut his eyes, to breathe in through his nose and out through his mouth. To do it again and again until he started to drift. And then a flutter of purple fabric splattered in blood billowed through his mind and his eyes flicked open.

Grabbing his pillows, he plonked them on top of his head, shoved his face into them and let out a giant *yawp!*

'Hamish?'

Startled, he ripped the pillows off his head to find Lola striding into his room, her short gown covering her from neck to knee but hugging everything in between. He was pretty sure she wasn't wearing much of anything underneath.

Great.

'Lola?'

'Are you okay?' She stood at the end of the bed, her forehead creased, her arms folded tight against her chest.

'Yes.' Hamish flopped onto his back and stared at the ceiling. It was that or ogle her. 'Just...can't sleep. Have you been skulking outside my door?'

'No.' He smiled at the affront in her voice. 'I was just passing to get a drink of water and I heard a noise. I thought you were...upset or something.'

He gave a harsh laugh, air huffing from his lungs. *Great.* Lola thought he was lying in bed, crying. It'd be emasculating if he wasn't currently sporting an erection the size of the Opera House.

He thanked God for his decision to keep his underwear on today and for the sheet that was bunched over his crotch.

'I'm frustrated,' he told the ceiling. *In more ways than one.* 'I need to sleep but my brain is ticking over and the fan is totally useless in this heat.' He raised his head again. 'We even have air-con in the country, Lola, what gives?'

'Grace and I moved into the apartment in the middle of winter. And there were fans...they're usually enough.'

'How do you sleep after nights on days like this?'

'Well, my room is quite a bit cooler than yours. Grace said I should take it because she didn't work nights on her job. But I have been known to get up and walk through a cold shower then flop on the bed wringing wet and let the fan air-dry me. That's almost as good as air-con.'

Hamish shut his eyes and suppressed a rising groan as his head fell back against the pillow. That image was not helping the situation in his underwear. Not one little bit.

'Are you dreaming about it?'

About her being wet and naked on her bed? He sure as hell would be now. But he knew that wasn't what she was talking about. He sighed. 'Yes.'

'You want to talk about it?'

'No.' What he wanted was to drag her down on the bed, rip that gown off her, roll her under him and sink inside her, and just forget about it all for a while. 'I don't want to talk about it. I don't even want to *think* about it. What I want right now is to just forget it so I can get to sleep. I *need* to sleep. I want it to *not* be forty degrees in this room so I can just *go to sleep.*'

She didn't say anything for a long time and a weird kind of tension built in his abdomen. Hamish lifted his head and immediately wished he hadn't. The way she was looking at him shot sparks right up his spine.

'What?' His voice was annoyingly raspy and he cleared it as her gaze roved over his body.

She nodded then, as if to herself, before saying, 'I can help you with that.'

Hamish swore he could feel his heart skip a beat. Where the hell was she going with this? Was she going to fix him a long cool drink or was she offering something else? 'What do you suggest?'

'My room is cooler and sex is not only the best sleeping pill around but I've generally found that if it's good enough it can also induce a temporary kind of amnesia. I can only surmise from the kind of sex we've already had together that the amnesia will be significant. What do you think?'

Hamish blinked. What didn't he think? There was no hope for his erection now.

He should decline. It was all kinds of screwed up and he knew how it'd mess with the boundaries they'd put in place. But he'd be lying if he said he didn't crave the solace—the oblivion—she was offering.

Didn't crave the white noise of pleasure, her breathy pants, the way she called his name as she came. Didn't crave the company of another human being, someone to hold onto in a world that seemed a little less shiny than it had yesterday.

Someone he wanted more than he'd ever wanted anyone. His heart rattled in his chest just thinking about being with Lola again.

'Please, Hamish.' She took a step forward, her features earnest. She'd obviously taken his silence as a pending *no* instead of a considered *hell, yes*. 'I know we said we shouldn't do this and we've both been trying to respect that. But…our jobs are… There's a lot of emotional pressure and sometimes we need an outlet. Let me do this for you. Let me be there for you the way you were there for me that night when I needed comfort and distraction. Unless you're too tired?'

Hamish gave a half laugh, half snort. 'Too tired for sex?'

She shrugged. 'I heard that's a thing.'

He grabbed the sheet bunched at his hips and threw it back to reveal how *not* tired he was. 'It's not a thing for me.'

Her eyes zeroed in on his underwear, following the ridge of his erection, and Hamish felt it as potently as if it had been her tongue. Her gaze drifted down a little then back up again, finally settling between his legs.

'So I see.' She dragged her attention back to his face and held out her hand. 'What are we waiting for?'

Hamish didn't have a clue. He vaulted upright, swung his legs out of the bed and rose to his feet, reaching for her hand. His pulse raced now as they headed across the hallway. The last time they'd done this it'd been the middle of the night. It'd been unexpected, spontaneous. There'd been haste, urgency. They'd groped blindly, they'd fumbled.

This was broad daylight, and premeditated.

She opened her door and led him inside where the heavy blinds at the window blocked out the light and the sparseness of the furniture and walls made it feel cave-like. And with the fan on high speed the temperature *was* several degrees lower. It wasn't cool exactly but the edge had been taken off the heat.

'Bloody hell,' he grumbled. 'I've been sweltering out there in the desert while you've been hibernating in a cave.'

She laughed and her hand slipped from his as she moved towards the bed. 'I thought you country boys could handle the heat.'

'What can I say? You've already made a pampered city slicker out of me.'

'*That* I find hard to believe.'

Hamish smiled as he watched her open a bedside drawer and bend over it slightly as she fished around inside. The gown rose nicely up the backs of her thighs and he didn't even bother to pretend he wasn't checking out her ass.

She found what she wanted and turned to face him, brandishing a square foil packet in the air for a second before tossing it on the bed. Then, as he watched, she tugged on the tie at her waist holding her gown in place. It fell open, revealing a swathe of skin right down her middle. The two inner swells of her breasts, her stomach, some lacy underwear and upper thighs. His mouth turned as dry as the dust in the cattle yards back home.

She smiled. 'You want to come a little closer?'

Hamish did, he really did. He strode over, his heart in his mouth as he stopped close enough to slip a hand inside her gown if he wanted. And he wanted. But he wanted to kiss her more. He wanted to kiss her until they both couldn't breathe.

He placed his hands on her face, cradling her cheeks, his eyes searching hers, looking for pity and finding only the softness of empathy. And a glitter of lust. He brushed a thumb over her lips and she made a noise at the back of her throat as she parted her lips. The breeze from the fan blew a curl from her temple across her face and he hooked it back with his index finger.

'You're so beautiful,' he whispered as he slowly lowered his mouth to hers.

Their lips met and her soft moan was like a hit of adrenaline to his system, tripping through his veins, whooshing through his lungs, taking the kiss from a light touch to a long, drugging exploration that left them both breathless and needy.

When he pulled back her lips were full and wet from his kisses and a deep reddish-pink. She looked like she'd been thoroughly kissed and damn if being the one to put *that* look on her face wasn't a huge turn-on. His hands slid to her shoulders, his thumbs hooking into the open lapels of her gown, which he slowly pushed back. The gown skimmed the tops of her shoulders before sliding down her arms, and falling off to pool at her feet.

Hamish sucked in a breath at the roundness of her breasts, at the light pink circle of her areolas and the way the nipples beaded despite the heat. His hands brushed from her neck to the slopes of her breasts, trailing down to the very tips before palming them, filling his hands with their fullness.

'Hamish.' Her voice was a breathy whisper and she swayed a little and shut her eyes as he kissed her again. Kissed her as he stroked and kneaded her breasts, kissed her until she was moaning and arching her back, her thighs pressed to his.

His hands slid lower, skimming her ribs and her hips, using his thumbs once again as a hook to remove her underwear, breaking off the kiss as he slid them down, crouching before her to pull them all the way down her legs. He looked up as she stepped out of them and her hands slid into his hair and he dropped a kiss on the top of each thigh, his nostrils filling with the heady scent of her arousal.

Hamish kissed his way back up, brushing his lips against her hip bone and her belly button and the underside of each breast and the centre of her chest and her neck then back to her mouth, groaning as she slid her arms around his neck and smooshed her naked body along the length of his, grinding her pelvis into him.

'Mmm…' he murmured against her mouth, his hands tightening on her ass. 'That feels good.'

'It'd feel better if you were naked too,' she said, her voice husky.

Hamish didn't need to be told twice and quickly pulled off his own underwear to stand in front of her naked, his erection standing thick and proud between them.

'Oh, yes,' she whispered, her hand reaching out to stroke him. 'Much better.'

Hamish shut his eyes as she petted him, her fingers trailing up and down his shaft, the muscles in his ass tensing uncontrollably, electricity buzzing low in his spine, his heart thumping like a gong in his chest.

Her fingers grew bolder, sliding around him, and he groaned again as he opened his eyes. 'Enough.' He grabbed her hand. 'I'm not sure how long I'm going to last and I want to be inside you.'

'God… Yes, please.'

Hamish lowered himself onto the bed and pulled her down on top of him, revelling in the easy way she straddled him, in the way his erection slid through the slickness between her legs, in the way she grabbed the condom and sheathed him, in the way her breasts swung and she moaned as he touched them, in the way her blonde curls blew around her head as she looked down at him.

His hands tightened on her hips. She was magnificent on top of him, so comfortable with her nudity and taking charge. She lifted her hips and took him in hand, notching his erection at her entrance, closing her eyes to enjoy the feel of it for a moment.

She took his breath away. 'You look like a goddess.'

She opened her eyes and smiled. 'You can call me Aphrodite.' And she lowered herself onto him.

Hamish groaned, watching her as he sank to the hilt inside her, watching pleasure spread over her face and satisfaction take over as she settled on him, her bottom lip caught between her teeth.

'Oh, yes,' she whispered, raising her arms above her head and sinking her hands into her hair, her breasts thrusting, her back arching.

She was gloriously unrestrained and she was his.

'*Now* you're Aphrodite.'

He moved then and she moved with him, her hands

still in her hair, rocking her hips, undulating her stomach, riding him like a belly dancer, taking his thrusts, absorbing them, consumed in the rocking and the pounding, building her, building him—building them—to fever point, the frantic whistle of the fan a back note to the wild tango between them.

Hamish's climax gathered speed and light and momentum, little daggers of pleasure burrowing into his backside, the tension in his stomach and groin starting to unravel, and he could almost reach out and touch the rapture. He slid his fingers between her legs, wanting her there with him, *needing* her there.

She moaned as he found the hard knot of her clitoris and she gasped as he squeezed it, the sensation jolting like a shock through her body, her internal muscles clamping hard around him.

'Hamish!'

She sobbed his name as the rapture took her, and he cried out to her too, as it collected him, his fingers digging into her hips as his spine electrified and his seed surged from his body. He pulsed inside her and she pulsed around him, the pleasure sweeping them along, ravaging them, their movements jerky, their dance disorganised, neither of them caring as they rode the rapture right to the very end.

It lifted as dramatically as it had descended, Lola collapsing against him, her curls spilling over his chest as she gasped for breath. She was hot against him but he didn't care. He was burning up too and moisture slicked between their bodies, but all that mattered was that they were burning up together.

She rolled off him eventually and Hamish groaned as he slid from her body. He turned his head to watch her. She looked utterly sated, a satisfied tilt to her lips.

There was a line of sweat on her upper lip as well as on her forehead and her chest and in the hollow at the base of her throat.

'So that first time wasn't a fluke, then?' she said, slurring her words a little, obviously sleepy.

Hamish chuckled. 'Nope.'

He assumed she knew how special that was. To be so *simpatico* with another person? To feel as if you *fitted* together. As if you were their *perfect fit*. He'd never felt it with another woman.

He shut his eyes, enjoying the thought and the coolness of the air from the fan drying his sweat and the stillness in his head, surrendering for a second or two to the tug of exhaustion, before rousing to dispose of the condom. Lola was already asleep, her body rosy from their contact, her blonde curls frothing around her head, a small smile still touching her mouth.

He crawled back in beside her—it never occurred to him to return to his own bed. Not now. This might only be a one-off but he was going to hold onto it for as long as he could.

He was going to lie down beside her and sleep—wonderful, wonderful sleep—and he was going to worry about the rest later.

CHAPTER TEN

ON HER LAST night shift, Lola was assigned to Emma who, although stable, still desperately needed a heart transplant. She'd been listed for almost six weeks now, which was truly pushing it, and there *would* come a point where Emma started to decompensate, despite medical technology's best efforts to keep her stable.

Then she'd be just another *died on the waiting list* statistic.

Which was tragic at any age but at twenty-three it was just too awful to contemplate.

Despite the underlying desperation of the situation, Emma was chugging along and Lola found her mind drifting back to Hamish. In her bed. They'd slept together three days in a row and she was counting on making that a fourth.

They hadn't talked about what had happened between them that morning after the bombing. Lola had just *understood* what he'd needed and hadn't been able to deny him. Not when he'd been *her* comfort, *her* solace, *her* soft place to land that first night they'd spent together all those months ago.

And she'd wanted to be that person for him.

They hadn't discussed sleeping together again either.

When she'd made the offer, it had been a one-time-only kind of thing.

The rest had just kind of happened.

They'd arrived home that next morning at the same time and it had seemed like the most natural thing in the world for her to join him in the shower, to soap him up, lay her hands on him, her mouth on him, until he had her up against the tiles, driving into her, withdrawing as he came because neither of them had thought about their lack of protection when things had started to get handsy.

And then he'd carried her through to her bed, both of them still wet, and they'd drifted off, their skin cooling under the roar of the fan, her heart happy. They'd woken twice during the day to join again, half-asleep but reaching for each other despite the fact she had to work that night.

Lola wasn't used to being gripped by such...attraction. Sure, she'd been with good-looking men, but she didn't need a *hubba-hubba* reaction to a guy to go to bed with him and sex had just been an itch to scratch. A fun but necessary biological function.

But these last few days had blown that theory out of the water. There was sex, there was *good* sex and there was *whoa Nelly!* sex. She'd had some of the first, quite a bit of the second but never any of the third. Until Hamish. He was the whole package—physically attractive and a magician between the sheets—and it had been totally consuming.

'Hey.'

Lola glanced up after finishing a suction of Emma's tracheostomy tube—a breathing tube had been inserted into her neck a few weeks ago—to find Grace approaching. She'd been here when Lola had arrived on shift but it didn't stop the spurt of guilt Lola felt every time she saw her friend, especially given the direction of her thoughts.

'Hey.'

Heat crept into Lola's cheeks despite telling herself she'd done nothing wrong. Hamish was an adult. He didn't have to check it was okay with his sister to sleep with Lola and Grace had already dismissed those concerns anyway. But, deep down, Lola knew that Grace would want to know.

It might not be one of the Ten Commandments but *Thou shall not sleep with your best friend's brother without at least giving her all the gory details* was ingrained in the female psyche.

Lola thanked God for the low lighting Emma's stable condition allowed at the bed space and smiled, determined to act normal, even if she did feel like she was wearing an 'I'm sleeping with your brother' sign around her neck.

'How are you?' Lola asked.

It wasn't a standard throw-away question. It was a genuine enquiry about what Grace was dealing with tonight. Just prior to Lola commencing, Wesley, who hadn't recovered or responded in the seventy-two hours since the bombing of the nightclub, had undergone his second set of neurological function tests and been declared brain-dead.

It was a tragic end to such a young life and had raised the death toll from the bombing to thirty-five. The one glimmer of hope from the situation was Wesley's parents, who had generously and selflessly consented for his organs to be donated.

And it was Grace's job to co-ordinate everything. Which was a massive undertaking. Everything from ensuring all the correct tests were done and protocols followed, to liaising with other teams and hospitals involved with the recipients, to choreographing the harvesting that was going to occur in a few hours, to being there for Wesley's family fell under Grace's purview in this instance.

'Are you okay?' Lola pressed.

She knew how difficult these cases were to deal with. How talking with bewildered and bereaved people looking for answers you couldn't give them was emotionally sapping. How being strong for them required superhuman levels of empathy and patience and gentleness and sometimes meant bearing the brunt of their grief and anger.

Just watching Wesley's distraught family as they came and went from his bedside had taken a little piece of Lola's heart. It was simply heartbreaking to watch and there wasn't one nurse on the unit tonight who wasn't affected by it.

Grace grimaced. 'I'm okay.'

A silent moment passed between them. An acknowledgment that the situation sucked, that Wesley's death was a tragedy about to spawn a lot of happy endings for people staring down the barrels of their own tragedies.

Organ transplantation was truly a double-edged sword.

Lola stripped her gloves off. 'Everything sorted now?'

Grace gave a half-laugh that told Lola she wasn't getting home to Marcus any time soon. 'Things are coming together,' she said, obviously downplaying how much still had to be put in place.

It didn't fool Lola an iota.

'But I do have some good news.' She tipped her head to the side to indicate Lola should meet her at the bottom of the bed.

Lola removed her protective eyewear and washed her

hands at the nearby basin before joining her friend at the computer station at the end of Emma's bed. 'I thought you might like to be the first to know,' Grace said, her voice low. 'Emma's a match for Wesley's heart.'

Lola stared at Grace incredulously for a moment. The possibility had been in the back of her mind but she'd dismissed it as being highly unlikely. Lola *had* seen it once before a few years back when the donor and a recipient had been on the unit together but it wasn't common.

'Really?'

Grace beamed. 'Really. They're ringing Emma's parents now.'

Lola's heart just about grew wings and lifted out of her chest. It was a moment of indescribable joy. *Emma was getting a new heart.* The backs of Lola's eyes pricked with moisture and her arms broke out in goose-bumps.

'That's…*wonderful* news.'

Grace nodded. 'Right? It's nice in this job when you get to give happy news.'

Lola gave her friend a hug because she was overjoyed but also because Grace probably needed it after all she'd been dealing with. Of course, it didn't take long for the logistics to dawn. To know that her night was suddenly going to get a lot busier, following all the pre-donation protocols and getting Emma ready for the operating theatre.

But the realisation that a usually anonymous process might not stay that way dawned the heaviest.

The truth of the matter was that families of ICU patients talked to each other. The unit had a very comfortable, well-equipped relatives' room, where people hung out. And talked. They talked about their loved ones— about the ups and downs, about the good days and the bad days, about the improvements and the setbacks.

Often they became *very* close, particularly in long-term cases like Emma's.

But donation was supposed to be anonymous. In most cases, donor families never met recipients. Usually about six weeks after the patient had died and their organs had been transplanted, the donor family was written to and given some basic information about the recipients in very generic detail.

Like, the right kidney went to a fifty-eight-year-old male who had been on the waiting list for ten years. Or the left lobe of the liver went to an eighteen-month-old baby girl and the remaining lobes were transplanted into to a thirty-one-year-old father of three.

But never names. Identities were always kept confidential. The whole process was ruled by a protocol of ethics and anonymity was strictly adhered to. It was too potentially fraught otherwise for recipients if donor families knew their names and where they lived. Also fraught for donor families.

If a recipient died due to complications after transplant—which did happen—what extra burden of grief could that put on already fragile families?

Organ donation was the ultimate altruistic gift and the lynchpin of that was anonymity.

Except now there were two families in the relatives' room—one whose son was brain-dead and about to have his organs harvested and the other whose daughter was about to get a heart transplant.

It wasn't going to take great powers of deduction to figure out the link.

'Have Wesley's family been interacting much with Emma's family?' Lola asked.

'Apparently not. They're still in that numbed, shocked stage and have kept to themselves. And Emma's family are down the coast for the night at some family thing so hopefully Wesley will be gone from the unit by the time Emma's family arrives back.'

'Fingers crossed we'll get lucky and neither will figure it out.' The other time it had happened, they'd managed to maintain the anonymity of the process. It had been touch and go for a moment but it had all worked out in the end. 'Are they going to use the Reflections Suite?'

Reflections was a self-contained unit two floors up that families of deceased patients could use to spend time saying goodbye to their loved ones, in private, before they were taken to the morgue. It was roomy with comfy chairs and couches and a kitchenette with a fridge. They were able to take all the time they needed to grieve as a family and be together in their loss.

Grace nodded. 'Yes. I'll go up with Wesley to the suite after the operation is finished and sit with the family for a bit if they want.'

Lola nodded. Grace was going to have a long, emotionally challenging night. 'Isn't that what the on-call social worker is for?'

'He'll be available to them too. But it's me they've been dealing with through this process so...' Grace shrugged. 'I want them to have some continuity and be able to answer any lingering questions they might have.'

'Yeah.' Lola nodded.

Caring for ICU patients meant caring for their families as well. And continuity, especially in acute situations, made everything much easier for grieving families.

Grace's pager went off and she pulled it off her belt, reading the message quickly. 'That's the Adelaide co-ordinator. Gotta go.'

Lola smiled. 'Of course. Go. I'll see you later.'

Grace darted off and Lola glanced at Emma and smiled before getting back to work. It was going to be another long night.

Lola was mentally exhausted as she entered the apartment eight hours later but her body was buzzing. In just a few days it had become scarily accustomed to Hamish being there and this morning was no different. In fact, it was probably worse.

They'd relaxed the rules about their roomie-only relationship and her cravings were growing.

Not even the prospect of telling him about Wesley's death seemed to put a lid on the hum in her cells. Lola knew Hamish was holding out hope that Wesley might make some kind of meaningful recovery, even though the news had been dire since the beginning. Hamish had asked after him every morning and Lola had filled him in on what she knew.

She doubted Wesley's death would come as much of a surprise but it would no doubt take a piece of Hamish's heart as it had taken a piece of hers.

'Hey, you.'

Lordy, he was a sight for sore eyes, lounging against the kitchen benchtop, a carton of orange juice in his hand. Her breath hitched as she pulled up in the doorway. He'd obviously just had a shower as his hair was damp and all that covered him was a towel slung low on his hips. His chest and abs were smooth and bare, his stomach muscles arrowing down nicely to the knot in the towel.

'I was hoping you'd still be in bed.'

He gave a nonchalant shrug but ruined it with a wicked grin. 'I've been for a run.'

'Of course you have.'

Lola laughed, feeling like an absolute sloth in his presence as she walked straight into his arms. His hands moved to the small of her back as hers slid up and over his shoulders on their way to his neck, revelling in the warm flesh and the taut stretch of his skin over rounded joints and firm muscles.

She sighed, grateful that the temperature had eased yesterday afternoon and she could get this close and personal without being a ball of sweat in five seconds flat. She pressed her cheek against a bare pec, the steady thump of his heartbeat both reassuring and thrilling. When he tried to break the embrace she held on harder.

'Lola? Everything okay?'

She could hear the frown in his voice and she pulled away slightly, gazing up into his face. His face did funny things to her equilibrium. How had his face come to mean so much to her in such a short time?

'Lola?' His hands slid to her arms and gave a gentle squeeze. 'What?'

Even with his brow creased in concern, his blue eyes earnest, she wanted to lick his mouth. 'It's Wesley.'

He didn't say anything for a moment but she was aware the second he knew what she was about to say. 'Oh.'

Lola stroked her fingers along the russet stubble decorating his jaw line. 'He was declared brain dead just before I started last night.'

'Yeah.' Hamish nodded. 'Guess that was inevitable.'

'Doesn't make it suck any less.'

He gave a half-laugh. 'No.'

Lola cuddled into him again, her cheek to his pec, hoping her body against his would be some kind of comfort. His arms came around her as he rested his chin on the top of her head.

'He'd be a suitable donor, right? Did his family consent?'

'Yes.' Lola broke away to look at him.

'Yeah?' Hamish brightened. 'That's fantastic.'

Lola beamed at him. She couldn't agree more. 'And guess what?'

He smiled. 'What?'

Strictly speaking, what she was about to tell him was breaking patient confidentiality, but healthcare professionals often did discuss patients past and present, particularly in overlapping cases where there'd been multi-team involvement, so Lola didn't have a problem divulging. And she figured Hamish would appreciate this particular silver lining.

'Guess who got his heart?'

He frowned for a moment but it cleared as quickly as it had formed. 'Your patient on the list?'

Lola nodded. 'She's in Theatre now.'

'Oh, God.' His smile almost split his face in two. 'That's…wonderful news.'

'The best.'

He kissed her then. Hard. And Lola melted the way she always did as her cares fell away and her body was consumed by the presence of *him*. His pine and coconut aroma fogged her senses. His touch dazzled and electrified everything in its path, drugging and energising in equal measure.

His fingers hummed at her nape, his lips buzzed against hers, the rough drag of his breath brushed like sandpaper over her skin. His heart thumped hard beneath her palm and the steel of his erection pressed into her belly.

She was so damn needy she wanted to simultaneously rub herself all over him *and* crawl inside him.

'Mmm...' He broke off and every nerve ending in Lola's body cried out at the loss. 'I missed you last night.'

Lola smiled. 'I have three days off now.'

He smiled back. 'Whatever shall we do?'

'Well...there is the Christmas shopping.'

'We *could* do that.'

Lola pretended to consider some more. 'We could take a drive along the northern beaches. Find a nice spot for a picnic?'

'Yep. We could definitely do that.' He ground his erection into her belly. 'I was thinking of something a little more indoorsy.'

The delighted little moan that hovered in Lola's throat threatened to become full blown as Hamish adjusted the angle of their hips and the bulge behind the towel pressed against her in *all the right places.*

'Oh, yeah?' She shut her eyes at the mindless pleasure he could evoke with just a flex of his hips. 'What did you have in mind exactly?'

'Something that doesn't require clothes for the next three days would be awesome.'

Somewhere in the morass of her brain Lola knew she should reject his invitation. Try and pull things back now their night duty stint was over. She was already dangerously attached to Hamish—three days of naked time with him would only make this insane craving she had for him worse.

Oh, but she *wanted* him.

Wanted to spend three days talking and sleeping and kissing and getting to know each other *really* well.

Lola tossed caution to the wind. Hell, it was Christmas, right? She grinned at him as she grabbed for the knot sitting low between his hips. 'I think clothes are overrated.' She pulled it and the towel fell to the floor, the thickness of his erection jammed between them.

Oh, yes, that was better.

She glanced at it before returning her attention to Hamish's face. 'I need a shower. I'm having very dirty thoughts.'

'But I like it when you're filthy.'

Lola grinned, kissing him quickly before shimmying out of reach, her fingers going to the buttons of her work blouse, undoing them one by one as she walked slowly backwards, opening the shirt when she was done so he could get an eyeful of her blue lacy bra.

'Come and get me,' she murmured, before turning tail and sprinting to the bathroom, a large naked man hot on her heels.

CHAPTER ELEVEN

EMMA WAS STILL ventilated when Lola went back onto the early shift after her days off and wild horses wouldn't have stopped Lola from requesting her to look after.

To say Emma was markedly improved was a giant understatement. She was breathing for herself and almost weaned off the ventilator. Her blood pressure was good, her heart rate was excellent, all her blood tests were normal and there were no signs of rejection. All her drains were out and her exposed surgical incision was looking pink and healthy.

She'd come a long way in such a short time.

Her eyes lit up when Lola said hello first thing and she reached for Lola's hand and gave it a squeeze.

'She remembers you,' Barry said.

Lola smiled. She had looked after Emma a lot these past weeks. Had held her hand, talked to her, reassured her. But Emma had been very ill for most of it and the drugs she'd had on board had often caused memories to be jumbled. Lola wouldn't have been at all surprised had Emma not remembered anything or anyone.

In fact, given the long, intensive haul she'd been through, it was probably not a bad thing.

'You look amazing, Emma,' Lola said.

Emma smiled and pointed to her tracheostomy, mouthing, 'Out.' The position of the tube in her throat rendered her unable to vocalise.

Lola laughed. 'Hopefully today, yes. After the rounds this morning, okay?'

She rolled her eyes and kicked her feet a little to display her impatience. 'I know.' Lola squeezed her arm. 'Not much longer now, I promise.'

'I told you, Emsy,' Barry said, kissing her hand. 'Soon.'

Lola smiled. Barry had come a long way too.

'You think she'll be on a ward for Christmas?' Barry asked.

Lola shrugged. Christmas was still a week away. 'That's the way to bet. *But—*'

'Did you hear that?' Barry said, interrupting Lola to beam at Emma. The way he looked at her caught in Lola's throat. 'You'll be out of here soon.'

'Maybe,' Lola stressed. She didn't want to rain on their parade but Lola had been doing this far too long not to be cautious about her predictions. 'Don't forget, it's one day at a time in here.

'We know, we know,' Barry said in a way that led Lola to believe they were already planning Emma's homecoming.

And Lola didn't have it in her to stop them. Inside Emma's chest beat Wesley's heart. His family's tragedy had become Emma's family's miracle and hell if Lola wasn't going to let them bask in that.

A few days before Christmas Hamish found himself sitting at the back of a packed cathedral in full uniform. He'd imagined a lot of different scenarios playing out during his urban stint in Sydney but attending a memorial service for the victims of a bombing had not been one of them.

Lola, one of the many hospital personnel in attendance, was by his side as the mayor talked about the tragic events that had unfolded that night and how the efforts of the emergency services had doubtless saved countless lives. He shifted uncomfortably in his seat, pulling the collar of his formal uniform shirt off his neck. It was stifling hot in the cavernous cathedral and praise such as this added to his discomfort.

He and everyone else who had attended that night and all the health care professionals who were caring for the injured—doctors and nurses like Lola and Grace—had just been doing their jobs.

Words like heroes and angels didn't sit well on his shoulders. He'd just done what he'd been paid to do.

A squeeze to his leg brought him out of his own head and he smiled at Lola, her hand a steadying presence spread over his thigh. He'd spent a lot of time in her arms avoiding thinking about the carnage of that night, but it was unavoidable today and he'd been discombobulated ever since meeting Wesley's parents earlier.

And somehow she knew it.

Jenny sat on his other side. She was rigid in her seat and tight-lipped, the buttons on her dress uniform as shiny as the tips of her black dress shoes. She shot him a small, strained smile as the minister at the front asked everyone to stand for the reading of the names.

They rose to their feet. Hamish knew how important these sorts of memorials were. That public grief, remembrance and acknowledgement brought communities together and paying respect helped people move on. He knew it would help him and Jenny move on from that night—eventually.

It still felt a little too raw right now, though, the girl in the purple dress still a little too fresh in his brain.

Abigail. That was her name. He'd seen it on TV.

Lola's hand slipped into his as the minister read the first name out and a candle was lit in their honour. He was so damn grateful to have her here. She'd become his distraction, his safe harbour, his soft place to land. She'd become vital—like oxygen and sunshine—and the thought of leaving her in a few weeks was like a knife to his heart.

Because he'd fallen in love with her.

The weird tension he'd been carrying in his shoulders for a while now eased at the realisation. If anything, it should have tightened because that was not part of *the plan*. Not that they'd talked about any plan. In fact, they'd studiously avoided it seeing that their last plan—to keep their hands off each other—obviously hadn't gone that well.

He should be worried. He should be grim. He should be nervous. Hell, he should at least be trying to figure it all out, work out his next step. But he was thirty years old and in love for the first time and right now, on this darkly emotional day, it was like a blast of light through the stained-glass windows of the cathedral.

It was enough.

The service ended fifteen minutes later and Hamish was finally able to breathe again. Jenny peeled off to talk to somebody she knew as they walked out into the fresh air and sunshine. Grace, who'd been up at the front supporting Wesley's family, waved and Lola's hand slipped from his as they headed in her direction.

Hamish missed the intimacy immediately and resentment stirred briefly in his chest before he got over himself. He didn't need Grace on his case as he tried to navigate this next couple of weeks. He kissed his sister on the cheek and she and Lola introduced the group of nurses they'd joined.

They made polite small talk for a few minutes but it was the last thing Hamish wanted to do. He wanted to be at home with Lola. He wanted to strip her out of her uniform and bury himself inside her and tell her with his body what he couldn't tell her with his words. Not yet anyway. Not until he'd figured out just how to do that without losing her in the process.

If that was even possible.

'You okay?' she asked, her voice low as the conversation ebbed and flowed around them.

Hamish nodded and smiled reassuringly. These people were clearly her work colleagues and friends and he needed to pull his head out from his ass. They'd all been part of the bombing and its aftermath in some way. 'Yes.'

'We'll, it's after twelve.' A male nurse who'd been introduced as Jay rubbed his hands together. 'Who's up for drinks at Billi's?'

There was a general murmur of, 'Count me in,' including from Grace and Lola.

'You, Hamish?' Jay asked.

Not really, no. He didn't want to go and psychoanalyse to death every part of that night, which was exactly what he knew would happen. It was inevitable when you got a bunch of health professionals together—it's what they did.

He just wanted to be alone with the woman he loved.

But Lola had already indicated she was going to the bar and he wanted to be wherever she was, even if it meant he couldn't touch her and he had to pretend everything was platonic between them. 'Um…sure.'

He glanced at Lola and smiled. But her eyes narrowed slightly and Hamish swore he could feel her probing his mind as she searched his face. 'Actually… I might take a rain-check.'

She turned back to Jay, the movement inching her closer to Hamish. He felt the slight brush of her arm against his, was conscious of their thighs almost touching.

'I still have some Christmas shopping to do and this is my only day off between now and Christmas.'

Hamish could have kissed her. Well…that was a given…but he *knew* she was blowing off her friends for his benefit and he seriously wanted to grab her and kiss the breath out of her. He sure as hell wanted to drag her beneath him and love her with all his strength.

All his heart.

'Oh. Right. Actually, that's a good idea,' he concurred, hoping he sounded casual and that his sister wasn't picking up on the mad echo of his heartbeat.

Grace glanced between him and Lola before cocking an eyebrow. '*You* want to go shopping instead of drinking beer?'

He shrugged. 'To be honest, I'm not sure I'm up to much company today.'

'Oh…absolutely. Of course.'

Hamish felt guilty as Grace's cynicism faded, to be replaced by an expression of concern. He didn't want her to worry about him but he'd say whatever he needed to say to be alone with Lola right now.

'Just don't let her drag you into a bookshop. You'll be stuck for two hours at the travel section.'

Everyone laughed, including Lola, before they said their goodbyes and quietly slipped away.

'Thank you,' he murmured as they headed for the car park. 'I really didn't want to make polite conversation today.'

'I know.'

Hamish sucked in a breath. It was simple but true. She did know. And he loved her for it.

Lola usually worked on Christmas Day. It was a good excuse not to go back to Doongabi and she got to spend it with people she really liked, doing what she loved. Instead of with people who wished she was different in a place that felt just as claustrophobic as an adult as it had when she'd been a kid.

And hospitals always went out of their way to make everything look festive and inviting throughout the season, and Kirribilli General was no different.

But this Christmas morning was different.

Good different.

Waking-up-in-the-arms-of-a-sexy-man different.

Hands touching, caressing, drifting. Lips seeking, tasting, devouring. Coming together in a tangle of limbs and heavy breathing, desire and December heat slick on their skin. Crying out to each other as they came, panting heavily as they coasted through a haze of bliss and floated back down to earth.

Hitting the shower to freshen up and cool off, only to heat up again as the methodical business of soaping turned to the drugging business of pleasure. Hamish kissing her, Lola kissing him back until she couldn't breathe, couldn't stand, slumping against the tiles for support, Hamish supporting her, urging her up, her legs around him, pushing hard inside her again and groaning into her neck as he came, whispering, 'Yes, yes, yes,' as she followed him over the edge.

And that was before they got to the best bit—opening the presents.

There were only a few beneath the tree. Grace and

Marcus's presents were the biggest—she'd bought them his and hers matching bathrobes as a bit of a joke present but they were top-notch quality and had cost a small fortune. They were coming over for lunch today and Lola couldn't wait to see the looks on their faces.

Hamish had also bought Grace a present and it was there along with the one Lola had bought him. It was just a novelty thing.

Nothing special. A snowglobe. With the Harbour Bridge and the Opera House planted in the middle. It had made her smile and she figured it'd be a memento of his time here.

And maybe he'd smile too every time he looked at it, the way he'd smiled when he'd talked about the innkeeper's daughter in Mykonos.

The biggest surprise, though, was Hamish's present to her, which had appeared a few days ago. In Lola's experience, men didn't really *do* presents for people they *loved*, let alone those they just…slept with.

Or whatever they were doing.

What that was, Lola didn't know. But an offer of solace had definitely turned into something more. Something she didn't want to over-analyse. Hamish's last shift was on the second of January and he was leaving on the third and starting back at his Toowoomba station on the fourth. Which meant they had just over a week left together.

Why mess up a week of potential good horizontal action—which she'd miss like crazy when he left—to put a label on something they'd already agreed couldn't go anywhere.

'So.' Lola, who'd thrown on shorts and a red tank top with 'Dear Santa, I've been very, very bad' splashed in glittery letters across the front, was pouring them both a tall glass of orange juice in the kitchen. A Christmas CD was playing 'Frosty the Snowman' in the background. 'What say we go out to the balcony with these and open our presents?'

Hamish wrapped his arms around her from behind. He hadn't bothered with a shirt at all, just boxers, which left a lot of bare, warm skin sliding against hers. Strong thighs butted up against the backs of hers as he lowered his mouth to nuzzle her neck and Lola almost whimpered at the pleasure of it.

'I'll grab the presents,' he said.

Lola followed him out with the drinks. She sat opposite him—all the better to see him—and placed the drinks down with a tapping sound on the tabletop. The balcony was still in shade and with the Christmas music drifting out through the open doors it was a pleasant morning.

Hamish swigged half of his juice in three gulps before handing over his gift. 'Ladies first.'

Lola, who'd already had a good feel of the present the moment he'd left the apartment, fingered it again. It was only palm-sized but quite heavy. She was dying of curiosity but also unaccountably nervous.

'No. Guests first.' She pushed his over. She'd rather break the ice with something gimmicky—have a laugh first. He started to protest but she shook her head. 'Please, Hamish, indulge me.'

He sighed dramatically but grinned and ripped the paper off. The boom of his laughter as the box was revealed had been worth it.

'Oh, my God.' He grinned as he pulled the plastic snowglobe out and shook it, holding it up between them. She watched him as his gaze followed the flakes fluttering down around the famous Sydney landmarks. 'This is awesome.'

'Yeah? You like it? I thought you'd appreciate something to take home from Sydney to remind you of the place. And the muster across the bridge.'

And her.

'Are you kidding? You know I'm nuts for all this tacky, tourist crap.' He grinned. 'It's perfect.'

Lola laughed. 'I think I win Christmas, then.'

'I think you do.' He shook it again as he held it up. 'I love it.'

His casual use of the L word caused a skip in her pulse as her gaze narrowed to the snow falling in the dome. When she widened her gaze he was staring through the globe straight at her.

'Now you.' He placed the snowglobe on the table and tipped his chin at the present he'd given her earlier.

'Right.' She smiled as she picked it up, her fingers fumbling with the paper a little, suddenly all thumbs.

Inside the paper was a plain, thick cardboard box that had been taped by someone who obviously had shares in a sticky-tape company. Lola glanced at Hamish. 'Seriously?'

He laughed as she sighed and started on the tape. 'It's fragile. I guess they wanted to protect it as much as possible.'

Fragile? What the hell could it be?

After a minute of unravelling layers of tape, Lola was finally able to open the lid. Inside was an object secured in bubble wrap and yet more tape. She pulled that out, working away at it, going carefully as she finally revealed the most exquisite glass ornament Lola had ever seen.

It was a jacaranda tree in full flower. The gnarled trunk and its forked branches were fashioned in plain glass. The flowers, a perfect shade of iridescent blue-purple, hung from the branches, frothing in a profusion of purple, each individual bloom a teardrop of colour.

Lola blinked as she placed it reverently on the table. It was utterly breath-taking. It was delicate and feminine and so very *personal*. She didn't keep trinkets because gypsies didn't do clutter, but she knew she'd take this to the ends of the earth with her.

'I…' She glanced at him. Nobody had ever given her such an exquisite gift. 'I don't know what to say… It's utterly…*lovely.*'

'Lovely' seemed like such a bland, old-fashioned word but it was actually perfect for the piece. It was pretty and charming and sweet.

It *was* lovely.

More than that, it was *thoughtful*. Only someone who *knew* her, truly knew her would know how much something like this would mean. And the fact Hamish knew her so deeply should have her running for the hills. But all she wanted right now was to run straight into his arms.

'You like?'

'I… It's perfect.' She dragged her eyes off its loveliness to glance at him as she deliberately echoed his words. 'I love it.'

'I guess that means *I* win Christmas.'

She laughed at the tease in his voice. 'Yeah. You totally do.' She sobered as her eyes followed the graceful reach of the branches before her gaze shifted to his. 'Oh, God.' She faux-groaned. 'And I got you a crappy snowglobe that cost ten bucks.'

'Hey.' He picked up his present and held it against his naked chest as if he was trying to cover its non-existent ears. 'Don't insult the snowglobe.'

Lola laughed. There was no comparison between the

two presents but he seemed just as chuffed with his gift as she was with hers.

He placed the snowglobe on the table. 'You want to see how well I can win Christmas in the bedroom?'

Lola's nostrils flared at the blatant invitation. But... 'I think you've already done that this morning. A couple of times.'

'I was just getting warmed up. Third time's the charm.'

Lola shook her head regretfully. 'I have things to prepare for lunch and a pavlova to make. Your sister's going to be here in three hours. And I think it might be a good idea if we don't look like we've spent all morning bouncing on a mattress together when she gets here.'

'I'll act my ass off, I promise. Not that I'll need to. She only has eyes for Marcus at the moment.'

Yeah. Grace was totally immersed in her new relationship, that was true. But women in love also had uncanny radar about other couples too.

'Lola Fraser, if you don't get your ass into that kitchen in the next thirty seconds, I'm going to take you remaining seated as a subconscious invitation to toss you over my shoulder, throw you on your bed and go down on you until you're singing "Ding Dong Merrily on High".'

Lola's stomach looped the loop at both the threat and the promise. 'Hold that thought,' she said as she rose and fled to the kitchen to the wicked sound of his low sexy chuckle and the jingle of bells from the CD.

CHAPTER TWELVE

THE TWO GUYS had insisted they'd clean up after Christmas lunch so Lola led Grace out onto the balcony. It was warmer outside now after several hours of the sun heating things up but there was still a nice breeze blowing in from Manly.

'Oh, my.' Grace reached for Hamish's present to Lola as she sat, turning it over and over. The sunlight caught the flowers and threw sparks of purple light across the glass of the tabletop. 'This is exquisite.'

'Yes.' Lola sipped some champagne, still stunned by the gift. 'Hamish gave it to me for Christmas.'

Lola was too caught up in the beauty of the piece to realise at first how still Grace had grown. How the light had stopped dancing on the tabletop as her hands had stopped moving. It wasn't until she spoke that Lola became aware of the situation.

'*Hamish* gave this to you?'

Lola glanced at her friend, a slight frown between her eyes at the strangled quality of Grace's voice. 'Yes.'

Grace's gaze settled on the tree for a moment before she placed it back on the table. 'I see.'

Her gaze flicked up to Lola, who frowned some more at the sudden seriousness of Grace's expression. 'What?'

'There *is* something going on between you, isn't there?'

Lola had known that Grace had been suspicious about her and Hamish a couple of times but she didn't see how a Christmas present could spark this line of questioning. Especially when she and Hamish had been impressively *chummy* throughout lunch.

'That would be stupid.' Lola trod carefully. They'd managed to keep the particulars of their relationship quiet from Grace so far. 'He's going back to Toowoomba in a week.'

'I've been watching you two for the last few hours. You've been knocking yourselves out trying to prove you're both just pals, but it's not working.'

Damn. Lola blinked, her brain searching for a rapid-fire response. She could just make out the low rumble of male voices inside over the sudden wash of her pulse through her ears and hoped like hell they stayed there until she had this sorted.

'I think you may be projecting there, Grace. Just because you're all loved up, it doesn't mean everyone else is.'

Grace sat back in her chair with a big, smug smile that was worrying and irritating all at once. 'You think I'm so caught up in my own love life that I don't notice anything else? It's been obvious today you two are sleeping together.'

Double damn. Lola swallowed, her eyes darting over Grace's shoulder to check they weren't getting any imminent visitors. She didn't need Hamish out here, making things worse. 'Obvious?'

'Sure. It's in the way you look at each other when you think the other isn't watching, all starry-eyed. And even if I was so blinded by my own feelings I couldn't see the blatantly obvious, I'd know from this.' Grace reached forward and picked up the tree again.

'It's just a Christmas present.'

'Lola.' Grace was using her don't-mess-with-me nurse voice. All nurses had one. 'This isn't *just* a Christmas gift.'

Lola glanced at the piece, a tight band squeezing her chest. 'He's…really grateful for my…hospitality these past couple of months, that's all.'

'And normally some guy you've been renting a room to would get you something for the kitchen or, better still, a gift voucher to a home appliance shop. Roomie Guy gets you practical and impersonal. He doesn't get you something pretty and frivolous. Something that's fragile and delicate and beautiful. And *meaningful*. He doesn't get you a work of art that speaks to you so deeply, that represents a place he knows you love, a place that's part of your shared history.'

Lola squirmed in her chair. She'd been so touched by the beauty of the blown glass, by its perfection, she hadn't thought about it having a deeper meaning.

Or maybe she hadn't *wanted* to.

'This is a gift of love, Lola.' Grace placed the sculpture down again. 'My brother is in love with you.'

Lola breath hitched as her gaze flew to Grace's face. *No*. How utterly ridiculous. 'He's just…a really thoughtful guy.'

She shook her head slowly. 'Trust me, I know him. He's really not. He's my brother and I love him but he's more the gimmicky gift giver.'

Lola thought about the T-shirt he'd bought Grace and his penchant for tacky snowglobes. Was Grace right? Adrenaline coursed through her system at the thought of it. She knew Hamish *liked* her. A lot. And it was reciprocated. They got on really well, enjoyed each other's company and they were magic between the sheets.

But they'd only known each other for a couple of months. It was just…fun.

Starry-eyed, Grace had called them. But really good sex *could* put stars in your eyes. It had certainly put stars in hers. And Grace's, for that matter.

'He's…going home in a week.'

'Yes.' Grace nodded, her expression gentle but earnest. 'Broken-hearted probably.'

Lola's blood surged thick and sluggish through her veins as she stared at the miniature glass sculpture. This wasn't the way it was supposed to be. They may have blurred the boundaries but he knew her attitude towards relationships and about her gypsy lifestyle. She'd thought he'd understood.

He *had* understood it, damn it. So Grace had to be wrong.

Lola was going to confront him about it as soon as Grace and Marcus had left. He'd deny it and they'd laugh over his sister's silliness and it'd be okay.

Although maybe they should *stop* sleeping together…

'More champagne, good women?'

Marcus's jovial voice coming from behind ripped Lola out of her panic. Her gaze briefly locked with Grace's, who was still eyeing her meaningfully before she turned and smiled. 'Yes, please.'

Hamish was there too, smiling at her, and the stars in his eyes blazed at her so brightly it was like a physical punch to her gut. *Crap.* She turned quickly back to escape their pull, her gaze landing squarely on Grace and her imperiously cocked *I told you so* eyebrow.

It couldn't be true. She wouldn't *let* it be true.

* * *

Hamish was standing at the sink, washing up, a couple hours later when Lola returned from seeing off their guests. 'Did they leave or did they make a pit stop in my bedroom for a quickie?' He grinned at her over his shoulder. 'I swear those two couldn't stop looking at each other.'

A faint smile touched her lips but it didn't reach her eyes. She folded her arms as she leant into the doorframe. 'That's exactly what Grace said about us.'

Hamish's smile slowly faded. Lola looked serious. In fact, she'd been kinda serious this past couple of hours. *This couldn't be good.* 'Does she know we've been sleeping together?'

'Yeah.'

'You told her?'

'No.' Lola shook her head. 'She guessed.'

'Impossible.' Hamish smiled, trying to lighten the mood. 'I acted my ass off today.'

She didn't return his smile, just dropped her gaze to the floor somewhere near his feet. 'It was your Christmas present to me.'

Hamish frowned. 'The tree?'

'She said it was a gift of love.' She raised her gaze and pierced Hamish to the spot with it, her chin jutting out. 'She said you were in love with me.'

It was softly delivered but, between the accusation in her tone and the look in her eyes, the statement hit him like a sledgehammer to the chest.

What the hell? Was Grace trying to sabotage his chances with Lola?

'Is it true?'

Of course it was true. But he hadn't wanted to tell her like this. Not that he'd given this moment much thought but he didn't want it to come when he was backed into a corner either.

Hamish dried his hands on the tea towel he had slung over his shoulder and turned round fully. 'Lola, I—'

'Is it true?' Her eyes flashed, her jaw tightened and her knuckles turned white as her fingers gripped her arms hard. 'I told her it was ridiculous.'

Hamish let out a shaky breath. She was giving him an out and he could see in her eyes that she wanted him to take it. He could pick up that lie and run with it and try and salvage something out of this mess. Paper things over, spend this next week with her as if tonight hadn't happened. Then take things slowly with her over the next year—settle into something long distance.

Woo her.

But loving her was bigger than that. Bigger than him and her. Bigger than any will for it not to be so. Too big to dishonour with denial.

Too *important*.

He rested his butt against the edge of the sink. 'It's not. Ridiculous. It's true. I've fallen in love with you.'

His lungs deflated, the air rushing out with the words. He'd held them in for too long and it felt good to finally have them out. He didn't realise they'd been a weight on his chest until they weren't there any more.

Lola, on the other hand, looked as if she'd picked up those words and was being crushed beneath them, her face running the gamut from shock to disbelief to down-right anger.

'But…that's not what we were doing.'

'I know.'

'I told you, I don't do relationships. We want different things.'

'I know.'

'This is just…sex, Hamish.'

'No.' He shook his head emphatically. God knew where they'd go from here but Hamish wasn't going to pretend any more that this had only been physical. And he wasn't going to let her pretend it either. It had been deeper than that right from the start.

Right from the first time she'd turned to him. Their connection had been forged that night and he knew she'd felt it too.

'It's never been just a sex thing, Lola.'

Her arms folded tighter, her lips flattened into a grim line. 'It has for me.'

A sudden rush of frustration propelled Hamish off the sink and across the kitchen, leaving only a couple of steps between them.

'Please don't lie to yourself, Lola. This is me, Hamish. I might not have known you for very long but I think you've let me in more than you've ever let anyone else in. You've told me about where you're from and your family and how you never fitted in and your Great-Aunt May and you've taken me into your bed time after time after time, even though you're the one-and-done Queen. Hell…you took me to your favourite place in Sydney. A place you've *never taken anyone else*. So don't pretend that all we've been doing is having great sex because that's ridiculous and we both know it.'

Hamish was breathing hard by the time he'd got that off his chest but he wasn't done yet either. If he was un-loading everything, he should go all the way. He took the last two steps between them and slid his hands onto her arms and said, 'And I think you have feelings for me too.'

Now he was done.

She gasped, her pinched mouth forming an outraged

O as she wrenched out of his grasp, pushing past him to pace the kitchen floor. 'Now *you're* being ridiculous.'

Hamish blinked at her vehement reaction. If he wasn't so sure about their connection, her dismissiveness might have cut him to the quick. 'Would it be so terrible, Lola?' His gaze followed her relentlessly back and forth as he leaned his shoulder on the doorframe. 'To let me love you? To let yourself fall in love with me?'

She stopped abruptly, her hair flying around her head as she glared at him. If anything, she was even more furious, her chest rapidly rising and falling. 'And how do you think that would work?' she demanded, her eyes wild and fiery.

'I don't know... I hadn't really thought about it.'

She gave a small snort. 'Well, think about it,' she snapped. 'Are you going to commute between here and Toowoomba or wherever the hell you end up?'

Hamish rubbed his hand along his scruffy jawline. 'I don't know.'

'Or are you going to move here?'

The rejection of that notion tingled on his tongue in a second. Sydney was a great place to visit but it'd drive him mad to live here permanently. The thought made the country boy inside him shudder. Also, he'd be putting his dream for rural service on hold. Maybe indefinitely.

But he could do it, especially if it meant being with her. 'Yes.' He nodded. 'I would move here.'

She gaped at him. 'You'd just give up all your dreams?'

'For you, yes.' He could get new dreams. What he couldn't ever get again was someone like Lola.

She was the *one*.

'If you were serious about being in a committed relationship with me,' Hamish continued, his thoughts starting to crystallise. 'Not if you're just going to keep me for a few months and discard me when your next wild adventure calls you. I'm happy to live with you wherever you want, but I'm not going to be just some filler, Lola, somebody to occupy yourself with between jaunts. I'm not going to be your *Sydney* guy.'

'God, Hamish...' She shook her head and started to pace again. 'I don't want you to give up your dreams.'

'Okay so...' Hamish shrugged. 'Come and live mine with me.'

She halted again. 'Oh, I see, so *I'm* supposed to follow you to Outer Whoop-Whoop.'

'I don't know. Maybe... Why not?' Hamish *didn't* know, but surely it was worth giving them a shot?

'Because I'm *not* going back to some speck on the map in the middle of bloody nowhere. I've paid my small-town dues, Hamish.'

'I'm not talking about forever, Lola. I'm talking about a couple of years. That's all. And it's not like it was when you were growing up in Doongabi. There's better roads and cars and more regional airports than ever being serviced by national carriers. Just because we might live in a small town, doesn't mean you're going to be *stuck* there. I'm not going to keep you a prisoner.

'You want to go to the nearest city for a week of shopping, go for it. You want to fly to Sydney to see the ballet or Melbourne to watch the tennis or the Whitsundays to lie on a beach and get a tan—great.'

She shoved her hands on her hips. 'I'm *going* to Zimbabwe in April.'

Hamish sighed. She was so damn determined to stay on the path she'd forged for herself. She been concentrating so hard on it she didn't realise she could change direction or forge a whole new path and that was okay. 'Then I'll carry your bags.'

She huffed out a breath, clearly annoyed by his logic. 'And what about my *job*?'

He shrugged. 'Rural areas are desperate for nurses.'

'But there won't be an ICU in the middle of nowhere, will there? Why should I let my skills languish?'

'Just because there won't be an ICU, doesn't mean there won't be patients who require critical care from time to time. Who are going to depend on you and what you do with what you have to keep them alive until they can be transferred to a major hospital. Think of the challenge and the experience you could come away with. I'm looking on it as a means to becoming a better paramedic, to push me, to challenge me. It could be the same for you. When was the last time you were truly challenged at work?'

An intensive care nurse had highly specialised skills but there was a lot of support in a big city unit with not a lot of autonomy.

She folded her arms and regarded him for long moments, which was a nice change from pacing and glaring, and for a second Hamish thought he might have won her over. But finally she shook her head.

'It's not just about moving to a small town, Hamish.'

He cocked an eyebrow. 'What, then?'

'I don't want to tie myself to one person at all but if I did, it wouldn't be a small-town guy. He'd have to be a kindred spirit. He'd have to have a gypsy soul, not someone who's content to live a small life with a side of snowglobe tourism.'

Her barbs struck him dead centre. She hadn't hurled them at him but he felt the bite of them nonetheless and a spurt of anger pulsed into his system. He didn't like her insinuation that because he wasn't as well travelled as her, he was unadventurous and lacking ambition.

Being happy with his life and his lot hadn't ever been a negative in Hamish's book. He'd never considered being content a *bad* thing and the fact that she was judging him for it was extremely insulting.

He may not be worldly enough for her but he knew people didn't get to pick and choose who they had feelings for—that just happened. And ignoring it was a recipe for disaster.

Whether Lola wanted to or not, she *did* have feelings for him. Feelings he suspected scared the living daylights out of her. And not just because she had them but because he was the opposite of what she'd always told herself she wanted.

Hamish took a steadying breath, shaking off her insult. 'I think you do want someone to tie you down. That you don't want to be a gypsy all your life.'

She shook her head vehemently. 'That's the most absurd thing I've ever heard.'

Hamish probed her gaze, holding hers, refusing to let her look away. The more he talked, the more convinced he was. 'Is it? I've never pretended to be anything other than a small-town guy, Lola, and yet you went there anyway. If you didn't really want this, want me, then why have you kept coming back? What the hell has this been?'

She took a deep breath before levelling him with a serious gaze. 'A mistake.'

Hamish wouldn't have thought two little words could have had so much power. Had she yelled them at him, he could have put it down to the heat of the moment, but she was calm and deliberate, her gaze fixed on his as she shot them at him like bullets from a gun.

He couldn't speak for a beat or two. Hamish knew that whatever happened between them after today he would *never* categorise their interlude as a mistake. He would look back at it with fondness, not regret.

But right now her rejection stung.

He nodded slowly. 'Right. Okay, then.' He pushed off the doorframe. 'I think I'm going to go and stay at Grace's tonight.'

There were only so many insults a man could take in one night. Lola had called him small town and insular and now a mistake. He couldn't work out if he was angry with her or disappointed, but he couldn't stay. They would either get into it more or they'd end up in bed together because sex seemed to be the only way they dealt with emotional situations.

And he didn't have the stomach for either.

A little frown knitted her brows and she opened her mouth. For a second Hamish thought she might be going to retract everything but her mouth shut with an audible click and her chin lifted. 'That might be best.'

Hamish nodded. Her dismissal hurt but what else had he expected? 'Merry bloody Christmas, Lola.'

CHAPTER THIRTEEN

IT WAS NINE that night when Lola answered the phone. She knew who it was before she even picked up. Aunty May always rang her on Christmas morning and where she was, in the Pyrenees, it was six in the morning.

'Merry Christmas, sweetie.' Her aunt's voice crackled down the line, not as youthful as it had once been but still shot with an unflappability that was uniquely May.

Lola almost burst into tears at its familiarity. She didn't, but it was a close call as she cleared her throat and said, 'Merry Christmas, Aunty May. How's the skiing?'

May launched into her usual enthusiastic spiel she went into when she was somewhere new and Lola was grateful for the distraction. She let her aunt talk, content to throw in the odd approving noise or question, not really keeping track of the conversation, her brain far too preoccupied.

Ever since Hamish had walked out so calmly a few hours ago, Lola had been able to think of little else. It had been an incredibly crappy end to such a great day. From the second Grace had mentioned the L word it had started to go downhill and had slid rapidly south.

Damn Grace.

And damn Hamish for ruining it even further by backing up his sister's outrageous claim. They'd had another week. They could be in bed right now, enjoying their last days together. Enjoying this day in the same way it had started.

But he had to go and tell her he loved her. Tell her he knew she had feelings for him too! The fact that he was right—there was something between them, although it couldn't possibly be *love*—had only compounded the situation.

'It's been a few years since I've done a black run but I'm very much looking forward to it.'

Lola tuned back in. 'It's just like riding a bike.' Aunt May had been skiing for the better part of fifty years—she could out-ski Lola any day.

May burst out with one of her big, hooting laughs. 'Been a while since I rode one of those too. Never mind… I've made some friends with a couple of hottie old widowers here so I won't be alone.'

And she launched into an entertaining description of the two gents in question in that irreverent way of hers that always kept Lola in stitches. Except for tonight. Because all Lola could think about was Hamish and how abominable she'd been to him.

Yes, he'd admitted he loved her and that had been a shock, but he hadn't deserved being told he was living a small life and that he was a mistake. As someone who'd made her fair share of mistakes she could confidently say none of them had felt as good as Hamish.

She'd even opened her mouth to apologise, to take it back, but then she'd realised it had been the perfect shield to fight the sword of his L word and she'd left it. But she hadn't liked herself very much.

And she liked herself even less now.

'Okay, sweetie. Are you going to tell me what's on your mind?'

Lola blinked. Aunty May was ten thousand kilometres away and they were speaking down a phone line but she still knew something was up. 'What? Nothing.' She forced herself to laugh. 'I'm fine. Just a little tired, that's all.'

'Lola Gwendolyn Fraser. This is me. When will you learn you can't fool your old Aunty May?'

Lola gripped the phone. It was some kind of irony that a woman who had been largely absent from her life knew her so well. They had that kindred spirit connection.

'Does it have anything to do with that guy who's been staying with you? What's his name again?'

'Hamish.' Even saying his name made Lola feel simultaneously giddy and depressed.

'That's right. Grace's brother.'

'Yes.'

'And you're in love with him?'

'No!' Tears blurred Lola's vision. 'I've only known him for two months.'

There was silence for a moment. 'You showed him your jacarandas, right?'

Lola was beginning to wish she'd never told May or Grace that particular bit of information. 'Yes, but I'm like you. A gypsy. We travel. We don't fall in love.'

'Poppycock!'

Lola blinked at the rapid-fire dismissal.

'It took me two minutes to fall in love with Donny.'

Donny? Who the hell was Donny? And since when had her spinster aunt been in love with anyone? 'Donny?'

'The one great love of my life.'

What the—? 'I...didn't know there'd been anyone.'

It was a weird concept to wrap her head around— her spinster aunt in love with a man. Lola had no doubt she'd been highly sought after but May had always been staunchly single.

'Well…it was a long time ago now.'

The wistfulness in her great-aunt's voice squeezed fingers around Lola's already bruised heart. 'What happened?'

May said nothing for a beat or two as if she was trying to figure out where to start. 'I was seventeen, working at the haberdashery in Doongabi, and this dashing young police officer moved to town. He was thirty. But when you know, you *know*.' She gave a soft chuckle. 'I fell hopelessly in love.'

'I see.' That was quite an age gap even for fifty-something years ago. 'And that caused a stir in the family? Or…' She hesitated. 'Didn't he reciprocate?'

Lola thought it the least likely option. May had always been a tall, handsome woman. Carried herself well, wore clothes well. But in the photos Lola had seen of her as a teenager she'd been striking, with an impish flicker in her eyes.

'Oh, he reciprocated. It was wonderful.' She sighed and there was another pause. 'But he was married. He had a wife and two girls who were joining him a little later. And I knew it and I embarked on a liaison with him anyway.'

Married? 'Oh.' Lola hadn't expected that.

'Yes. Oh… So I left. The day before his family were due in town. I was afraid if I stayed I wouldn't give him up, I wouldn't end it. That I'd risk my family's reputation and his marriage and break up his home because I was young and selfish and loved him too much.'

A lump lodged in Lola's throat. May was rattling it off as if it was something that had happened to somebody else but she couldn't hide the thickness in her voice—not from Lola.

'I'm so sorry. I didn't know.'

'It's fine.' May cleared her voice. 'As I said, it was in a whole other lifetime.'

'Is he still—?'

'No.' Her aunt cut her off. 'He died ten years ago. But you know…' She gave a half laugh, half sigh that echoed with young love. 'I would give up everything I've ever done, every place I've ever been, to have spent my life with him.'

Lola sat forward in the chair. *'What?'*

'Oh, yes. I've been with other men, Lola. Even loved a few of them. But not like Donny. He was always the one.'

'But…you've had such a wonderful life.'

'Yes, I have. I've been very lucky.'

'Right.' Lola nodded, feeling suddenly like she was the elder in the conversation having to point out the obvious. 'You've been to so many places. Seen so many things. Your life has been so full.'

'No, sweetie, it hasn't. I've been living a half-life. There's always been something missing. So promise me not to make the same mistake I did, choosing adventure over love. If this man loves you and if you love him, as I suspect you just might, be open to it. Humans are meant to love and be loved. We mate for life. And a gypsy caravan is big enough for two.'

Lola was too stunned to speak. Her whole world had just shifted on its axis. Not only had her great-aunt had a torrid affair with an older, married man but she'd have traded her gypsy life for a second chance with him.

'Lola? Promise me.'

Her aunt's voice was fierce and strong and Lola was

spooked by the sudden urgency of it, goose-bumps breaking out on her arms. 'I promise.'

Lola was pleased to be back at work the next morning. Between what had happened with Hamish and the conversation with her great-aunt, her head was spinning. May—spinster of seventy-five years—had loved a married man she'd gladly have given everything up for. And Hamish *loved* her.

Loved.

On such short acquaintance. And having being warned that she didn't *do* love.

The whole world had gone mad.

At least work was sane. She knew what she was doing there. What was expected of her. And people didn't ask more than they knew she could give. She could care there, she could give a piece of herself, but she didn't have to give them *everything*. They didn't demand her heart and soul.

Only her mind and body. And *that* she could do.

'Lola, can you take Emma today, please? She's due to be transferred to the ward around eleven so can you make sure all her discharge stuff is completed by morning tea?'

'Yep. Sure can.' Lola leapt up from her chair in the staffroom, eager to throw her body and mind into a full, busy shift. And she was excited to be the nurse looking after Emma on her last day on the unit.

Everything since the transplant had gone swimmingly well and Lola was thrilled about Emma's transfer. Two months was a long time to be on the ICU and all the nurses had grown fond of Emma and her lovely supportive family.

For so long it had been touch and go and to see her

leaving the unit with a new heart and a new chance at life was why Lola did what she did.

'Hey,' Lola said as she approached Emma's bed to take handover from the night nurse. The background noise of beeping monitors and trilling alarms and tubes being suctioned formed a comforting white noise that blocked out the yammering in her brain.

'Hey, Lola.'

Emma's voice was still husky but she beamed at Lola. She'd lost weight, was as weak as a kitten and looked like she'd been in a boxing ring with her smattering of scars, nicks and old bruises, but the sparkle in her eyes told Lola everything she needed to know. Emma's spirit was strong, she was a fighter. And she was going to be okay.

'I'll just get handover and then we'll get you all ready for your discharge to the ward.'

'Now, those are some beautiful words,' Emma quipped. The small white plaster covering her almost healed tracheostomy incision crinkled with her neck movement.

Lola took handover. It was short and quick compared to the previous weeks that had required twenty minutes to chronicle all the drugs and infusions and changes as well as the ups and downs of the shift.

'How did you sleep?' Lola asked a few minutes later as she performed her usual checks of all the emergency equipment around the bed.

Emma may be leaving in a few short hours but certain procedures were ingrained for Lola. It was important to know everything she might need in an emergency was here, exactly where it was located and that it was in full working order.

Patient safety always came first.

'Wonderfully.'

Lola laughed. 'Somebody should have warned me I was going to need sunglasses today to block out the brightness of your smile.'

'I am pretty excited about leaving this dump,' Emma said with a smile.

Lola sighed and clutched her chest dramatically. 'People never want to stay.'

Emma grinned. 'I'll come back and visit.'

Lola grinned too as she put a stethoscope in her ears. 'Make sure you do.' She placed the bell on Emma's chest and listed to her breathing. A patient assessment was performed at the start of every shift.

'You want to know what I got for Christmas?' Emma asked as Lola removed the earpieces. 'Besides a new heart?'

Lola cocked an eyebrow—Emma was vibrating with excitement. 'Of course.' Hopefully it'd help take her mind off what Hamish had got her. The little glass jacaranda tree had caused a shedload of problems.

Emma held up her left hand and wiggled her fingers. The oxygen saturation trace on the monitor went a little haywire because the probe was on that hand but that wasn't what caught Lola's attention. A big, fat diamond ring sparkled in the sunshine slanting in through the open vertical blinds covering the windows.

'Barry asked me to marry him and I said yes.'

Lola blinked as the refraction shone in her eyes. Damn it, was the whole world conspiring against her at the moment?

'Crikey.' Lola kept her voice light and teasing as she took Emma's hand and inspected it closely, her heart beating a little harder at the expression of pure joy on her patient's face. 'Did he rob that bank he works for?' Barry was a teller at a bank in the city.

Emma laughed. 'I'm afraid to ask.'

Lola smiled as she released Emma's hand. 'Well, I'm thrilled for you. If anyone deserves a bit of happiness it's you.'

Emma held her hand out to admire the ring, wriggling her fingers slightly to get a real sparkle going. 'To think I was never going to do this. Marriage and all that stuff.'

Lola had turned to grab a pair of gloves from the windowsill behind so she could remove the arterial line from Emma's wrist, but she stopped and turned back. 'Oh?'

Maybe this was why she felt such an affinity for Emma? She too didn't want to tie herself down.

'Yeah.' Emma dropped her hand to her stomach. 'Baz and I have only been going out for ten months and he's asked me twice to marry him now but I always felt like I was a bad bet for a guy. Why would I inflict a woman with a dodgy ticker on someone I supposedly loved without an easy out for him? Better for him to just be able to walk away, for us both to be able to when things got tough.'

'I see.'

'Barry's kinda hard to shake, though.' Emma grinned. 'He was determined to stick around. To show me that he was here for the long haul as well as the short haul if that's the way it panned out.'

Lola nodded. 'He's been very dedicated, Emma. He was here every day.'

'Yeah, I know. But even with my new heart…well…' Emma grimaced. 'The potential for complications is real, right? Rejection, infection, complications from medication…and how long will it last till I need another one? But when he asked me yesterday morning to marry him, all that just fell away and love was all that mattered.'

A lump the size of Emma's bed lodged in Lola's throat.

Isn't that what May had essentially said last night too? If Lola didn't know better, she'd say the universe was trying to tell her something.

Just as well she didn't go in for all that spiritual crap.

'Sure, my life's potentially shorter than that of other women my age and it might not all be smooth sailing, but none of us are guaranteed a long life, are we? I mean, I don't know how old my donor was but he or she didn't get a say in their life coming abruptly to an end, right?'

Lola nodded. It was still a miracle to her that they'd managed to pull off having a donor and a recipient on the same unit without either being aware of the other.

'Life's short, I know that better than anyone, so why shouldn't I get to live my life fully? Like other people? To love like other people. To share my life, no matter how long it is, with someone else? And I think I owe that to my donor. To live my life *fully*. Why should I restrict myself to a half-life?'

A half-life. Just as May had said last night.

'Of course you do,' Lola said, a little spooked that Emma appeared to be channelling her great-aunt. 'You deserve all the good things, Emma, and I think it's exactly what your donor would have wanted.'

Emma smiled and grabbed her hand. 'So do you, Lola.' For a second Lola's heart stopped—maybe her patient actually *was* channelling Aunty May—but then Emma glanced around the unit at the general hubbub. 'All the nurses do. You're freaking angels.'

Lola gave her usual self-deprecating smile. 'Okay, well, there's no time to shine my halo at the moment.' She squeezed Emma's hand before withdrawing it, all business now. 'I've gotta spring you out of here.'

Emma nodded and sighed and went back to looking at her engagement ring.

CHAPTER FOURTEEN

THERE WAS A knock on Lola's door later that afternoon. She'd just shoved the ice cream in the freezer and ripped into a chocolate bar. She might as well have one of those too if she was about to consume a one-litre tub of ice cream, right?

The knock came again and she put the bar down with an impatient little noise at the back of her throat. 'Coming.'

Her pulse accelerated as she walked towards the door—what if it was Hamish? She had no idea what his plans were for his last week. Was he coming back? His stuff was still all here, or was he going to move in with Grace for his remaining time?

She felt sure if it was him he'd probably just use his key but maybe, after their words yesterday, he didn't want to intrude uninvited. Her heart did a funny little giddy-up at the thought. It'd only been twenty-four hours but she missed his face.

It wasn't Hamish.

It was the police. Two of them—a man and a woman, both in neat blue uniforms and wearing kindly expressions.

Lola frowned. 'Can I help you?'

The woman introduced them. 'Are you Miss Fraser?'

'Yes, that's right...' Although she felt rather stupid being called 'miss' at the age of thirty. 'Lola.'

'You are the next of kin for a May Fraser?' she clarified.

The hair on Lola's nape prickled. 'Yes. She's my aunt. My great-aunt.' Lola had been down as May's emergency contact for the last ten years. 'Is something wrong?'

Had her aunt fallen on that black run and broken something? Her leg? Or a hip? She was going to be really cranky with herself if she had. But then something worse occurred to her. The police didn't usually come around just to tell someone their loved one had been injured in a foreign land.

But...what if it was more serious than that? What if there'd been an avalanche? A surge of adrenaline flew into Lola's system.

'Could we come in?'

The question was alarming. 'Please just tell me here.' Because if they could tell her here, *whatever it was*, on the doorstep, then it couldn't be too bad, right?

Lola didn't notice the barely perceptible exchange of glances that passed between the two police officers. 'I think it would be better if we came in, Lola,' the male officer said gently, his smile kind.

Oh, God. Dread burrowed into her veins and the lining of her gut and the base of her skull but Lola fell back automatically to admit them. Once they were sitting, the male officer took up the baton and delivered the news she'd been expecting.

'I'm sorry to have to inform you, Lola, but your Aunt May passed away earlier today.'

Every cell and muscle in Lola's body snap froze. Aunty May was...*dead*? The pounding of her heartbeat rose in her ears as tears sprang to her eyes, scalding and instant.

May was dead.

'Did she…have a skiing accident?' Lola wasn't sure if it was the right thing to ask but her mind was a blank and it seemed logical given what she knew about May's whereabouts and her intended activity.

'No.' The woman took over now as if they were some kind of grief tag team and for a second Lola thought how horrible it must be to deliver this kind of news as part of your *job*.

Lola had sat through many end-of-life conversations in hospitals, holding the hands of distressed and grieving people. But this? Out of the blue like this? Everything chugging along then *bam*! Strangers on your doorstep.

'She was found in her bed,' the woman continued. 'She didn't turn up to meet some people she was going to go skiing with and they raised the alarm. Hostel staff entered her room to find her still in her bed. At first they thought she was sleeping but they couldn't rouse her. She'd died some time during the night in her sleep.'

Lola shook her head. Died in her sleep. *No.* Whenever she'd imagined her aunt's death it'd been her doing something adventurous when she was ninety-seven.

Going out with a bang, not a whimper.

'But… I was just talking to her yesterday.' Which was a stupid thing to say given her medical background—she knew how quickly and unexpectedly death could come knocking. 'She was fine. Are you sure?'

May's words from the phone call came back to her now and Lola shivered. They'd spooked her a little yesterday but even more so now. May's insistence that Lola promise her to give love a chance felt like some kind of portent today.

Was that only twenty-four hours ago?

Had her great-aunt *known* she was not long for this world?

Goose-bumps feathered Lola's arms at the thought.

'Yes. I'm afraid so.' The man again with his gentle voice. 'It's been confirmed by all the appropriate officials.'

'Could it have been...some kind of foul play?'

It seemed like a bizarre thing to ask but no more bizarre than her bulletproof aunt dying in her sleep.

The police officers took her question in their stride. 'The local authorities say that your aunt was lying peacefully in her bed wearing her sleep mask.'

Lola almost laughed at that piece of information. May used to collect the sleep masks from airlines and swore by them as an antidote to jet-lag. She'd never travelled without one.

'There'll be an autopsy, of course, but they're expecting to find natural causes.'

Lola nodded, the medical side of her brain already making guesses. It had probably been a massive stroke or a heart attack. It wouldn't have been a bad way to go, a quick death, taking her in the night. But the thought May had died alone was like a knife to Lola's chest.

It would have been the way her aunt would have wanted it—dying as she'd lived—but Lola wished she'd been able to hug her one last time and she thanked the universe for that phone call yesterday. She was grateful for the time they'd spent chatting, for having spoken to her beloved aunt one last time.

Even if May's words hadn't sat easily on Lola's shoulders.

The officers talked more about procedures and passed over some pamphlets regarding relatives who died overseas. 'Is there someone we can call for you, Lola? Some-one who can be with you now?'

Hamish.

His was the first name that popped into Lola's head and a tidal wave of emotion swamped her chest. Her fingers curled in her lap as she thought about the solid comfort of his arms around her, about him holding her, keeping her together while her insides leaked out.

But she couldn't. Not after their argument. Grace came to mind next but as she had lied to her best friend about sleeping with her brother *and* ignored six phone calls from her in the last twenty-four hours, she didn't feel able to suggest that either.

Of course, Grace wouldn't care about any of that in the face of this news. But Lola wasn't exactly thinking straight at the moment.

'Um, no.' She shook her head. 'I'm good. I'm fine.' Her mouth stretched into a smile that felt like it had been drawn on her face in crayon.

'We don't like leaving people alone after this kind of news,' the male officer said. 'Especially at Christmas.'

Between the events of yesterday and working today, Lola had forgotten it was Christmas. 'It's okay. Really. I'm a nurse, I work at the Kirribilli in ICU. I'll be fine.'

That information seemed to relax them both.

'I'll ring my mum,' Lola assured them. 'May is *her* aunt. And we'll go from there.' She smiled more genu-inely this time, realising that her last attempt had probably frightened the hell out of them. 'I'll be fine, I promise.'

They left with her assurances but the last thing Lola felt like right now was talking to her mother. She *would* ring her—in a while. Right now she felt too numb to use her fingers, to use words. She needed time to wrap her head around the fact she was never going to see her favourite person in the whole world ever again.

Lola sat on the couch and fell sideways, pulling her legs up to her chest. Tears pricked at her eyes. May was gone. No more Christmas Day phone calls. No more postcards. No more random drop-ins. No more *National Geographic*-like pictures or entertaining foreign swear words or endlessly fascinating anecdotes from her travels.

May hadn't just been some distant, eccentric great-aunt. She'd been Lola's family. She'd been the one who had understood her when no one else had. She'd been Lola's sounding board, her shoulder to cry on when life in Doongabi had seemed like it would never come to an end, and had championed her desire to travel and see the world.

Lola realised suddenly she was already thinking of May in the past tense and pain, like a lightning bolt, stabbed her through the heart with its jagged heat, stealing her breath. The first tear rolled down her cheek. Then the next and the next until there was a puddle.

And the puddle became a flood.

Hamish stood indecisively outside Lola's door much the same as he had almost two months ago now. Nervous and unsure of himself. He'd been furious when he'd walked out yesterday and while he'd calmed down significantly, he was still a little on the tense side. He couldn't remember ever knowing a woman he wanted to shake as badly as he wanted to drag her clothes off and kiss her into submission.

He got it, she was used to keeping her relationships in a box, one where she made all the rules and had all the control.

But to not be open to something more? Something different? Something deeper?

Something *better*?

It was ironic that Lola had left Doongabi partly because everyone she'd known had been stuck in their ways and yet she was proving to be just as immovable.

He knocked, wary of his reception. Not knowing if she was even home. He knew she'd worked an early shift today, which meant she'd normally be home by now, but maybe she'd made other plans.

And what was he going to say if she *was* home? What was his plan? Hamish knew what he wanted. He wanted to come back here for his last remaining days. Back into Lola's house and her bed and her *life* and make plans with her. Plans about how their future might work out. It wouldn't be easy to come up with something they were both happy with but he knew they could do it if they put their minds to it.

If they both committed.

But if Lola didn't want any part of a future with him? Could he live here for the next week and pretend he was okay with her decision? Pretend he wasn't dying a little each day?

Whatever…they needed to have a conversation which was why he'd come now and not earlier when he'd known she'd be at work. They'd both had twenty-four hours to mull over what had gone down yesterday and he could sit and brood and look obsessively at the picture he'd taken of her that day with jacaranda flowers in her hair, or he could confront her.

He'd chosen confrontation. It was time to lay their cards on the table.

Hamish knocked again. When she still didn't answer he sighed and fished in his pocket for his keys. He'd have preferred to enter by invitation but if she wasn't home it wasn't going to happen. And, if nothing else, he needed his clothes for work tomorrow.

He inserted the key into the lock. He'd just grab his bag and go. Ring her later and see if they could make a time to talk. He entered the apartment and pulled the door shut behind him, the ghosts of a hundred memories trailing him as he traversed the short entrance alcove that opened into the living room.

'Hamish?'

Her head and torso suddenly popped up from the couch and scared the living daylights out of him. Hamish clutched his chest to still his skyrocketing pulse. 'Damn it, Lola.'

'Sorry.'

'I knocked but...'

It was then he noticed her red-rimmed eyes and her blotchy face in stark relief to the pallor of her skin. She looked...awful. Lost and scared and small. Like someone had knocked the stuffing out of her. Not the strong, feisty Lola he was used to.

Was this grief...over him? Over them?

And why was the thought as gratifying as it was horrifying? What the hell was wrong with him?

'Lola?' Hamish took a step towards her but stopped, unsure of how welcoming she'd be to his offer of solace. 'Are you okay?'

Her short hysterical-sounding laugh did not allay his concerns. She shook her head, her curls barely shifting it was so slight. 'Aunty May died.'

Her words dropped like stones into the fraught space between them. 'What?' *Her aunt was dead?*

He was at her side in three strides, their animosity forgotten as he sank down beside her, his hand sliding around her shoulder and pulling her to him. She didn't argue or jerk away, just whimpered like a wounded animal and melted into his side.

He eased them back against the couch and her arm came around his stomach, her head falling to his shoulder. Hamish dropped his chin to her springy curls, shutting his eyes as he caught a whiff of his coconut shampoo in her hair.

'You want to talk about it?'

She shook her head. 'Not yet.'

So he just held her. Held her while her tears flowed, silently at first then louder, choking on her sobs, her shoulders shaking with the effort to restrain herself and failing. Eventually her sobs settled to hiccupping sighs and she was able to talk, to tell him what had happened.

'I'm so sorry,' Hamish murmured, still cradling her against him, his lips in her hair. He knew how much Lola's great-aunt meant to her.

Lola nodded. 'I thought she'd be around for ever, you know?'

'Yeah.' He dropped another kiss on her head. 'I know.'

She seemed to collect herself then, pushing away from him slightly as she scrubbed at her face with her hands. 'Sorry for crying all over you.'

'Don't.' Hamish cupped her cheek, wiping at some moisture she'd missed. 'I want to be here for you, Lola. You *have* to know that.'

He wanted to be here for her for ever. If she'd let him.

Emotion lurked in her big green eyes, waiting for another surge of grief. They slayed him, so big and bright with unshed tears.

So…damn sad.

'Hamish.' Her hand slid on top of his as their gazes locked. She absently rubbed her cheek into his palm and tiny charges of electricity travelled down his arm to his heart. From there it was a direct line to his groin.

Which made him feel like seven different kinds of deviant.

Traitorous body! *This wasn't about that.* This was about something deeper and more profound.

Comfort. Not sex.

Yet the two seemed to have a habit of intertwining where they were concerned. Even now he could feel the threads reaching out between them, twisting together, drawing them nearer.

Her breathing roughened and Hamish responded in kind. A strange kind of tension settled over them, as if the world was holding its breath. Her eyes went from moisture bright to a rich, wanton glitter.

'Lola.'

It was a warning as much for himself as for her. They couldn't keep doing this, letting desire do their talking. She was grieving. And he wanted to give her more than a quick roll on the couch. They *mustn't* let their hormones take over.

'I missed you last night,' she said, her voice barely louder than a whisper.

Apart from *I love you* she couldn't have chosen better words to say to him, especially when they were full of ache and want and need. Her voice was husky and it crawled right inside his pants and stroked.

'Lola.'

He was only a man. And he loved her.

She shifted then, moved closer, pressing all her curves back into him again as her mouth closed the gap between them. Their lips met and he was lost.

Gone. Swept away.

In her taste and her smell and the small little sounds

of her satisfaction that filled his head and rushed through his veins like a shot of caffeine.

Hamish's other hand curved around her face, sank into her hair as he kissed her back, his nose filling with the smell of her, his tongue tingling with the taste of her. She moaned and he half turned and their bodies aligned and he totally lost his mind.

He'd missed her too.

It was a crazy thing to admit. It had only been twenty-four hours but he hadn't been able to stop thinking about her, to stop wanting her, to stop wishing he'd just shut the hell up and not pushed for more.

It wasn't fair that one woman had so much power but that was love, right? You laid yourself bare to one person. Laid yourself bare to their favour as well as their rejection.

'God… Hamish…'

Her voice was thick with need as she slid her leg over the top of his and straddled him. She kissed along his neck and pulled at his shirt and he was drowning. Happily. Being sucked down into the depths of Lola's passion, dying in her arms, every part of him aching to give her what she wanted. What she needed.

And to hell with what he wanted, what he needed.

But somewhere, something was fighting back. A single brain cell screaming at him to *stop, stop, stop*. To have some respect. For himself. And for Lola.

Groaning, Hamish wrenched his mouth away from her kiss, from her pull. 'Wait.' He shut his eyes and panted into her neck as her hands fell to his fly, her fingers not waiting one little bit. And he wanted her hand on him so damn bad.

'Stop.'

He shifted, grasping for sanity, for clarity as he tipped

her off his lap. Ignoring the almost animalistic moan from Lola, he pushed to his feet and strode to the opposite side of the room. Shoving his hand high up on the wall for support, Hamish battled to control the crazy rattle of his heart and the crazier rush of his libido.

'I can't.'

She made a noise that sounded like another sob and Hamish whipped around. He couldn't do this if she started crying again.

She wasn't. But she *was* annoyed.

'I'm sorry.' It seemed like the least he could say given the frustration bubbling in her gaze and how hard her chest rose and fell.

She rubbed a hand over her face as she exhaled in a noisy rush. 'Hell, Hamish. I just…needed some comfort.'

'Yeah.' An ironic laugh rose in his throat but he choked it back. 'That's what we do, you and I, when we're feeling emotional. We have sex. That's the problem.'

'Why is it a problem?'

Her casual dismissal was like the slow drip of poison in his veins, eating away at him. 'Because we don't talk, Lola. We just take our clothes off and let our bodies do the talking. And I need more than that now. We need to start using our mouths to communicate, not our bodies.'

She blinked at him like she couldn't believe what was coming out of his mouth. But he meant every word.

'I love you. I want to *be* with you. I want to be in your life—*part of your life*—not just the person you turn to when you need some distraction between the sheets.'

Hamish broke off, his heartbeat flying in his chest. Was he making any sense? It all seemed totally jumbled inside his head.

'You want me to help you with the funeral arrangements and repatriation of May and being there when you talk to your family and rocking you as you cry yourself to sleep tonight? I can do that. I *want* to do that. I want you to lean on me, Lola. I want it all.'

She looked at him helplessly and Hamish felt lower than a snake's belly. Denying her didn't give him any satisfaction. But it would be too easy to slip into their old routine. Find himself in the kind of relationship he *didn't* want, and he couldn't bear the thought. His insides shrivelled at the prospect.

He wanted to be all in. And if that wasn't on the table then he needed to be all out.

'I...can't deal with this now, Hamish.' She rose from the couch and paced to the open balcony door. The last rays of afternoon sunlight slanted inside, gilding her shape. 'Can you please just go?'

Hamish nodded. He'd dumped a lot on her today, on top of the news about May. Which was an awful thing to do but, damn it, she drove him crazy. He wanted to be her *person*, not just a warm body with the right anatomical parts.

He sighed. 'I'll just grab my stuff and go. I'll be at Grace's until my plane leaves on the third.'

She nodded, her back erect. 'Okay.'

Hamish waited but she didn't turn around no matter how hard he willed it. 'I'll ring you tomorrow to check on you.'

She nodded again but didn't say anything, a stiff, forlorn figure in the fading gold of the afternoon light. It was like a knife to his heart to walk away. But a wise man knew when to choose his battles and live to fight another day and he was going to fight for Lola.

Even if it meant playing the long game.

CHAPTER FIFTEEN

THE APARTMENT WAS silent as Lola let herself in at almost ten thirty on New Year's Eve. Her shift had finished at nine but with the road closures around Kirribilli because of the New Year celebrations, she'd had to take public transport to work. Which had been fine on the way to the hospital but on the return journey the buses had been loaded with families trying to get home after the early fireworks. Add to that the detours in place and the trip had been much longer than usual.

Throwing her bag and a bundle of mail on the coffee table, Lola used the remote to flick on the television. Every channel was showing New Year revelry in Sydney, from shots of the foreshores to the concert on the steps of the Opera House. She settled on one channel and headed for the kitchen.

Grabbing the fridge door, Lola paused as her gaze fell on May's postcard. Her heart squeezed as she pulled it off and read it again, smiling at May's inimitable style. It still punched her in the gut to think she was never going to get another postcard from her aunt to brighten her day and make her smile every time she saw it.

The last few days had been a flurry of activity, making the arrangements to repatriate her aunt's body and coping with all the associated paperwork and legal requirements. Which had been a good thing. Something to keep Lola's mind off Hamish and how much she missed having him around.

May's body was expected back in Sydney in four days and Lola was travelling with her to Doongabi. May hadn't made any specific funeral requests, just that she be cremated and that Lola scatter her ashes somewhere wild and exotic.

Lola didn't think May would mind going home after all this time, especially knowing that her aunt had left out of propriety, not animosity. It wouldn't be her final resting place, Lola would make sure of that, but funerals weren't for the dead. They were for the living. And the town and the Fraser family wanted to be able to grieve her passing, even if it had been over fifty years since May had left.

Including Lola's mother, who had been surprisingly helpful with all the arrangements and genuinely upset at May's passing. Lola had always thought her mother had disliked her aunt for her gypsy ways and for seducing Lola to join the dark side, but her mother's grief had been raw and humbling and had made Lola look at her mother in a different light.

She put the postcard back on the fridge with a sigh, knowing without a shadow of a doubt that May's last written communication would stay right where it was for ever. Opening the door, Lola grabbed the half-empty bottle of wine and poured herself a glass. She was going to sit on the balcony in the dark and watch the revellers whooping it up at the park across the road.

She was going to think about everything that had happened this past year. About May and her mother and going back to Doongabi. About the explosion at the night club and Wesley and Emma.

And Hamish.

From their first meeting on the bridge to him walking out of here the other day, rebuffing her need for comfort. She was going to *wallow* in all of it. Probably even cry over it a little.

But when the clock struck twelve, that was it. A new year. A clean slate. Looking forward. Not back. And there was a lot to look forward to. Seeing family again. A job that she loved. Her trip to Zimbabwe. And maybe it was time to take a sabbatical and do some more extensive travelling. Her aunt was gone, someone had to pick up her mantle.

Someone had to take May's place.

Work would probably let her take a year off without pay. And even if they refused, she could quit. It wasn't like she couldn't get another job again on her return to Australia. She was highly skilled. She could go anywhere with a hospital and pick up a job.

From Sydney to some two-bit town way out past the black stump. Which brought her squarely back to Hamish.

And just how lonely she felt suddenly, her life stretching out in front of her, a series of intersecting roads and her walking down the middle. All by herself.

Lola had never felt lonely before. Serial travellers made friends wherever they went but were also happy with their own company. When had she stopped being happy with her own company?

Maybe it was to do with her aunt's death? Knowing she was out there somewhere in Lola's corner had counteracted any isolation Lola might have felt without May in her life. But deep down she knew it was Hamish—she'd only started feeling lonely since he'd come on the scene.

Damn the man.

To distract herself, Lola contemplated going out. Throwing on her red dress and getting herself dolled up and hitting Billi's. She could probably still make it before the countdown. Flirt with some men, do some midnight kissing.

But the thought was depressing as all giddy-up. The truth was, she didn't want to be with just anyone tonight, kiss just anyone. She wanted Hamish.

Lola scowled and stood up. *It would pass.*

It was just a break up-thing, the loss of the familiar. Which was why she didn't do relationships. No relationships, no break-ups. No feeling like death warmed up on New Year's Eve or any other night for that matter.

They were too different, she reminded herself. They wanted different things. It would never work.

She went and poured herself another glass of wine, picking up the mail off the coffee table as she passed. But she didn't open it straight away, distracting herself instead with her phone and friends' social media posts.

All round the world, it seemed, people were in varying stages of preparation for the New Year. Lots of overseas friends stared back at her from photos full of happy, smiling people, all having a great time together. She tried to smile too, to feel their joy, but she felt nothing except the heavy weight sitting on her chest.

It was grief, Lola understood that, but knowing that didn't make it any easier.

She should have volunteered to work the night shift tonight instead of the late shift she'd filled in for as at least it would have kept her mind on other things. Like how she and Hamish had requested this night off so they could sit on the foreshore together and watch the fireworks, show the country boy some real city magic.

The thought made her smile, which made her annoyed,

and Lola grabbed for the mail. Maybe a few bills might help keep her mind off things until the fireworks went off and her slate was magically cleaned. She hadn't checked the box since before Christmas so she had quite a stack to deal with.

Most of it was bumf from advertisers. There were three bills, though—it was the season for credit cards after all—and a letter from the local elected representative wishing his constituents all the best for the festive season.

And there was a postcard. From May.

Lola's heart almost stopped for a moment before it sped up, racing crazily as tears scalded the backs of her eyes. It was of a snow-covered mountain, the peak swirled with clouds. The caption on the front read, 'Beauty should be shared.'

On the flipside, May had written, 'One of nature's mighty erections.' Then she'd drawn a little smiley face with a tongue hanging out. Lola burst out laughing and then she started to cry, the words blurring. Her aunt had signed off with, 'Merry Christmas, Love, May.'

'Oh, May,' Lola whispered, turning the card over again to look at the picture, her heart heavy in her chest and breaking in two. 'I'm going to miss you.'

The mountain stared back at her, and so did the words. *'Beauty should be shared.'* May's strange insistence from their Christmas Day phone call that Lola choose love over adventure, replayed in her head. *'A gypsy caravan is big enough for two.'*

Lola's heart skipped a beat as the words from the postcard took on a deeper meaning. *Beauty should be shared.* Was her aunt reaching out from beyond the grave? The feeling that May had somehow known she wasn't long for this world returned.

Suddenly Emma's words joined the procession in Lola's head.

'Why shouldn't I get to live my life fully? Like other people? To love like other people. To share my life, no matter how long it is, with someone else. Why should I restrict myself to a half-life?'

Lola shut her eyes as the words slugged hot and hard like New Year's Eve fireworks into her chest. Oh, God. That was what she was doing. She was restricting herself to a half-life. Choosing adventure over love.

Yes, love.

Because she *did* love Hamish Gibson. No matter how much she'd tried to deny it. How much it scared her. And it did scare her because they were so different and she knew squat about being a couple. Squat about being grounded after being a gypsy most of her adult life.

But he'd crept up on her, slid under all her defences, and her heart was full of him. Bursting with him. And now she couldn't imagine her life without him.

She didn't know what shape her life would take next, all she knew was that two wise women had given her advice this festive season and she'd be a fool to discard the lessons they'd imparted.

She chose love. She chose a full life.

If she hadn't already blown it.

Lola stood. Not stopping to think about what she was doing next, she was already on her phone, ordering a cab, which would probably cost her a fortune in a surcharge on New Year's Eve but she'd had two glasses of wine and she didn't care. She grabbed the postcard off the table and strode into the living room, snatching her keys out of her handbag before heading for the door.

She *had* to see Hamish. She had to tell him she loved him and beg him to forgive her and hope like hell she *hadn't* blown it. Because now Lola realised she was living a half-life and she wanted her full life, *with Hamish*, to start immediately.

Lola arrived at Grace's apartment with fifteen minutes to spare before midnight. She knew Marcus and Grace had gone to some fancy party in the city so they wouldn't be here. She also knew Hamish wasn't working.

Because they were supposed to be together tonight.

She just hoped like hell he was at the apartment and not out somewhere whooping it up, because he wasn't answering her calls or her texts. If he wasn't here she didn't know what she was going to do, but if it meant she had to sleep outside this door all night, torturing herself with images of who he might be whooping it up with, she would.

Lifting her hand to knock, the door opened before she got a chance to make contact and Lola pitched forward. Right into Hamish's chest. His hands came out to steady her.

'Lola?'

'Hamish.' He smelled *so* good—coconut and pine—that for a second she just stood in the circle of his arms and breathed him in.

Too quickly, he eased her away and Lola noticed he had his keys in his hands. 'You're on your way out?'

'Yes.' His grin was really big, and that impossibly square jaw of his was looking absolutely wonderful covered in ginger scruff. 'I was coming to you.'

He kissed her then, pushing her against the open doorway, and Lola *melted*, moaning deep in the back of her throat, her hands going up around his neck to shift nearer, to bring him closer. Her head filled with the scent of him and the sound of his breathing and the taste of beer on his breath.

'Oh, I missed you,' he muttered, and his words filled her head too, making her feel dizzy.

Intoxicating her.

She was drunk. Drunk on the feel and the taste and the smell of him. On his heat and his hardness. But... they had to talk first.

There were things he needed to hear, things she needed to say. And if they kept this up there'd be no talking. There'd be nudity in the hallway and sex on the doorstep. God knew, she wanted him badly but she had to prove to him she *could* talk with her mouth, not just her body.

Lola pulled away, placing a hand on his chest as Hamish came back in for more. Their breathing was heavy between them as his gaze searched hers. 'We need to talk.'

'Lola, I don't care.' He dropped his lips to her neck and nuzzled. 'I don't bloody care.' His words were muffled and hot on her neck and Lola's eyes felt as if they'd rolled all the way back in her head as he teased her there, his tongue and his whiskers a potent combination.

'I've held out for as long as I can and I just don't care any more. You win. Whatever kind of relationship you want, I'm in. We don't have to talk ever. I just need you too bloody much.'

His words were like a rush to her brain. And places significantly south. But they didn't give her any great satisfaction. She'd treated him like a sex object. Like a life support for a penis and that had been wrong.

'Hamish.' Lola broke away again.

He pulled back, his pupils dilated with lust, his breathing raspy. 'Come to bed with me. Let me show you how much I missed you.'

And he kissed her again, long and drugging, and she

clung to him, blood pounding through her breasts and belly and surging between her thighs as the dizziness took her again. The man could definitely kiss. He sure as hell made it hard to stop.

But. This was important. It was their future.

Lola pushed hard against his chest this time and Hamish groaned as he pulled away again. 'You accused me of not wanting to talk.' She was panting but determined to see this through. 'And you were right. So I'm going to do this properly. We're going to *talk*. And then you can take me to bed and do whatever you want with me.'

He searched her gaze for a moment before breaking into a smile. 'Whatever I want?'

Lola's heart swelled with love. 'Anything.' She'd give this man anything.

He grinned. 'You're on.' Then he stepped back, grabbed her hand and urged her inside. 'Let's go to the balcony. I won't be tempted to take off your clothes out there. *Probably.*'

Lola laughed. She didn't care where they talked, only that they did, and she followed him out to the balcony with its view of the Manly foreshore in the distance. She could hear the distant noise from New Year's Eve revellers floating to her on the balmy night air.

Hamish stood at the railing, his arms folded across his chest as if he couldn't be trusted not to touch her, and Lola smiled. She settled against the railing too, leaving a few feet between them.

'Speak.'

She didn't speak. Instead, she reached into the pocket of her work trousers—because she hadn't stopped to change—and handed over May's postcard. He took it impatiently, staring at the picture. 'What's this?'

'It's a postcard from May.'

'Well, yeah, I figured that. I mean why are—?'

'I got it today. It's postmarked the twenty-first.'

He glanced at her swiftly. 'Oh, Lola.' He took a step in her direction and stopped. 'Are you okay?'

Lola nodded. 'I am, actually.'

'It's kinda freaky, yeah?'

'Yeah.' Lola smiled. 'A little.'

'Listen, I've been thinking. I could come with you... to Doongabi...keep you company.'

Hamish no doubt knew about all the funeral arrangements. She'd only responded in a perfunctory manner to his texts and hadn't answered any of his calls, but Grace was up to speed with all the details.

Lola's heart filled up a little more at Hamish's offer. 'You have to be back at work in Toowoomba.'

'I'm sure I can figure it out with my boss.'

'Well...yes, thank you. I'd like that.' She took a step towards him. There was only about a foot between them now. 'I'd like to introduce my family to the man I love.'

She could hear Hamish's breath catch and caught the blanching of his knuckles as he gripped the railing. 'The man you love?'

'Yes.' Lola nodded and her heart banged in her chest. This was it. The moment of truth. 'I love you, Hamish. I'm so sorry it took me this long to see it. That I was so blind to it, too wedded to this idea of being a gypsy, too frightened to deviate from the path I'd set myself all those years ago, to see what my heart already knew.'

'You *love* me.'

He was very still suddenly and Lola rushed to reassure him. 'Yes. *God, yes.*' Her hands were trembling and she folded her arms to quell the action. 'It took a postcard and some words from Aunty May and my heart trans-

plant patient to realise that I've only been living a half-
life and a gypsy caravan is big enough for two and I want
to share mine with you.'

'You do?'

'Yes.' Stupid tears threatened and Lola blinked them
back. She was done with crying. 'And I treated you like
a…sex object—'

His laugh cut her off. 'Well, that bit wasn't so bad.'

Lola laughed too. 'That bit was pretty damn good.
But it was wrong of me. You were *always* more than
that. You were the guy who made me laugh. The guy
who held me when I was sad. The guy who watched *Die
Hard* with me. The guy who bought me the most beautifully perfect gift I've ever been given. I've been falling
in love with you all this time and lying to myself about
it because I've been single for so long I don't know how
to be part of a couple.'

'Lola.' Hamish took that one last remaining step and
brought his body flush with hers, his hands sliding pos-
sessively onto her hips. He smiled. 'You should stop talking now and kiss me.'

Lola shook her head, pressing a hand between them
as worry that she might screw things up grew like a
bogeyman inside her head. 'I mean it, Hamish, I don't
know how to do this. And we're so different, we want
different things. I still don't know how we're going to
work it all out.'

He smiled gently. 'Do you love me, Lola?'

She nodded. 'Yes. *God, yes.*'

'Do you want to be with me? In the forever kind of
way.'

'Yes,' she whispered. 'I want forever with you.'

'Good answers, *City*.' He smiled and Lola relaxed and
fell in love a little more. 'All that matters is that we love

each other. We can work the rest out. Sure, it'll take compromise and we'll probably argue a little and go back and forth a hundred times over the same old things but as long as we're committed to staying together, we can overcome anything. We'll be all right, Lola, I promise.'

Suddenly, Lola knew he was right. She could feel it in her bones. Because nothing was more important in her life than Hamish. And she knew he felt the same way about her.

They were going to be better than all right. They were going to be freaking amazing.

'Now.' Hamish removed her hand from his chest and urged her closer. 'Are you going to kiss me or what?'

Lola smiled, lifting on her tippytoes to kiss the man she loved, twining her arms around his neck and sighing against his mouth as their lips joined and everything in her life clicked into place.

In the distance the countdown started and they were still kissing as the crowd yelled, 'Happy New Year!'

The first firework shot into the sky with a muted *thunk* and exploded seconds later in an umbrella of red sparks. Lola and Hamish broke apart, laughing. She stared in wonder at the fireworks and at Hamish.

'I think I just saw stars.' Lola laughed up at him as the night sky erupted into a kaleidoscope of noise and colour.

He grinned. 'Me too. Now, let's go make the earth move.' And he tugged on her hand and led her to his bedroom.

EPILOGUE

A COOLING HARBOUR breeze blew cross the park on the warm November morning. Flurries of electric purple jacaranda flowers swirled and drifted to the ground, carpeting the road and the footpath and the edge of the park where the ceremony was being held in a stunning lilac carpet.

'Do you take this woman...?'

Lola's hands tightened in Hamish's as she smiled up at her soon-to-be husband and her heart did its usual *ker-thump*. It had been his idea to have the marriage service here, in this place she loved so much. And, if it was possible, her heart expanded a little more.

Having Grace and Marcus joining them to make it a double wedding was the icing on the cake. They'd already said their vows and were waiting eagerly for Lola and Hamish to get through theirs so they could all be declared husbands and wives.

Grace was looking radiant in her figure-hugging cream lace creation, her gorgeous red hair piled into a classy up-do. Marcus was darkly handsome in his suit and still only had eyes for Grace.

Lola had chosen a more gypsy-style dress of embroidered cotton that flowed rather than clung. It had shoe-string straps and fluttered against her body in the breeze, the garland of jacaranda flowers in her loose, curly hair the perfect finishing touch.

'I sure as hell do.'

The wedding guests—a mix of friends and both families who'd travelled to Sydney for the occasion—laughed at Hamish's emphatic answer and Lola's heart just about burst with happiness. He was breathtakingly sexy in his fancy suit with his purple shirt. His clean-shaven jaw was as rock solid as always, his reddish-brown hair flopped down over his forehead as endearingly as always and his bottomless blue gaze was full of promises to come.

It had been a whirlwind year—falling in love, getting engaged and planning a wedding in such a short space of time but, as Aunty May had said, when you knew, you *knew*.

Hamish hadn't gone back to Toowoomba, he'd stayed on in Sydney to complete his course, finishing it while Lola had been in Zimbabwe then joining her there for the last week, taking Aunt May's ashes with him. Together they'd scattered them from a canoe across the mighty Zambezi River, a place as wild and free as May herself.

Tomorrow they were leaving for two weeks in London before heading to western Queensland. Hamish was taking up a two-year rural post and Lola had a job at the local hospital. *And* she was looking forward to it.

It had taken her very little time with Hamish to learn that home was wherever her heart was and her heart would always be with him. They'd even talked about having children when they returned to Sydney.

Children!

Lola had always assumed she'd remain childless, like May. Now she couldn't wait to be running around after a little blonde girl and little boy with cinnamon hair. She'd been a lot of places and seen a lot of things but what she craved most now was home and hearth and family.

It was official, she was a hundred percent, head-over-heels gone on Hamish Gibson.

'And do you take this man…?'

The celebrant was smiling at her. Grace was smiling at her. Her mother was smiling at her. And Hamish… Hamish was smiling at her.

'Yes,' Lola said, her eyes misting over. 'For ever and ever.'

More laughter but Hamish squeezed her hands tighter and, as the jacaranda flowers twirled around their heads in the breeze, she knew she'd never spoken truer words.

He was hers. And she was his.

For ever.

* * * * *

SEDUCED BY THE SHEIKH SURGEON

CAROL MARINELLI

CHAPTER ONE

IT WASN'T BECAUSE of lack of opportunity for there had been plenty of them.

In fact, here was one now!

A late spring storm had come from nowhere and lit up the London sky.

Adele stood at the bus stop across the road from the Accident and Emergency department, where she had just finished working a late shift. The rain battered the shelter and she would probably be better off standing behind it. Her white dress, which was not designed to get wet, clung to her and had shrunk to mid-thigh and her shoulder-length blond hair was plastered to her head.

She wore no mascara so she was safe there—Adele wouldn't be greeting Zahir with panda eyes.

It was ten at night and she could see the blinkers on his silver sports car as he drove out of the hospital, turned right and drove towards her.

Surely now? Adele thought, as she stepped out from the supposed shelter just to make sure that she could be seen.

Surely any decent human being who saw a colleague standing shivering and wet at a bus stop, caught in a sudden storm, would slow down and offer them a lift home.

And when he did Adele would smile and say, 'Thank

you,' and get into the car. Zahir would see her clinging dress and wonder how the hell he had not noticed the junior nurse in *that* way before.

And she would forgive him for a year of rudely ignoring her. Finally alone, they would make conversation and as they pulled up at her flat...

Adele hadn't quite worked out that part. She loathed her flat and flatmates and couldn't really see Zahir in there.

Maybe he would suggest a drink back at his place, Adele thought as finally, *finally*, her moment came and the silver car slowed down.

She actually started to walk towards it, so certain was she that their moment had come.

But then he picked up speed and drove on.

No, his car didn't splash her with water, but she felt the drenching of his repeated rejection, just as if it had.

He must have just slowed down to turn on his radio or something, Adele soon realised, for Zahir drove straight past her.

How could she fancy someone as unfeeling as him? she wondered.

It was a conundrum she regularly wrangled with.

She couldn't console herself that he didn't like women.

Zahir dated.

A lot.

On too many occasions Adele had sat at the nurses' station or in the staffroom as he'd taken a call from whoever his latest perturbed girlfriend had been.

Perturbed because it was Saturday night and they were supposed to be out and Zahir was at work. Perturbed because it was Sunday afternoon and he had said several hours ago that he was only popping in to work.

Work was his priority. That much was clear.

During Adele's last set of night shifts he had been called in when he hadn't been rostered on. Wherever he had come from had required him to wear a tux. He had looked divine. For once he had been utterly clean shaven and his thick black hair had been slicked back. Adele had tried to stammer out the problem with the patient that she and Janet, the nurse unit manager, had been concerned about.

It had proved to be a hard ask.

'He was seen here this afternoon and discharged with antibiotics,' Adele said. 'His mother's still concerned and has brought him back tonight. The paediatrician has seen him again and explained it's too soon for the antibiotics to take effect.'

'What is your concern?' Zahir asked.

His cologne was heavy yet it could not douse the testosterone and sexual energy that was almost a visible aura to Adele. His deep, gravelly voice asked pertinent questions about the patient. She loved his rich accent and each stroke of a vowel he delivered went straight to her thighs.

'Adele,' he asked again, 'what is the main reason for your concern?'

'The mother's very worried,' Adele said, and closed her eyes because mothers were always very worried. 'And so am I.'

Zahir had gone in to examine the patient when a stunning woman had walked into the department. Her long brown hair and make-up were perfect despite the late hour. Dressed in silver, she had marched up to Janet and asked in a very bossy voice exactly how long Zahir would be.

'Bella, I said to wait in the car.' Zahir's curt response

had made the beauty jump. Clearly she only spoke like this out of his earshot.

Janet smothered a smile as Bella stalked off. 'Gone by morning,' she said to Adele.

Zahir had asked that Janet send in Helene to assist him.

More experience was required.

Adele had none.

Well, not with men but it seriously irked her that even after a year of working in Accident and Emergency he seemed to treat her as if she had just started.

And she had been right to be worried about the child.

Zahir performed a lumbar puncture and viral meningitis was later confirmed. The little boy was admitted and ended up staying in hospital for five days.

Not that Zahir told her.

There was never any follow-up for Adele.

And yet, for all his faults in the communication department, Zahir was the highlight of her working day.

Of all her days.

Well, no more, she decided as his car glided past.

He was arrogant and dismissive and it had been outright mean of him not to stop and offer her a lift—she refused to fancy him any longer.

Adele's world was small, too small, she knew that and was determined to do something about it.

The bus finally arrived.

Actually, two of them did. The one that was late and the one that was due.

Spoiled for choice, Adele thought as she climbed onto the emptier one and said hello to the driver.

There were some of the regulars on board and there were a few others.

Adele was a regular and knew she could zone out

for the next half-hour. She rested her head against the window as the bus hissed and jolted its way through the rain, and as it did so she went to her favourite place in the world.

Zahir.

Her conundrum.

She had no choice in her attraction toward him, she had long since decided. She had fought it, tried to deny it, tried to do something about it and she had also tried to ignore it.

Yet it persisted.

It simply existed and she had to somehow learn to live alongside it.

Maybe it was because he was completely unobtainable, she considered as someone started to sing at the back of the bus.

Yes, she needed to get out more and she was starting to do so. On Friday night she had a first date with Paul—a paramedic who had made his interest in her clear.

Just say yes, everyone at work had told her.

Finally she had.

Except it wasn't Paul that she wanted to go out with.

It was, and felt as if it always would be, Zahir.

His name badge read, 'Zahir, Emergency Consultant.'

The patients did not need to know he was Crown Prince Sheikh Zahir Al Rahal, of Mamlakat Almas.

Her heart hadn't needed to know that either. She had felt its rate quicken the moment she had seen him, before she had even known his name.

At first sight, even before their first introduction, this odd feeling had taken residence in Adele.

His hair was black and glossy, and his skin was the

colour of caramel and just as enticing. The paper gown he'd worn had strained over wide shoulders. There had been an air of control in the resuscitation room even though it had been clear that the patient's situation had been dire.

He had glanced up from the patient he'd been treating and for a second his silver-grey eyes had met Adele's and she had felt her cheeks grow warm under his brief gaze.

'I'm just showing Adele around the department.' Janet, the nurse unit manager conducting the interview, had explained.

He had given just the briefest of nods and then he had got back to treating the critical patient.

'As you can see, the resuscitation area has been updated since you were last here,' Janet had said. 'We've now got five beds and two cots.'

Yes, it had been updated but the basics had been the same.

Adele had stood for a moment, remembering a time, several years previously, when she had been wheeled in here and, given that Janet had been with her on that awful day, she had perhaps understood why Adele had been quiet.

Janet had made no reference to it, though; in fact, as they'd both walked back towards Janet's office she'd spoken of other things.

'That was Zahir, one of our emergency consultants,' Janet said. 'You'll have come across him when you did your placement.'

'No.' Adele shook her head. 'He wasn't here then. I believe he was on leave.'

'He's been working here for a couple of years now but, yes, he is away quite a lot. Zahir has a lot of commitments back home so he works on temporary contracts,' Janet explained. 'We always cross our fingers that he'll renew. He's a huge asset to the department.

'I've worked with his brother, Dakan,' Adele said.

They both shared a smile.

Dakan had just completed his residency and was a bit wild and cheeky, and she knew from the hospital grapevine that Zahir was the more austere of the two.

Of course she had heard about his brooding dark looks and yet she had never expected him to be quite so attractive.

Adele hadn't really found anyone that attractive before.

Not that it mattered.

There had been no room in her life for that sort of thing, not that Zahir would even give her a second glance.

'So,' Janet said as they headed back to her office, 'are you still keen to work here?'

'Very.' Adele nodded. 'I never thought I'd want to work in Emergency but during my placement I found that I loved it...'

'And you're very good at it. You shall have to work in Resus, though.'

'I understand that.'

As a student nurse Adele had struggled through her Accident and Emergency placement. She had dreaded going into the room where, even though her mother hadn't died, Adele had found out that she was lost to her.

Janet, knowing all that had gone on, had been very patient and had given Adele the minimum time in Resus and had looked out for her when she was there. Now, though, if Adele wanted to make Accident and

Emergency her specialty, there could be no kid-glove treatment.

'Are you sure it won't be too much for you?' Janet checked.

'I'm sure.' Adele nodded. She had given it a lot of thought and she explained what she had come to realise during her training.

'Really, my mother was in Theatre, in Radiology and ICU. For some reason the Resus room hit me the hardest but I've come to understand that there are memories of that time all over the place.'

'How is Lorna doing now?' Janet asked carefully.

'She's still the same.' Adele gave a strained smile. 'She's in a really lovely nursing home, the staff are just wonderful and I go in and see her at least once a day.'

'That's a lot of pressure.'

'Not really.' Adele shook her head. 'I'm not sure if she knows I'm there but I'd hate her to think I'd forgotten her.'

Janet wanted to say something.

Years of visiting her mother at *least* once a day would take its toll, she knew.

But then Janet understood why it would be so hard for Adele to move on. After all, she knew the details of the accident.

Janet had been working that day.

They had been alerted that there had been a motor-vehicle accident and that there had been five people injured and in the process of being freed from the wreckage of the cars.

Lorna Jenson, a front-seat passenger, had been in critical condition with severe head and chest injuries.

The driver of the other car had abdominal and head injuries and had been brought into Resus too. His wife and daughter had escaped with minor injuries but they had been hysterical and their screams and tears had filled the department.

And finally, as Lorna had been about to be taken to Theatre for surgery to hopefully relieve the pressure on her brain, Janet had gone in to speak with her eighteen-year-old daughter who'd lain staring at the ceiling.

Adele's blonde hair had been splattered with blood and her face had been as white as the pillow. Her china-blue eyes had not blinked, they'd just stared up at the ceiling and her lips too had been white.

'Adele?' Janet checked, and Adele attempted to give a small nod but she was wearing a hard cervical collar. 'Can you tell me your full name?' Janet asked as she checked the wristband. She had been busy dealing with the critically injured patient and had to be very sure to whom she was speaking.

'Adele Jenson.'

'Good.' Having confirmed to whom she was speaking, Janet pressed on. 'I believe that Phillip, the consultant, has been in and spoken with you about your mother.'

'He has,' Adele said.

Phillip had been in and had gently told her just how unwell her mother was and that there was a real possibility that she might not make it through the operation.

His glasses had fogged up as he'd looked down at Adele and told her the grim news.

Adele didn't understand how the doctor had tears in his eyes and yet hers were dry.

Now Janet was looking down at her.

'She's going to be going to Theatre very soon.'

'How's the man…?' Adele asked.

'I'm sorry, Adele, I can't give you that information.'

'I can hear his family crying.'

'I know you can.'

'How badly are they hurt?'

'I'm sorry, Adele. Again, I can't give you that information, it's to do with patient confidentiality.'

'I know it is,' Adele said. 'I'm a nursing student. But I just need to know how he is, if he's alive.'

'It's very hard for you.' Janet gave her hand a little squeeze but gave her no information. 'I wondered if you'd like me to take you in to see your mother before she goes up to Theatre.'

Adele tried to sit up.

'Just lie there,' Janet soothed. 'We'll wheel you over on the gurney. I can take that collar off you now, Phillip just checked your X-rays and says your neck is fine. It just had to be put on as a precaution.'

Gently she removed it.

'How do you feel?' Janet asked.

'I'm fine,' Adele said, though, in fact, she felt sick and had the most terrible headache, possibly from sitting in the car as the firefighters had used the Jaws of Life to peel back the roof. The noise had been deafening. The silence from her mother beside her had been far worse, though.

Janet could hear the sound of police radios outside the curtain and one of them asking if they could speak with Adele Jenson.

'Just one moment,' Janet said to Adele. She took the police to the far end of the corridor, well out of Adele's earshot.

'I'm just about to take her in to see her mother. Can this wait for a little while?'

'Of course,' the officer agreed. 'But we really do need to speak with the other driver.'

'*Learner* driver,' Janet said, and with that one word she asked that they tread very carefully.

The officer nodded.

Janet left them then and wheeled Adele in to see her mother.

At the time Janet was quite sure Lorna wouldn't make it through surgery.

But she did.

Now Lorna clung to life in a chronic vegetative state.

And her daughter, Janet rightly guessed, was still paying the price for that terrible day.

CHAPTER TWO

'THAT WAS SOME storm last night,' Janet said.

'You're telling me!' Helene responded. 'Hayden was driving and I had to get him to pull over.'

Adele was on another late shift and they were sitting at the nurses' station. They had been discussing annual leave before the conversation had been sidetracked.

Adele really wasn't in the mood to hear about Helene's son's driving lessons.

Again!

Helene had, a few months ago, come back to nursing after a long break away to raise her perfect family, and she spoke about them all the time.

'Did you get home okay, Adele?' Janet checked.

'I did,' Adele said, glancing over at Zahir, who had his back to her and was checking lab results on the computer. He was wearing navy scrubs and his long legs were stretched out. He was still taking up far too much space in her mind. 'A lovely man stopped and gave me a lift.'

She watched as Zahir briefly stopped scrolling through results but then he resumed.

'Who, Paul?' Janet asked, because they all knew that Adele had a date with him tomorrow night.

'No.' Adele shook her head. 'It was just some random

man. As it turned out, he'd escaped from police guard in the psychiatric unit, but I didn't feel threatened—he didn't have his chainsaw with him.'

Janet laughed. She understood Adele's slightly off-the-wall humour. 'You got the bus, then.'

'Yes, I got the bus.'

Chatter break over, they got back to business.

'Adele, you really need to take some annual leave.'

Janet placed the annual leave roster in front of her and Adele frowned as Janet explained. 'Admin don't like us to hold too much over and further you haven't taken any in the time you've been here.'

'Nice problem to have!' Helene said.

'What about September?' Adele suggested, because there were several slots there and Janet nodded and pencilled a fortnight in then. 'You need to take two weeks before that, though.'

The trouble with that was it was now May. The upcoming summer months were all taken. In fact, a couple of months ago Adele had cancelled her leave when Helene had won a competition to take her perfect family on an overseas holiday.

'How about the first two weeks of June?' Janet suggested. 'There's a spot there.'

'But that's only three weeks away.'

'That will give you time to book something last minute and cheap,' Janet said. 'I've been telling you to take some leave for ages, Adele.'

She had been.

'What might you do?' Helene asked once Janet had gone.

'I have no idea,' Adele admitted.

The truth was, even if she could afford to jet off to

somewhere nice, she could not bear the thought of leaving behind her mum.

And a fortnight without the routine of work wasn't something that Adele wanted either.

She didn't like the flat where she lived, and, feeling guilty about acknowledging it to herself, neither did she want to spend even more time at the nursing home.

Perhaps she could do some agency work and try to get enough money together to start looking for her own place.

'How is Mr Richards now, Adele?' Zahir asked about the patient whose notes she had been catching up on when the subject of annual leave had arisen.

'He's comfortable.'

'And how are his obs?'

'Stable,' Adele said.

Mr Richards was on half-hourly obs and they were due, oh, one and half minutes from now.

Basically, Zahir was prompting her to do them.

Well, she didn't need him to remind her, as he so often did, but she said nothing and hopped down from her stool.

Mr Richards had unstable angina and as she did the observations Adele smiled down at the old man, who was all curled up under his blanket and grumbling as the blood-pressure cuff inflated.

'I want to sleep.'

'I know that you do,' Adele said, 'but we need to keep a close eye on you for now.'

His blood pressure had gone up and his heart rate was elevated. 'Do you have any pain at the moment?' Adele asked.

'None, or I wouldn't have, if you'd just let me sleep.'

Adele went to tell Zahir about the changes but was

halted by a very elegant woman. She had a ripple of long black hair that trailed down her back and she was wearing a stunning, deep navy, floor-length robe that was intricately embroidered with flowers of gold. Around her throat was a gold choker and set in it was a huge ruby.

She was simply the most stunning woman Adele had ever seen.

'I am to meet with Zahir…' she said to Adele. 'Can you tell him that I am here?'

Adele would usually ask who it was that wanted to speak with him but there was something so regal about her that she felt it would be rude to do so. As well as that, she had heard Zahir asking Phillip to cover him for a couple of hours as he and Dakan were taking their mother out for afternoon tea.

This was surely his mother—the Queen.

'I'll just let him know.'

There was only Zahir in the nurses' station now. He was still on the computer but just signing off. 'Zahir,' Adele said.

'Yes?' He didn't turn around.

'There's a lady here to see you. I think that it might be your mother.'

'Thank you,' he stood. 'I shall take her around to my office. When Dakan comes, would you tell him where we are?'

'Actually…' Adele halted him. 'I was just coming in to tell you that Mr Richards's blood pressure and heart rate are raised.'

'Does he have pain?'

'He says not, he just wants to sleep.'

'Okay.' Zahir glanced at the chart she held out to him. 'Could you take my mother to my office and have her wait there?'

'Of course,' Adele said. 'What do I call her?'

'I answer to Leila!'

Adele turned and saw that Zahir's mother had followed her into the nurses' station. 'I apologise.' Adele smiled. 'Let me take you through...'

They walked through the department. Leila said how lovely it felt to be in London and to be able to go out with her sons for tea. 'Things are far less formal here than they are back home,' she explained. 'I prefer not to use my title when I am here as people tend to stare.'

They would stare anyway, Adele thought. Leila was seriously beautiful and it was as if she glided rather than walked alongside her.

'I thought you'd have bodyguards,' Adele said, and Leila gave a little laugh.

'My driver is trained as one but he is waiting outside. I don't need bodyguards when I have my sons close by.'

'Zahir's office is a little tucked away...' Adele explained as they walked through the observation ward, but then she frowned as she realised that the Queen was no longer walking beside her.

She turned around and saw that she was standing and had her fingers pressed into her forehead.

'Are you okay?' Adele checked.

'I'm just a bit...' Leila didn't finish. Instead she drew in a deep breath and Adele could see that she was terribly pale. 'Could you show me where the restroom is?'

'It's there,' Adele said, and pointed her to the staff restroom. 'I'll just wait here for you, shall I?'

Leila nodded and walked off and Adele waited for her to come out.

And waited.

Perhaps she was topping up her make-up, Adele decided, but then she thought about how pale Leila had suddenly gone and Adele was certain that she had been feeling dizzy.

She was loath to interrupt her. After all, Leila was Zahir's mother and she was also a queen.

But, at the end of the day, she was a woman and Adele a nurse and she was starting to become concerned.

Nursing instinct won.

She pushed open the door and stepped in but there was no Leila at the sink washing her hands or doing her make-up. 'Leila?' Adele called into the silence.

'Please help me...' Leila's voice came from behind the cubicle door.

'It's okay, I'm here.' Adele took out the coin that she kept in her pocket for such times. She turned it in the slot and pushed open the door, relieved that it gave and that Leila wasn't leaning against it, as had happened to Adele in the past.

'Don't let my sons see me bleed,' Leila begged.

'I shan't.'

She was bleeding and on the edge of passing out.

'Put your head down,' Adele told her. 'Has this happened before?'

'A couple of times. I am seeing a doctor on Harley Street.'

Adele didn't want to leave her sitting up in case she passed out, but neither did she want to lie her on the floor. She opened the main door to the rest room, at the same time as keeping an eye on her. She saw Janet bringing a patient into the obs ward.

'Janet!' Adele called out in a voice that made the other woman turn around immediately. As she did so Adele ducked straight back into the cubicle, knowing that Janet would follow her in.

'Just take some nice big breaths,' Adele said to Leila.
As Janet entered, Adele brought her up to speed.

'This is Leila, Zahir's mother. She's bleeding PV.'

'I'll go and get a gurney.'

'Janet,' Adele added, before she dashed off, 'she doesn't want Zahir to see.'

It was all swiftly dealt with. Leila was put onto a gurney and oxygen given. Adele put some blankets over her to make sure that she was covered before they wheeled her through.

Of course Zahir had finished with Mr Richards and was making his way to his office as they passed by.

'What happened?' he asked and then he gave a look at Adele as if to say, *I left her with you for five minutes!*

'Your mother fainted,' Adele told him as they walked quickly into the department.

'Maria,' Janet called out to the female registrar who was on duty today.

'I will take care of my mother,' Zahir said as they arrived at the cubicle.

He started to walk in but Adele blocked his path.

Well, she hardly blocked it, because she was very slight and he could easily have moved her aside or stepped around her, but there was something in her stance that was a challenge. 'Zahir!' Adele said, and she looked up at him and, for only the second time in twelve months of their history, their eyes met properly.

'Adele, let me past.'

'No,' she said, and stood her ground. 'Zahir, there are some things a mother would prefer her son didn't see.'

As realisation hit he gave a small nod. 'Very well.'

'We've got this,' Adele reassured him.

He was like a cat put out in the rain but reluctantly he stepped back. 'Could you keep me informed?'

She nodded.

Poor Leila, Adele thought as she got her into a gown and did some obs. Leila point blank refused to allow Adele to remove her jewellery.

Janet inserted an IV and Maria ordered some IV fluids. In a short space of time Zahir's mother was starting to look better.

'I've been unwell for a while,' she explained. 'I came over last month to have some time with my sons but I also had some tests done. I'm supposed to be having a hysterectomy tomorrow. I don't want my husband to know.' She took a breath. 'As awkward as it might be, I was going to tell my sons today at afternoon tea.'

Maria went through her medical history but at first Leila was very vague in her responses.

'How many pregnancies have you had?' Maria asked.

'I have two children.'

'How many pregnancies?' Maria asked again.

'Three,' Leila said, and Adele saw a tear slip from her eyes and into her hair. 'I don't like to speak of that time.'

Maria looked at Adele, whose hand Leila was holding, in the hope Adele could get more out of her. 'The doctor needs to know your history, Leila. She needs to know about your pregnancies and labours and any problems you have had.'

'My womb causes me many problems. I got pregnant very quickly with Zahir but he was born prematurely. It was a very difficult labour.'

They waited for her to elaborate but she didn't.

'And the next pregnancy?' Adele prompted.

'It took five more years to get pregnant and then I had Dakan. Again it was very difficult, he had very large shoulders. Two years later, I was lucky and I fell pregnant but my body did not do well... I had the best healer and a specialist *attar* but there was little they could do for me.'

'*Attar*?' Adele checked.

'He makes up the herbs the healer advises. I took the potion every day yet I still felt very unwell, and I started to vomit.'

'At what stage of the pregnancy?' Maria asked.

'He said I had four months left to go,' Leila answered. 'I was getting worse and I insisted that I be flown to a medical facility overseas. My husband and the healer were very opposed to the idea but I demanded it. In Dubai they said that I had to deliver the baby and that my blood pressure was very high. I called my husband and he said the healer had told him it was too soon and that the baby would die and that I needed to come home. Fatiq flew to Dubai to come and bring me back home...'

Leila started to cry in earnest then. 'But by then I had delivered and the healer was right. A few hours after my husband arrived our son died.'

'I'm so sorry,' Adele said.

'I have a picture of him.'

Adele got Leila's bag and watched as she took out her purse and showed them the tiniest most beautiful baby. 'We named him Aafaq, it means the place where the earth and sky meet.'

'It's a beautiful name,' Adele said, and she looked at a younger Leila and a man who looked very much like Zahir and was probably around the age his son was now.

They were both holding their tiny baby and he was off machines.

'What a beautiful baby,' Adele said.

They were a beautiful family, Adele thought, despite the pain. The King's arm was around his wife and he was gazing down at his son and you could see the love and sorrow in his expression.

'We cannot even speak of Aafaq,' Leila sighed. 'There is too much hurt there to even discuss that time. I think that my husband blames me for turning my back on the healer and yet he loves me also. I want for us to be able to speak about the son we lost but we can't. Aafaq would have been twenty-five years old next month and time still hasn't healed it. I miss him every day.'

It was so sad, Adele thought, and she continued to hold the older woman's hand as Maria examined her. A while later an ultrasound confirmed fibroids and Maria went through the options.

'We have a private wing here and I can speak with the consultant gynaecologist, Mr Oman. Or you can be transferred to the hospital you're already booked into, though I doubt they'd operate tomorrow. You might need a few days to rest and recover from this bleeding.'

'I think I would rather stay here but I shall discuss it with my son. Will you speak with him, please?' Leila asked Maria. 'He will be so worried and I am so embarrassed.'

'Stop thinking like that,' Adele told her. 'Zahir is a doctor, he deals with this sort of thing all the time.'

'Adele's right,' Maria said. 'Can I tell Zahir that you were already planning to have surgery?'

'Yes.' Leila nodded. 'But please don't mention what I said about Aafaq.'

'I shan't. Do you want him to come in when I've finished speaking with him?'

'Please.'

'Check first, though,' Adele called, as Maria left. 'I'm just going to help Leila freshen up.'

Adele left to make preparations so that she could give Leila a wash and change of sheets. When she came back into the cubicle Leila was staring at the photo but then she placed it back in her bag.

It must be so hard for her, Adele thought, not to be able to speak of her son. She wondered if Zahir even knew about the baby his mother had lost.

'Were you going to tell your husband after the operation?' Adele asked as she washed her.

'Yes,' Leila said. 'I might even have told him before or got one of my sons to. I know it is hard to understand our ways,' Leila said. 'Most of the time I am very grateful for the care I receive. There are times, though, that more is needed.'

Aafaq had been one of those times, Adele guessed.

Soon she was washed and changed.

'Thank you for caring for me,' Leila said.

'It's my pleasure. I'm just going to take your blood pressure again.'

She was doing just that when Maria checked that Leila was ready to receive visitors and a concerned-looking Zahir and Dakan came in.

They came over and Zahir gave his mother a warm embrace and spoke kindly to her in Arabic.

'It's okay,' he said. 'You could have told me that you have not been well.'

'I have been trying to deal with it myself.'

'Well, you don't have to. You have two sons who are doctors.'

'The healer seems to think…'

What was being said, Adele did not know but she watched as Zahir's jaw gritted.

'Zahir, don't just dismiss it out of hand. The potion

helped at first but in the end was not working. It was the same when...' She didn't finish.

Zahir looked down at his mother's swollen eyes and he knew that she would have been asked about previous pregnancies.

And he knew that subject must not be raised by him.

'When things were getting no better, the healer suggested that when I was in London perhaps I could see someone.'

Zahir frowned. 'He suggested it?'

'Yes,' Leila said, 'but please don't tell your father that. I don't want the healer to get in trouble.'

It was a long afternoon that stretched into the evening. Dakan got paged to go to the ward and Zahir saw patients while keeping an eye on his mother.

Mr Oman came and saw Leila. It was decided that she would be admitted to the private wing and that surgery would take place on Monday.

'For now we'll have you moved somewhere more comfortable and you can get some rest.'

He spoke with Zahir on his way out. 'You know that I shall take the very best care of her.'

'I do. Thank you.'

'Try not to worry. It will be a laparoscopic procedure and there will be minimal downtime.' Mr Oman said.

Zahir knew that.

It was a straightforward operation that his mother had had to travel for ten hours to get access to.

Dakan came in to visit again and they persuaded their mother that Fatiq, the King, needed to be informed as to all that had happened today, and finally she agreed.

'Go easy on him, Zahir,' Leila said, for she knew how they clashed, especially on topics such as this. 'He will be so worried and scared for me.'

Zahir nodded.

And at the beginning of the call, knowing how deeply his parents loved each other and the shock this would be, he was gentle. He sat in his office, explaining as best he could what had happened and that his mother would have surgery on Monday.

'No,' his father said and Zahir could hear the fear in his voice. 'I want her here. Last time she went into hospital…' He didn't finish.

They never did.

That topic was closed for ever.

'Zahir, if anything should happen to her—'

'She needs surgery,' Zahir interrupted, but they went around in circles for a while, with Fatiq insisting that surgery was unnecessary and that the healer could sort this.

Zahir bit back the temptation to tell his father that the healer had been the one who had suggested it.

That had surprised Zahir, yet it pleased him also.

Perhaps some progress could finally be made.

'She is seeing one of the top surgeons in London,' Zahir said. 'I will ensure that she gets the very best of care and shall keep you informed.'

The call ended and Zahir replaced the receiver. He squeezed the bridge of his nose between finger and thumb and took a deep breath to steady himself. He was so angry with his father about the health care back home and it was a battle they had fought for way more than a decade.

It was the reason he was here.

CHAPTER THREE

'ARE YOU OKAY?'

Her voice was soothing.

Pleasant.

He opened his eyes and there, standing at the office door, was Adele.

Zahir thought he had closed it and was uncomfortable that she'd caught him in an unguarded moment.

'I'm not about to have my second Al Rahal faint on me today?' Adele checked, and Zahir gave a reluctant smile.

'No.'

'We're just about to move your mother to the private wing.'

'Good,' Zahir said, and then glanced at the time. 'You must be finishing up. Thank you for all your help with her today.'

'You're welcome.'

'Who's taking her up to the ward?'

'I am,' Adele said.

His mother had insisted on keeping Adele around and, because queens were something of a rarity, the rules had been relaxed.

'She wants to know if you've spoken with her husband.'

'Tell my mother that he knows. I'll come and speak

with her on the ward. I just have a couple more patients to see.'

It took ages to settle Leila into the private wing. She was lovely but extremely demanding and by the time Adele had everything to the Queen's liking and had handed over it was way past the end of her shift and she was exhausted.

'I shall see you in the morning,' Leila checked as Adele wished her goodnight.

Zahir had come in to check that his mother was settled too.

'No.' Adele shook her head.

'But you said you started tomorrow at seven.'

'Yes, but I work in Emergency.'

There was an exchange in Arabic between mother and son. A rather long one and finally Zahir translated what was being said.

'She wants to know if you can nurse her. I've just explained that that is not how things work.'

Leila spoke now in English. 'I want Adele to be my nurse.'

'She's very used to getting her own way.' Zahir gave a wry smile and then went back to speaking in Arabic.

His mother was adamant and, seeing that she was getting upset, Adele intervened.

'Leila, I would love to care for you but it isn't my specialty and I'm already rostered on to work in Accident and Emergency tomorrow. They're very short of staff. I can come and visit you, though.'

'You'll visit me?'

'I'd love to.' Adele nodded. She often caught up with patients once they were moved to other wards and few were more interesting than Leila. 'I can come in during my lunch break tomorrow. For now, though, you need to get some rest. It's been an exhausting day for you.'

Adele headed down and changed out of her scrubs and into jeans and a T-shirt. It was well after ten and she had missed her bus and would have to wait for ages for the next one.

It wasn't the first time it had happened and it certainly wouldn't be the last.

It was, however, the first time that the silver sports car that usually glided past pulled in at the bus stop.

The window slid down and Zahir called out to her.

'The least I can do is give you a lift home.'

Even though Adele was still sulking about last night, she knew it would be petty to refuse.

Finally she sat in the passenger seat.

'You don't drive?' Zahir asked.

'No.' Adele shook her head. 'There's no real need to in London.'

She gave her regular excuse, but the truth was that since that awful day even the thought of getting behind the wheel made her feel ill.

'Surely it's better than getting a bus late at night?'

'Maybe.' Adele gave a shrug.

Perhaps she couldn't afford a car, Zahir thought. He had heard that she was saving up to move out of her flat.

He would buy her a car, Zahir decided.

It was as if cultures had just clashed in his brain.

That was what his family would say—buy her a car, repay the debt, return the favour tenfold—and yet he knew that she would find such a move offensive.

Today was not a debt that needed to be repaid to Adele.

It was her job. Nursing was what she did.

And she did it very well.

It wasn't her fault that he was terse with her at times.

It was necessary for him to function.

She entranced him.

She was funny and open and yet private and deep.

Adele was the woman he kept a distance from because she was the one person he would really like to get to know.

And no good could come from that.

'I really am grateful for all your help today,' he said.

'I was just doing my job.'

'I know, but you helped my mother a lot. I know that she would have been scared, given that she is so far from home, and that she would have needed someone to talk to.' Zahir hesitated. He thought of his mother's eyelids, swollen from crying. He hoped she had given her full history to the doctors. 'Did she mention that she lost a baby?'

Adele frowned as Zahir glanced at her. From the way Leila had asked that it not be mentioned, Adele had assumed Zahir didn't know about his brother. She thought about it some more and realised he would have been about seven when it had happened.

When she didn't answer the question, Zahir elaborated.

'I don't really know the details,' he admitted. 'It's a forbidden subject in the palace. I just know she was having a baby and that she flew to Dubai. Then my father left and they all returned. Aafaq is buried in the desert but to this day…' He glanced at her again, hoping he might glean something.

Anything.

'You need to discuss that with your mother,' Adele

said, though there was regret in her voice. She knew how it felt to be kept in the dark. She could still clearly remember trying to get information out of Janet. It was awful knowing someone held facts that were vital to you but could not be shared. 'I'm sorry.'

'I know,' Zahir admitted. 'And I'm sorry to have put you in that situation. I just hope she has been frank with Mr Oman.'

Adele didn't answer.

Zahir respected her for that.

'Just here,' Adele said, and they pulled up at a large building with heavy gates.

'Again—thank you again for your help with my mother today.'

'No problem. Thank you for the lift.'

'Any time.' Zahir gave an automatic response.

She let out a short, incredulous laugh. For a year he had driven past her; last night she had been drenched and he'd utterly ignored her. And, yes, it might seem petty but she would not leave it unsaid. 'Any time you feel *obliged* to, you mean.'

Zahir stared ahead but he was gripping the steering-wheel rather tightly.

He knew that Adele was referring to last night.

Of course he had seen her.

It had taken all he had not to stop.

'Goodnight, Zahir.'

She got out and opened the gates.

Zahir knew he hadn't dropped her at her flat. This was a nursing home. He knew that Adele's mother was very ill and that she visited her often.

He had never delved.

Zahir had wanted to, though.

He wanted to explore his feelings for Adele. He wanted her more than he had ever wanted anyone.

But he had been born to be king, which meant at all times he kept his head. His emotions he owned and his heart had to remain closed until marriage.

And he would marry soon hopefully.

It was the last bargaining tool he had with his father.

King Fatiq wanted a selection ceremony to take place and for Zahir to choose his future bride.

There were several possibilities and the union must be the one to best benefit the country, yet Zahir had refused to commit himself so far.

Only when he had free rein to rebuild the health system in his own country would Zahir choose a bride. His father had resisted but Zahir was now thirty-two and the King wanted his son married and home.

And so Zahir chose to remain aloof in relationships, knowing, hoping, that at any given time his father might relent and summon him home and the work on the health system in his country could truly begin.

There was nothing aloof about his feelings for Adele, though.

It could only prove perilous to get involved with her.

The last time he had been home he had sat in the desert and asked for a solution.

Always he asked for help regarding Aafaq and the clash with his father, and always he asked how best to serve his people. Lately, he had asked about Adele.

There could be no solution there, Zahir knew.

Yet he had asked for guidance and in the quiet of deep meditation the answer had been the same.

Have patience.

In time the answers will unfold.

Do what is essential.

Zahir's patience was running out.

He watched as Adele pressed the buzzer and then she turned around and frowned.

She was surprised that the man who left her standing in the dark night after night seemed to want to see her safely inside.

Within a matter of moments she was walking into the nursing home and towards her mother's room.

'Hi, Adele.' Annie, one of the nurses, had just finished turning her mother and smiled at Adele as she came in.

'I know that it's late but I couldn't get here this morning and...'

Adele stopped herself. They always told her that she didn't need to give a reason if she couldn't come in. Tomorrow she wouldn't be able to—she was on an early shift and, even though the nursing home was close by, she was going out on that date with Paul.

The trouble was she wasn't particularly looking forward to it.

'Hi, Mum,' Adele said, and took a seat and held one of her mother's hands.

Lorna's nails were painted a lovely shade of coral. Adele did her mother's finger- and toenails each week. Her once brown hair was now a silver grey. Adele had used to faithfully do her roots but in the end she had stopped that.

Oh, she knew she had to get a life and yet it was so hard not to come in and visit.

And people simply didn't understand.

Lorna had been so vibrant and outgoing. A single mum, she had juggled work and her daughter, along with an active social life. She'd had a large group of friends and at first they, along with relatives, had filled the ICU waiting rooms and then later they had come by to visit when Lorna had been on the ward.

Over the years those visits had all but petered out.

Now the occasional card or letter came and Adele would read it out then add it to the string on her mother's wall. Lorna's sister, Adele's aunt, came and visited maybe once or twice a year. Another friend dropped in on occasion but apart from that it was just Adele.

And so she brought her mother, who lay with her eyes closed, up to date on what was happening in her life.

'I finally my got my lift from him,' Adele told her mum. 'It was very underwhelming.' It really had been, she thought. 'Anyway, I'm over Zahir. I really do mean it this time. I'm going out with Paul tomorrow night. He's one of the paramedics,' Adele explained to the silence. 'He's asked me out a few times and I decided maybe I should give him a chance after all. I guess I'm not going to like everyone in the same way I do Zahir.'

It really was time to get a life.

But then she told her mother the real reason she had stopped by after work.

It wasn't just that she might not be in tomorrow, there were bigger reasons than that for her being here tonight.

If her mother would just squeeze her hand or blink or do one thing to acknowledge that she knew Adele was here, it would help.

This was agony, it truly was, sitting here day in, day out, and yet she was all her mother had.

But Adele made herself say it out loud.

'Mum, I've got some annual leave that I need to take and I'm thinking of going on holiday.'

It was a huge thing for her to say.

Yet she knew she couldn't live this life for ever.

To pay for the nursing home and the legal fees when the other family involved in the accident had sued, the family home had been sold and Adele now shared a small flat with Helga and James.

Adele had deferred her studies for two years, but they had been spent dealing with the aftermath of the accident. She hadn't had a holiday in years. Any weekends or leave had always been taken up with other things, such as university, work, visiting her mother, getting the house ready for the market or dealing with lawyers, doctors and real estate agents.

Finally, when her mum had been placed in this home and things had started to settle, Adele had started her role in Accident and Emergency.

Now she felt as if she was coming up for air and she simply wanted to get away and maybe just grieve for her mother.

Of course she would still visit, Adele thought as she walked the small distance home to her flat.

But she had to work out some sort of balance.

Helga was in the kitchen, making an enormous fry-up for herself and James, and she had her music up loud.

Adele was so tired but she lay on her bed, trying not to think of what she had just told her mother and trying to consider where to go on holiday.

Greece perhaps?

She woke to that thought.

Adele took out her laptop and looked at several destinations and then saw a wonderful package deal for the South of France.

Oh!

It was more expensive than she had planned for.

Then again, she hadn't really planned to be going away.

Walking towards the bus stop, she saw that a one-bedroom flat nearby had just come up for rent.

Perhaps the money would be better spent moving out than on two weeks overseas.

Arriving at work, she smiled at Janet, who was waiting for the rest of the early-shift staff to arrive before they had handover, which wouldn't take long, given that the place appeared dead.

Zahir was sitting on hold on the phone and not looking in the sunniest of moods.

'How's the holiday planning going?' Janet asked as Adele came over.

'I've seen something nice for the South of France.'

'Ooh, la la,' Helene said as she joined the group. 'Will you go topless?'

'I might.' Adele said. 'And I might find myself a nice French man...'

'What about Paul?' Janet checked.

'Oh, yes.' Adele said, her voice a touch deflated.

'You've got your hot date tonight!' Janet reminded her, and Adele rolled her eyes. 'Where's he taking you?'

'No idea.' Adele shrugged.

Zahir tried to ignore the conversation. Adele was going out on a date, well, of course she was.

She was beautiful, seriously so, and it had nothing to do with him what she did in her free time.

But this wasn't her free time.

'Is it appropriate,' Zahir said tartly as he hung up the phone, 'to be discussing topless bathing and dating in a corridor.'

'Er, Zahir.' Janet, who knew a thing or three, and

had been enjoying winding him up, answered with her own version of tartness. 'There are absolutely no patients around. I can handle my nursing staff, thank you.'

She smiled as Zahir stalked off.

Oh, yes.

She knew full well that he liked Adele.

CHAPTER FOUR

IT WAS A busy morning and lunchtime soon came around. Adele made good on her promise to visit Leila.

'You are looking so much better.' Adele was delighted to see the other woman sitting up and that she had some colour in her cheeks. Her hair was up and, despite wearing a hospital gown, she looked amazing.

'I am feeling it,' Leila agreed. 'Thank you for all your help yesterday. Honestly, I shudder to think what might have happened. We could have been at afternoon tea!'

'Don't think like that.' Adele smiled.

'It's hard not to,' Leila sighed. 'There's not much else to do here. It is so nice to have you come and see me. I am used to being very busy. To just lie in bed is so frustrating. Zahir and Dakan have been in, of course, and the nurses here are very kind, but I am so bored.'

'Will your husband come and visit you now that he knows you're having surgery?'

'No.' Leila shook her head. 'He does not like hospitals.'

It must be lonely for her, Adele thought.

'He was going to send one of my handmaids but I have told him not to. I have asked Dakan to bring my embroidery from the hotel. That will take my mind off things.'

Leila was so easy to talk to. She was the complete opposite of Zahir, who, Adele guessed from the little she had gleaned, took after his father. Leila was more open and outgoing, rather like Dakan.

'So you have days off this weekend?' Leila asked.

'I do.' Adele nodded. 'Then I'm on night duty for a fortnight.'

'They must be tiring,' Leila said, and then looked at Adele and saw the smudges under her eyes and her pale features. 'Though you look tired now, even before you have started your night duty.'

'I am tired,' Adele admitted, and not just to Leila but to herself. It had been an exhausting few years and Janet was right to insist that she take her leave. 'I've got a holiday coming up.'

'That's exciting. Are you going anywhere nice?'

'I haven't decided yet. I'll have a think about it this weekend.'

As they chatted Adele revealed that she was going on a date that evening.

'A first date.' Leila beamed.

'I'm actually not looking forward to it,' Adele admitted. 'I'm thinking of cancelling but I can't come up with a good enough excuse.'

'What do your parents think of him?' Leila asked.

'They...' Adele paused. 'I think your idea of a first date and mine are a little bit different, we're just going out for dinner.'

'Oh, yes.' Leila nodded. 'I sometimes forget. By the time I had my first date with Fatiq he was already my husband.' She laughed.

'Had you met him before you married?'

'Yes, there was a selection ceremony two months before the wedding. I knew though that I would be chosen. Or rather I hoped. From when I was a little girl I always knew who I would marry. I told him that I came with conditions, though,' Leila said, and tapped the ruby at her throat.

Adele guessed Leila meant she had told Fatiq that she must be kept in splendour.

'Well, I can't see myself ever marrying Paul,' Adele admitted. 'I can't even picture getting through dinner.'

'Your parents haven't met him, then?'

'No.' Adele shook her head. 'My parents divorced when I was very young and my father has never had anything to do with me.'

'And your mother?'

'She was in an accident,' Adele said. 'She's very unwell and is in a nursing home. I see her every day.'

'And you're visiting me too!'

'No, I *like* visiting you,' she said, and then closed her eyes on the sudden threat of tears.

Adele never cried but she was suddenly close to it now as she had practically admitted the truth—she didn't like visiting her mum.

Leila's hand went over hers.

It was unexpected and also terribly kind, given what she had just said.

'She can't talk or react,' Adele told Leila. 'She's just a shell of herself. I don't even think she knows that I'm there.'

'You know that you're there for her, though,' Leila said. 'That's the important thing.'

Finally, someone who understood, Adele thought.

Her family, friends and colleagues all encouraged her to step back. Even the nursing staff at the home gently implied that Adele didn't need to visit quite so much.

Adele knew that she had to sort out her life—she

didn't need to be told that but it was so nice to have someone understand.

'I'm worried about going on holiday,' she admitted.

'Can I tell you something?' Leila offered. 'I want to have a holiday. I love my country and my people but because of certain ways…' She hesitated and then explained. 'Always there must be a royal in residence. Fatiq was already a king when we married so I never even had a honeymoon. Now one of my sons steps in if we have to go away for formal occasions. Usually it is Zahir, but both of them have busy lives, so they only return when they must. I know that a holiday would be rejuvenating. I dream of having some time away with my husband to replenish myself, although I can't see it ever happening. Take some time for yourself, Adele, and you will return refreshed and better able to take care of your mother.'

It helped to hear that.

The wise, gentle words made Adele feel better about taking a short break.

'I must get back to work.' It had been nice talking and before she went Adele wished Leila well for her operation on Monday.

'I doubt you'll be up to visitors on Monday night but I'll come in after my shift on Tuesday morning.'

'I shall look forward to it,' Leila said. 'Enjoy dinner tonight.'

Adele did.

Her date went well, in fact. Paul was nice, and perfectly fine, except she didn't fancy him.

Not a bit.

And it neither started nor ended with a kiss.

It just wasn't there.

For Adele at least.

Monday came and in the afternoon Adele lay in bed, trying to get some sleep before her night shift.

Then Helga and James started to row.

Again.

She had gone to look at the one-bedroom flat, along with many others. She had put an application in and all Adele could do now was hope.

Oh, Leila was right, she needed a break.

She had two weeks of night duty to get through and then the world was her oyster.

Not quite.

She sat up and reached for her laptop and checked her bank account.

Still, it didn't stop her from daydreaming. She liked the look of Greece though she was still considering the South of France when an advert for exotic honeymoon destinations caught her eye.

Well, not the honeymoon word. Adele couldn't even get the excitement up for a second date. Paul had called over the weekend, suggesting that they go to the movies, but she had said no.

There was no point.

No, it was the destination that had her pause.

Mamlakat Almas.

That was where Zahir was from.

Adele clicked on it and immediately she was swept away.

She found out that the name translated to Kingdom of Diamonds.

It looked incredible. Adele watched a short film. It was taken from the air and she saw the azure water and the pristine white beaches. From snatches of conversations when she had worked with Dakan and from the odd comment Zahir had made, she had thought it was all ancient buildings and desert. And, yes, there was all of that—the film led her through the desert and she saw a caravan of camels and Bedouin tribes as well as colourful souqs. The city skyline, though, was modern, with golden high-rise buildings that shimmered in the sun.

And there, most beautiful of all, was Qasr Almas.

Diamond Palace.

Zahir's home.

It was spectacular—an imposing white residence with beach and ocean on the one side yet the desert started directly behind and spread into the distance.

The palace was dotted with stones, rubies, emeralds, and sapphires and some diamonds too.

Adele wanted to see it and she wanted to be there in the souqs and especially out in the desert.

She read the comments and most agreed it was an amazing destination. There was a certain magic to it, many said, and it was perfect for a honeymoon or romantic getaway.

Then Adele read the negative comments and they were all pretty much the same.

Don't get taken ill there!
Bring your own medication!

And one was aimed at a tour guide.

He couldn't even answer why the palace is called Diamond Palace and yet it is mainly coloured stones.

Oh, she would love to go there.

Right now, though, she needed to sleep.

It was bad enough trying to sleep when she was working days—her flatmates liked to party hard, it didn't matter what day of the week. Trying to sleep during the day was almost impossible—there were doors slamming, arguments breaking out. After a fitful sleep Adele woke to the sound of the television blaring and loud chatter from the kitchen as supper was being made.

She was tired before her shift even started. It was going to be a very long night.

Zahir also wasn't having the best of days.

While he was grateful that his mother's operation had gone smoothly, he was furious that it had to come to this.

There was only one small hospital in his home town. Zahir had had several architects working on plans for a new one, yet his father had halted him every step of the way and in the end the project had been abandoned.

The whole health system in Mamlakat Almas needed to be addressed and better ways implemented.

The main reason that Zahir and his brother had chosen to study medicine had been so that they could knowledgeably implement the changes that were needed, yet they were thwarted at every turn. Their father refused to move forward and over and over he came up with reasons why the plans for the hospital could not go ahead.

Zahir had now had enough.

Finding out that his mother had had to travel to another country just to get suitable treatment did not sit well with him.

He looked at his mother, drowsy from anaesthetic, and was told by Mr Oman that surgery had gone well.

'I'm surprised she waited so long,' the surgeon commented.

Zahir was sure his mother had been struggling for a long time and it meant his mood was not the most pleasant as he made his way back to the emergency department after visiting her.

And Zahir's already dark mood did not improve when he saw a woman holding a large bouquet of flowers asking one of the nurses if they could be delivered to Adele Jenson.

'She's not on duty till tonight,' the nurse said, taking the flower arrangement. 'But I'll see that she gets them.'

Once the delivery woman had gone a debate took place as to who had sent the flowers.

'She had a date with Paul on Friday,' someone said.

Zahir did not want to think about that but the flowers seemed to follow him everywhere.

They were in the nurses' station as he wrote his notes. And when, having checked on his mother again in the late afternoon, he went to make a drink, someone had moved them through to the staff kitchen.

He went to his office to make a call to his father.

The King.

He sat at the desk for a long moment, thinking hard. There was a lot on his mind. Admin were demanding his signature on a new contract, as they had every right to do.

Zahir knew, though, that he needed to go home and not just for a visit this time.

He was thinking of going head to head with his father so that he could get the hospital under way.

There was another reason, though, that he hadn't signed his new contract—Adele.

The attraction had been instant and troublesome. He

could still vividly remember the first time he'd laid eyes on her. Working on a patient, usually nothing could have drawn his attention, yet for a fleeting moment she had.

Her china-blue eyes had met his and Janet had explained that Adele was there for an interview.

He hadn't wanted her to get the job.

That was how much he was attracted to her. Even before they had spoken, he would have preferred that they never had. Of course she had been given the role and two weeks later he had walked into the nurses' station to the sound of her laughter and her fresh fragrance.

'Zahir,' Janet had said. 'This is Adele. She is a graduate nurse...'

'Adele.' He had responded with a brief nod.

'Hi!' She had smiled.

'Adele did her training here,' Janet had explained, 'so she's familiar with the place.'

Zahir had shut her out at every possibility. He'd asked for more senior staff when possible. He'd ignored her slightly wacky humour and had not rewarded it with a smile.

He'd dated sophisticated beauties and he'd told them upfront that he was in no position to settle down.

Currently he was dating Bella.

That was about to end and he knew Bella sensed it. He had used the excuse of his mother being sick this weekend not to see her and now she had come up with tickets to the theatre next week.

He would end it before then.

Soon he would marry a bride considered suitable.

Of course he would be consulted, but the effect of her laughter on the edge of his lips would not be taken into consideration. Neither would the fact that the mere scent of her made him want to turn around.

There would be a more logical thought process when it came to the selection of the future Queen. Perhaps her country would have a considerable army, for it would be a marriage of countries rather than hearts. Of course Zahir was not considering Adele for such a role. Yet, on sight, his guard had gone up and he'd known he'd have to be wary of the attraction he felt.

It was an attraction so intense that over the last year every time he had driven past her at the bus stop he had wanted to slow down and tell her to get in. Not to take her home but to take her to his bed.

To make slow, tender love to her.

Yes, he had slowed down the car once, but the sight of her in that short wet dress had been too much.

She was a relentless assault to his senses and six feet three of turned-on sheikh had decided it was safer to drive on.

It was hell to drive past her and leave her standing in the dark. It was hell to work alongside her.

It was hell.

And perhaps time away was needed before self-control ran out.

Nothing could come of them, Zahir knew that. It was the reason that he kept his distance.

His feelings for Adele were serious and that was why he held well and truly back. But it was getting harder to do so.

And it was another reason why it might be better to return to his country.

Zahir rang home.

'I have just come from visiting the Queen.' Zahir spoke formally with his father. 'She is doing very well.'

'How long until she can come home?' The King asked.

'Not until she is ready,' Zahir said. 'I have spoken

with Mr Oman and usually it would be several weeks before she could fly but, given she will be on the royal jet, I don't expect it to be that long. And I shall accompany her, of course.' He took a breath and then told his father what he had decided. 'I am not renewing my contract at the hospital. I'm coming home to sort out the building of the new hospital. I'm going to be speaking with architects over the coming weeks. I shall do my best to find someone who can understand the need to respect our traditions, as well as incorporate the new. When I return things will immediately get under way.'

'Nothing is to get under way without my permission.'

'Too many lives have been lost,' Zahir said. 'Your delay in implementing changes has caused your own wife to collapse. What about all our people?'

'I am King.'

'And I am Crown Prince and I refuse to do nothing until your death. I shall be returning with the Queen and change will happen.'

'Don't speak of this now, Zahir. Not when I am concerned for my wife—'

'No,' Zahir interrupted. 'You can no longer ignore that fact that there are better ways. The Queen collapsed while she was visiting me at work. What if she had been at a formal dinner or a royal event? Luckily she was in a hospital at the time.'

Zahir let out a tense breath, embarrassed on behalf of his mother as to how events could have panned out.

He was so grateful that Adele had dealt with things so discreetly.

Adele.

All roads led to her.

Even in the middle of a difficult conversation he

smiled at the memory of her blocking his path as he had tried to get into the cubicle to care for his mother.

Then his smile faded and he returned to the subject.

'We shall discuss this in person,' Zahir said to his father. 'For now, know that she is resting comfortably and that she is receiving *excellent* medical care.'

'If you are returning then there shall be a selection ceremony and a wedding.'

'You know where I stand on that,' Zahir said. 'I will not marry and have children when I cannot ensure adequate health care for them.'

Zahir hung up.

He saw a few more patients and then went through to the staffroom. Those flowers really were following him. They had been placed on the table and the word 'Adele' had been written on a sheet of paper, as well as an arrow, a row of hearts and a lot of question marks.

It was tease from the other nurses, informing her that she would need to explain!

Zahir did not want to hear it.

Adele walked into the staffroom fifteen minutes before the start of her shift to the beautiful sight of Zahir stretched out and asleep on a sofa. His mouth was slightly open, he needed to shave, but she'd prefer that he did not. But then her heart sank when she saw the large floral arrangement and the note with her name on it. Not for a second did she hope that the flowers were from Zahir. With trepidation she opened the card and read the message.

Adele
    Thanks for a great night. Hope to do it again very soon.
Paul x

Unlike their date, there was a kiss at the end.

Zahir awoke to the sickly scent of flowers and to Adele's blue eyes as she stood in the middle of the staff-room.

She looked over as he stirred and wondered what it would be like to wake up beside him.

'You got flowers.' He stated the obvious.

'I did.'

But not from you, her eyes accused.

Never anything from you.

Not even a smile.

'How is your mother?'

'She's doing well.' Zahir stretched his long body. 'The operation went smoothly.'

'That's good.' she said, wondering how the mere sight of him stretching had her on slow burn. How a night being wined and dined by a friendly and good-looking Paul couldn't garner a kiss, yet she could happily go over and straddle Zahir right here and right now.

Honestly!

She had never slept with anyone but she could almost feel the pull in her groin to walk over to him, to bend her head and to kiss that sulky mouth.

He sat up and she was very glad that he did.

'My mother said that you have been visiting her and are going to see her again.'

'I just thought with her being so far from home—' Adele started to explain, but Zahir cut in.

'I appreciate it,' he said, and then abruptly stood and left.

It didn't feel as if he appreciated it, Adele thought as he stalked off.

Still, she wasn't visiting Leila to earn favours from him.

She liked his mother and enjoyed their conversations.

Adele missed talking with her mum so much and Leila helped with that.

Zahir went home and it was a quiet night in Emergency, which made it a very long one. By morning, all Adele wanted was to go to sleep but she remembered she had promised to visit Leila.

'Don't forget your flowers,' Janet called out as she left.

Blasted things, Adele thought, but then she decided they might brighten the room up a little for her visitor.

'Flowers!' Leila was wearing a gorgeous nightgown, had all her jewels on and was back to looking stunning. She smiled when Adele knocked on her door and quickly dabbed her eyes with a handkerchief. 'You shouldn't have.'

'I didn't,' Adele admitted. She knew Leila had been crying. 'The man I went out with on Friday sent them.' She rolled her eyes.

'Do tell.'

Adele did.

Well, a little bit.

'It didn't go well.'

'Why?'

Because he wasn't your sexy son!

'It just didn't,' Adele said. 'I kept wanting to check my phone. That's not a good sign, is it?'

Leila laughed.

'Then he called over the weekend and asked me out again and I said no. I thought he'd got the message but he sent these. I didn't want to look like an idiot on the bus, and I thought they might cheer you up.'

'Well, they have.'

They were like a snowflake in a snowstorm, though, Adele thought as she looked around.

There were flowers everywhere.

'How do you feel?' she asked Leila.

'I had a lot of pain in the evening but they changed my pain control and now I feel much more comfortable. I've just had my first drink of tea. I asked Mr Oman when I can go back to the hotel. He says not for a few more days.'

'You've got on your jewels.'

Leila nodded. 'I was appalled when they told me I had to have them off for surgery. I insisted they were brought to Recovery and I was to wake up with them on.'

Adele smiled.

'Adele,' Leila said, 'I've been thinking.'

'About what?'

'Well, I need a private nurse and I would very much like it to be you.'

'I'm on night shift for the next couple of weeks,' Adele said.

'No, I'm not talking about back at the hotel. I mean for you to fly back with me. You said that you wanted a holiday.'

Adele's shocked expression was misinterpreted.

'I wouldn't be making too many demands on you,' Leila said quickly. 'I would just feel safer knowing I had a nurse for those first few days at home, and then you could do what you wanted. I would page you if required. You would have your own wing with its own beach and of course you would be well reimbursed.'

'Leila…' Adele didn't know what to say.

She was stunned to be asked and very flattered too.

And the more she thought about it, the more excited she felt.

There, in her chest, was something that had been missing for so long—the hope of adventure.

The thought of Zahir didn't enter her head. Not at that moment. He would be here, working. This had nothing to do with him.

It was the thought of a holiday at such an exotic location. Yes, it would be a working holiday perhaps but that suited Adele even better—it didn't have to be a holiday *or* a new flat, she could have both.

Yet hope was dashed even before it took form.

'Ah, Zahir!'

Adele, who had been perched on the bed, hurriedly stood up as Leila greeted her son. He was dressed in a suit for now. No doubt later he would be wearing scrubs, but for now he was all glossy and freshly showered, and the scent of his cologne as he came over was more heady than a room full of flowers. 'I was just saying to Leila that I need a private nurse and she had told me that she has some annual leave coming up. I thought—'

'I will arrange your nurse,' Zahir interrupted, and his voice was terse.

'I don't need you to arrange anything,' Leila said. 'I would like Adele—'

'Adele is a junior emergency nurse. I shall find a surgical nurse who specialises in women's health to take care of you. In fact, I already have. She will be looking after you when you go back to the hotel.'

'Zahir!' Leila reprimanded her son.

'It's fine.' Adele halted them. Her cheeks were on fire and she was angry and hurt at Zahir's cutting words. Clearly he didn't even think her capable of nursing what would by then be a two week post-op patient. 'It was lovely of you to think of me, Leila... I really do have to go now.'

She said goodbye and gave a very brief nod to Zahir.

'Zahir,' his mother admonished once they were alone. 'You were very rude to speak like that in front of her.'

'I work with Adele.' He shrugged. 'I shall find a more suitable nurse. Anyway, perhaps *you* were the one who was rude. Adele might already have plans.' He tried not to think of her topless on a beach in France and then he thought of Paul. 'Maybe she wants to go away with her boyfriend...'

'Rubbish,' Leila said. 'She doesn't have one. In fact...' She gestured to her locker and those flowers really were following him everywhere because Zahir caught sight of them as Leila continued to speak.

'She had a disastrous date on Friday. She said all she wanted to do was to check her phone. She spends all her spare time taking care of her mother and I want to do something nice for her.'

Zahir held in an exasperated sigh.

There was a debt to be paid and his mother had now come up with a way to pay it.

'I shall think of a more suitable way to thank her,' Zahir said, and then he asked a question. 'Why do you want Adele?'

It was a question he had asked himself many times over the past year.

'I find her easy to talk to and she knows about...' Leila shook her head and lay back on her pillow and closed her eyes. 'It doesn't matter. I'm going to have a little rest now. I've been up since five.'

The subject was closed.

So many subjects were closed.

He could see that she had been crying and Zahir thought about what Adele had said to him in the car: *You need to discuss that with your mother.*

He didn't know how to, though.

He could speak with grief-stricken parents, he could tell someone, with skill and care, that they did not have long to live.

Yet this was a conversation that was almost impossible to start. From seven years old he had been warned not to ask questions. Not to upset his mother or anger his father by bringing the subject of his brother up.

But they weren't at the palace and things had been left unsaid for far too long.

'I miss him too,' Zahir said to his mother, and he watched her face crumple. 'I know I never saw him, but I still think of him and when I go to our desert abode I pray for him each time.'

As Leila started to cry he let her and then after a while she asked him something.

'Could you pass my bag?'

She took out her purse and Zahir saw his brother for the first time as his mother spoke. As he finally found out what had happened Zahir wasn't in doctor mode, or crown prince mode, he was just remembering the sadness and the silence that had returned with his parents to the palace and he looked at the tiny, beautiful reason why.

'Zahir, I had to tell the doctor about Aafaq and Adele was there when I did so. I don't want to go through it all with another nurse. I am very tearful at the moment. I know that. Mr Oman says it is to be expected after such an operation and it may continue for a few weeks. Maybe the nurse you arranged can care for me at the hotel—'

'You don't need to be in a hotel,' Zahir said. 'Please come back to my home.'

'Your home is in Mamlakat Almas,' Leila told him. 'I would prefer to stay in a hotel.'

Despite being more open than Fatiq, she did not approve of his lifestyle here. Leila did not like the fact that Zahir and Dakan dated when there was an array of brides waiting for them to choose from.

Staying in a hotel was her protest.

'Please let me have Adele care for me.'

'I'll think about it,' he said.

Adele was all he could think about of late.

He had been about to head to Admin to tell them he was taking the last fortnight on his contract as leave and that he would not be renewing it.

The ramifications of a relationship with Adele had long troubled him—his father frowned on his lifestyle here and certainly any serious relationship would be even more frowned upon. It would be dire indeed if anything happened in Mamlakat Almas. He could never choose Adele. The rift it would create between him and his father would be irreparable.

The King was a stickler for tradition and those traditions did not allow for a woman without a title who had dated before.

He could well be exiled and unable to fulfil his duty to his country.

No, he did not want to consider his mother's request.

He was trying to get away from Adele.

Not bring her to his home.

CHAPTER FIVE

FOR A MOMENT there Adele had thought that her luck was finally changing.

You make your own luck, Adele told herself.

She just didn't know how.

It was her second week of nights and she couldn't wait for them to be done and for her two-week break to commence.

She was still smarting at Zahir.

It was six p.m. and there was a staff accreditation that Adele needed to have signed off. She wanted to get it done before she went on annual leave.

She wasn't going to the south of France. Despite the offer still being available, it remained too expensive, so she had decided she would take the Eurotunnel to Paris.

In the morning she would book it.

It really was time to move on with her life, while still including her mother.

And she *was* going to have a holiday romance.

Absolutely she was.

She was tired of her lack of a love life and that she was twenty-four years old and still a virgin.

And, as she went over to the nurses' station and Zahir didn't even acknowledge her, she decided was tired of having feelings for someone who thought so little of her.

He looked immaculate. He was wearing his suit and clearly hoped to get away quickly.

'Zahir,' Meg asked, 'is there any chance of you staying back?'

'I can't,' he said. 'I have to finish at six. Bella is waiting for me to pick her up. We are going to the theatre.'

Ouch, Adele thought.

'I just need to write up this drug regime and then I'll have to go,' he said.

With all the drama of his mother being sick and settling her into the hotel, as well as the constant calls back home, he had forgotten to tell Bella they were over. Zahir did not want to put it off for even one more night. He would tell her tonight soon after the curtain came down.

Helene came in then, all ready for staff accreditation too before her night shift.

The staff rotated, and did two weeks of nights every twelve weeks or so.

'You made it!' Janet smiled.

'I nearly didn't.' Helene gave a dramatic sigh. 'I took Hayden out for a driving lesson this afternoon and I've decided I'd rather pay for an instructor. I actually value my life. Honestly, he's—'

'Adele.' Janet halted Helene's latest rant about her son. 'Could you get the annual leave roster from my desk?'

Janet had seen Adele's eyes shutter.

It wasn't Helene's fault. She didn't know.

Few did, but Helene loved to give dramatic blow-by-blow accounts of her day, and with her son just learning to drive, it must be pretty hellish for Adele.

'You know Adele's mother isn't well?' Janet checked with Helene once Adele had gone.

'Yes…'

'She suffered a severe head injury. Adele was at the wheel of the car—she was learning to drive at the time.'

'Oh, no.' Helene cringed. 'I didn't know.'

'Of course you didn't, she doesn't really talk about it. Just know that she's had the most awful time.'

Zahir said nothing.

He finished writing up the chart and headed to his office.

There was Adele coming towards him with the roster.

'Adele…' he said, but she didn't stop walking.

In fact, she brushed past him.

She was on the edge of tears at what Helene had said and she never broke down. Right now, she knew, Janet would be having a discreet word with Helen. And she was fed up too with Zahir. She was tired of smiling only to never have it returned, and being offered the dream job just to have it snatched away by him had been the final straw.

At least she hoped that it was.

She was over him for good.

Oh, no, she would not turn around.

'Enjoy the theatre,' she called over her shoulder, and there was a jealous barb in her tone.

She was cross with him and hurt by him and too weary to not let it show.

Still, she had a fun couple of hours spent with mannequins being signed off on her CPR technique. Having found out she was going to Paris, Janet had remembered a beret she had in her locker and had put it on Ken, the mannequin, when it was Adele's turn.

'Ooh, Ken,' Adele said in a terrible French accent as

she knelt over him, 'Why do you just lie there so still? Let's get this heart racing…'

Janet was laughing loudly and then looked up at the open door. 'Oh, Zahir, I thought you'd gone.'

'I'm just leaving now.'

She got more reaction out of Ken, Adele thought as, blushing, she massaged his chest.

The best bit was supper was provided!

Maria came in and grabbed a couple of sandwiches. 'I'm about to go home,' she said. 'Janet I tried not to admit anyone, but I've got a patient that needs to be in the obs ward overnight. Her name is Gladys Williams. She's eighty and had too much to drink and fell and hit her head. I can't send her home.'

'Of course not.' Janet said.

They were low on staff numbers and would do their best to keep the observation ward closed for as long as possible.

At nine they hit the ground running.

Gladys would have to wait to be admitted. For now her gurney was parked in the corridor where the staff could keep an eye on her without her taking up a cubicle or having to open the observation ward.

She lay there, singing, and didn't seem to mind at all.

'It's supposed to be a Tuesday night!' Helene moaned as the place started to look more like Accident and Emergency on a Saturday after the pubs had turned out than a weeknight.

A group of young men, all the worse for wear, were creating a bit of a ruckus in the waiting room. The security guards were in there, watching them, as Adele called one of the men through.

It wasn't even ten o'clock and the place was full.

She put on some gloves and peeled back the dressing that the triage nurse had put over his eye.

'Sorry, Oliver,' she said as he winced. 'That must hurt.'

It was a nasty cut and was going to require a lot of stitches.

Phillip came in and introduced himself and then took a careful look at the wound.

He was a nice doctor, calm and laid back, and Adele would always remember how kind he had been to her the day he had broken the awful news.

Phillip never referred to it and Adele was grateful for that.

Now, though, she understood the tears in his eyes that day. Phillip was very much a family man and he had a daughter close in age to Adele.

'I want to take my time to suture this,' Phillip told Oliver. 'Which means you might have to wait for a few hours until I'm able to give it the attention it deserves.'

The patient nodded.

'For now, Adele will put on a saline dressing to keep it moist. Adele,' Phillip asked, 'is the overnight ward open?'

'It's about to be.' Adele nodded.

She was going to take Gladys around after this.

'Well, why don't we admit you there?' Phillip said to his patient. 'You can get some rest and then when the place is quiet I'll come and suture you.' He turned to Adele. 'Hourly obs, please.'

'Sure.'

Adele started to dress the laceration as Phillip wrote up his notes and then he opened up the curtain to head out to see the next patient.

It was then Adele heard an angry shout. 'There he is!'

It all happened very quickly after that.

A group of men—not the ones from the waiting room—had come into the corridor and had found who they were looking for.

They barged Phillip aside, and he was knocked to the floor and trampled over in their haste to get to Oliver.

Unfortunately for Adele, she was now the only thing between them and the man they wanted. As Oliver went to jump down, the gurney moved and the punch aimed at Oliver hit Adele's cheek. She fell to one side, her fall broken by a metal trolley to her middle.

It was over in seconds.

The security guards hauled the men out of the cubicle and Adele found out the police had already been alerted as soon as the group had burst into the department.

She could hear the sirens.

Janet moved her away from the drama and onto the computer chair at the nurses station and Adele just sat there, feeling her eye and trying to work out what had just happened.

'You'll be okay,' Janet said as she checked her eye.

And then Adele remembered Phillip and that he had been knocked to the floor.

'How's Phillip?' she asked.

'He's a bit winded. He's in his office. Helene's with him.'

No work was getting done.

The night manager was on her way down and would arrange cover. Ambulances would be placed on bypass for now as the department dealt with what was, unfortunately, not a particularly rare occurrence.

Helene came around then and brought Janet up to date. 'Phillip's okay,' she said. 'Just a few bruises and his glasses are broken.'

'Is Zahir on his way?' Janet checked.
'He's fifteen minutes away,' Helene replied.
Zahir would make it in ten.

CHAPTER SIX

ZAHIR WAS TAKING Bella home when the phone call came in.

Rather, he was taking Bella back to her apartment.

They had loosely dated for a few weeks and though he had been upfront from the start—that they would go nowhere—Bella seemed to have completely blanked out that particular conversation.

When she had rung to say she had tickets to the theatre, Zahir had told her that he was considering going home.

'I could come over and visit.'

For Zahir it was by far the worst suggestion she could have made.

But it wasn't the rules of his land that made him end things.

He just couldn't ignore his feelings for Adele any more and he was certain that they were reciprocated. Perhaps it wasn't such a foolish idea for her to see where he lived.

If he was going to fight for them.

Zahir had never run from a challenge, yet he knew this was perhaps an impossible one.

Now he chose to face it.

Zahir hadn't rushed from Emergency to take Bella out.

Instead, he had stopped by to visit his mother.

After that he had dropped in at Emergency to hopefully speak with Adele but she was busy making out with a mannequin and making others laugh.

And at the theatre, instead of watching the performance, he had sat in the dark, thinking about Adele and what she had been through.

Who was he to deny her a holiday?

He loved his homeland very much.

Oh, there were problems. Serious ones at that. Yet there was a certain magic to Mamlakat Almas that Adele deserved to experience.

He knew, even if she would be looking after his mother, that she would be beautifully taken care of at the palace. He thought of the golden desert and the lush oases. He thought of steam rising from hot springs and the majesty of the stars at night. How, no matter how many problems you had, the night sky held you in such awe that it reduced them. So much so that sometimes you simply forgot your troubles completely.

Adele could certainly use that.

And as for the two of them?

He didn't know the answer—just that they could not end without a chance.

He was just about to launch into his *it's not you, it's me* speech with Bella when his phone had rung.

Seeing that it was the hospital, he took the call, hoping that there wasn't a problem with his mother.

It was Helene and she sounded somewhat breathless.

'Zahir, there's been a gang fight in the emergency department and some of the staff were in the middle of it. A couple have been injured, not seriously, though.'

'Who?' Even as he asked the question he was executing a U-turn.

'Phillip. He's got a few bruises and his glasses are broken. Adele has a black eye and is a bit winded, and Tony, the security guard, was kicked.'

As they approached the hospital Zahir could see blue lights from several police cars and vans outside the ambulance bay.

'Wait here,' he said to Bella as he pulled into his reserved spot.

Bella though had no intention of waiting in the car, he soon realised, because as he arrived at the nurses' station he turned and saw that she had followed him in.

'It just came from nowhere,' Janet explained to Zahir as he looked around the chaotic department. 'We were already busy. I don't think they intended to hit out at the nursing staff or the doctor. I'm sorry we had to call you in.'

'You were right to call me in,' he said. Phillip was in no way fit to see patients and, as well as that, the staff deserved to be treated at times like this by the most senior staff.

He could see that Adele was sitting in a chair with her arms folded over her stomach. Her eye and cheek were swollen and she looked angry.

'Where's Phillip?' Zahir asked.

'He's in his office. Tony's already in a cubicle.'

'I want Adele and Phillip both in gowns and in cubicles.'

Zahir would do everything to keep this completely professional. As Janet was taking Adele to get changed, Bella chose her moment to speak.

'How long do you think you'll be?' she asked, and Zahir turned impatiently.

'Why don't you get a taxi home? I might be a while.'

'I'm happy to wait in your office.'

Adele heard the brief exchange as she made her way to the cubicle.

Janet had been wrong, it would seem. Bella hadn't been *gone by morning* and never had Adele felt more drab in her baggy scrubs and showing the beginnings of a lovely black eye.

She could hear the sounds of the police radios and tried not to think back to the last time she had been in a cubicle, waiting for a doctor to arrive.

As he waited for Phillip and Adele to get changed, the receptionist, as was protocol, brought up Adele's old Accident and Emergency notes. He flicked through them and tried to be objective. He read about an eighteen-year-old nursing student with minor injuries who had been the driver in a high-impact motor vehicle accident.

Phillip had wanted to admit her to the observation ward but the patient had refused and said she wanted to go and wait near Theatre.

There was a self-discharge form attached to the notes that Adele had signed.

Everything was there, even her muted reaction when Phillip had broken the news that her mother was critically ill, was noted.

It just didn't seem enough, Zahir thought.

Yes, the notes were detailed but there was a brevity to them, to all patient notes here, that Zahir could not logically explain to his colleagues.

First he checked in on Phillip. He now had spare glasses on but there was a small cut over his eye and a nasty bruise on his back. He checked Phillip's abdomen. 'Any tenderness?' he asked.

'A bit,' Phillip admitted.

'I would like his urine checked for blood,' he said

to Janet, and then spoke with Phillip. 'I would like you to stay in overnight.'

'It might be better,' Phillip agreed. 'Meredith will get a fright if I come home in the middle of the night.'

Tony, the security guard, was next and he wanted to get back to work but, having examined him, Zahir said that he should go home.

'Adele.' He came in to see her with Janet. 'I'm so sorry that this happened.'

She didn't respond.

'How are you feeling?'

'Fantastic!' Adele knew her sarcastic response was perhaps a bit harsh but what hurt more than the bruise was that, after a year of being ignored, now that she was a patient he was finally being nice to her.

He went through everything and asked if she'd been knocked out.

'No.'

He went through all the allergies and her medical history and Adele answered him in a monotone.

'Are you on any medication?'

'No,' Adele said. 'Just the Pill.'

She didn't add it was the pill of perpetual hope, hope that one day she would be doing what seemingly every other twenty-four-year-old had already done.

It really wasn't the best of nights.

He picked up the torch and checked her pupils' responses. He tried not to notice unshed tears, but he could see her pain. Oh, his findings were not evidence based, but he could see that there were years of agony there.

'I need to look at the back of your eye.'

He picked up ophthalmoscope and Adele stared

ahead as he moved in close. She managed not to blink and then thankfully it was over.

She felt as if he had just stared into the murky depths of her soul.

His fingers gently probed the swelling around her eye.

'It's a soft-tissue injury,' Zahir said.

'I know.'

'It needs to be iced but you are going to have a black eye. Is it painful?'

'No.'

It was the truth. It didn't really hurt, as such. What pained her more was the shock of what had happened and the indignity of Zahir now being kind to her.

'I need now to look at your stomach,' Zahir said.

'I was just winded.'

'Adele,' Zahir said, 'this will probably go to court and my notes need to be thorough. Lie down, please.'

She did so and Janet covered her neatly with the blanket before lifting her gown. He examined her abdomen and she answered the question before he asked it.

'There's no tenderness,' she said as he probed her stomach. And then she gave a wry laugh.

She hadn't just been talking about her abdomen—there had never been any tenderness from him.

'Did I miss the joke?' Zahir asked, and he gave her a smile as he covered her with the blanket.

And maybe because she was hurting so badly she was allowed to be a little bit mean too.

'I don't need your small talk and your pleasant bedside manner, Zahir,' she told him. 'We don't get on, let's just keep it that.'

She glanced to Janet, who gave her a small smile as if to say, *You get to say what you want to tonight.*

Janet had seen for herself the way that Zahir was with her, though she knew it had nothing to do with them not getting on!

'I would like you to stay in the observation ward to-night,' Zahir said.

'Well, I'd prefer to go home.'

'Who is there to look out for you?'

Adele thought of Helga and James and closed her eyes as Janet spoke. 'I'm not putting you in a taxi to go home to those flatmates tonight. I'm not going to be argued with on this, Adele.'

'Is Phillip going home?' Adele asked.

'Phillip is staying here tonight too,' Zahir answered the question. 'He doesn't want to upset his wife by turning up in the middle of the night.' His mind was made up. 'You're staying in and then I'll sign you off for the rest of the week.'

Adele would far rather have gone home but instead she had to lie there listening to Phillip snoring and Gladys, who was now in the opposite bed, first singing and later talking in her sleep.

And then she too started to snore!

As well as that there was a lot of chatter coming from the staffroom as people went for their breaks.

Yikes, she would be quieter in the future when she took her break, Adele decided.

A light was shining from the desk and Adele asked if the curtain could be pulled around her.

Then, just as she drifted off, it was time for her hourly observations.

And then, a while later, from the other side of the curtain came the balm of Zahir's voice as he asked the night nurse for an update.

'How's Gladys?'

'Sobering up.'

'How's Phillip?'

'His obs are all fine, he's sleeping soundly. What happened with Tony?'

'He was discharged home.'

And then he asked about her.

'What about Adele?'

'Her obs are stable, she's not sleeping very well, though.'

'Okay.'

Zahir went off to see some more patients.

It was an exceptionally busy night but in between seeing patients he made his *it's not you, it's me* speech to a very put-out Bella.

Normally he would have seen her home, but tonight he could not leave the department and he could not string her along so she had gone home in a taxi.

Now, as the day staff started to trickle in, Zahir made coffee.

And he took one in to Adele.

She was finally asleep, not that anyone took such a thing into consideration in the observation ward!

'Adele.'

He watched as she woke up and opened both eyes, and he was pleased to see that her eye had not closed over.

'How are you feeling?' he enquired.

'A bit sorry for myself,' she admitted. 'And I'm sorry if I was rude to you last night.'

'I get it.'

'I doubt it.' She sat up and saw that he was placing a mug of coffee on her locker.

'Ooh, I really am getting the royal treatment this

morning,' she said, and then smiled at her own joke and Zahir found that he did too.

'I've discharged you,' he said. 'Roger comes on at seven and I shall bring him up to speed with all that happened last night and then I shall drive you home.'

'I don't want you to drive me home, Zahir,' she said. She didn't.

All she needed was to get away from him, from the torture of being crazy about someone. He had been horrible to her, rude to her, and while she understood that he might not fancy her she loathed the sudden false niceness.

'I'm going to call a friend to come and get me,' Adele said.

'No, you're not,' Zahir refuted. 'We need to talk.'

'About?'

'We shall discuss things in the car.'

He made no secret that he was taking her home. In fact, when Phillip asked Adele how she was getting home, Zahir responded that he would take her himself.

And, really, no one gave it a thought.

Janet had offered her a lift and so had Helene and a couple of other staff too.

Of course her colleagues were concerned.

The mood was sombre and assaults on staff were not good for morale.

'Here.' Janet had fetched Adele's clothes from her locker and brought her a towel and the little overnight pack that Gladys and Phillip would be getting too.

It contained a tiny bar of soap, a minute tube of toothpaste, a toothbrush and a little plastic comb.

Adele freshened up and pulled on the tube skirt and top she had worn yesterday and slipped on shoes.

Zahir was waiting for her at the desk and speaking with Janet.

'I'm on my holidays!' Adele smiled. 'Do you think I'll pull?' And it made Janet laugh as she stood there with a huge black eye.

'Have a wonderful break, Adele,' Janet said, as Adele walked out in the clothes she had arrived in, trying not to be just a little more disillusioned with the world.

'Send us a postcard…'

They walked out and Adele winced at the bright morning sunlight.

'You're not very good at parking your car,' Adele commented, because it was over the line and at an angle.

He did not tell her the reason—that on hearing she had been injured he had hit the accelerator and when he had arrived he had practically run in to see how she was.

Instead, he held open the door for her.

Adele got in and a moment later he joined her.

'We meet again,' she said.

As he drove past the bus stop Zahir thought of all the times he had driven on, pretending not to have noticed her there.

And so did Adele.

She didn't understand why he briefly turned and smiled.

She didn't smile back.

'Are you sulking?' he asked.

'Yes, I'm sulking.'

'Are you warm enough?' he asked, because he had the air conditioner on up high.

'You can stop being nice now,' she said. 'I'm not your patient any more.'

'No, you're not. Adele, I have spoken with my

mother. If you are still interested, she would love you to be her private nurse.'

'I don't need you feeling sorry for me, Zahir.'

'I spoke to her last night, before the incident.'

He had.

Zahir had thought long and hard about it.

He had been avoiding Adele for twelve months now and it had got him precisely nowhere.

He wasn't used to avoiding anything, yet his feelings for Adele could challenge a lifetime of thinking and centuries of tradition.

Wasn't he asking his father to do the same?

It was time to face things.

'On Monday she will fly home to Mamlakat Almas. A car would collect you at six in the morning and you would meet her at the airport…and you would return to England on a commercial flight two weeks later.'

Adele frowned.

'You don't have to worry about a uniform or what to wear, everything will be provided.'

She turned and looked at him and for the first time since last night she properly smiled. 'What does that even mean?'

'Just bring what you feel you want to. We are very used to having guests in the palace and accommodating them.'

'Oh.'

'And if you are worried about something, there will be someone who can advise you. It really will be relaxing and you need that. Especially after last night.'

Excitement started to ooze in, like jam squeezing out a sandwich as you took a bite, but Adele did what she could to rein it in for now as the car pulled up at her flat.

'I will do some studying up on hysterectomies…'

'Adele.' Zahir smiled. And in her direction too! 'It's a holiday. My mother will just need a little encouragement to walk, especially on the plane, and some reassurance, but we both know a private nurse is a touch unnecessary. She is, though, a queen. The second week would be yours to completely enjoy.'

'I want to see the desert,' Adele admitted.

'I'm sure it will be arranged.'

There was such energy between them, he knew that she felt it and how confused she must be by his cool treatment of her.

'You should go in,' he said, as still they sat outside her flat. 'Get some rest. You didn't sleep much last night.'

'I had Gladys singing and Phillip snoring.'

He said nothing, he was too deep in thought.

It was Adele who broke the silence.

'Thank you, Zahir. I know you didn't want me there but I really will take care of her.'

'I know you will. You will love my country. It really is magical.'

'I don't believe in magic,' Adele said. She had stopped believing in magic and miracles a very long time ago.

She had prayed so hard for her mother's recovery, and had later downgraded that plea to just the tiniest sign that her mother knew she was near.

Zahir looked at her bruise. 'You need to ice your eye.'

'I will.'

'And use some arnica cream.'

'Okay.'

For a second there she felt as if he was going to examine it again but though he raised his hand, he changed his mind.

And then, in that moment, she felt his resistance.

He hadn't been about to examine her.

Experience counted for nothing in this equation, for Adele had none, but she was quite sure then that she had been about to be kissed.

Maybe it was the knock to her head that was causing irrational thoughts.

Lack of sleep.

Too much want.

She needed to go, she knew, because she wanted to reach over and kiss him, and if she was reading things wrong she would never get over the shame.

She opened the car door and then, as she started to get out, she realised that she still had her seat belt on.

There could be no dignified exit, though, when there was a pulse beating between your legs.

She went to undo her belt.

He went to do the same.

For a year he had relied on self-control.

It was dissolving.

Zahir looked into the blue eyes he had wanted to explore since the very first day he had seen her.

She just stared back at him.

And then she remembered Bella, all beautiful and no doubt waiting in his home.

'How was the theatre?' she asked in a voice that was oddly high.

'Terrible,' Zahir said, though he knew what she meant. 'Bella and I broke up last night.'

'Because?' Adele asked.

'Because of this.'

Do what is essential, he had heard in the desert.

He had interpreted that as avoiding her, that it was

essential to resist her. Now, though, it was essential that they kiss.

For Adele, after such a horrible night, came the sweetest, most unexpected reward.

The feel of his lips on hers.

He kissed her softly and was careful of her sore face.

And as she moaned to the bliss, he slipped in his tongue and she tasted perfection. She discovered all that had been missing and why a kiss had never worked till now.

It had needed to be his.

There was silence in her mind and the sensual soothing of his tongue. Her hand went to the back of his head, and she felt that silk hair on her fingers.

There was utter relief as he kissed her, soon replaced by the yearning for more.

He kissed her deeper and his hand slid from her waist to the stomach he had touched last night.

And now there *was* tenderness as his hand slipped into her T-shirt and her skin was traced by him.

She knew then the hell he had gone through.

Trying to be friendly and to treat her as a patient.

And she knew now the reason for his seeming disdain.

His hand came up to her small breast and he stroked it through her bra and all this within a kiss.

'Does that explain things better?' he asked, as he moved his mouth a fraction away.

It did.

'Do you understand now why I didn't stop the car the other night?'

His hand was still on her breast and the ache between them could not be soothed by his soft caress.

'You should have,' she said.

'I would not have been tender then.'

'That would have been fine,' she said, and now she got the reward of his smile.

And always he was honest and upfront and explained to women that it could never come to anything.

It would possibly be fairer to say that now.

Yet he could not.

He removed his hand from her breast but hers was still on the back of his head and possibly it would require surgery to remove it, for she wanted to feel his lips again.

'Adele, this would be very much frowned upon back home.'

'I'm not going to tell your mum,' she teased, but now Zahir did not smile.

'I am returning home with the Queen.'

She swallowed and now she removed her hand and sat there and stared out of the window rather than at him. 'Because you don't trust me?'

'No,' Zahir said. 'I was always going to return with her. Do you see why I didn't want you there?'

She did.

'Why did you change your mind?' she asked.

'Because otherwise it would have been goodbye.'

She didn't understand.

'Go in,' he said.

'I don't want to.'

'Go in,' he said again. 'I will see you on Monday.'

'And?'

He didn't know.

All Zahir knew was…they had been awoken.

CHAPTER SEVEN

'READY FOR THE OFF?' Annie, her favourite nurse at the care home, asked on the night before Adele flew to Mamlakat Almas.

'I am!'

'You're eye's looking a lot better.'

Adele had been icing it regularly and using the arnica cream that Zahir had suggested. The spectacular purple bruise had now faded to pale yellow.

Sometimes she felt as if she had dreamt their kiss.

As if her mind, tired of nothing happening, had manufactured it.

Yet she knew it had been real and though the last few days had been busy she had dwelt on it regularly.

Hourly.

Maybe every five minutes or so!

Even though Zahir had said everything would be provided, she had spent a small fortune on underwear, nightdresses, dressing gowns and slippers in case she had to go the Queen at night.

It was very hard dressing for mother *and* son, Adele had thought as she'd closed her case on her hopefully subtly sexy lingerie.

But then she also knew there would be no furtive kisses or hot sensual Arabian nights.

She would be working and Zahir had told her anything more would be very much frowned on at his home.

And, from the little she knew, things were different there and her lovely new underwear had no hope
of being seen.

Still, it was better to be safe than sorry!

'It will just be for two weeks,' she told her mum as
she kissed her goodbye.

Yet it was about more than a two-week break. Adele
knew that by taking this step she was if not cutting the
cord then loosening it a touch.

Annie did too.

'You know we'll take good care of her.'

'I know that you will and I'll call every day.'

As she left the nursing home Adele felt different.

Of course she would be back and she would always
visit but this was a huge step in reclaiming her life.

It was very hard to get to sleep and it felt that as soon
as she did her alarm went off.

The car duly arrived and Adele was only too happy
to close the door on the flatmates from hell.

She had bought some linen trousers and a long-
sleeved top for the journey and then regretted it as her
trousers had already crumpled while waiting for the
car to arrive.

The driver made small talk as he drove her to Heath-
row, but they took a different entrance from the main
one. Soon she was in a very plush room and there was
Leila but there was no sign of Zahir.

Leila had the pale, sickly pallor of someone who had
spent time in hospital and indoors but apart from that
she seemed well. 'I am so pleased to see you, Adele.'
She beamed. 'This is Hannah, one of the nurses who
has been taking care of me at the hotel.'

There was a detailed handover.

Leila had seen Mr Oman for a post-operative check-up the day before and Adele was told that he was very pleased with her progress.

'This is his phone number,' Hannah said, as she went through the file. 'You are to ring him if there are any concerns. Here is a course of antibiotics for Queen Leila, if he feels it necessary for her to take them. However, Mr Oman also said that he has full faith that the healers can care for her from this point on. He has written a letter for them. They can also contact him with any concerns that they might have.'

Hannah said goodbye and Adele looked out at the royal jet, scarcely able to believe that soon they would be boarding.

'I am so excited to be going home,' Leila said. 'Zahir and Dakan should be here soon.'

And here they were.

Always, *always*, he looked immaculate.

Just not today.

His suit looked a bit rumpled, as if he had slept in it, and he really needed to shave.

Oh, she hoped he didn't!

Adele hadn't seen or heard from Zahir since they had kissed, and she tried to remember how she used to greet him before...

That's right, she'd smile and he'd ignore her!

It had worked for twelve months and it worked now, for Adele smiled and Zahir duly ignored her.

It was Dakan who returned her smile.

In fact, he came over. 'My mother's ever so pleased that you're going home with her. I brought some antibiotics just in case they were required...'

'It's okay,' Adele said. 'Mr Oman has already taken care of that.'

'These are for you,' Dakan said, 'in case you need them. Are you allergic to anything?'

'No but—'

'Adele, believe me, you don't want to get ill there. I'm sure Zahir has got some with him but he may well be busy or away. Have these with you just in case.'

'Thank you.'

A flight steward came out to greet Leila and Dakan went over to his mother and they embraced.

Leila's eyes filled with tears and, though they spoke in Arabic, it was clear to Adele that Leila found it hard to say goodbye and that she wanted both of her sons home.

It was time to board and Leila did so without fuss, though she needed a little help with the steep stairs.

Adele felt dizzy with anticipation as she boarded the royal jet and Leila greeted the captain, co-pilot and the rest of the crew.

They greeted her so formally—even Hannah had called her Queen Leila—that Adele realised the great privilege it had been to talk to Leila so informally.

The Queen and Zahir sat in a lounge area and Adele did what she could to make Leila comfortable. She gave her a little cushion to put over her incision and helped her to strap in for take-off.

'Are you wearing your anti-embolism stockings?'

'I am.' Leila nodded, and lifted the bottom of her robe to show that she was.

'Good,' Adele said.

Adele was guided a little further back to a gorgeous leather seat that was set apart from the lounge, but she would be able to watch the Queen and would hear her if she called. She was told that her room was further down at the rear of the plane and she could sleep there later.

Adele had thought maybe it would be small jet, but it was huge, and lavishly furnished.

Still, she tried to focus on Leila.

It was the most rapid take off. Almost as soon as Adele sat down the plane started moving and before long they were levelling out. Adele looked down and saw they were already over water and when she noticed Zahir looking at her she gave him a small smile.

This was normal to him.

It was a huge adventure to her.

Once they were able to move around Adele found her room. It was small but there was a very comfortable-looking bed and a small shower. It was like first-class travel and this was just for the staff! There was a muslin nightdress laid out for her on the bed.

As well as that, hanging up was a coral-coloured robe and some pretty jewelled shoes.

She thought about what Zahir had said about everything being provided and it felt as if she had entered another world.

She came out and Zahir was on his computer and was chatting with his mother when the meals were served.

Adele took her cues from the flight stewards. She was seated to the rear and would take her meal there, whereas Zahir and Leila ate at a polished table.

Adele chose a lovely mint soup and a small bread roll for starters but her stomach was too tied in knots to have a main course.

Dessert was a light, pale custard with a rich rose-water syrup over it.

She saw that Zahir had declined dessert.

A foolish mistake, Adele thought, and closed her eyes in bliss at the taste and then opened them to see him.

He made her blush.

With one glance from Zahir she felt heat in her face.

Once the meals had been cleared away, Zahir declared he was going to bed.

He went into his suite, stripped off and showered.

He hadn't slept last night. He had gone out but had soon returned to his apartment and drunk cognac, wondering when, if and under what circumstances he might return to England.

He pulled on black silk lounge pants and closed his eyes but sleep would not come.

Zahir, in an attempt to drag his mind from Adele and those awful linen trousers, made a couple of phone calls to some architects and tried to line up some meetings.

One of them, Nira, sounded promising and she had some questions that she put to him.

Adele, on the other hand, tried not to think of Zahir asleep a matter of metres away as Leila took out her sewing.

'Come and see this, Adele,' Leila said.

'Oh!' Adele walked over and looked down, and saw that the Queen was embroidering a small square. The silks were so rich and the stitching so detailed it really was exquisite. 'It's beautiful. What are you making?'

'A blanket,' Leila told her. 'I have been making it for many, many years.' She took out a few squares from the sewing bag for Adele to see. They were all different, and each one was a work of art in itself. They ranged from flowers, to delicate letters, to beautiful coloured birds.

'These must take hours and hours.'

'They do,' Leila agreed. 'It is a stitching technique

that has been passed on through generations. Each square has a different symbol or flower...soon I shall put them all together. It has been a labour of love.'

Soon, though, Leila put away her embroidery and declared that she was very tired. 'I don't understand why, though, I slept well last night.'

'You were up early,' Adele pointed out.

'I am always up early.'

'It's your first proper outing since surgery, so being tired is to be expected,' Adele said.

'Well, I'm going to go to bed, if you could come and help me.'

'Of course, but you do need to walk around first.'

The Queen wasn't sitting in cramped economy class but she had just undergone abdominal surgery and that was a major risk factor for embolisms.

'You're bossy,' Leila moaned, and then she smiled at Zahir, who had come out of his room and was on his phone.

Of course, Leila didn't nearly faint at the sight of Zahir in black silk lounge pants and a naked torso.

That would be Adele.

And neither did Leila care that his hair was wet from the shower and that his feet were bare.

That would be Adele too.

Oh, she tried not to notice him speaking in Arabic into his phone as he opened up the laptop he had left in the lounge.

Finally Adele walked Leila to her room and it was Adele rather than Leila who breathed out a sigh of relief as she closed the door on Zahir.

It was as beautiful as any five-star hotel.

There was a large walnut dressing table and a pretty lemon-coloured bed, which had been turned back.

Adele helped Leila to change into a nightgown and then Leila sat on the edge of the bed and Adele helped her with her legs.

Really, she was unsure whether Leila could not manage or simply was not used to doing it herself.

'I'll come and wake you in a couple of hours so that you can do some leg exercises.'

'Very well. If I need you or I am concerned about something I shall have a stewardess alert you, but now it is time for you to get some rest too, Adele,' Leila said. She could be bossy too! 'There should be a robe for you to change into before we land. There will be more of a selection for you when we get to Mamlakat Almas. Could you please dim my light on your way out?'

Adele did so.

'Thank you,' Leila said. 'Now you go and relax.'

It was incredibly hard to, though, especially when she came out of the Queen's bedroom and saw that Zahir was still talking on the phone.

She went to sit on her allocated seat and then changed her mind and decided to head to her own room, but Zahir ended the call then.

'Adele, come and sit in the lounge.'

'No.' Adele shook her head. She was blushing, but not from embarrassment. She was heated and turned on just at the sight of him and the memory of their kiss. Sitting on a sofa with him dressed in next to nothing had no chance of ending well.

He knew what was on her mind.

'No staff will come unless they are summoned.'

'What if your mother gets up?'

He smiled.

'My mother doesn't get out of bed without the help of a maid. You'll know when she wants to get up! Come on.' He gestured with his head for her to join him. 'We need to talk.'

They did and so Adele went over.

She went to sit on a chair but he patted the seat on the sofa beside him and rather tentatively she sat down.

'I was just speaking with an architect and arranging to meet.' He pointed to his laptop screen and she saw building plans.

'I'm not returning to London, I haven't renewed my contract,' Zahir, rather bluntly, told her. 'I am hoping to bring about change to the health system...' He gave a small mirthless laugh. 'Actually, there *is* no real system.'

'None?'

'There is one small hospital but it is under-resourced and overstretched. Most doctors stay a month and leave and I don't blame them. My father is resistant to change.'

'When you say you're not coming back, for how long?'

'Maybe never.' And he was brutally honest then. 'I have long held off on marriage, but my father will insist on it if change gets under way.'

And just as that evening when she had seen the flowers, and had known they had not come from him, today she knew that marriage could not apply to her.

'There are many traditions and legends and rules in my land,' Zahir explained. 'I could take the whole flight to tell you about them and only then would we scratch the surface. The main thing I am trying to explain is that I cannot see my country accepting you. That is why I have done nothing about us.'

'Zahir, I don't want to live there,' Adele said. 'I would never leave my mother for a start, but we could have had a year, Zahir. A whole year of...'

And she felt like slapping his cheek for his restraint. 'Now you're leaving, just as I find out you wanted me all along. Why did you tell me all this now when there's nothing we can do? Why did you say to your mother I could come when you knew you were going to marry? Why kiss me…?'

'Would you prefer that I hadn't?' he asked. 'I could have left, and let you carry on assuming that I disliked you. You could have had your holiday in France and returned and found out I had gone…'

She tried to picture it and she didn't like what she saw.

'Perhaps I would have returned in a few years' time and by then I'd be married, perhaps you would be too.'

And she sat there.

'All I can tell you is that I was not ready to say goodbye and had you not come today, it would have been goodbye, Adele.'

'What happens now?'

He shrugged his broad shoulders.

'That's no answer.'

'Because I haven't been to the desert to ask for a solution.'

No, she did not understand their ways.

Neither, fully, did he.

He had sought solutions under the sun and the stars on many occasions.

The answers were always the same but in various orders.

Do what is essential.

Be patient.

In time the answers will unfold.

Yet they hadn't.

He did not want his father to die, yet that was the only solution that Zahir could see.

'Adele, it was either say goodbye in the car that morning and you would never know how I feel, or bring you to my home. I chose the latter.'

Adele looked into his beautiful eyes and she was now very glad that he had.

To have never known his kiss, to have never sat here looking him in the eye, as painful as it might prove, she was glad to be here.

There was an ache for contact and he solved that with his thumb, running it along her bottom lip.

'I want to kiss you,' he said, and he looked at her mouth as he spoke.

'Someone might come.'

'Not unless I summon them.'

And she looked at his mouth too.

'Leila might call. Anyway, I'm working.'

'If you are needed they will buzz through to your room.'

She half expected the oxygen masks to suddenly ping down, she felt so light-headed.

'This might be the last chance,' Zahir said, and he saw the struggle in her eyes.

'Just a kiss?' Adele checked, because just a kiss surely couldn't be wrong.

'Just that,' he said.

She stood on legs that felt unfamiliar and walked the length of the lounge and past the Queen's room.

There were no staff around, the only sounds the engines and her own pulse whooshing in her ears.

She stepped into the small bedroom and told herself that there was no chance they would be caught.

Yet she knew this was wrong.

Zahir came in then and turned the lock on the door.
All this for a kiss.

'One kiss,' Adele said, as he went for the drawstring
of her linen pants.

'Just one,' Zahir said, and her thighs were shaking
as she stepped out of her clothes.

She lifted her arms and he peeled off her top.

He unhooked her new and very lacy bra and peeled
it down her arms and his eyes took in her small breasts
and looked down at her stomach.

Her knickers were silver and tiny and he could see
the dark blond hair peeking out the top.

And Adele could see him hard beneath black silk.

She looked at his solid chest and broad shoulders.
With this kiss their skin would make first contact. She
lowered her head to taste his broad muscled chest.

'Don't waste your one kiss there,' he said.

His voice was gravelly and thick with desire and
Adele felt as if hands had closed around her throat because she was struggling to breathe.

He moved her so that her back was to the wall and as
she went to reach for him he took her wrists and raised
them so that they were above her head and then he held
them against the wall. He looked at the lift of her breasts
and how she was shaking with arousal.

'You're presumptuous,' Adele accused, and he smiled
a slow smile.

'I am.'

He restrained her yet his own restraint was gone and
he kissed her so hard that their teeth clashed.

One kiss, which made Adele twist against the restraint of his hands as she fought for her chance to hold
him and drag him in.

He denied it.

One kiss, where their chests finally met, and she wanted to move her mouth just to taste his shoulder but that would break the deal of one kiss.

Her breasts flattened against him as he crushed her.

His erection slid against her stomach and she wanted it lower. He just bored into her and, with a craving for more contact, with nothing else for it, she attempted to hook her leg around him, but he widened his stance so that her foot dropped to the floor.

But now he was lower.

His tongue moved with the same motion as his groin and it was still one kiss but it had been spiced with dynamite.

Her jaw ached with tension and that tension slid to her neck and raced down her spine. Her thighs pressed together and Adele was rocking her groin into him. As she started to shudder he released her hands.

She held him between them as she came, and he felt the rip of tension and the stilling of her tongue, the slight squeal that he swallowed as she gripped him hard.

And it was still just one kiss as he silvered her palm and fingers and Adele felt him hot on her stomach as they pressed into each other.

Then he kissed her back but not to reality, for that was lost to her now.

And then he was gone.

CHAPTER EIGHT

ADELE SHOWERED AND put on the little muslin robe and, quite simply, she crashed.

She fell into a deep, dreamless sleep and yet woke with instant and absolute recall and with a curious absence of guilt.

She just lay listening to the hum of the plane and tried to understand how she was feeling.

It was disorientating.

Not just that she was on the way to a strange land but the might of his want and the rage of her desire.

There was no compass, no goalpost, no promises made, other than that he would ask the desert for solution.

Adele got out of bed and looked out of the window and there below her were the golden orange sands that Zahir would be communing with soon.

'I'd like the solution too,' she said, not quite tongue in cheek, because it was so vast and so endless that she first glimpsed its power.

She dressed in the pretty coral robe and put on her jewelled slippers and then looked at her reflection in the mirror on the door.

Adele barely recognised herself—not just her clothes, she should surely be on her knees in guilt and shame.

Yet she smiled.

Her intercom buzzed and she was informed that the Queen was awake and would like some assistance.

Adele knocked and went in and then blinked in surprise when she saw that Leila was in the bathroom, relaxing in a deep bath with taps made of gold.

There were bubbles up to her neck and she smiled as Adele came in.

'I didn't know you could have baths on a plane,' Adele admitted.

'You can have anything,' Leila said. 'The maid ran it for me, though I do need your help to get out.'

Adele helped her to step out and once Leila was dry Adele checked her wounds. There were three small ones from the laparoscopic procedure and all looked dry and healthy.

'I still have trouble with the stairs,' Leila admitted.

'It's quite a big operation,' Adele said. 'I think you're doing very well.'

'I am a bit nervous to go home,' Leila admitted as Adele helped her to dress. 'My husband has been so concerned. We've never been apart for so long and of course he is cross that I never told him I was having surgery. My husband is such a...' She stopped herself from saying anything more.

'You can talk to me,' Adele said. 'I would never break your confidence.'

'Even with Zahir?'

'Especially with Zahir,' Adele said. 'You're my patient and he's not your doctor, he's your son. If I have any concerns I would speak with Mr Oman.'

'My husband is very stubborn and Zahir wants to make changes,' Leila said. 'Maybe I am worrying over nothing. I am a bit weepy. It says in the leaflet to expect to be.'

She handed the leaflet to Adele and she read it as the Queen spoke.

'I don't have to worry about not doing housework or heavy lifting,' Leila said.

'And no intercourse for six weeks,' Adele added.

She would not avoid subjects just because Leila was a queen.

'Poor Fatiq.' Leila smiled and then she surprised Adele. 'Poor me. I do think six weeks is a bit excessive.'

Adele remembered her time in training and often the women would joke that they'd consider it a little holiday, or ask if the doctor could change it to ten weeks instead.

No wonder the Al Rahal brothers came with reputations. It would seem that the whole family was highly sexed.

'I hate sleeping alone.' Leila pouted.

'You can still share a bed.' Adele smiled but Leila shook her head.

'We have to sleep separately till I am healed. It was the same when I had my babies.'

Oh, no, Adele thought. At the time they must have needed each other most they had been apart.

'Once I am home I shall meet with the healer,' Leila told Adele. 'I'm sure I will feel brighter then.'

The Queen had selected a gown in a very deep shade of fuchsia and for someone who had just had surgery she looked stunning.

'I am going to do my make-up,' Leila told Adele, 'and then I'll be out.'

Adele sat in her seat and breakfast was served. She watched as Leila came out and took a seat at the gleaming table and then she turned her head and smiled.

And Adele fought not to.

It was Zahir.

As he walked past she quickly averted her eyes and looked out at the ocean.

He was wearing black robes and a *keffiyeh* that was tied with a rope of silver.

She looked again and saw that his feet were strapped in leather and that he was holding a scabbard that contained a long sword, which he put down on the sofa with the same ease Adele might put down her bag.

She had only ever seen him in a suit or scrubs, sometimes in jeans if he came in at night...

Adele had known the day they had met that he was a crown prince, but she had never really given it proper thought.

He had always been Zahir, Emergency Consultant, and the man she'd had a serious crush on.

Not any more.

Before her eyes he had become Crown Prince Sheikh Zahir Al Rahal, of Mamlakat Almas.

And that was scary at best.

Breakfast was cleared and they all took their seats.

Now the jet descended and to the right she could see a glittering ocean and then a palace. As beautiful as it was, Adele knew that soon, if they were discovered, she might not be welcome here.

As they landed she watched as he picked up the leather scabbard from the sofa and put it on.

The hilt of his sword was jewelled and for a brief second he looked up and their eyes met.

She was used to him flicking his gaze away.

Now she knew why.

Adele stood by Leila's side to help her down the steps as the cockpit door opened.

The Queen had wrapped a scarf around her head and over her mouth and Adele attempted to do the same with hers.

The wind gave her the first taste of the desert.

Her scarf slid straight down and the hot air burnt in her lungs and she thought of the traditions and legends that Zahir had touched upon.

She doubted the desert was welcoming her.

CHAPTER NINE

THEY WERE DRIVEN the short distance from the runway to the palace.

As the car slowed to a halt Adele was pleasantly surprised when the door opened and she realised that it was Fatiq who had rushed to help his wife out of the car.

Leila gave a small cry of delight when she saw him and he was clearly pleased to see his wife and greeted her warmly.

For a moment Adele relaxed and she almost forgot he was a king.

But then she saw the look he shot at Zahir and she would never forget again.

They came into the entrance and Leila smiled at Adele. 'I am going to go up to my suite. You will be taken care of.'

'Thank you. Would you like me to help you up the stairs?' Adele offered.

'I will be fine.'

As Fatiq helped Leila up the steps she paused and held onto her stomach midway and bent over a little and he looked down at Zahir again.

Zahir stared back and Adele could feel the stand-off between the two men and it gave her goosebumps.

'Samina will take care of you from now,' Zahir informed her, and he walked off. She watched as guards opened two large engraved doors, which he went through.

The palace was splendid, and Adele had only seen the entrance.

There was a gentle, cool breeze and tiny humming-birds were taking nectar from flowers even though they were inside. She looked at the dark staircase and ancient walls and heard the delicate sound of fountains.

She was shown to her suite and, as Leila had said, there was a stunning array of gowns for her to choose from.

Samina gave her some lessons, such as how to tie a scarf so it did not slide down and how to greet the King or Queen if they passed in the corridor.

'We have a system,' Samina explained. 'If Queen Leila needs you, she will summon you with this...' There was a small tablet by the bed. 'If you are not in your suite the message will go directly to your phone.'

It was a surprisingly modern system, yet there was nothing modern about her suite which was beautiful.

There was a velvet rope above her bed, which Adele was told she was to use to summon meals. There was a carved stone stairway that led down to her own beach and, as she walked through the large lounge, Samina opened some shutters and Adele looked down at a stunning mosaic pool below that was hers to enjoy.

'It is very private,' Samina explained. 'You can swim and if you want refreshments brought out to you, just pull the bell on the wall there.' She pointed down to it. 'Would you like supper here in your suite or down by the pool?'

Adele chose the pool.

It was so tranquil.

Even here tiny hummingbirds hovered and sipped nectar from the flowers, yet despite the gorgeous surroundings Leila couldn't quite relax.

She had seen the look Fatiq had given his son. He blamed Zahir for his wife having surgery.

Adele was starting to understand just how resistant the King was to change.

And that left her and Zahir nowhere.

She called the nursing home and was told that her mother appeared comfortable and that there was no change.

There never was.

Later, Leila paged her and said that the palace healer would like to meet with her.

Samina took Adele through to the King and Queen's wing and showed her to Leila's room.

Outside was a robed man, who followed Leila inside.

He was introduced to her as the palace healer. Adele gave him the letter that Mr Oman had written and he read it and then spoke a little with Leila.

After he had gone she and Leila enjoyed a gentle stroll around the gardens. The sun was starting to set and there was the lovely sweet fragrance of jasmine.

'Is it good to be home?' Adele asked.

'So good,' Leila said. 'I will enjoy the peace for now. Things are going to get very busy soon now that Zahir is back. My husband wants to move ahead with a selection ceremony so that Zahir can choose his bride, but I have said I am too weak for that just now. In a month's time perhaps.'

And, yes, as much as it had hurt to hear it from Zahir, she was glad he had warned her so that she did not hear it first from his mother.

* * *

In the first few days, while Adele had worried she might be unnecessary, blissful as it was to mainly relax, she realised that Leila had been right to request a nurse to care for her in her home.

The Queen had some minor post-operative problems, which Adele was pleased to reassure her often happened.

'I shall call Mr Oman and see if you need antibiotics.'

'I want to speak with the palace healer also.'

Leila had seen him on the day she had arrived home but it had been a brief visit.

This was a more comprehensive consultation. He came to the Queen's chambers and they spoke at length. Leila translated what was said.

'He suggests that, starting tomorrow, I walk barefoot on the sand and that shall help my genitals and get me grounded.'

Adele blinked.

'He wants me to take a course in the healing baths. I have to have another woman come with me. That will be you. He is also going to speak with the *attar* and have him prepare a remedy.' Leila spoke with him again but they both were looking at Adele. 'He says you carry too much tension in your solar plexus.' Leila gave her a smile. 'I agree.'

Adele nodded yet she was troubled, especially when a maid came to her room the following morning with a muslin bathing dress that she was to wear under her robe and also a slender vial from the *attar*.

'This is for the Queen?' Adele checked, deciding that she would call Mr Oman before she administered it.

'No,' the maid said. 'The Queen already has her remedy. This has been prepared for you. You are to keep it at body temperature and carry it in your robe, and take a sip morning and night.'

'For me? But what's in it?'

The maid didn't answer and, troubled about what the Queen had been given, Adele decided to call Mr Oman. She was surprised to find he had already had a long conversation with the healer.

'Yes, he discussed it with me,' Mr Oman said. 'I agree that Leila should be out in the sun and the herbs he recommends are an excellent choice. Make sure she completes the antibiotics.'

They had a gorgeous morning, walking barefoot on the beach, and then Adele helped Leila down some stones steps. The healing baths were cut into rocks and filled by the ocean, and they took off their robes and got in.

It was bliss.

Unlike the ocean, here the water was calm and there was just the occasional gentle lulling wave.

'I needed this.' Leila closed her eyes and lay on her back and Adele found she was soon doing the same. 'The nurse at the hospital put salt in my bath, but of course it cannot match the magic of the ocean.'

Colour was returning to Leila's face and as the days passed, Adele realised just how tense she herself had been because she was starting to unwind.

Maybe she should try the remedy.

Adele didn't know why, all she knew was that she felt relaxed here.

That afternoon, when Leila had gone for a rest, instead of walking towards the beach, as she did most afternoons, Adele headed to the desert-facing side of the palace.

And it was there, for the first time since arriving, that she saw him.

Zahir was driving out through his own private exit when he saw Adele.

Her hair was blonder from swimming in the ocean and her cheeks were pinker. She looked very beautiful in a lilac robe and silver scarf.

He slowed the car to a stop and got out and she walked towards him.

'Am I not supposed to be here?' Adele checked.

'You can walk anywhere,' he said, 'unless it is gated. Don't worry, you cannot accidentally access the royal beach or gardens, they are all guarded. Just wander as you please.'

'I shall, then.'

He looked amazing in his robes and the *keffiyeh* brought out the silver in his eyes. He no longer had stubble on his jaw, it was way more than that, and he was simply beautiful.

'How has your time here been?' he asked her.

'Amazing,' Adele said. 'I can't say I've really been working…'

'My mother is very pleased that you are here. She said you have been liaising with Mr Oman.'

Adele nodded.

'And she says that the healer prescribed you a remedy.'

'He did,' Adele said. 'I don't know whether I should take it. I don't know what's in it.'

Zahir smiled and when he did, her stomach turned

into a gymnast, because it didn't just somersault, it felt as it was tumbling over and over.

'Do you have it with you?' he asked, for he knew how things worked and that a potion should be carried by the recipient and kept at body temperature.

She nodded and went into her robe and handed over the vial.

He read the intricate writing that she could not understand.

'It's fine to drink, though just a sip morning and night,' Zahir told her. 'Do you know, my father and I were just talking and he pointed out that both Dakan and I have never been ill? He is right. I remember when I was studying medicine and I joined the rugby team. I strained my shoulder. I was new in London and I was surprised that they strapped it and suggested pain and anti-inflammatory medication. I ended up at a Chinese herbalist.'

'Did it help?'

'Yes,' Zahir said. 'It did.'

He had returned to Mamlakat Almas so gung-ho and demanding yet he could see the rapid improvement in his mother and he was quietly pleased that the healer had taken some time for Adele also.

She carried pain.

Emotional pain.

It was something he could both see and feel and something modern medicine had little room for.

He had seen it when he had shone the torch into her eyes, but he had expected to see it then. She had been hit after all. But the pain he had seen wasn't acute.

It was chronic.

Layer upon layer of pain.

He could only imagine his colleagues' reactions if he had written that in his notes.

'I am just going to look at the site for the new hospital.'

'Are the plans going well?'

'No,' Zahir admitted. 'Would you like to join me?'

'Is it allowed?'

'Of course,' he said. 'If the hospital goes ahead we would need nurses. Why wouldn't I seek your opinion?'

He was giving her the same explanation he would give his father. The truth was, he wanted some time with her.

It had been a long week, knowing that she was here and wondering how she was doing but being unable to enquire.

It was lovely to be out with Zahir.

He drove the car through ancient, dusty streets and then through a very modern city, at least in part.

There was an eclectic mix of ancient and modern. The most fashionable boutiques were housed in ancient buildings and there were locals and tourists, bikes and old cars along with sports cars and stretch limousines. Then there were towering modern hotels.

'We have everything but a workable health system,' Zahir told her. 'We have a good education system yet our best brains travel overseas to study medicine and few want to work back here once they have.'

They drove a little further and came to a small, run-down-looking building.

'This is the medical centre,' he explained.

They walked in and he spoke with a nervous receptionist who quickly summoned someone, a young woman, who showed them through the facility.

There was some very basic equipment and an occasional gleaming piece of machinery.

'Dakan and I bought these defibrillators last year. The trouble is, we need to train people in their use. It is a multi-faceted problem. This is the theatre...'

They stepped in and Adele could see why the Queen would seek treatment elsewhere.

'What do you see happening?' Adele asked. 'Tear it down and start again?'

'No.' He shook his head. 'This building should be the gateway to the new, though that is not my idea...' He led her through and they walked outside. The heat hit them like an open oven door and, in contrast to the busy street at the front, to the rear there was a vast expanse of nothing and they looked out to the desert.

'Like most cities, it is overcrowded and there is a clamour for space, yet this land had been held back for generations. The architects and advisors of the time knew that the city would one day need more room. I cannot build anything, though, without the King's approval. I want a facility that incorporates both traditional and modern medicine. I want them combined.'

'It would be amazing,' Adele said. 'What about the healers? Would they agree?'

'We are all healers,' Zahir said. 'It is time to put ego aside and to exchange knowledge and respect each other's ways. It was the palace healer who suggested my mother seek treatment elsewhere.'

They walked through the building and out to the car.

'I should get you back,' Zahir said.

He made absolutely no reference to the two of them and she looked out of the car window at a large sun in a pink sky. 'I'd love to see the desert.'

'I will see that it is arranged,' Zahir said.

They both knew that it wasn't what she had meant.

She'd wanted to know if he had sought solutions about them, but more than that she wanted to go to the desert with him.

CHAPTER TEN

IT REALLY WAS a wonderful, relaxing time.

In the morning Adele and Leila would swim gently and then lie on their backs in the healing water and talk.

Adele was now taking the tonic that the *attar* had prepared and she had never slept better. She was starting to awake refreshed, instead of wanting to pull the covers over her head and go back to sleep.

Sometimes she would see Zahir and they would walk on the beach or go for a drive.

They spoke about things but not about them, and though she ached to know if there was any progress or hope for them, she was also grateful that they didn't discuss it. It meant she could meet Leila's eyes when she returned.

One afternoon, as she and Zahir walked on the beach, Adele looked over at the glittering palace.

'How come it's called Diamond Palace when there are so many other stones?'

He didn't answer her.

'Zahir?'

'When you're ready to know, you shall.'

Zahir asked about the car accident she had been involved in.

'Did you see my notes?'

'Yes...' he nodded '...and also I heard Janet tell Helene.'

'I don't really like to talk about it.' If he could simply choose not to answer then so could she!

They walked in silence for a moment and she looked at the sparkling water and at the gorgeous palace ahead and wished she could stay here for ever.

It was Zahir who broke the silence.

'Do you know, I was going to buy you a car for helping my mother?'

Adele smiled. 'It wouldn't have been appreciated. I can't drive. I was only learning when it happened.'

'I could give you lessons,' he offered. 'I taught Dakan to drive when he first came to London. He's rather arrogant...'

'Like you.'

'Of course, and I doubted he would pay much attention to a driving instructor. I would be very patient with you, Adele.'

'I know you would,' she said, and she thought about it. He was very calm and controlled and if there was anyone who could teach her to drive it would be him, but she shook her head.

'After the accident I promised I would never get behind the wheel of a car again. I meant it. I just don't want to.'

'Fair enough.'

She liked it that he accepted her decision and didn't try to dissuade her.

And, Adele realised, she could tell him what had happened that day.

She wanted to.

For the first time she wanted to tell someone who

wasn't a lawyer or a police officer or an insurance representative.

'I'd only had a few lessons,' Adele said. 'I was on a main road and trying to turn into a street against oncoming traffic,' Adele said. 'I'd done it at the same spot the previous week, except this time it was rush hour and there was this wall of traffic coming towards me.'

She stopped walking and so did Zahir.

Adele couldn't both walk and talk as she recalled that day.

'I kept missing the gap in the traffic and realising afterwards that I should have gone then. I was starting to panic and the cars behind me were getting impatient and sounding their horns.'

He saw unshed tears but today he was grateful that they did not fall, for it might kill him to listen to this and watch her weep and do nothing. Given they were in view of the palace, he was very glad that Adele didn't cry as she told her tale.

'Mum suddenly said "Go…" and even as I went, even as I put my foot down, I knew that I'd made a terrible mistake. She said, "To hell!" and everything went slowly. I knew then that she had been telling the drivers who were sounding their horns to go to hell. I sent her there, though…'

'And yourself.'

Adele nodded.

'It was an accident, Adele. A terrible accident.'

'I know,' she agreed. 'And for the most part I've forgiven myself. I just…'

'Say it.'

She couldn't.

'You can say it to me,' he offered more gently.

'I think it would have been easier if she'd died.'

And she looked up into silver-grey eyes and they accepted her terrible truth.

'It would have been harder for you at first,' Zahir said, 'but, yes, easier on you in the end.'

'I don't know how to move on.'

'You already are,' he said. 'Moving on is just about going forward, not necessarily pulling away.'

And they started to walk again.

Slowly she started to heal.

The evenings were hers for relaxation and enjoyment and at night she would check on Leila's wounds and give her her tonic.

It was blissful.

A bliss Adele never wanted to end, but time was starting to run out and on her last Friday she and Leila lay on their backs in the salty sea water and Adele closed her eyes against the sun and just floated.

Leila was pensive beside her.

'My husband has to go on a royal visit to Ashla— a neighbouring country—tomorrow,' Leila said. 'I am thinking of joining him.'

Adele turned her head in the water. 'Will there be a lot of formal duties?'

'Not for me,' Leila said. 'Just one dinner on the Sunday night. I like visiting Ashla, we always have a nice time when we go there. We would return on Monday morning.'

That was when Adele flew home.

Her time here had raced by but now it was ending. Oh, it would be wonderful to see another country, but she loved her mornings in the healing baths and the occasional time spent with Zahir.

It was dawning on Adele that she might not see him after today and nothing had been solved.

Not a thing.

There was no solution.

'When would we leave?' Adele asked.

'Oh, no.' Leila shook her head. 'I do not need you to come with me. You can have the holiday you so deserve. I think a couple of days away with Fatiq are in order. Things are very strained between us.'

It was a huge admission and when Leila finally made it Adele gave it the attention it deserved and stood up in the water.

'Leila?'

'I love him very much. Today, though, is a difficult day and the build-up to it has been harder than usual.'

Adele remembered what had been said the afternoon Leila had collapsed. 'Is today Aafaq's birthday?' she checked, and Leila nodded, and then she too stood in the water and told Adele something that perhaps she should not.

Yet she could no longer hold it in.

'Things are very tense between Fatiq and me, Adele.'

'Birthdays and anniversaries are the worst. Well, I haven't lost a child and my mother's still alive but I know how much they hurt,' Adele said.

Indeed they did.

'Separate rooms aren't helping matters,' the Queen admitted.

'Does that have to be adhered to?' Adele gently enquired.

'I don't know.' Leila gave a helpless shake of her head.

'What about when you go away?'

'Oh, it will be separate apartments there,' Leila said. 'I cry every night.'

Adele was worried, not just for Leila but for Fatiq too.

They were grieving for their son but not together, and the rules kept them apart at a time when they needed to hold each other most.

And Leila spoke then about her tiny son, and how his little feet and toes had been just the same as his brothers. How hard he had fought to live. 'He wanted to live, just as much as I wanted him to live,' she said. 'I want his life to have meant something wonderful—instead, year by year, it is proving to be the death of our marriage.'

Adele didn't know what to say.

'Oh, we would never break up but we are growing further apart and this operation hasn't helped. Maybe I should have carried on with the healer.'

'Leila,' Adele said, 'you collapsed. And am I right in guessing that it wasn't the first time?'

'You are right.'

'You needed the surgery. I am so sorry you are hurting so badly today.'

'I will miss Aafaq for ever,' Leila told her.

'Of course you will.'

'It has helped to speak of him on his birthday. Usually I just deal with it alone and so does Fatiq. One day I hope we can speak of him but I can't see it happening. This evening Zahir is taking me to the desert so that I can visit Aafaq's grave. Usually I go by myself.'

'What about Fatiq?' Adele asked, and then corrected herself. 'I mean, the King. Does he go and visit the grave?'

'He went this morning.' Leila said. 'Alone. He's so...'

Her face twisted in suppressed anger and Adele watched as she fought to check it.

'He's grieving,' Adele said. 'It manifests in different ways.'

There was a sad atmosphere back at the palace and, late afternoon, as Adele lay by the pool, she looked up and saw a helicopter. She guessed it was the Queen and Zahir.

It was.

He held his mother's hand as they were taken deep into the desert and he held her shoulders as she stood dry-eyed and pale at her son's grave.

Zahir looked at the small stone his father must have placed there earlier today.

'I wish we could celebrate his life,' Leila said. 'Yet all it does is tear us apart.'

Zahir knew his mother was referring to her marriage.

'Adele says that he is grieving,' Leila continued. 'That it manifests in different ways. I just thought he was angry with me.'

'He is grieving,' Zahir said, and he was glad that his mother had had Adele to talk to.

But soon she would be gone.

Now that he had seen a photo of Aafaq, now that he had spoken with his mother, it hurt even more to be here, and yet he would work through it.

Zahir prayed for his brother, for the tiny Prince who had never had a chance to serve his people.

He himself, on the other hand, did have a chance, yet it was being denied to him.

Still there was no hint of solutions.

He knelt in prayer and every fibre in his body strained for a sign, for a glimpse as to what he should do.

Be patient.

Do what is essential.

In time the answers will unfold.

Yet *still* they hadn't.

He picked up sand from his brother's grave and pocketed it.

And then he put his arm around his mother and walked her back to the helicopter.

She was drained and tired and Zahir was again glad that Adele was at the palace because she greeted the Queen with a gentle smile and he knew that his mother was in good hands.

Adele walked up the many stairs with Leila and on the way she saw Fatiq and lowered her head as she had been instructed to.

'Fatiq,' Leila called to her husband, and there was a plea in her voice. Adele would happily melt away if only these two would talk, would embrace, but then the King spoke.

'Layla sa y da.'

Goodnight.

Adele checked Leila's wounds and they had all healed. She gave her her potion and Leila lay in the vast bed and looked so alone.

'You're going to cry when I go, aren't you?' Adele said.

Leila nodded.

'Would you like to cry with me?'

And she did. She cried for her tiny son who should be a man and her husband who seemed to be moving further away from her every day.

And Zahir heard it.

Walking in the grounds, he heard his mother weeping and he wanted to go upstairs and shake his father.

There must be change.

He was no longer patient.

CHAPTER ELEVEN

LEILA SEEMED MUCH better in the morning.

'Look,' she said to Adele when she came in to check on her.

They would not go to the healing baths today as the King and Queen were flying off and Leila was preparing for her trip.

She held out a small square of fabric to Adele. 'I made this last night.'

There were tiny rows of gold and reds and above dark navy and dots of stars and there in the centre was a small silver heart.

'Where the earth and sky meet.' Adele smiled. 'For Aafaq.'

'It is beautiful, isn't it?' Leila said. 'I put all my love into it.'

Her maid came in to dress her and Adele witnessed a very regal Leila. She wore a cream gown with a sash and when they went downstairs Fatiq was wearing a military uniform.

All the staff lined up to formally bid them farewell as it was official business they were leaving on.

'I will be back on Monday morning,' Leila said to Adele, 'in time to say goodbye. You are to enjoy your days off. Do you have plans?'

'I want to go to the souqs and to see the desert,' Adele admitted.

'Well, there is a driver at your disposal, just take some time for yourself.'

'You do the same,' Adele said.

Fatiq went to his office to say goodbye to his son. 'You are now ruling.'

'Not really,' Zahir said. 'If I make any changes over the weekend, you will simply veto them on your return.'

'Then don't make changes,' Fatiq said, and turned to leave.

'Father...' Zahir called him back, not as a king but as a father. 'Please go gently on my mother. She is recovering from surgery...'

'She is recovering from an unnecessary procedure. She left the palace laughing and smiling, yet she has returned unable to climb the stairs unaided and she weeps each night. Now, with the help of the *attar* and the healing baths, she is slowly starting to recover. It does little to enamour me to your modern ways. However, I do think, on my return, we could consider plans for a birthing suite at the hospital.'

It was the tiniest concession but a possible step forward.

Zahir didn't trust that it would transpire.

'As well as that,' the King said, 'I think we should hold the selection ceremony soon. I was going to invite Princess Kumu...'

'Don't extend any invitations,' Zahir said. 'Not without my consent, for it would not look good if Princess Kumu and her family came to the palace and I was not here.'

Zahir had fired a warning shot and he watched the clench of his father's jaw.

Yes, he was warning that he might leave.

The King did not respond to the threat from his son, just walked out of the office, and Zahir followed him.

They bade farewell and Zahir stood there as his parents were driven to the airstrip.

He watched them take off.

Zahir was now the ruler.

There was no point working on the hospital in his father's absence, he knew that.

Yet change would be implemented.

'Ask Adele to come and speak with me in my office,' Zahir said to Bashir, a royal aide.

His office looked out over the desert and he put his hand deep in his pocket and felt the sand he had taken from his brother's grave.

'You asked to see me?' Adele said, and the sound of her voice lifted his soul and he knew he was right to do what he was about to.

He nodded and turned.

'How about I show you the desert?'

'Is it allowed?'

'I am the ruler,' Zahir said. It didn't fully answer the question. 'If you want to call the nursing home and enquire about your mother, you should do so now, because there will be no reception out in the desert.'

'How long will we be there?'

Zahir didn't answer.

'Should I bring anything?'

'No.'

She called the nursing home and spoke to Annie. 'How is she?'

'She's the same. When are you back?'

'On Monday.' Adele hesitated. 'Annie, I'm going into the desert, I'm going to be out of range…'

And she thought of Zahir's words and she told herself that she was simply moving forward, not pulling away.

'We'll take care of her, Adele,' Annie said. 'You go and have a wonderful trip. Time in the desert, out of range, sounds magical to me.'

It was the most exciting adventure of her life.

Adele sat next to Zahir in the helicopter and they put on headphones; she was lifted into the sky and for a moment felt as free as a bird.

The palace was on the edge of the desert and soon all that was beneath them were golden sands.

'It's amazing,' Adele said into her mouthpiece. 'Just miles and miles of nothing.'

'No,' Zahir said, 'there is so much more to see.'

She just drank it in but Zahir was right—there was more.

The helicopter hovered and descended and she looked down at the sand dunes and saw a caravan of camels and their long shadows. It was truly mind-blowing to think that in this huge expanse there were people surviving and going about their business.

They flew over vast canyons and then the helicopter hovered as Adele took in a sight she had never thought she would—a desert oasis.

It was the most wonderful thing she had ever seen.

'There is a hot spring there.' Zahir's voice came through the headphones. 'Birds gather and drop seeds…'

It *was* magical.

Adele was starting to believe in magic again.

'And people live there?' she asked, because there was an array of white tents set beside the hot springs lake.

'That is the royal desert abode. Would you like to see it from the ground?'

She nodded.

The closer they got the more Adele's excitement grew.

The helicopter landed and they ran under the rotors but soon the sand gave way to a rich lush moss that surrounded the water.

It was nothing like she had ever seen or imagined.

She had thought the desert abode was a tent in the middle of nowhere; instead there were trees, delicate flowers and the lake was a dazzling azure.

It was paradise.

'Do you miss coming here when you're away?'

'I do,' Zahir admitted. 'I miss home all the time, but not the politics.'

There was a herd of white Arab horses and they were magnificent.

'Do you ride?' Zahir asked.

'Very well,' Adele said, and then laughed at her own joke. 'That's a lie. I've never even been on a horse.'

He pointed to a large tent by the lake and told her it was the royal one.

'So who lives in the other tents?'

'There are maids and the horsemen and a falconer.'

'Where's your harem?' Adele teased.

'Over there.' Zahir pointed as they walked towards the main tent. 'There is a tunnel from their tent that leads to the royal suite.'

'Are you serious?'

'Yes?'

'And do you…?'

'I came of age in the desert, Adele.'

She was sulking as they reached the royal abode. Or

she was trying to, but it was so beautiful that she forgot to be cross as she removed her shoes. The floors were covered with Arabian rugs and the walls and ceilings were lined with cascading white silk.

She took out her phone and Zahir smiled.

'Are you so bored on our date that you are checking your phone? I don't think that's a good sign.'

'Did your mother tell you about my date with Paul?' Adele laughed. 'Well, I'm actually checking for reception.'

There was none.

And her phone didn't tell her the time either.

'There are no clocks...'

'We go by the sun and the stars,' Zahir explained. 'The main reason for coming here is to get away from all things modern. I agree with my father on that point. Here is for introspection and to seek guidance. It is a haven from the modern world.'

'It's actually quite freeing,' Adele admitted.

It was and she told him why.

'You know, I always have this knot of dread—what if I miss a call and it's about my mother? The first thing I do is check my phone, yet while I've been here...' she shook her head unsure she could explain, '...it doesn't matter.'

'Tell me.'

'Well, I've always put off having a holiday. I convinced myself I'd panic all the time in case something happened and I couldn't get to her.'

'You know, if there was any change then I would get you straight home.'

'I know.' Adele nodded. 'But, rather than panicking, I've found...' She didn't know how best to explain it. 'I'm ten hours away at best. It's actually nice to know if something happens I won't have to deal with it. I now understand why people kept suggesting that I take a proper break.'

'Good for you.'

'Anything could happen,' Adele said, 'and we wouldn't know.'

And then she met his eyes and they told him that anything could happen and she wouldn't mind at all.

She wandered around. There was the royal suite with cascades of crimson silk and on one wall a red velvet curtain. Above the bed was a velvet rope.

'I doubt that summons breakfast,' Adele said.

'It doesn't.'

'Does that ring in the harem?'

'It does,' Zahir said.

She was tempted to pull it just to see some sultry beauty come through the curtain.

Adele did so and Zahir smiled and put her out of her misery. 'The harem was disbanded before my parents married. I believe it was a condition she insisted upon when she attended the selection ceremony.'

And she remembered Leila tapping at her ruby and telling Adele that she had made demands of her own.

Now she understood the demands Leila had made had not been about keeping her in splendour.

'Good for her.' Adele smiled.

And she thought of Fatiq, who really loved his wife. She just wished she could help there, but knew that there was nothing she could do.

A maid served them some tea and pastries and they sat on cushions. They were alone, finally alone, and she never wanted it to end. 'When do we have to go back?'

'When we choose to,' Zahir said. 'Would you like to

go riding? It will be sunset soon. I can have them prepare a gentle horse.'

'That sounds amazing.'

It was.

They went on a slow walk along the dunes and a huge orange sun turned the sands and the sky to molten gold. The colours meant it was like being in the middle of a furnace, yet with the setting sun a soft wind circled them.

The sky darkened and the first stars started to appear as the air cooled. Adele wanted more of the desert.

She wanted more of Zahir.

'Will Leila know...' Adele asked '...if we stay here tonight?'

'The staff are discreet. It might eventually filter back but you will be long gone by then. But I think she will understand when I tell her I have feelings for you. Deep ones.' He was honest. 'I can barely get my father to agree to an X-ray machine, I very much doubt he would allow you to be my bride.'

'I could never leave my mother.'

'I know,' Zahir said. 'So for now all we have is this time.'

'For now?'

'I told you, I have asked the desert for a solution.'

Which didn't seem a lot to hang hope on, Adele thought.

Perhaps she'd sighed because Zahir looked at her and smiled.

They arrived back at the oasis and when she'd thought there could be no more surprises she watched the steam rise from the hot waters as it hit the cold night air.

'Do you want to go in?' Zahir asked.

Often, too often, Adele had wondered how it might happen—a kiss that grew out of hand, as had been the case on the plane, or he might sneak her to join him in the royal suite. Never had she envisaged the absolutely certain, almost calm way he dismounted and held out his hand to help her down.

And she knew this was it.

They had withheld and resisted but finally they were alone and there was nothing now that could stop them.

Though there was one thing perhaps, Adele thought as he lifted her down and for a slow, sensual moment her body slid over his.

If Adele told him this was her first time, she knew Zahir might well reconsider.

And she didn't want that.

He held her against him and she could feel that muscular body and the roughness of his robe.

'You're sure?' he checked.

'Very.'

He turned her around and undid the zipper of her robe and it slipped to the ground.

A nearly full moon lit them and Adele could feel his eyes on her as she took off her underwear.

'It's cold,' Adele said.

'Then get into the warm water.'

The water came up to her shoulders and she stood and watched Zahir undress.

First he removed the scabbard that held his sword and dropped it to the ground, and then he disrobed and removed the leather straps from his feet. And then as he stood and she saw that magnificent body fully naked he strode with purpose to the waterside. She wondered if perhaps she ought to tell him.

No.

She lay on her back in the water and gave him full view of her body, and as he stared down she parted her legs and she felt her stomach tighten as he stared.

It was too late to be shy, she decided, and she would never regret this magical night in the desert.

He joined her in the water and Adele stood. They faced each other for a moment and then he reached over and she slid through the water to the demand of his hands.

The air was cold above the water but their kiss was warm and deep and his beard was rough and sexy.

His hands were over her skin, feeling her breasts, cupping them, and then teasing her nipples. Then down to her waist and then to her buttocks. All this as her arms wrapped around his neck. His mouth was so beautiful and she explored it. The steam had made their faces damp and their mouths slid easily.

She could feel him nudging at her stomach and one hand moved from his neck just to hold him again.

He lifted her so that her legs wrapped around his waist and she could feel the nudge of him at her centre and held him there. It made her kiss him harder as his hand slid to her sex and he felt her warm and slick.

And then they stopped kissing and she stared deep into his eyes, and they were back to their first meeting.

Somehow they had known even then that they were meant to be.

Their kiss was deep and her body pliant. Her arms were loose enough around his neck that he could guide her.

He positioned himself, one hand at the base of her spine and the other around himself so he could take her fast and deep, and she now stared into his eyes.

No kissing.

Just watching and waiting for him.

Yet he did not slide inside her easily, as he had planned to.

Adele made throaty noise at the bliss of intimate pain.

And Zahir realised that this was her first time as he seared into her, and though she moaned in pain she ground down in acceptance.

She was tight and the pleasure for him was intense. He felt her mouth bite his shoulder and he held her hips and thrust in hard. He knew from her moans that she gladly suffered an erotic mix of pain and bliss.

He was not gentle, he was rough, delivering the pleasure that made her thighs shake and her calves ache as they gripped him.

Her cold mouth came up to his and her tense lips were on his as he took her ever more deeply.

He angled himself and she stiffened at the new sensations he aroused and then she moaned because he stroked her inside so exquisitely.

They were surrounded by stars; they were there when she looked up and they were reflected on the water as she rested her head on his shoulder as he took her faster. They were bathing in the sky, that was how it felt; they were two stars locked now in eternal orbit.

Adele felt the swell and the hot rush of him deep inside and he moved her as she pulsed around him.

They were sweating in the cold air and heat below and she took every drop he delivered and then he stilled her with his hands and they kissed until she again rested her head on his shoulder.

'Why didn't you tell me?' he asked, still inside her.

'You might have said no.'

Zahir shook his head. 'Never.'

CHAPTER TWELVE

'I HEAR ABOUT you going out on dates?'

They were back in the tent, lying on the opulent bed and still wet from the hot water. She could see the bruise her teeth had made on his shoulder and she felt sore but sated.

'Yes, I've had many first dates.' Adele smiled.

He didn't ask about her being on the Pill and she remembered telling him that she was when she'd been hit.

She knew she had missed taking a couple of them. When she had stayed overnight at the hospital and possibly the day after that she hadn't taken it.

There was no point saying anything yet, though.

There wasn't exactly a glut of pharmacies in Mamlakat Almas.

She would deal with that later.

Adele had everything she wanted in this moment and many more times throughout the night.

She came to his hand and he came to her mouth.

They spent the night making love rather than waste a moment sleeping. Together they made up for lost time.

But all too soon morning started to creep in.

Zahir pulled back a drape and he dressed in his robe and left the tent as Adele lay there, watching the stars disappear and the day invading in a glorious riot of yellows and pinks.

'We'll leave soon,' he said when he returned from wherever he had been.

She didn't want to leave.

She had never felt more at peace than here in the desert.

'Are you looking forward to going home tomorrow?' Zahir asked.

'I'm...' Adele couldn't answer. She wanted to see that her mother was okay but she wasn't looking forward to it as such. And she wanted to sort out where she lived. She loved her career but just couldn't quite envisage Zahir not being there.

No, she couldn't answer honestly because the truth was that she wanted to be here, sharing his bed.

He saved her from lying with a kiss but she could hear the maids setting up for breakfast in the lounge and she pulled back.

'Where did you go?' Adele asked.

'To visit my brother's grave. I always do when I am here. I finally spoke with my mother about all that happened.'

'That's good.'

'I can see now that she had pre-eclampsia,' Zahir said.

'I'm sorry that I couldn't tell you.'

'No, I respect that you didn't,' Zahir said. 'I know that you think my father must be mad but...'

'It must be so difficult for him,' Adele broke in.

Her response surprised Zahir but Adele had given it a lot of thought. 'The one time your mother stepped outside tradition he lost his son.'

He thought about that as Adele went to bathe.

She came back pink and dressed in a silver robe and neither wanted to leave, so they lingered over breakfast.

She drank a lovely infusion of hot lemon and mint and they ate sweet cakes and he saw that she was holding back tears.

'It isn't over,' he said. 'We have tonight. You will be in my bed back at the palace.'

She shook her head.

'The staff aren't going to say anything. They are good people and we will be discreet. My parents won't find out for ages and I am fully prepared for that.'

It wasn't that so much that troubled her.

It was the next day when she went home.

CHAPTER THIRTEEN

FOR LEILA THE hope that a weekend break might help her marriage soon faded.

And being away from home had been more tiring than she had anticipated.

In the morning, unable to face another day and night smiling and being gracious, she asked Fatiq to make their excuses and to fly them home.

'That is impolite,' Fatiq told her.

'I don't care,' she said.

Leila was through with being polite.

Fatiq had strode into the palace, not best pleased.

'Inform Zahir that I am back.'

And Bashir knew, because whispers had swirled through the palace, that Zahir was not here and neither was Adele.

Neither was the pilot who had taken them into the desert yesterday afternoon.

'I believe that Zahir is out,' Bashir said.

'Where is he?' Fatiq demanded.

Bashir did not answer.

Leila certainly did not need to know where their son was—he was a man after all.

'I am going to have some tea and then lie down,' she

said. 'Bashir, would you have Samina disturb Adele and ask her to come and see me.'

Leila had the most terrible headache and it had been a strained time away with Fatiq.

'Of course,' Bashir said.

Oh, they delayed and played for time, and by the time the Queen had taken some morning tea and was slowly climbing the stairs, Samina came to her with the answer.

'Your Highness, Adele is not in her wing.'

'Where is…?'

And the Queen stopped herself from asking the question when she saw the conflict in Samina's eyes.

'Actually, don't trouble Adele.' She knew. 'I gave her the weekend off.'

'Where is the nurse?' Fatiq was coming up the stairs behind his wife.

'She likes to walk on the beach,' Bashir said.

Poor Bashir did his best too.

But the King was no fool. He climbed the stairs right up to the turret and looked out at the splendid view and then came back down.

'Where is the Crown Prince?' Fatiq asked. 'He needs to be informed that I am back.'

Bashir was sweating and Samina's eyes were wide as he answered the King.

'I believe that Zahir has gone to the desert abode.'

'Fetch Queen Leila's nurse,' the King said in a voice that had even the little hummingbird hovering at the fountain falter.

Oh, Leila would not be getting her lie-down!

'You are dismissed for now,' she said to Bashir, rather than have him answer that Adele too was at the desert abode, and she followed her husband back down and into his office.

'He took her to the desert!' an enraged Fatiq said to his wife as soon as they were alone.

'Adele always said that she wanted to see it. Perhaps he is giving her a tour. There might have been a sandstorm.'

The King gave a derisive snort, which told Leila what he thought of that. 'The palace staff are embarrassed. Thanks to your nurse—'

'My nurse,' Leila interrupted, 'saved *me* from embarrassment.'

She was angry too but she was also conflicted.

Zahir always kept to the rules.

Now, were it Dakan who was home she might have been better prepared for such goings-on.

But Zahir?

A short while later there was the sound of the helicopter and they stood at the window and watched it descend.

Leila watched the helicopter land on the lawn and saw Zahir and Adele disembark.

They were relaxed and laughing and there had been no sandstorm, neither had this been an innocent tour.

They were lovers, she could see that it was so, and so too could Fatiq.

And then Zahir must have seen the royal jet for he stilled and put a protective arm around Adele.

The King sucked in his breath at the public display of affection.

Leila watched as Adele startled and turned as if to run.

'My parents are here,' Zahir told her.

'They can't find out.'

He looked up at the office window.

They already have.' He took charge immediately.

'Come. We will go in by my private entrance and I shall take you this morning to the airport myself. You don't have to face them.'

Adele had never even set foot in his wing.

And now she sat on his bed with her head in her hands and she felt mortified.

'Can you say we got stranded, or that we slept apart…?'

'I'm not going to lie, Adele,' Zahir said. 'My only regret about what went on is that it now makes things difficult for you.'

'And impossible for us,' she said.

'Not necessarily.'

'Somehow I don't think there's going to be a solution here,' she said, and it was a jibe at the faith he had that things would turn around.

But he remained calm.

'Adele, it is better they know. Not yet, of course, but in the long run it is better than doing and saying nothing and marrying a neighbouring princess simply to appease him. I am not going to apologise for last night.'

His only regret was that Adele would be embarrassed and he would now do his best to handle that.

He left her on his bed and walked down the stairs towards his father's office. He nodded to Samina, who was crying, and he gave a small nod to Bashir. He knew they would have done their best to cover for him and Adele.

One of the guards gave him a small grim smile of quiet support as he opened the door and admitted Zahir to face a very angry king and a rather strained queen.

Zahir returned the guard's smile.

And then he stepped in and took charge.

'We shall speak later,' Zahir informed them by way

of greeting. 'Right now I am going to take Adele to the airport. Clearly it will be uncomfortable for her to remain here.'

'You don't even try to hide it,' the King shouted in exasperation. 'You don't even attempt to come up with a polite excuse!'

Zahir's response was calm. 'I refuse to hide any more that I have feelings for Adele. I have been doing just that for the past year and it has got me nowhere. I have driven past her, drenched in a storm at a bus stop, and told myself I was right to do that, that it was essential to keep my emotions in check. I have ignored her, I have tried to remove myself from her and I refuse to do so any more.'

'You have free rein in England,' the King retorted angrily. 'And I know full well that you and Dakan use every inch of it. You know not to bring those ways here.' He looked at Leila and of course he now made it her fault. 'Now, if there were still a harem none of this would have happened...'

'This isn't about sex!' Zahir said.

And Leila blinked in confusion, not at what Zahir had just said but at his words before.

'Zahir, I don't understand,' she admitted. 'Why did you drive past her when she was drenched from a storm? I taught you better than that.'

He did not answer and Leila's heart broke for her son as she realised the reason was a love that could never be.

Never, because she looked at Fatiq and he had become a stranger.

'We shall leave by my private exit,' Zahir said to his father. 'There is no need for Adele to receive your disdain.'

He walked out.

'I expected better from Zahir,' Fatiq said.

'Why?' Leila retorted. 'He is his father's son. Remember how you used Bashir's ladder to come to me after the selection ceremony because you could not wait for the wedding night?'

The King said nothing.

'We had the biggest premature baby that this kingdom has ever seen,' Leila now shouted. 'Zahir's shoulders nearly killed me and we had to smile and pretend he was small.'

'At least we were betrothed.'

'Barely,' Leila snarled.

It had been the night of the selection ceremony that they had first made love and she had told him that night that if he wanted her then the harem was to be gone.

Fatiq had readily agreed.

They had known on sight they were in love, Leila thought.

Look at them now.

Oh, she ached for her son and Adele.

And she ached for herself and her husband too.

Zahir spoke with Samina and told her to pack Adele's things and then to arrange to have them put in his car. He told Bashir to move Adele's flight forward by a day.

Then he headed to his suite.

'Should I go down and apologise?' Adele asked.

'No,' he said. 'You have nothing to apologise for.'

'I'm her nurse!'

'Adele, we didn't exactly do it in a cupboard while she was breathing with the aid of a ventilator.'

That made her smile.

'No,' she admitted.

'You were on holiday by then and she was away in

another country, trying to sort out the disaster of her own relationship while I was working on mine.'

And he acknowledged then to Adele that he knew the trouble his parents' marriage was in.

'He's so stubborn, so set in his ways...'

'You're not,' Adele said. She had thought Zahir was at first, but she had seen how open he was to discussion and change and how calm he was under pressure and she loved him so very much.

'I don't know how to help them,' Zahir said. 'Every time I bring up change he gets angrier...'

'Maybe he's scared to be proved wrong.'

Zahir dismissed that.

'He's not scared of anything. Come on,' he said. 'We shall leave by my private exit.'

Except it was not so easy to leave quietly.

Samina came and informed Zahir that the Queen had requested that the car be bought to the main entrance and that the Queen wished to bid farewell to Adele herself.

'Don't apologise,' Zahir told Adele again. 'Not just because you have done nothing wrong but because it would acknowledge that something occurred.'

He saw her frown.

And now he smiled.

'Just wish her well.'

Oh, Adele did.

She loved Leila very much; she was so much more than a patient to her.

If ever there was a walk of shame, though, this was one, Adele thought as she went down the palace steps with Zahir by her side.

The King was nowhere to be seen but a strained-looking Leila stood at the bottom of the stairs to say goodbye to her guest.

She was supposed to have helped her to feel better; instead, Adele could see the tension in her features and she could not meet her eyes.

'Zahir,' Leila said, 'perhaps you could wait for Adele in the car.'

Adele screwed her eyes closed and pressed her lips together because she wanted to say how sorry she was yet Zahir had told her not to apologise.

'Thank you for the care you have given to me,' Leila said.

Adele's cheeks were on fire and still she could not bring herself to meet the Queen's eyes.

'I am going to miss our lovely walk and talks,' Leila said.

'So am I,' Adele said. Oh, how she would!

'I have a small gift for you,' Leila told her, and her voice was a little shaky but she remained dignified as she handed Adele an intricately engraved wooden box. 'Please open it.'

'I don't think I deserve a gift,' Adele said.

'You do.'

'No,' Adele said, 'I don't.'

'How could I be cross with you for loving my son?' Leila whispered, and then spoke in a clearer tone. 'Please accept my gift.'

Adele opened the box and was dazzled. A stunning sapphire that was beyond anything she had ever seen, let alone touched, was being given to her.

'It comes from the palace wall, from the same guest room where you stayed,' Leila explained. 'In a few weeks' time a ceremony will take place and the hole where your stone was will be filled with a diamond. One day, generations from now, the *qasr*, I mean the palace, will live up to its original name. The only requirement to accept this gift is discretion. We don't need the world to know or understand our ways. Adele, please accept it and I trust you to keep the spirit in which it was given.'

'I shall,' Adele said. 'Thank you.'

It was agony to get in the car.

Adele didn't want to go home, she simply didn't want to ever leave, but she climbed in and Zahir was silent as he drove off. He looked down at the box she held in her hands.

'You understand what the gift means?'

'I do.' Adele nodded. 'What happens in the palace stays in the palace.'

Zahir gave a small smile at her interpretation and nodded. 'Pretty much.'

Through dusty ancient streets he navigated the vehicle and she looked at the glittering city skyline that was so modern in comparison with the villages she had seen from the sky. And she remembered the comments she had read about Mamlakat Almas and the suggestion that it was best not to get sick here.

'I don't know how long I shall be,' Zahir said, 'but know this isn't the end.'

And she looked out of the car and at a city that needed a hospital and a modern health care system to be implemented. Zahir had a fight on his hands to do that.

'It has to be the end.'

'I know you don't share my faith but I have asked for a solution.'

'There isn't one.'

She would not cry when she said goodbye.

And she didn't.

'Can I ask that you don't call me?' Adele said.

'I need to know that you get home okay.'

'Well, turn on the news tonight and if there haven't been any plane crashes, you can assume that I did.'

'I will be back in London at some point.'

'And very possibly married.'

'No.'

'Zahir, you know there are going to be repercussions. This country needs to change and your father will use anything he has at his disposal and so will you...'

Would he?

Could he turn his back on Adele and take a wife if it meant better care for his people?

'I shall address things with my father.'

'Why?' Adele said. 'I can't come here. I'm not leaving my mother.' And it wasn't just that. 'After this morning I could never face your parents again.'

It was impossible, and safer to end it.

'I've had the most wonderful time of my life,' Adele said.

'I'll see you in London.'

'I shan't be your mistress, Zahir.'

'Liar.' He smiled. 'I might have to reinstate the harem and keep you there.'

How could he make her smile even now?

Yet he did.

There could be no kiss or embrace for they were in public and so she walked off and went straight through customs and she did not turn around.

And still she did not cry.

Not on the plane because it would be so loud that they would have had to divert to the nearest airport as she wailed.

And not even when she landed.

To terrible news.

CHAPTER FOURTEEN

LANDING IN LONDON, Adele told herself that she should be looking forward to seeing her mother; instead, she was resisting listening to a message that Zahir had left on her phone.

There was also one from the estate agent, informing her that the flat was hers.

That call she returned.

And then, before she went to the underground to take the tube home, she rang the nursing home and told them that she was home.

'Hi, Adele,' Annie said. 'We weren't expecting you back till tomorrow. How was your holiday?'

'It was wonderful, thank you,' Adele said. 'How's Mum?'

And she waited for the familiar answer—that she was comfortable and that there was no change. Instead there was a pause.

'You need to come in, Adele.'

No, her mother wasn't dead, but there was something that Annie needed to discuss and not over the phone.

Adele went straight there.

She didn't even stop to drop her suitcase back at the flat and she sat with it beside her in the nurses' office.

'When she had her hair washed last week, the nurse

noticed a lump on her neck. We spoke with her GP and a biopsy was done. Adele, we did discuss telling you...'

'I understand why you didn't.' Adele said. She was grateful for the thought they had put into it. Of course she would have rushed back and for what? To sit by her mother's bed and await results.

She wouldn't have had the time with Zahir, even if it had come to such an embarrassing end.

'When do the results come in?'

'Dr Edwards expects to have them back tomorrow when he does his rounds.'

Adele sat by her mother's bed and held her hand.

'I'm back,' she said, but of course there was no response.

There never had been since day one.

And then, only then, did Adele allow herself the bliss of listening to Zahir's voice as she turned on the message he had left on her phone.

'Call me when you land,' he said in his lovely deep voice that felt like a caress. 'Let me know how you are.'

She didn't, because she needed him so much now and it would not be fair to tell him so, knowing there was nothing he could do.

No, she had no faith in the desert offering a solution.

And she sat by her mother's bed.

'Call me when you land... Let me know how you are.'

She played it over and over and over some more.

And the next day, after picking up the keys to her new home and signing the lease, she listened to it again before she went back to the nursing home for Dr Edwards's round.

'It isn't good news, Adele.'

He was terribly kind and as Adele sat in the office

he gently explained that it would be wrong to send her mother for invasive tests and treatment.

Nature would take its course.

'I want her to have pain medication,' Adele said.

'Of course.'

'I want to be sure that she's not in any pain.'

'We'll do all we can to ensure she's comfortable.'

It was Adele who was the one in pain. There was a wash of guilty relief that finally there was an end in sight and that was so abhorrent to her that she was propelled to her feet.

'I'm going to go and sit with her,' she said.

And as she did she held her phone to her ear.

'Call me when you land,' Zahir said in his lovely deep voice that felt like a caress. 'Let me know how you are.'

Adele hit delete.

And then she gave her mother a kiss and headed out to the office. 'Annie, I need to update my contact details.'

She had deleted his number and blocked him and by tomorrow she would be at a different address.

And the day after that she would be back at work.

'Wow!' Helene said as a suntanned Adele came into the changing room. 'How was Paris?'

'Fantastic.' Adele smiled.

'Good God, how hot was it?' Janet said as she took in Adele's sun-bleached hair and brown limbs.

'Pretty warm?'

'Are they having a heatwave?'

'I think they were.'

'Where's our postcard?' Janet checked.

'It must be on its way.'

She didn't tell them about her mother and she certainly didn't tell them she had been in Mamlakat Almas.

Instead she was brought up to date.

'Zahir didn't renew his contract,' Janet informed her as they walked around to the nurses' station, 'so we're rather short-staffed, though what's new?'

Everything, Adele thought.

The place felt different without him, though her home life was better, of course, now that she lived alone.

The days just seemed to limp by, though.

For Zahir they did too.

She had been gone almost a month and there was no progress that Zahir could see.

In any direction.

He was working with Nira, the architect, and she had some wonderful suggestions but his father just knocked back every one and it incensed Zahir.

'Why are you so opposed to this?' he demanded of the King.

'Our scholars are the basis of your system. We were the forerunners, and that wisdom I refuse to lose. I consult with the Bedouins and the elders, not with you.'

Zahir walked out.

His father was right. His culture had contributed so much to modern medicine. Surely they could marry ancient and modern. Other countries managed it and yet his father blocked him at every turn.

He found himself on the beach, and he strode in the pristine white sand and looked out to the stunning gulf and he did not know the solution.

He looked up at the palace and saw that a long ladder was resting against the wall that led to the suite where Adele had resided.

Up the ladder a man went, and beneath it were the elders, all watching as the small ceremony occurred.

From early times the elders, with little evidence, had believed that Mamlakat Almas was a land of diamonds. Rubies and other precious stones had been panned from the rivers and later mined. So convinced were they, despite evidence to the contrary, that the kingdom held the most precious stones, that when the palace had been built it had been named Diamond Palace. Its walls had been dotted with precious stones with the promise that one day diamonds would be discovered. They had been and now, when a guest stayed at the palace, they were presented with a stone from the wall and it was replaced with a diamond.

There were rare exceptions.

On the night of the selection ceremony the Sheikh Prince would meet with the elders and the King. A diamond would represent each bride and when the Sheikh Prince had made his selection he would hold the diamond in his palm and show his choice to the King. If the King endorsed the decision he would place his palm over the chosen stone and it would then be presented to the future bride.

That should be Adele's stone.

Zahir strode over, and his shout halted proceedings and he told them to hand over the stone.

Adele's stone.

The elders frowned and tried to argue with him but Zahir was having none of that.

'I am the Crown Prince of Mamlakat Almas,' he reminded them. Not that it counted for much as his father had the final word after all, but for now he put his hand on the hilt of his sword. 'You can take it up with him later, but for now you are to give me the stone.'

They did so.

He put it into his deep pocket.

He made his way back to the palace and he saw his mother sitting in the lounge, taking tea.

Leila was doing her sewing and, despite the tension in the palace, she was looking forward to tonight. It had been six weeks since her surgery and she and Fatiq had a romantic meal planned.

Maybe when they shared a bed again it would be easier to communicate and his mood would improve.

All was seemingly well and yet she could not relax. She looked up when she heard Zahir stride through.

'Zahir?'

'I am going into speak with the King.'

And her heart sank because she had dreaded this moment and yet she had anticipated its arrival.

Two proud, immutable men, both of whom thought they were right.

And she loved them both.

The huge wooden doors to the study were closed and the guards were outside and she gave them a look that told them they had better not attempt to halt her.

One bowed and opened the door and she stepped into a heated exchange and listened as his son stated his case.

'Even the healer has opened his mind. He and the *attar* have liaised with Mr Oman and they have worked well together to return the Queen to full health.'

'She wouldn't have been so ill were it not for the surgeon. You have never had a day's ill health in your life,' the King again pointed out.

He refused to understand and Zahir shook his head.

'I will not sit back and do nothing. If you refuse to implement the changes I have suggested then I am returning to London. At least in England I can save lives. I will return when you either give me the authority I need, or on your death…'

'Zahir,' Leila said in a shocked tone, and he turned and looked at his mother.

'Tell me another choice,' Zahir said.

Leila had spent many nights awake, trying to come up with one, and she gave a sad shake of her head.

Zahir had not finished, though.

'I shall be taking this stone and asking Adele to marry me.' He held out his palm to his father, who should now place his palm over the stone, in acceptance of Zahir's choice.

Fatiq did not.

'Adele would make a wonderful queen.' Zahir fought for her, for them.

'She brings nothing,' Fatiq said.

'Adele was like a breath of fresh air to this palace,' Zahir countered. 'She has emotional charity and that is a rare gift indeed.'

'I will never endorse that marriage.'

'Well, I don't need you to.' He did not look at his father as he answered; instead, he turned to his mother when she asked him a question,

'You love her, don't you?'

'Very much,' Zahir said. 'And she loves me.'

The King had other ideas, though. 'Adele only wants you for your riches. She persists because…'

Zahir closed his eyes and still did not turn as he spoke.

'Adele does not persist. She has cut off all contact. She has blocked me from calling her. I had somebody go to her home but she has moved. Anyway, her mother is very sick so she cannot be here.'

'So this is just an excuse for you to turn your back on your people?' Fatiq said.

Leila addressed her husband then.

'Zahir has never made an excuse in his life,' Leila told him, and she gave her son a small smile.

'Is that why you did not stop for her when you were driving because you knew where it might lead?'

Not just bed, Zahir could have handled that. It had been more that it would lead to this.

To standing in his father's office and being told he could not marry the woman he loved.

'I loved her then,' he said to his mother.

'And is this love the reason you did not want her to come here and be my nurse?'

Zahir nodded. 'It was. But I have found out that she is essential to me.'

And they were the words from the desert.

Zahir was so angry at his father but as he went to walk out he remembered what Adele had said, and the sympathy she had shown for his father.

'I spoke to Adele about Aafaq,' Zahir told his mother and he saw her face flinch.

'I told Adele it was not to be discussed with you,' Leila said.

'She did not tell me anything. When I asked her a question she said I should speak with you, and I did. And when I visited my brother's grave, as I do every time I return to the desert, I again sought a solution. When I returned to the tent I said how angry I was about the health system here and how frustrated I was by the complete lack of progress. Adele said that she understood my father's plight.'

Now he turned around.

'This is not to be discussed,' the King warned.

'Then we won't discuss it,' Zahir said, 'but you will listen.'

'No, I saw what your machines did to my son.'

'They kept him alive till you got there,' Zahir said, and he now fought to be gentle for he could see his father's pain. 'My mother had a condition called pre-eclampsia. The only treatment is delivery. That is it. They can try to hold off delivery for a few days, but by the time she arrived at the hospital it was too late for that.'

'Zahir,' Leila said, 'please don't.'

'Yes,' Zahir said. 'He needs to hear this. Had she got there earlier they would have given my mother steroids in the hope of maturing the baby's lungs and they would have given her treatment to bring her blood pressure down to avoid her having a stroke. And though my mother cannot remember much more about what happened, I know that had the pregnancy continued she would have had a stroke or a seizure. I know, from all I have studied, that had my mother been here she would have died. She would have been buried in the desert with her son in her womb. I *know* that. You would have lost them both,' Zahir said. 'You would have lost your Queen.'

'I don't believe that,' Fatiq said.

'Then I can't help my people. I shall return when my hands are untied.'

He put the stone into his pocket. He felt the sand from the desert and, as had been promised, yet not in neat order, the answers came to him.

He thought of Adele and what she had said, that maybe his father was scared to be wrong.

For if he was wrong, didn't that then mean his pride had killed his own son?

'Father, I don't believe modern medicine could have

saved Aafaq back then. Maybe now, twenty-five years on, he might have stood a better chance. I have seen the photo of him, and from my mother's dates most babies born at that stage died back then.'

Fatiq said nothing.

'You could make Aafaq's death mean something. He could be the catalyst for change—'

'Go,' the King interrupted. 'Go to the woman who you put before your people.'

'If that is your opinion then you don't know me.'

Zahir was done.

Fatiq remained in his office, but Leila walked with her son to the royal jet.

'It had to be said,' Zahir told his mother, and he put his arm around her as they walked.

'I know it did,' Leila agreed. 'I have been trying to keep the peace and it has got us nowhere.'

'You'll come and see me in London?' Zahir checked.

'Of course I shall.' Leila smiled. 'Give my love to Adele.'

'I will.' He looked at his mother. 'You'll be okay?'

'Zahir, I am not scared of your father. The only thing I fear is that I have lost him. I love him so much. I am angry at his resistance to change, but now maybe I can see why he resists. Your father and I need to talk about Aafaq, and you need now to be with Adele.'

Zahir nodded.

He did.

Finally his patience had run out.

There was no answer, he could not fight for a solution any more.

He looked down at the desert as he flew over it. He wished he were down there, just for one more day.

There was so much guidance he needed and now

he had his parents' marriage to add to an increasingly growing list.

And his upcoming marriage.

He reached into his robe and took out Adele's stone.

There was but one regret with Adele.

The night he had left her alone in a storm.

It had gone against everything he believed in.

How he wished he could take that night back.

And yet, would she have been ready for the strength of his desire?

At least then, by the time his mother had fainted, they might have faced the upcoming problems as a couple.

Then again, things had unfolded in time.

A word came to him.

Resolution.

There could be resolution at least for him and Adele.

He would focus on that for now.

CHAPTER FIFTEEN

ADELE SAT BY her mother's bed and held her hand.

The room was silent and, apart from the diagnosis, nothing had changed.

Yet everything had.

'You're going to be a grandmother,' Adele told Lorna. 'I found out this morning...'

She wanted to cry.

Yet she was scared to.

She was terrified to break down only to have no reaction from her mother. She was scared that Lorna might fail the final test Adele had set long ago—that desperate tears might awaken her.

She didn't want to know the answer and yet she couldn't hold it in any more.

She started to cry from the bottom of her soul and she rested her head on her mother's chest and held her hand as she wept.

There was no reaction from her mother, no arms went around Adele, and there was no attempt to reach out to her daughter in her plight, no tiny squeeze of her hand.

Adele lifted her head and watched her own tears splash on her mother's face and crying brought her no comfort.

None at all.

So she stopped.

'I'm going to be okay,' she said to her mum. 'I know that I shall be. It's good news really...'

It was.

A baby was good news.

Yet it was so scary too and she did not know how to tell Zahir.

She simply did not know.

It was a rainy summer day and she got off the bus and went into work to start her late shift.

The department felt different without Zahir there. It just did. Adele put her bag in her locker and closed it and then rested her head on the cool metal. She straightened up when Helene came in.

'I've lost my pen,' Helene said.

'Here.' Adele handed her one.

'How did Hayden do on his driving test?' she asked, because she had heard Helene saying he'd taken it yesterday but she had stopped talking when she'd seen Adele.

'He passed.'

'That's good.'

They had avoided the subject and sort of danced around it but Adele refused to play life like that any more.

And she was healing because as she walked around with Helene Adele felt her warped humour seeping back.

'Hey, Helene,' she said. 'Now that Hayden's passed, would you maybe give me some lessons?'

And she watched Helene's slight bulge of the eyes at

the thought of Adele behind the wheel and then Adele laughed.

'You're wicked.' Helene smiled.

'I am.'

'Oh, by the way,' Helene said, 'Zahir called this morning. He wanted to speak to you.'

'Probably something about his mother.' Adele shrugged and feigned nonchalance but her cheeks went bright pink.

She couldn't hide for ever, but she did not want him calling her at work and if he did so again Adele would tell him not to.

Before or after she told him that she was pregnant?

Maybe she would be his London love after all, she thought.

She just could not see any other solution.

Zahir could.

To Dakan's utter shock.

Zahir had just come back from Admin, having signed a new six-month contract, and they sat in the canteen of the hospital and Dakan shook his head as Zahir spoke.

'You can deal with it if you so choose,' Zahir said. 'I have an architect lined up. Her name is Nira and you are to meet with her next week.' He looked at his brother's taut features. 'Or not.'

'Why not you?'

'I am tired of speaking with architects, only to have every suggestion they make knocked back by our father.' Then he told his brother what he had done. 'I will no longer be returning to cover any royal duties. Not until our father backs down. I have told him that that role now falls to you.'

'I have a life here.'

'Your duty is back there,' Zahir said calmly. 'I have always returned at short notice, but no more. You will now fill that role.'

'I never thought you would turn your back on our people,' Dakan said.

'And I never would,' Zahir replied. 'I shall rule when it is my time but until then it falls to you, or not...' He would wait this out, Zahir had decided. His silence and removal would hopefully force change. Dakan was the royal rebel, charming, funny and yet, Zahir knew, more than capable of filling the role of Crown Prince in his absence.

'You can't just swan in here, meet me for coffee and tell me...' Dakan started, but then halted as they heard the emergency chimes.

'Major incident. Could all emergency staff and the trauma team make their way to Emergency.'

It went on repeat and Zahir stood.

'You don't work here.'

'As of half an hour ago,' Zahir corrected him, 'I do.'

He strode down the corridor, and ambulances were already pulling up and patients were being wheeled in.

Most of them were crying children.

He headed straight into Resus, where Janet was busily setting up.

'What's coming in?'

'I'm not sure. We've been told it was a car versus school bus,' Janet explained. 'We haven't got a clear idea of the number of injuries or their severity yet, but given that it's a school bus I didn't want to wait and see.'

'Good call,' Zahir said as he put on a paper gown.

'You're back?'

'I just signed my contract. I'm fine to be here.'

Janet didn't really care right now whether or not he

had signed it. Zahir's hands were more than welcome, today especially.

The driver of the car arrived and she was extremely agitated and distressed,

'Try and stay calm,' Zahir said, but the woman kept crying and trying to sit up despite the fact she was wearing a hard cervical collar.

'Adele.' Janet called for Adele to come in and take over as she needed to be out there, triaging.

Adele walked into the resuscitation area and she saw him, his shoulders too wide for the paper gown. He looked up and just for a second their eyes met and this time he smiled and greeted her.

'Adele.'

And she wanted to run to him, to ask how and why he was there, but right now the patient was the priority and required all her attention.

The rest would all simply have to wait.

'I don't know what happened…' The driver was sobbing. 'A school bus. Oh, my God—oh, my God…'

'You're going to be okay,' Adele told her, and asked her name.

'Esther!' she said through chattering teeth, but it was an irrelevant detail to her right now. 'How badly are they hurt?' she begged. 'Please tell me how many are hurt?'

'We don't have that information, Esther,' Adele said. 'We're taking care of you.' She started to undress the woman. 'Zahir…' Adele said as she undid Esther's jeans.

Esther had wet herself.

'Can you open your mouth for me?' Zahir said, and he shone a torch inside. 'She has bitten her tongue. Esther?' he said in that lovely calm voice. 'Do you suffer with seizures?'

'No,' Esther said. 'Please can someone find out how many are hurt...?' And then she stopped begging for information and gave an odd, terrified scream, which Zahir recognised. Patients often experienced an aura before a seizure. It might be a terrible smell, at other times a feeling of impending death and fear, and often they let out a scream as they dropped, though Esther was already lying down.

'Help me roll her onto her side,' Zahir said.

And they did just that as Esther started to seize.

They hadn't worked together often, Zahir had made sure of that, but he found out now that they worked together very well.

He suctioned the airway as Adele pulled up drugs and soon Esther was postictal and snoring loudly while being closely watched.

And information was starting to emerge.

Paul, the paramedic, came in.

'We've just brought in the passenger. Apparently she and Esther were chatting when she let out a scream and started to fit.'

'Thank you,' Zahir said.

And other information was revealed.

He saw a worried look on Adele's face when the radiographer stated the usual—that if anyone was pregnant they should step outside.

And he thought of a night in a desert and of the magic the desert had made, whether you believed or not, and of course there might be consequences.

'Adele,' he said. 'I'll stay with Esther.'

Zahir was here and though there was no time to

catch up or to ask how or why, her world just felt better knowing he was near.

And later, Adele sat with Esther, who was awake now, distressed and crying.

'I don't know what happened,' she said. 'I need to know how the children are.'

'I honestly don't know,' Adele said. It was the truth. Janet had said she was to stay with Esther. She hadn't sought information; truly it was easier not to know what was going on than to have to withhold it from her patient.

It sounded as if the department was calming down.

There had been the sounds of crying and frantic parents arriving but the only person who had been bought into Resus since Esther's admission was a cardiac patient not related to the accident.

It could be good, or there could be other hospitals dealing with injuries.

For now, Adele focused on Esther.

Her toxicology screen was back. It would seem no drugs and certainly no alcohol had been involved.

Sometimes accidents happened.

Terrible, terrible things happened and there wasn't always someone to hang the blame on.

Except ourselves.

She thought of Fatiq and was quite certain now that he blamed himself for the death of his son.

For years she had beaten herself up over what had happened with her mother.

Now she ached for Esther.

One of the security guards called out that the news cameras had arrived and Esther closed her eyes in dread and fear.

'I can't face this...'

'You can,' Adele said.

She had.

Adele remembered seeing the images of her accident on the evening news as she'd sat waiting to find out if her mother would make it through surgery.

'*Four members of a family have been taken to hospital and another woman is in a critical condition after a learner driver...*'

Adele went with Esther while she had an EEG and she sat with her for a long time until finally she fell asleep.

Janet left her alone.

She was a healer too and knew Adele needed this.

Later, much later, Adele heard the sounds of police radios and them asking Zahir if they could speak with the driver now.

'Adele.' Janet put her head around the curtain.

'It's time to go home.'

Adele shook her head.

'Yes, Adele, it's time to go home.'

Esther opened her eyes as Adele stood.

'I have to leave now,' Adele said. 'But I'll come and see you in the morning.'

Moving forward didn't necessarily mean pulling away.

Whatever the outcome.

Tomorrow Esther would know a friendly face.

CHAPTER SIXTEEN

ADELE STOOD IN the summer rain at the bus stop and waited.

Not for the bus.

She let two go past.

It was like standing in a warm shower and she was drenched right down to her underwear.

But finally she saw his silver car indicate and turn and Zahir drove towards her. She hung off the bus stop and swung her bag.

She saw the whiteness of his smile and then he slowed down and stopped. The window slid down and she walked over and stood there.

'Get in.' he said, as he had wanted to for so long.

She lowered her head and peered into his lovely plush car and then at the lovely, sultry man.

'You might not be able to afford me,' Adele said.

'Get in,' he said again.

She did.

And the world, and all that was going on in it, could wait for now.

This was about them.

About two stars who belonged, who connected, and together they shone brighter.

She was soaking wet and her clothes clung to her

and he undid his seat belt and kissed her hard against the soft leather.

She dripped water all over him and the windows steamed up.

His hands roamed over her breasts and went up her wet skirt and between her legs. Then he peeled her wet body from his and started the car.

'That's what would have happened had I stopped that night.'

'Pity you didn't,' she retorted.

They drove through wet streets and the air was thick and potent. She asked no questions so he could tell her no lies.

Adele didn't want to know about the palace just yet and she didn't want to speak of her mum, or find out about Esther.

Tonight had been waiting so long.

And he asked no questions either.

Zahir had only one thing on his mind.

She discovered his home was a very plush apartment and she sat in the passenger seat as he got out. She wondered how he might have explained her arrival that wet, stormy night.

Zahir, she soon found out, explained himself to no one.

He greeted the doorman and told him that the keys were in the ignition and would he please park his car. He walked a very bedraggled Adele through the foyer.

There was another couple in the lift, and he wished them goodnight as they got out at the fifth floor. He pressed the button again for the eighth floor, the only sign of his impatience for he had pressed it once already.

He opened the door to his apartment but as they stepped in he asked but one question.

'Would you still be here now had I stopped the car that night?'

He deserved an honest response.

'I'd have been on my knees by now.'

For being so crude she was hauled over his shoulder and marched through his apartment and thrown onto his vast bed.

He removed her knickers and skirt and kissed her up her thigh with a rough unshaven jaw. Adele dealt with her top half herself. He kissed her very deeply, and there were a couple of fingers there too as he explored her intimately and so *thoroughly* that her feet pressed into his shoulders.

And she thought of that night and that he had not stopped and she shouted it this time.

'Pity you didn't,' she sobbed.

He kissed her again and when she came to his mouth he made her his again, and not gently.

Jacket on, tie on, he just unbuckled and unzipped and took her hard. He was fully dressed, she was naked and it was utterly divine.

There was not a thought in her head except how she loved this man and how the world could disappear when it was just them.

Zahir got up on his elbows and thrust faster and she moaned and held his face in her hands, just because she had to. His hips thrust harder and he moved into that delicious point of no return and she watched his grimace and felt the rush of his release. She was rigid to the very soles of her feet as she came.

He did not collapse onto her afterwards, he just stared deep into her eyes. Sometimes she felt as if he was looking deep into her soul.

He was.

There was pain there still, but there was the shine of fresh happiness and a little ray of hope.

And he would make it grow.

'You haven't paid me,' she teased as he stood and zipped up.

'Here.' He went in his pocket and tossed her a diamond. If it had come from anyone other than Zahir she would have known it was false.

She slipped between the covers and sat there examining it, too stunned for words. He went out for a few moments and returned with two very welcome mugs of coffee.

'I really am getting the royal treatment,' she said, as he put a mug down by what was now her side of the bed and he undressed and joined her in it.

'We're getting married,' Zahir said.

'Has your father given his permission?'

He shook his head.

'We can't, then…'

'We can. I'm going to be here with you in England. I've signed a new contract.'

'No…' It was Adele who now shook her head. 'You belong there.'

'And one day I shall be, but for now I will do what I must do and that is to marry you. I can't live in a jewelled palace and live a charmed life when I cannot help my people. I shall return when I am able to do so and I hope that when I return it will be with you as my Queen.'

It had become, to Zahir, as simple as that.

He would do what he felt was essential and trust that patience would serve him well and that the answers would unfold in time.

'Dakan can fill in for me until then. I am prepared to wait it out. I was speaking to him at the hospital today just as the alert came. He's not best pleased.'

And the rest of the world trickled in.

'How's Esther?'

'She's doing well. It would seem it was her first epileptic seizure. Thankfully there was no one seriously injured...'

He watched as she closed her eyes in relief and knew that today would have brought up a lot for her.

'How is your mother?' he asked, and he expected to hear that there had been no change.

'She's dying,' Adele told him. 'And please don't say sorry because I don't deserve it. To be honest, I feel a bit relieved.'

It was the most terrible admission and she felt his hand take hers.

'Who do you feel relieved for?'

'Myself,' and then she thought harder. 'I feel relieved for her too. She's had no life since the accident.'

He took her in his arms and his hand explored her flat stomach. It was wonderful to think there was a life starting in there.

'Did you tell your mother she was going to be a grandmother?'

'How do you know?' She turned in his arms. 'I think I forgot to take my Pill when I got hit—'

'Adele,' he interrupted, 'I took you to the fertile waters by the royal tent...' He smiled. 'No Pill was going to save you.'

'Were you trying to get me pregnant?'

'Truth?' He looked at her. 'That night there was nothing on my mind but you.' He kissed her long and slow.

'But, yes, in taking you to the desert I knew one way or other that it would bring things to a head.'

'You're okay with it.'

'I am thrilled,' he said, and he kissed her again.

'Did I tell you how much I love you?' he asked. 'And how much I always will?'

He didn't have to.

She already knew.

Zahir took the stone and held it in his palm. 'In my country, when the choice is made, the Prince holds the chosen diamond in his palm. The King is supposed to place his palm over the stone.' He held out his hand. 'I don't need his acceptance, Adele, just yours.'

It was overwhelming.

Centuries of tradition she could wipe away with a sweep of her hand. But then she looked from the stone into his silver-grey eyes.

Zahir was better than that. Even now, loving her, he was preparing to one day return to his people, but with her by his side.

'I thought the desert hated me when I arrived,' Adele admitted. 'I felt, if it found out about us…'

'We made love in the desert, Adele, and it has given us the greatest gift.'

She looked up and smiled.

'I'm not just talking about the baby, Adele. We returned and we were caught, yet our night together confirmed our love. There's no need to be scared for the future.'

She wasn't now.

There was hope and there was excitement and there was a love that had proved to be undeniable so she lifted her hand and placed her palm over Zahir's.

They were together now.

'You don't belong on the palace wall.' He told her what he had been thinking that day as they had walked on the beach. 'You belong on the inside, as my Queen.'

And one day you will be, Zahir hoped.

CHAPTER SEVENTEEN

IT WAS TO be the tiniest of weddings.

The staff at the nursing home would be their witnesses and Adele and Zahir would marry by Lorna's bedside.

When Zahir made a decision, it was made, and he wanted Adele as his wife. The problems that the marriage might create he would deal with in the fullness of time.

Right now all he wanted was for their union to be official.

He had informed his father, who had terminated the call, as Zahir had expected him to. The formal invitation that Zahir had had delivered to the palace would have been torn up, he was quite sure.

He pulled up outside the nursing home at ten to two in the afternoon and was told by a smiling Annie that Adele wouldn't be long and that the photographer was already there.

They had worked so hard to ensure that even though this wedding was small it was beautiful.

Lorna's hair was back to brunette and her nails had been done and she was wearing a gorgeous nightdress. The room was decorated with flowers and after the brief service there would a lavish meal for the nursing-home staff and guests.

And, whatever the consequences, it would be done. As was right.

'Lorna's ready to be mother of the bride,' Annie said.

'Could I speak with her, please?' Zahir asked, and Annie nodded and pulled the curtains around them.

Zahir sat down by Lorna's bed. He understood how poor her condition was yet he understood Adele a little better because he spoke to Lorna as if she could hear him.

Just in case she could.

'Today I am marrying Adele,' Zahir said. 'I know that you must have your reservations, as at some point I will be a king and there will be many demands on both myself and Adele. I want you to know that I will do everything I can to support your daughter with that transition. I know that she will be a wonderful queen. I want you to know that I am not taking her from you. You need your daughter now and Adele needs to be here with you. We are so looking forward to the baby's arrival. Know that I shall take the best care of them.'

And Zahir understood Adele a little better still.

There was no response, no flicker of the eyes, no squeeze of the hand to say that she understood.

Poor Adele, Zahir thought, and poor Lorna.

'You have my word that I shall take care of her,' Zahir said.

And his word was worth a lot.

He came out from behind the curtains and startled, for there, instead of his bride, stood two very unexpected guests.

His mother and father had come.

Not to protest, Zahir quickly realised, for his father was wearing a suit and his mother embraced him.

They had heard all that he had just said to Lorna.

'Adele is pregnant! That is so wonderful!' Leila was beaming and always she surprised Zahir, because in her own way she fought for change. Her acceptance of the news made her husband step forward and shake his son's hand.

'We want to show that you have our support,' the King explained. 'And you do.' The King looked at his son. 'It is time for change.'

He had waited so many years to hear those words yet right now Adele was his top priority.

'I cannot come back just yet,' Zahir explained. 'Adele's mother is very ill.'

'We heard. Tomorrow an announcement will go out that you have married and that there will be a formal celebration back home, when the time is right...' Leila said.

'Who is in residence?' Zahir frowned, because his mind never moved far from duty. 'Is Bashir acting...?'

'No, Dakan is in residence,' Leila said. 'And he has full rule. Your father and I are taking a holiday together. Our first... I remember saying to Adele that I hadn't had one.'

And then Leila stopped talking as the bride arrived.

She wore a slip dress in pale ivory and flat shoes, and she was carrying a bunch of jasmine that Zahir had had sent for her from his home. She was a bride fit for a king.

'Leila!' Adele said. 'Fatiq!'

Oh, she broke with protocol, she was so grateful to them for being here.

Her eyes filled with tears as Leila embraced her and

congratulated her on the wonderful news that she was expecting a baby and Fatiq, handsome in a suit, smiled too.

'I hope it's a girl,' Leila said. 'A boy would be wonderful but I love to shop for girls.

And, in her own unique way, Leila had removed any pressure on Adele to produce a suitable heir.

'Our people will be very surprised,' Leila said, 'but they will be happy.'

'Our people will be surprised too,' Adele said, and Zahir smiled.

They hadn't told anyone at work.

That news would be shared on Monday and she could not wait to see Janet's expression when she explained the need for a new name badge.

Yet she wouldn't have to wait, for there were two more guests at this very special wedding.

Janet and Helene, dressed to the nines, had just arrived too.

'They worked it out,' Zahir said.

'Of course we did.' Janet smiled at Adele. Then she went to see Lorna, who she had nursed on such a black day.

Leila clapped her hands to get things under way. 'I have brought a gift for your mother, and also something that you should wear on your wedding day,' Leila said. 'There are certain traditions that must be upheld.'

And it would seem there was going to be a delay, as the bride, according to Queen Leila, was not quite ready.

Adele went back, with the Queen, to the room she had dressed in.

'I can't believe that you're here,' Adele said, as Leila took out a sheer veil and started to arrange it.

'I can,' Leila answered. 'Believe me, Adele, I choose my battles wisely.'

'Battles?'

'There are some advantages to being a queen. When I get angry, I get very, very angry, and I told Fatiq that things were finally changing, that I never thought that I would see the day that I was absent from my son's wedding, that I had played by the rules but no more, that I had collapsed and still he would not consider a modern health system.'

'And he listened?'

'Not at first,' Leila said.

'But Zahir had spoken to him about Aafaq. Adele, he blamed himself, he was holding onto so much guilt and grief. We cried together for the first time and I think he came to understand that he would have lost us both and it was not his fault that Aafaq died. But, Adele, he is a very proud man—he had to be the one to make the decision and yet he is stubborn. I wanted my family to be together again so I decided to move things along.' Leila smiled a secret smile. 'Do you want to be my nurse for two more minutes?'

Adele frowned.

'You said I could confide in my nurse.'

'I'd love to be your nurse for two more minutes.' Adele smiled.

Leila nodded. She would say this once and once only. 'The day Zahir left was six weeks after my surgery. We had a romantic dinner planned but of course I was very upset that night. Well, six weeks turned into seven...'

Adele let out a gurgle of laughter.

'And if you ever say that to Zahir...'

'Oh, I never shall,' Adele said.

'Well, Fatiq asked if there was anything I could think

of that might help me to feel better. I had just turned to
my sewing and remained in my own room at night. I
said perhaps a cruise, some time away, and that maybe
a little romance might help me to return to my once
happy self. But, of course, Zahir had gone and Dakan
said he would only step in if he had free rein with the
hospital. And then seven weeks turned to eight and the
King suggested that maybe Dakan should take over,
maybe a new system was in order! It had to be his idea,
of course.' Leila rolled her eyes and then smiled. 'And
now here we are and we are about to take a long over-
due honeymoon!'

Adele was delighted. Leila had gone on a sex strike,
and it was perhaps the funniest thing she had ever heard.

'You are no longer my nurse now,' Leila warned.

There would be no more confiding but Adele felt as
light as a feather as she set to join a wonderful family,
one with a very powerful queen!

Leila laughed too but then she became serious.

'I will do all I can to guide you too,' she said. 'I have
never had a daughter and my mother did little to prepare me for the role. I shall not let that happen to you.'

It meant so much to hear that.

'Are you going on honeymoon too?' Leila asked.

'Not yet,' Adele said. 'I don't have any annual leave
until September and Zahir has only just come back,
but anyway...'

'You have this time with your mother,' Leila said.
'I have a gift for her. One thing you must understand
is that when a favour is done or something precious is
given...' She faltered. 'You are a precious gift to our
family, Adele.'

'I see,' Adele said, though she didn't.

Leila left her then and Adele took a moment to breathe.

Their parents were here, together, to witness this day, and she felt as if the earth had moved just for her. And her friends were here too.

She walked out and her eyes should have first gone to Zahir but they were drawn to her mother's bed. The quilt that Leila had been working on for so many years, each stitch created with love, was over her mother's bed. The gorgeous silks, the complex beauty, and Adele knew that Lorna was wrapped in love for ever.

Adele wore a veil when she hadn't expected to and as she stood before Zahir and he pulled it back, her smile was wide.

There was love and peace in this room and she felt it all around.

She looked into Zahir's eyes as he made his vows in English. He more than met her gaze now.

He held it and it felt like a caress as he told her he loved her.

'I will do all I can to provide for your heart and to hold your trust as we share the journey ahead.'

He looked deep in her eyes and saw there was still pain, but he was patient and would work to see it lessen.

And Adele made her vows to him.

'You made me believe in love at first sight.' She believed in magic too now, for how could she not? 'I have and always shall love you.'

And that was it. They were husband and wife and Zahir, very thoroughly, kissed his bride.

They posed for official portraits and Adele knew they were important ones. Without the King smiling at their side, it would have sent a message of disapproval to his people.

Oh, Fatiq smiled beside his wife.

They were *finally* off on their honeymoon tonight!

There was a little party afterwards, and the oldies put on some music. Annie had hung up a disco ball so that light bounced off the walls.

Janet and Helene sat on Lorna's bed and told her about the magic being made.

The King and Queen were dancing dreamily, and a few of the residents too.

And, of course, Adele and Zahir danced.

The lights flickered and they felt again as if they were bathing in the sky.

Two stars locked in eternal orbit.

They were simply meant to be.

EPILOGUE

LORNA HAD DIED soon after the wedding.

There was no sense of relief for Adele.

She didn't even know how to cry.

Lorna had been buried wrapped in the blanket but still Adele had not been able to cry.

A month later they had returned to Mamlakat Almas for a formal celeration to mark their marriage and then come back to London so that Zahir could complete his contract.

The baby would be born in England.

When Adele was six months pregnant they went back for a flying visit. Even though they would be there for just one night, Zahir had made sure that there was the necessary equipment and staff on hand should something happen.

It was supposed to be a brief visit, a duty visit, but just before they returned to the UK Adele had finally broken down.

This time, she had arms to hold her as she cried, but not with remorse or guilt. She simply wept for the mother she had lost.

It has been a long time coming and the grief did not fade with her tears.

The flight was delayed, of course, and Adele lay on

their bed and tried to fathom that she was going to be a mother and that hers was gone.

Zahir was patient.

Yet his concern was deep and so was his love.

The *attar* prescribed a blend of herbs to nurture both baby and mother and also a slight calmative, and that helped a little.

On the morning that they were due to fly back to London they lay in bed and Zahir stared out at the desert, feeling the kicks of their baby beneath his hand when Adele stirred.

'Adele,' Zahir asked, 'are you looking forward to going home?'

Half-asleep, she answered him honestly.

'This is home.'

She loved England and would always go back to visit friends but Mamlakat Almas felt like home.

She stretched and turned to face him and, more awake now, she smiled, still unable to believe that she could wake up with him every morning. 'What time do we leave?'

And Zahir had come to a decision—the choice would be Adele's.

Dakan had moved mountains, his goal to get the birthing suite ready should Adele need it.

Zahir could feel how much more relaxed she was here.

'Do you want to stay?'

'Stay?' Adele checked. The baby was due in eight weeks and soon it would be too late to fly.

'Maja is a good obstetrician, she is one of the best...'

Dakan had made sure of that and Zahir would not even consider it if he did not trust Maja.

'We could have the baby here?' Adele checked.

'If that is what you want,' he agreed.

And Adele thought about it and realised she very much did.

It was the most wonderful time. Mornings were spent in the healing baths with Leila.

They spoke about Aafaq, yet Adele still couldn't speak about Lorna. Sometimes they just floated in silence. Adele, who had been without a mother for so long, loved that she had guidance and support from Leila.

Afternoons she would walk barefoot on the sands with Zahir and at night she would lie in his arms and try to comprehend how far they had come.

It was peaceful, it was gentle, it was bliss.

And then, two weeks before her due date, Adele woke up and looked out at a red desert sky.

'What time is Maja coming to see you?' Zahir asked.

'At midday,' Adele answered, but then she asked him something. 'Do you think she knew I was having a baby?'

All those hours, all the years talking to her mother without so much as a sign that Lorna could hear and yet she asked him now.

'I do.'

'You're just saying that.'

'No.' Zahir shook his head. 'Did you tell her about me...?'

'You were all I spoke about for a year.' Adele gave a soft laugh but then it changed. 'I miss that.'

It had seemed agony at the time but Adele now missed those times with her mum.

'Of course you do,' he said. 'I spoke to her on our wedding day and just like you had said there was no response, no sign she understood, yet she held on until she knew you were okay...'

'I don't know.'

Adele didn't know what to think.

'Talk to her again,' Zahir said. 'Maybe in your head. Have those conversations that you miss.'

Adele did.

She walked on the beach and in her head she chatted to her mum and told her how much she loved her.

How sorry she was.

And some tears fell and then she smiled. 'You'll be pleased to know I have a driver now.'

Zahir was right.

It helped to talk to her mother again. For years there had been no response but now she could feel the breeze on her face and the sand at her feet and she could talk to her whenever she wanted to.

Then Adele saw Leila walking towards her and she always made her smile.

Leila had nearly finished the blanket for the baby.

It was complete, save for one square, and she was trying to squeeze the baby's name out of Adele.

Adele wasn't telling; instead, they chatted about Maja's visit today.

'She thinks it might be wise if I deliver soon, given that the baby is so big.'

'Good,' Leila said. 'Hopefully you will be prescribed more time in the healing baths after you have the baby. I was there for weeks afterwards. You know how I suffered in my labours. Both Zahir's and Dakan's shoulders...' And then she hesitated but a little too late, for Adele had frowned.

'I thought that Zahir was premature?'

'He had very big shoulders,' Leila said quickly. 'Even at seven months.'

Then she looked up at the palace and saw the ladder against the wall and she smiled at the memory of Fatiq climbing up it to be by her side.

'This is the stone I received the night after the bridal selection,' Leila said, and she pointed to the ruby that she wore around her neck for Adele to admire.

And she gave a tiny, almost imperceptible wink.

Yes, what happened in the palace stayed in the palace, but those last tweaks of regret about her walk of shame left Adele then as she realised she that Zahir hadn't been premature in the least.

They laughed.

Zahir was working in his office when he took a moment to enjoy the lovely view and saw his mother and Adele walking on the beach.

He loved his country.

Always.

And he loved the changes that had been made and the care that had been taken of Adele. He could see her calm and relaxed and happy and walking with his mother.

He watched as Adele and his mother stopped walking and started to laugh.

Adele was doubled over with laughing and it was nice to see.

Leila carried on walking and talking and then turned as Adele failed to catch up.

He watched his mother walk back towards Adele.

That was all Zahir saw.

He swiftly made his way through the palace and down to the beach.

'I'm here,' he said, and then he stopped talking as Adele looked up and smiled in relief.

They shared a gentle kiss on the beach where she had first told him all that had happened and as they looked at each other he could see in her shining eyes the healing that had taken place.

And he knew then that they had been right to stay.

Samina helped Adele into a fresh gown and Zahir walked her down the palace stairs. When she bent over midway, Adele remembered the glare that had passed between father and son when Leila had doubled over.

Things were so different now.

The birthing centre was beautiful and the bliss of an epidural could not be overstated.

'Adele,' Maja told her, 'you need to have a Caesarean.'

She had come to realise that and so too had Adele and Zahir after a lot of very unproductive pushing.

It had always been a real possibility.

Adele was slight and Zahir was not and this was rather a large baby.

She thought of Queen Leila and what she had gone through and was so grateful for all that had changed.

Adele stared at the ceiling as she was moved through to the theatre and Zahir was by her side.

'The staff are praying for a calm and wonderful delivery,' a nurse explained, 'and then they will come in.'

Their ways really were beautiful, Adele thought.

Zahir was utterly calm and sat by her head and held her hand. He chatted as if they were sitting at a bus stop, rather than about to become first-time parents.

He calmed her in a way no one else ever could.

And she loved his patience and also his occasional

impatience when a solution wasn't forthcoming at his pace and he pushed things along.

She loved his almost unwavering belief that the answers would unfold in time.

And she loved, most of all, how essential she was to him.

As he was to her.

It was a moment like no other.

She heard the gurgle of the suction machine and felt the odd sensation of tugging and then heard the sound of tears.

Lusty, healthy tears and they were gifted with a small glimpse of their son.

He had thick black hair and was a big, angry baby indeed. Adele laughed when she saw him and knew, as fact, the Caesarean had been necessary.

'Go over to him,' Adele said to Zahir, and he gave her a kiss and then did so.

The staff were a little nervous as Zahir approached.

He was not only a doctor but would one day be king and so too would his new son.

'He is beautiful, Your Highness,' Maja said. It was the proudest moment in her career to have delivered the future king. She was so pleased that he had been born safely here in Mamlakat Almas.

He was crying very loudly and a nurse was wrapping him up and preparing to take him over to Adele.

'Can I take him?' Zahir asked her.

That would be a yes.

He took his baby and rested him in his arm. He looked down at his son, who stared back and calmed in such a firm hold.

Zahir went over to Adele and sat on the stool, putting the baby's head by hers and watching them meet.

And he saw tears flow freely from Adele's eyes.

He was the most beautiful baby, with navy eyes and thick black lashes and he didn't look like a newborn. He was stunning and he had her heart just like that.

And the name they had chosen was absolutely right, Adele thought as she felt his little fat hand reach out for his mother.

'Azzam…' Adele said, and she kissed him.

And later, much later, sitting in bed, holding her baby with Zahir by her side, the baby was introduced to his family and Leila finally got to know his name.

Azzam.

Royal Prince Sheikh Azzam Al Rahal, of Mamlakat Almas.

It would be stitched onto a little square tonight and placed in the centre of his blanket.

The palace healer also came to visit Adele and he thought she might need at least eight weeks of the healing baths.

'Maybe ten,' he said, and gave Adele a smile.

'Your mother will be delighted,' Adele said to her husband when the healer had left.

They were breaking one old tradition, though, and Adele would be back in Zahir's bed on her first night home.

'Once you have finished your course in the healing baths, we shall have to see about a honeymoon.'

'Where?' Adele said.

'You choose.'

And she thought of an oasis in the desert but she would not be forgetting to take her Pill this time.

She could not have been happier.

Neither could Zahir.

And later, after she had fed him and Zahir was settling him down, she called Janet to share the happy news.

'It's a beautiful name,' Janet said. 'What does it mean?'

'It means determined,' Adele said, and then Zahir smiled at her and she met his gaze. He walked to Adele and sat on the bed, took her hand as she explained further.

'Resolved.'

* * * * *

ONE HOT NIGHT WITH DR CARDOZA

TINA BECKETT

To John, as always.

CHAPTER ONE

AMY WOODELL ADJUSTED the single strap of her teal gown one last time as she entered the swanky hotel. She'd ripped out the stitches and resewn it in an attempt to pull up the hemline just a bit. But it hadn't quite solved the problem.

In her rush to pack for her trip to Brazil, she'd brought the wrong shoes. The heels on her silver slingbacks were about an inch shorter than the black stilettos she normally would have worn. But she'd been a last-minute addition to the people who'd be attending the summer lecture program at the fabulous Hospital Universitário Paulista. And between a rushed itinerary followed by flight delays, there'd been no time to go shopping. She'd added a silver-linked belt to her waistline as an additional way to keep her dress from dragging the floor.

Glancing through the palm trees and lush tropical decor, she spotted a familiar face in the crowd. Krysta, wasn't that her name? The customs and immigration line had been long, but fortunately she'd met Krysta, who was also part of the group of visiting doctors—a specialist in otolaryngology and facial reconstruction. They'd hit it off almost immediately, the other woman's friendly nature helping put her nerves at ease.

Amy's mom's sudden death six months ago had put her life into a tailspin, making her realize how little firsthand knowledge she'd had about her mother's heritage. Being in Brazil—her mom's home country—made her feel connected to her in a way that defied logic. And she had an uncle she'd never even met, who supposedly lived on the outskirts of São Paulo, according to an address in her mom's things.

Well, she was going to make the most of these three months! And if she could adopt a little bit of her mother's philosophy of living in the moment, even better.

Heading toward Krysta and hoping against hope that the other woman remembered her from the immigration line, she surveyed the room. Round tables were topped with silk damask tablecloths and huge flower-strewn topiaries. The colors and lush tropical theme were like something out of a pricey travel magazine. It was gorgeous.

So were the people.

And Amy had never felt more out of place.

Her eyes met those of a man across the room, his lean physique and good looks making her steps falter for a minute. He stood straight and tall, his black hair melding with his equally black clothing; everything from his suit to his tie to the tips of his polished shoes were dark.

She shivered. He could have been the angel of death or a grim reaper—albeit a gorgeous one—here to mete out swift justice. All he lacked was a scythe. He did have something in his hand, although she couldn't quite tell what it... When she realized she was rooted in place...and that she was staring—*staring!*—she forced her feet back into motion.

Oh, Lord.

Maybe he hadn't noticed. She chanced another quick peek and was thankful to see him talking to some cute blonde, his mouth curving to reveal a flash of white teeth. Her insides gave a deep shiver.

Probably his wife, Amy.

Who thankfully hadn't noticed a strange woman ogling her husband.

She made it to Krysta and forced a smile, although she was suddenly feeling even less sure of her place here. And her reaction to a complete stranger? Ridiculous.

Although if she had been her vibrant, larger than life mother, she would have marched right over and introduced herself to him. Laughed at his jokes. Fluttered her lashes at him a time or two. Cecília Rodrigo Woodell had never met a stranger. Something that used to embarrass Amy. But not anymore.

"Wow, this is quite a welcoming party. I don't know if you remember me. Amy Woodell?"

Krysta nodded. "Of course I do. You're a physical therapist, right?" She got the attention of the woman next to her. "Amy, this is Flávia Maura. She actually works in the Atlantic Forest with venomous snakes and spiders. She's here to give a lecture."

"Nice to meet you. I hate to admit it, but snakes kind of terrify me." She held up her palm, where two small scars were still visible. "Pygmy rattlers are pretty common in Florida. So are pools. And the two of them seem to find each other. A lot."

Flávia shifted her attention from something in the crowd back to Amy and Krysta, smoothing her palms down the front of her dress as if suddenly ill at ease in it.

"Yes, I'm familiar with rattlesnakes. But I'll admit the only snakes that disgust me are the ones that strut around on two legs, brag about their *avô*'s contributions to this hospital and spend much of their time insulting others."

She sent a glare back into the crowd. "But that's neither here nor there. And hopefully neither of you will have to deal with that particular *cobra*." The bits and pieces of Portuguese mixed with her English made the statement sound slightly sinister.

The image of Tall, Dark and Reaperish popped up in her head. Was Flávia talking about him? She'd kind of been looking off in that general direction. If so, Amy should be doubly glad she wouldn't have to work with him. Or flutter her lashes at him.

Although that smile hadn't made him look like a snake. Or even a jerk. But then again, looks could be deceiving. As she'd found out from her job. And her last boyfriend, who'd appeared to be totally into her. Until he wasn't. She'd learned the hard way that "ghosting" was actually a real phenomenon.

From now on she was going to keep things between her and men light and simple. Maybe somewhere in the neighborhood of "fling" territory. And the Reaper? That glance he'd given her had been anything but light or simple.

Flávia smiled. "I see movement by the podium. I think they're getting ready to give the welcomes. *Até logo.*"

"Nice to meet you, Flávia." Amy smiled back before turning to Krysta. "See you soon, too, I hope," she said with a light touch of Krysta's arm. She then began to circle the tables, waiting for further instructions. She almost tripped over the hem of her dress before yanking it up again. Ugh!

The wait was longer than she expected it to be, but just as she was trying to decide whether or not to find Krysta again, someone at the front of the room tapped the microphone. "We want to take a moment to welcome our visiting doctors and lecturers. We're very excited about this year's summer lecture program."

She shifted her weight. She wasn't a doctor. Furthering her education had been on the back burner for a long time, but recently she'd started giving it serious thought and had included that fact on her application.

The speaker's English was excellent. Since there were people here from all over the world, it made sense that they'd address the group in that language. Despite having a mother who was Brazilian, Amy unfortunately hadn't taken advantage of practicing her Portuguese. So, she'd pretty much stuck to short simple phrasings since she'd arrived, although she could understand most of what was said.

"If you haven't already done so, please consult the seating chart at the entrance to find your place. Dinner will be served shortly, so if you could take your seats as soon as possible, that would be appreciated."

Amy took a deep breath and headed over to the seating chart just as someone else was getting there. Sensing someone to her left, she turned with a smile to introduce herself. It quickly faded. It was the Reaper. And up close, those flaws she expected to see were nonexistent. Also nonexistent was the blonde he'd been with moments earlier. She forced herself to speak.

"Hello. I'm Amy Woodell."

"Ah, so you are our physical therapist? I have been wondering about you."

The way he said "our" in that gruff, accented English gave the words a sense of intimacy that made her swallow. It served to reinforce her weird initial reaction to him. She forced her lashes to stay put until her eyes burned with the effort.

Stupid, Amy. Probably married. Remember?

"Yes, I guess I am. And am I the only one?" She slid a thumb under her the strap of her dress, afraid it might slide down.

"You are indeed. I'm Roque Cardoza, the head of orthopedics. We'll be working together, it seems." He glanced at the seating chart. "And sitting together. Shall we go?"

Working? And sitting? Together? Oh, no!

She blinked a couple of times in rapid succession, her composure beginning to crumble as they made their way to the table. He had a cane in his left hand. Had he injured himself? Not that she was going to ask. "It's very nice to meet you. I'm anxious to get started."

Actually, she was anxious to be anywhere but here, suddenly.

"Yes. As am I."

She shivered. It had to be the language that gave everything that smooth seductive air. She could get addicted to listening to him. And the way his eyes remained fastened to her face the whole time he'd addressed her… But not in a creepy way. Not like how she'd sized him up earlier.

Her thumb dipped out from under her strap, almost wishing it *would* slip, just so they could be on equal footing as far as staring went. Her eyes dropped to his ring finger, but it was empty. Not even a hint that one had been recently removed, although that meant nothing. Lots of people chose not to wear their wedding bands. And it didn't look like staff members had brought their significant others to the soiree, since they didn't seem to be paired up that way.

Roque indicated her seat and waited for her to take it before sliding into his own, propping his cane against the table. He hadn't used the cane to walk and there was no orthopedic boot on his foot, and he'd certainly had no problem maneuvering into his chair. In fact, he was…

Nothing. He was nothing. And he definitely wasn't light. Or simple. Her two new requirements in a man.

Time to squash those fling thoughts that kept circling her head like vultures looking for any sign of weakness.

She turned her attention to the person in the seat to her right. The woman was another visiting doctor from London who specialized in sports medicine.

"The doctor you were speaking with also specializes in sports medicine, I hear, so it'll be interesting to hear things from his perspective."

Was he listening?

"Some of my early physical therapy work was at a center specializing in sports injuries. Those are hard, since most athletes need the affected area of the body in order to perform adequately. Sometimes they never completely recover."

"Yes. Sometimes that is the case. No matter how much physical therapy they may receive." The comment came from Roque. So he *was* listening. And his words had a strange, almost angry quality to them.

Anything she might have said in response was halted as dinner plates were brought around to the tables.

She knew this dish. "This looks like shrimp in coconut milk, like my mom used to make."

"Your mother is Brazilian?"

Amy glanced at him. "Yes. I think she called this *camarão no leite de coco*."

"Very good. So you speak Portuguese as well?"

"I understand a lot. But I'm sorry to say I only

have survival-skill fluency as far as speaking goes. My tongue gets tripped up."

His fingers came to rest on the table. "If you understand the mechanics, then it's only a matter of practice for the tongue. Soon it remembers exactly how to move."

She gulped as those vultures continued to circle. Everything he said carried a double-edged whammy that made her senses reel. She'd gotten all kinds of sly innuendos while working on male patients over the years. Both married and unmarried. But she wasn't getting those vibes from Roque. At all. He wasn't doing it on purpose.

And yet she found her body reacting to them—to *him!*—and that horrified her.

"I don't think I'll be here long enough to get in that kind of practice." She decided to rope those vultures and jerk them out of the sky. He was one of the first men she'd actually sat down to talk to in Brazil, so it made sense that she might notice him more than she normally would.

After her mom died, she'd realized how much life the woman had exuded. How many chances she'd taken in the living of it, and how little of herself she'd held back. When Amy was a kid, she'd struggled with having a mother who was so open, so friendly. But only now was she wishing she had a little more of her mom's joie de vivre. Fully embracing any and all opportunities. Including in the area of love.

And Roque?

Not one of those opportunities. Especially if he was involved with someone.

And if he wasn't?

She was only here for three months. If she met someone else, someone other than a man she'd be working with, why not have a little fun? And this time, she'd have no expectations. Unlike her last relationship.

Her mom had met Amy's father while he was in Brazil on business. They'd fallen in love instantly. Before they knew it, they were married, and Amy's mom had uprooted herself from everything she'd known to be with the man she loved. He'd died five years later, and her mom had stayed in Florida to be close to his grave. And now she was buried next to him.

Not something Amy could imagine herself doing. Florida was one of the last links she had with her parents. She actually worked at the hospital she'd been born in.

"If the hospital administration finds out that you understand the language, I can guarantee they will use that to their advantage."

"And if they don't know?"

"Vão descobrir, com certeza."

She took a bite of shrimp, the rich luscious flavors rolling around in her mouth. Swallowing, she said, "They won't find out. Not unless you tell them." Too late she realized that he'd spoken to her in Portuguese.

"I think I will not have to tell them... Amy." Her name came out sounding like "Ahh-Mee," all musical and so horrifyingly attractive.

She licked her lips, trying to maintain her grip on what little composure she had left.

He was right. There was no way she could keep her knowledge of the language a secret. But the truth was, she was embarrassed to speak. She hated making mistakes of any kind. And yet Roque's English wasn't perfect, and he was still willing to try in order to be understood. And at a hospital like Paulista he was probably called on to speak English fairly often. "You're right. I'll give myself away, won't I?"

"Yes. Most assuredly."

She smiled at him, feeling silly all of a sudden. What would her mom have done in this situation? She would have tackled that language barrier and conquered it, just like she'd done when she'd married her father. While her mom had always maintained her accent, she'd spoken English very well. "Well, I won't try to hide it, then."

One side of his mouth kicked up. Not quite as big as the smile he'd lavished on the blonde, but it transformed the rugged lines of his face in ways that made warmth pool in her stomach.

She took a deep breath and dug into her food, hoping to take her attention off the man beside her. Just in time, too. Because the next speaker was at the podium giving instructions on how the scheduling would work. She forced herself to listen, since she didn't want to be lost tomorrow, when things got under way. It seemed those who were not giving lectures would shadow a staff member for the first half of their stay in order to learn the ropes. Then they would be given more latitude and allowed to have input in patient care.

That was exciting. From the information she'd seen online, Paulista would rival any hospital she'd visited in the US.

"For those of you who have just arrived, there is an envelope on the table listing who you'll be paired with. There will be two or three visiting medical professionals shadowing the same staff member. Who knows, you might even be sitting at the same table with them."

There were a few chuckles at that comment, but Amy didn't share in the mirth. Her hands suddenly turned to ice, her fork stopping halfway to her mouth.

She spotted the envelope the woman had mentioned. Cream-colored and tipped with gold, it shouldn't look ominous, but it did. Knowing she couldn't simply drop the fork and dive for the list, she forced herself to pop the shrimp into her mouth and chew as the person to Roque's left drew the sheet from the envelope and glanced at it. The man then passed the paper to Roque, while Amy struggled to swallow her food.

The orthopedist didn't even glance at the names. Instead, a muscle in his jaw flickered and one brow edged up, and he handed the sheet to her, eyes meeting hers and lingering.

Oh, God! Why? Her and...the Reaper?

That's why he'd mentioned working together. She hadn't thought he'd meant so closely together. Amy forced herself to look at the paper in her hands...to find her name. But it was all a pretense. And there it was in black and white: Roque Cardoza, Amy Woodell and two other names.

She didn't know how she'd expected this thing to work but had assumed there'd be some kind of short orientation as a group before listening to the various lecturers and participating in treatment as opportunities arose. But to work closely with someone she was already uneasy with? For half of the three-month stint? That was a whole month and a half. Of watching every move the man made.

She passed the sheet to the woman next to her. Why couldn't she be with Flávia and Krysta?

Because they were both lecturing.

The woman she'd spoken to a few minutes earlier smiled. "It looks like I'm in your group, and I've met the other man on the list as well. He's on the far side of the table."

Okay, so at least that was something. "That's great." But there was no conviction in her voice.

The speaker addressed them again. "So once you've finished dinner, find your group and set a meeting time and place for tomorrow, if you would."

Roque leaned over. "Looks like you're stuck with me for a little longer. But don't worry. I won't tell anyone your little secret."

Little secret?

The words made her heart skip a beat. Then another. Had he guessed what he did to her? Her face became a scorching inferno. "I'm not sure what you mean."

"That you understand Portuguese." He frowned. "Is there some other secret I should know about?"

Her shoulders sagged and her strap actually started to slide down her shoulder. She shrugged it back into place.

"No. No other secrets." *Liar.* "And since we both agreed it would be impossible to keep my Portuguese under wraps, I guess it doesn't matter."

Somehow she got through the rest of the meal, which was followed by a luscious crème brûlée for dessert. Then people were getting to their feet, and groups formed all over the room, the sounds of excitement building in the air.

Except the air where she was sitting.

"So here we are." Roque stood, not reaching for his cane.

She scrambled to her feet as well. "Yes, we are." *It's only six weeks, Amy. You can do this.*

The sports medicine doctor introduced herself to the group as Lara Smith. And a man with light brown hair came over and shook Roque's hand and then hers. "I am Dr. Peter Gunderfeld. You must be Dr. Cardoza and Dr. Woodell?"

Everyone in her group was a doctor. Except for her.

"Just Amy, for me." Her uneasiness about her decision to come to Brazil grew. These people were all brilliantly talented in their respective fields, from what she was discovering. Maybe she should have just planned a vacation to the country and skipped the summer lecture program.

"You can call me Peter, then."

"And Lara is fine with me."

"I am Roque."

The pronouncement landed like a hammer, although she was sure he hadn't meant it to.

They went through a few moments of exchanging social pleasantries about where they were from. She already knew Lara was from England. And Peter was from Munich, Germany.

Roque was from Rio de Janeiro, originally. She had noticed a difference in his speech patterns as opposed to her mom's, who was from São Paulo. Many of his *s*'s had the "sh" sound characteristic of the famous city.

"Did you know that the name Florida comes from the Portuguese word meaning 'flowered'?" Roque's mouth curved slightly. She forced her gaze not to dwell.

"I did." This would be a perfect time to ask what his name meant, but that might be a little too personal.

Peter had no problems sharing personal information, however. He was married with a two-year-old daughter.

"It had to have been hard to leave them at home," Lara said.

"Yes. But they're going to meet me here the last week of our stay, and then we'll vacation in Iguaçu Falls."

"Good choice. Foz do Iguaçu is worth the visit." Roque glanced at Amy. "I hope you and Lara added extra time on to your trip as well."

She hadn't really thought about that. She already

had her return ticket, in fact. Maybe she should check to see how hard it would be to switch the dates.

"I've been to Brazil several times actually. And no husband or kids to bring," Lara said, smiling at Peter. "So I'm just here for the conference."

Roque hadn't commented on his relationship status, and Amy wasn't about to ask nor share hers. Not only was it not any of her business, she didn't want him thinking that she was interested in him like that.

She wasn't.

Those thoughts about flings and the flutters in her belly were strictly animal survival instincts. Nothing more. If she stuck to work topics, it should be easier to view him as a colleague and not as a person whose speech patterns did crazy things to her libido.

Maybe she did need to hook up with a good-looking man and knock some of this stuff out of her system. It had been ages since she'd had sex.

She wasn't going to number Roque in with the possible candidates for that, though. Her gaze scouted the room, and while she saw several other attractive men, there was no pull toward them.

Well, all that meant was that she wasn't shallow, right?

Hmm…and yet she'd been glued to almost every word that came out of Roque's firm, sexy mouth.

She rolled her eyes.

The man picked that moment to glance at his watch. "I have an early day tomorrow. Do you all know your way to the condominium?"

"Yes. The Fonte Cristalina, right?" Amy had already dropped her luggage off at the apartment build-ing the hospital had put them up in. It wasn't fancy, but it was clean and had a gorgeous view of the city.

"Yes." Roque looked from one to the other. "It's within walking distance of Paulista. But it's better to do that during the day. So, let's meet in the hospital lobby at eight in the morning?" There was a slight furrow between his brows now, though.

"Very good. I must go call my wife," Peter said. "See you tomorrow."

"And I'm meeting a friend for a nightcap," Lara added a second later.

Amy said her goodbyes. Was she the only one feel-ing lost at sea?

Maybe Roque sensed some of her thoughts because he stayed where he was. "Would you like me to drop you off at the apartment complex?"

"Oh, no, it's okay. I can catch a cab. There are some out front, I'm sure."

"Very likely." He moved sideways to let some-one through, which put him way too close to her for comfort.

Amy took a quick step back, and a sharp tug at her shoulder was followed by a distinct ripping sound. Then things began a slow slide. Straight down. In-cluding her mind.

Oh! Oh, no!

She grabbed at the bodice of her dress just as the shoulder strap flopped uselessly over the top of her hand.

Roque turned…stared at her shoulder, before

glancing down at where his foot was planted on her hem. His face turned a dull red.

"*Merde!* I am sorry, Amy. I did not realize."

Her name came rough-edged off his tongue, and she shut her eyes as hot embarrassment rained down on her. She knew she hadn't stitched the strap enough, but hadn't given much thought to it. A huge mistake.

Just like this whole damned trip.

"It's okay, but I'd better find that cab now."

"I will take you home. It's only right."

The thought of running out of the hotel holding up her dress was mortifying, so she decided to accept his offer. "Thank you. Could you stand in front of me for a second, though?"

His head tilted sideways, but he shifted until they were face-to-face, and much, much closer than they had been last time.

Hot flames licked at her innards, and she had a hard time catching her breath. "I—I kind of meant for you to turn the other way. I want to tuck my strap into my dress so it's not as obvious."

This time, his eyes did what she'd wanted them to do earlier. Trailed over her bare shoulder and lower before coming back up to meet her gaze. That muscle in his jaw twitched the way it had when he'd handed her the list of names, but he said, "Of course," before turning away from her, shielding her from prying eyes.

She quickly shoved the strap into the front of her dress, hoping it didn't cause any awkward bulges, then she clamped her right arm across her chest and picked up her clutch purse. Where were those few lost pounds when you needed them?

"Okay, you can turn around now."

He did, his glance going back to her shoulders, now bereft of any fabric. "I will pay for the damage I caused."

No, he wouldn't. Because the real damage wasn't anything that could be seen with the naked eye.

"It's my fault. I tried to alter the length on my own, when I should have bought higher heels. I'm just glad it happened at the end of the evening rather than at the beginning."

"I know a very good seamstress. It would also be free."

Oh, God! Maybe he really was married. She could picture him trying to explain to some faceless wife how he'd practically stripped one of his charges naked in front of an entire room of doctors.

Well, not naked. But almost. She didn't have a bra on, since the dress had one built into it. "I'm sure that's not—"

"It is my mother. It would take her little time to make it right. She could even arrange for a fitting to adjust the length, if you would like. Her shop is at my parents' home."

Somehow the fact that his mom was the seamstress made her relax. "That would be an awkward conversation, wouldn't it?"

"No. She's come to expect me to be a little more… clumsy than I used to be."

Inadvertently, her glance shifted to the cane. "You're not clumsy. It was an accident."

He was the most elegant, graceful man she'd met in a long time, whatever the reasons for that cane.

"Yes, well, be that as it may, I do insist on making it right."

Amy had a feeling he wasn't going to let it go. "At least ask your mom if she'd mind, first, before just assuming she'll say yes."

"I will. But I know she will not mind." He gave her that slow smile of his. The one that devastated her senses and made it hard to think beyond it. "Let me do this for you, Amy. This one small thing."

It wasn't a small thing. Not to her. But if she tried to keep arguing the point, he was eventually going to realize there was something more behind it. Something that made her wary of him—wary of working on his team for the next three months. Wary of shadowing him for half of those three months.

So all she could do was agree and say a fitting wasn't necessary, and hope that once the dress was returned, she could forget about this incident once and for all. Maybe then she could focus on her real reasons for coming to Brazil. Those had to do with her mom and finding her uncle. And her career, of course.

And none of those things included the man in front of her.

CHAPTER TWO

DAMN, WHAT HAD he done?

The very physical therapist he'd tried to veto having on his team seemed to be a nice person. But she carried an air of fragility that socked him in the gut and made him wish he'd stuck to his guns. But the physical therapy department was running short-staffed at the moment and couldn't spare anyone to participate in the summer lecture program.

And then he had to go and ruin her dress. And when he'd misunderstood and stood face-to-face with her, almost touching, and definitely close enough to...

Close enough to nothing!

This damned leg. Even as the thought went through his head, a phantom pain shot through his thigh. One that had nothing to do with his reaction to her. Or that dress.

He stepped on the gas as the drive to the apartment seemed to take forever, even though it was less than three blocks away. Part of it was due to navigating in heavy traffic. But also because his peripheral vision kept checking the top of her dress to make sure it hadn't crept any farther down. If that happened, he might have to do a major reboot of his sanity. Because as he'd gazed at her in that room full of people, he'd found himself wishing it would. Which was ridiculous. Not to mention unprofessional.

They finally arrived, and Roque pressed the code into the security box at the front of the building, waiting as the heavy garage door swung open to allow his Mercedes to slide past. It closed behind them with a sense of finality, trapping him in the space with her.

He forced himself to say something in hopes she wouldn't guess where his thoughts were straying. "The hospital bought several apartments in this condominium for visiting doctors or VIP patients coming in from other areas of the country. So everyone's staying at the same place."

"That makes sense." Her dress seemed to edge down a millimeter, and his mouth went completely dry.

He found a parking spot. "Would you like me to wait while you take off the dress?"

"Excuse me?"

A flare went off in his head, sending up an alarm that the rest of his body failed to heed. His thoughts about it sliding down were evidently starting to come out in his speech. "I did not mean in the car, of course. I meant in your apartment. You could bring the dress back down to me, unless you prefer to bring it to the hospital."

Yes, the sooner she was out of sight, the sooner he would be able to get that image out of his head. But he was pretty sure it would reappear—along with a few others—the second he went to sleep tonight.

"Oh, of course." She hesitated. "I'd rather not bring it to the hospital, if that's okay with you. Why don't you come up to the apartment and I can give it to you there? It's really not necessary to have your mom repair it, though."

"It is to me. And if you're okay with it, I'll come up. It will save you the trip back down."

Why the hell had he just offered to do that? Hadn't he just thought how glad he'd be to have her out of sight?

"Okay, great." Still keeping her arm across her dress, she turned sideways and tried to hit the button on her seat belt, struggling with getting her hand that far back.

Roque reached over to hit the release latch for her, his sleeve brushing her bare arm as he did and catching a light floral scent that seemed to cling to her skin. He swallowed. "Wait there."

Getting his cane from the back and climbing out of the car, he came around to her side, the tension in his jaw making itself known in his leg. He leaned a little of his weight on the cane's handle. No wonder he'd stepped on her dress. Maybe this was some elaborate joke perpetrated by karma after his response to his mom's nudging at dinner last night. She'd asked about him meeting someone special. He'd bluntly told her he wasn't interested in meeting anyone—special or not so special. Less than twenty-four hours later, he'd stepped on someone's dress and found his thoughts riveted to all kinds of "what if" scenarios.

Well, he needed to un-rivet them. *Now.*

He forced his steps to quicken, opening her door and pulling the webbing of the seat belt away from her, taking care not to touch her, this time. "Can you get out on your own?"

Deus do céu, he hoped she could.

She swung her legs out of the car and planted them on the ground, but his low-slung car wasn't helping her.

"Here. Give me your hand." He gritted his teeth and forced himself to add the obvious, "The left one."

You're a funny, funny guy, Roque. As if she's going to give you the other one.

She let him pull her up from her seat, her grip on his firm and warm and lingering maybe a second longer than necessary. Then stood in front of him, her head tilted to look at him, the overhead lights shining on cheeks that were slightly pink and far too appealing. "Thanks, I appreciate it."

"The least I can do." And it was. Especially since his thoughts were now having to run some pretty impressive evasive maneuvers, like a footballer trying to stay just out of reach of his opponent. Which in this case happened to be common sense.

She followed him to the elevator. His steps still felt a little off, but he draped his cane over his arm. And he wasn't quite sure why. He wasn't ashamed of that hitch in his stride. Was he?

And when he'd stepped on her dress. Was he being

prideful by not using it? And if he had used it, could he have avoided this whole damn mess?

"Did you hurt your foot?"

Her question came out of nowhere, seeming to echo his earlier musings as the elevator doors opened. "What floor are you on?" He stalled for a few seconds, trying to collect his thoughts.

"Four." She licked her lips. "I'm sorry. I shouldn't have asked that."

"No, it's okay." He pushed the button for her floor, and leaned against the wall to look at her. Her arm was pressed against the neckline of her dress, and he noticed two tiny scars on her hand. Very lickable scars.

Hell, where had that come from?

He forced his attention back to her question. "My injury… It seems I am not only good at tripping over dresses, but my own two feet. It's an old sports' injury."

"Which sport?" Her gaze flicked over his chest, down his abdomen…

He cleared a throat that was suddenly dry. *"Futebol."*

Her eyes were now on his thighs and it was as if she could see right through his clothes. And pretty soon, she was going to see something that was visible despite his clothing.

"Have you had physical therapy?"

The shock of her question hit him like a bucket of ice water, scalding him in a way that heat couldn't touch. If she only knew. Yes, he'd had therapy. And more therapy. All it had done was pile more grief onto an already existing wound. It seemed every female he met thought they could magically fix him and put him back to rights.

His jaw tightened until twin points of pain appeared. "Are you offering me your professional services, Amy?" He made it as clear as he could that she was overstepping her boundaries.

"No. I'm sorry. You're an orthopedist. Of course you have."

"It happened a lifetime ago. And it's permanent. What you see is what you, and everyone else, gets. All the physical therapy in the world won't change it."

Diabos. Why had he gone on the attack? She was trying to help. She wasn't like his ex-therapist or any of those women he'd gone out with who'd shown a morbid interest in his damaged leg.

He moved a step closer, so he could touch her hand. "I'm sorry. That came out badly."

They arrived on the fourth floor before he could explain further. She got out in a hurry and stuck her key into the lock of the nearest door, only to jiggle it. She took it out and tried again. "That's weird. It worked earlier. I'm not sure why it's not this—"

The door opened, and the doctor from the gala appeared.

Amy recoiled a step. "I'm so sorry. I must have the wrong…" She glanced at the key. "Heavens, I do. The key says 402. I've only been up here once."

Lara had a glass of wine in her hand, and when her eyes met his, they widened.

Perfect. She was probably wondering what he was doing coming up to Amy's apartment straight from the party.

As was he.

Should he tell her why? That he'd almost ripped Amy's dress off her at the party and had now come here so she could remove it the rest of the way? That sounded pretty damning actually.

"There were no cabs left." The lie flew off Amy's tongue with incredible speed. Evidently she wasn't any more anxious to give the real reason for his visit than he was. But anyone who'd thought about it long enough would realize, there'd been a whole fleet of taxis parked outside the venue. Even if there were no cabs, it didn't explain why he'd come up in the elevator with her. Or why the strap to her dress had suddenly disappeared. Maybe Lara hadn't noticed how she was dressed.

Amy's chest rose as she took a deep breath. "And actually, my dress strap ripped, and Roque's mother is a professional seamstress, so he offered to have her sew it back together for me."

He blinked. She'd backtracked. Why?

"Oh, that was nice of you," Lara murmured.

"Anyway, sorry for disturbing you. See you in the morning."

The other woman smiled at them and said good night, closing the door and leaving them alone in the corridor.

Roque couldn't contain a grin. "I've never known anyone who can make even the truth sound like a lie."

But when she swung around to look at him, her face was white as a ghost.

She whispered, "You don't care that she might think we've come up here to…?"

He wasn't about to admit that he'd entertained a thought or two himself.

"No. I really don't. I don't worry about what people think of me."

At least he hadn't until a minute ago when he saw the look on her face.

"My mom was like that. It must be pretty freeing."

"Freeing? I don't understand."

"Never mind." Amy moved to the next door down, double-checking the number, and inserted her key into the lock. This time it turned smoothly, opening to a white-tiled corridor and living room just beyond it. She entered, motioning him in behind her.

Roque followed her into the space, glancing around.

"Make yourself at home. I'll just go and change. There's not much in the refrigerator, since I haven't made it to the grocery yet."

"It's okay. I don't need anything."

Her suitcases were in the living room and one of them was open wide, a pair of—*diabos!*—lacy pink briefs hanging over the side of it. His gut immediately tightened and all the thoughts he'd banished came rushing back, followed by a few thousand more.

She hurried over and kicked the offending garment into the case and quickly folded it closed.

What she couldn't close was the part of his brain

that had imprinted itself with that image, making him wonder what other forbidden wonders she had hidden in her luggage.

Which was none of his business.

Setting her bags upright, she wheeled one of them toward a room to her left. "I won't be a minute." With that, she shut the door with a thump.

Her panties!

She leaned against the back of the door, shutting her eyes in horror.

Oh, God, they'd been lying there right in front of him! Not minutes after being seen—and recognized—by her neighbor, someone she would have to work with day in and day out. At least for the first month and a half.

But her underwear! Why had she left that case open?

Well, she hadn't expected to have a man in her apartment on her first night.

Or the second or third nights. And now that she knew who was living next door, probably no other night, either. Any hookups would now have to happen "off campus," so to speak.

Roque might not care what people thought, but she did. Far too much. And she certainly didn't want him to hear secondhand that she was entertaining men in one of the hospital's apartments.

Entertaining men? What was this? The 1920s?

Opening her eyes, she went over to the bed and hefted her suitcase onto it, one-handed. This was ridiculous. He couldn't see her now. She let go of her dress, and sure enough, the top of her bodice slid past her waist. Quickly finding a pair of yoga pants and a loose-fitting T-shirt, she opened the side zipper on her dress and let it slither the rest of the way down.

There, are you happy now?

She glared at the garment at her feet, stepping out of it and tossing it onto the bed with a little more force than was necessary.

She then dug through her bag, aware of a little time clock ticking in her head as she tried to find her bra. She blinked. She'd worn one on the flight over, so it had to be here somewhere. Or another one. That maybe she'd packed in the other suitcase that was still in the living room. Or not?

Ack. She'd left the bra she'd traveled in in the bathroom when she'd changed for the party, since she hadn't needed it for the dress. She was not leaving this room to go grab it and waltz her way back to the bedroom with it dangling from her fingertips. That would be almost worse than him seeing her underwear. Although maybe he hadn't noticed.

Oh, he'd noticed, all right. His eyes had been right on them.

So what to do? She'd always been small up top, wishing as a teenager that she had more oomph in that department. But right now, she was glad she didn't. She pulled the T-shirt over her head. It was black and loose. Peering into the bedroom mirror, she decided you couldn't really tell as long as you weren't staring at her chest.

So hauling her yoga pants up over her hips and sliding her feet into a pair of flip-flops, she took the decorative comb out of her hair, tired of it digging into her scalp.

"I don't worry about what people think of me." Wasn't that what he'd said?

Well, maybe she could practice a little of what he—and her mom—preached. She shook her hair out, trying not to care that it was curling in all kinds of crazy directions. She then folded her dress in as small a ball as possible and shoved it into one of the plastic grocery bags she'd included in case she had any wet clothes to pack on the return flight.

There. She was ready.

Sucking down a quick breath, she opened the door and sauntered into the living room as if she hadn't a care in the world. As soon as she saw him, she wished she hadn't agreed to let him take the dress. He was lounging on her sofa, both arms stretched out over the top of it, looking as fresh in his dark suit as the moment she'd laid eyes on him. And she was…

Not caring what people thought, that's what she was.

His glance trailed over her hair, before arriving at the plastic bag in her hand. "Is that it?"

"Yes." She handed it to him. "Thanks again."

"For ripping your dress?"

Maybe. Could it be that this little mishap had provided a way to break the ice? To give her that little flaw in his perfection that she'd been searching for?

"You make a pretty intimidating figure—did you know that?"

His head cocked. "No. I didn't."

"I think even Peter and Lara felt it." Although he wasn't intimidating in a bad sort of way, like whoever Flávia had been referring to.

"Then I'll have to work on that."

He uncurled himself from the sofa and stood over her, and there it was again. That shiver of awareness. And whether it was because of the T-shirt fabric brushing over her bare skin or her reaction to him, her nipples tightened as a swirl of sensation spiraled down her belly to points below. She had to fight the urge to hook her arm back over her chest like she'd done while holding up her dress.

"You don't have to work on anything. I'm sure it's just part of being in a different country." Why on earth had she said anything to him? "Pretty much everything is intimidating to me right now."

"Don't be intimidated, Amy. You'll find Brazilians are quite *amigáveis*."

"I know they're friendly. I didn't really mean that."

"What did you mean, then?"

"I'm not sure. I just feel a little bit out of place. Everyone I've met has been either a doctor or an expert in their field."

"You are an expert in your field, or you wouldn't be here."

She hadn't thought of it like that. She'd heard the vetting process was tough and was actually surprised that she'd gotten in, even if it had been because someone else had dropped out. "Well, thank you. But not really."

"Don't sell yourself short. The team decided you were right for this position."

Something caught her attention. "The team. But not you?"

"The heads of the departments are given a list of applicants that are *préselecionados*... I think you say it as 'short-listed,' yes? And then the selections are made. You were on that list."

He was evading the question about whether or not he had wanted her. Or was he?

"But I only got on afterward, when there was a cancellation."

"There was no cancellation. The powers that be were merely trying to find where best to place you. The physical therapy department couldn't spare anyone to oversee your month-and-a-half shadow period. So you are now with me. I almost said no. Until I read one of your case files. It made me change my mind."

He almost refused to work with her? And if he had, she'd still be sitting in the States.

She did not want him to see how much that stung.

He changed his mind, Amy. That counts for something.

"Which case file?"

"The spina bifida patient who went on to practice martial arts."

Bobby Sellers. She almost hadn't included him, because he hadn't been the stellar success story she felt the hospital was looking for. But he'd touched her life. And when he told her he'd always wanted to break a board in tae kwon do, something her mom had insisted on her participating in, it had struck a chord. And she'd helped him work toward that, even going as far as attending the event where Bobby had indeed broken his board. It had brought her to tears.

"But why that case?"

"It showed that you are able to think outside the box—that you don't keep pushing where it will do no good. You tweaked the prescribing doctor's treatment plan slightly to include your patient's own personal life goals. That is exactly what I want to see at Paulista. Things don't always follow a prescribed path. As the saying goes, medicine is sometimes more art than science."

"I believe that as well. We have to look at patients as a whole, not as a conglomeration of symptoms. We have to help them adapt and change when the body won't cooperate."

He smiled and stood, leaning on his cane a little more than he had been. "And *that* is why I said yes. I should go. *I* might not care about what people think, but I have a feeling you do. And since Dr. Smith knows I'm here in your apartment…"

Yes, it was time for Roque to go. But not because of Lara Smith. Or the fact that the pink scrap of lace peeking out of her suitcase was going to haunt him for days to come. He was pretty sure she wasn't wearing a bra under that T-shirt. But none of that was what drove him to say goodbye. It was because of the vulnerability he'd seen in her when they were talking about how she'd gotten into the program.

He'd sensed a bit of imposter syndrome, and he probably had fueled that even more with his honesty. But he hadn't wanted to work with someone like the physical therapist he'd been assigned after his surgery. He didn't want a fix-it mentality. He wanted someone with the ability to set realistic expectations for his or her patients. In the end, Roque would not have agreed, if the candidate absolutely didn't meet that qualification. His patients were too important to him.

But to have stepped on her dress.

Hell. He definitely did not have the coordination he'd had back in his days with Chutegol, his football club. But then again, his injury had resulted in muscle and nerve damage, and although you wouldn't know it from the single long scar on his outer thigh, the damage to the underlying structures had ended his football career. Fortunately, he'd earned enough from his five years of playing to put himself through medical school.

"Well, thank you for coming."

Amy's voice cut through the fog of his thoughts, and he swung his gaze to her, avoiding looking at her chest.

"I will let you know when it is done." He held up the bag containing the real reason he was here. His mother would be happy to repair it for her. But not without a question or two, or a mention of their earlier conversation, which made him wonder if he'd been right to offer her services. After having women throw themselves at him during his football days, and the messy breakup of his engagement, and then the pass his physical therapist had made during treatment, he was leery of believing someone could be interested in *him*...as someone who came from simple roots, who'd worked hard for everything he had. So his relationships were short and sweet, and very, very superficial. No one who would try to "fix" whatever they thought was wrong with him.

So yes, his mother would ask some pointed questions.

But Roque took care of the mistakes that he could. And the ones he couldn't? Well, he walked away from them.

Amy wrapped her arms around her midsection. "The dress was my fault, so don't worry about it. Like I said, it's too long. I shouldn't have worn it."

The image of her with her forearm clamped across her chest to keep her bodice from falling down swam in front of his face. Were all her undergarments pink? And lacy?

Damn. Talk about mistakes. Maybe this was a bigger one than he realized.

"The dress was—*is*—quite lovely." His phone buzzed on his hip. Glancing at the readout, he frowned. Enzo Dos Santos? He hadn't heard from the owner of the football club in ages, other than a quick note saying he'd had a cancerous lesion removed from his jaw. Had things gone south? He let the call go to voice mail, making a note to call his friend back once he got back to the car. "I'll let you know when my mom has had a chance to look at it."

What he wouldn't tell her was the hoops he was sure to have to jump through before his mom actually got down to work.

"Well, thank you again."

"You're welcome. I'll see you in the morning." Roque had been dreading this three-month rotation, but there was now a weird sense of anticipation he hadn't felt in a while. One he didn't like and halfway suspected was due to the woman whose dress he'd stepped on. She was here for three months. Why risk letting things get messy, when they could stay in a neat and tidy box. And where he'd have no more mistakes to correct. So he said his goodbyes and walked out of her apartment, glancing at Lara's door and wondering if she was staring out her peephole with a stop watch. Ridiculous. Roque did not care what people thought.

Except for the owner of his former football team. When he got to his car, he tossed Amy's dress into the passenger seat and slid into the vehicle, taking out his phone and scrolling through his missed messages. Then putting all thoughts of his rotation charge out of his head, he dialed Enzo's number and waited for the man to pick up his phone.

CHAPTER THREE

HE'D GIVEN HER a choice. Take the morning off or scrub in on an emergency Achilles' tendon surgery.

It had been an easy choice. Scrub for surgery.

The surgical mask felt strange and confining, but it was also a different experience. She could now see why people said the eyes were the window to the soul.

Roque glanced at her, brows raised. "Are you sure you wish to be here?"

"Absolutely." She wondered why Lara and Peter were not in the room as well. Maybe because they both saw surgical procedures day in and day out, and a complete rupture of the tendon was probably no big deal for them. But it was to her. It would give her a glimpse into what went on before a patient arrived on her physical therapy table.

"Let me know if you have any questions, since I'll be speaking in Portuguese once we start. I'm going to do a percutaneous repair rather than opening his leg, to reduce the chance of infection."

"And if you need to graft part of the tendon?"

He looked surprised. "Good question. This case is

fairly straightforward. If the ends of the tendon were say…shredded, I would then open the leg and fold down a portion of the *gastrocnêmio*… In English—?"

"Gastrocnemius?"

"Yes, that is it."

The corners of his eyes crinkled in a smile that made her swallow. Without being able to see his mouth or the rest of his face, and with his emotions being translated by his eyes, it forced her to watch carefully. That had to be why her own senses were taking in every millimeter of movement and multiplying how it affected her.

"We would use a portion of that tissue to reinforce the repair. To make it less likely to rupture a second time."

"But you don't need to this time?"

"No. This patient is still in school and young and healthy. He should be able to return to football, once he lets the injury heal completely." He glanced around the surgical room where the other personnel appeared to be waiting on a signal from him. "Let's get started. You can ask more questions as we go."

She answered with a quick nod.

His words hadn't been a dismissal. So why had it felt that way? Maybe because she knew he'd almost said no to her being in the program. And because she'd been way too caught up in their exchange of words and hadn't been quite ready to end it.

A natural reaction, Amy.

Of course she'd be interested in learning as much as she could. And she wanted to show Roque that she absolutely should be here, despite any reservations he might have had in the beginning.

The orthopedist walked over to the patient who was already prepped for surgery and under general anesthesia. He motioned for her to join him by the table, while a nurse with a tray of surgical instruments stood on his other side. Amy watched as he made two tiny incisions on either side of the leg, using forceps to enlarge the holes slightly. He gave a running commentary in Portuguese, which she surprisingly understood, only missing a word or two here and there. "I'm going to place sutures under the skin in a figure-eight motion, catching the upper part of the tendon and using the suture material to draw it down to meet the other half."

He then ran the needle through the first of the incisions and out the second hole. When he ducked back in, he allowed the point of the needle to tell him where to make the next small cut, repeating the process down the leg until he reached the other end of the tendon. His long fingers were sure and precise, almost dancing over the surface of his patient's skin.

Not a good analogy, because her brain immediately opened up a side-by-side screen, putting her where Roque's patient was, with those fingers sliding up the back of one of her calves in a way that had nothing to do with surgery. She blinked away the image, trying to force her eyes to focus on what was happening in front of her.

"Almost done."

Amy glanced up at the clock, shocked to see that

only about ten minutes had gone by. And the procedure was a lot more straightforward than she'd expected it to be. Somehow he found the tendon under the skin without any kind of imaging equipment, seeming to go by feel. But there'd been no hesitation. How many of these had he done over the course of his career? Enough to make it seem like a piece of cake.

Roque tugged on the two ends of suture line and she could almost see the ends of the tendon pulling together beneath the patient's skin, just like the ripped seams of her dress's strap would be pulled back together as his mom stitched it. An odd comparison, but it really was what had happened. Only this man's leg was alive, and a ripped tendon couldn't just be cast aside like a piece of clothing.

"These sutures are absorbable, whereas the ones I'll put on the outside will need to be removed." He tied off the inner stitches, and was handed another threaded needle, which he used to close each of the tiny holes he'd made in the skin. He glanced at her. "And that's it. Not very exciting."

Yes, it was. Too exciting actually. But not in the way he meant. Roque's eyes were brown, but without his dark clothing on, they had almost an amber hue that she hadn't caught last night. Or maybe because she'd been too busy taking in the man as a whole rather than being fixated on one small part of him.

No, not fixated. But when she scrambled around for another word, she suddenly couldn't find one.

That was a problem for later, because she couldn't exactly think straight right now.

"Thanks for letting me watch the procedure. I've done the physio for several Achilles' reattachment patients. It's a long slow process in the States."

He nodded, pulling his mask down and thanking his team, before responding. The curve of his mouth set off a line in his left cheek that had probably been a dimple when he was a child.

He wasn't a child anymore, though. He was all man.

"The process is long here as well. Andreu, our patient, won't be able to play for six months and will be in a boot for several weeks."

She sighed. "Six months can seem like forever to someone so young."

"Yes. It can seem like a lifetime. But at least *his* outcome should be a good one."

The cryptic words made her heart ache, because she knew who he was referring to.

As he moved toward the back of the room, his steps seemed a little slower, the hitch she'd noticed earlier was more pronounced. He'd left his cane outside, probably to avoid contaminating the room. It was on the tip of her tongue to offer to go ahead of him and retrieve it for him, but no one else in the room had volunteered. Maybe it was a touchy subject. And as a physical therapist, she knew that the more people could do for themselves, the better.

A thought struck her. "Was this your first surgery of the day?"

"No, my third."

"What?" She pulled off her own mask and gloves,

discarding them in the trash can next to the door and glancing at the clock on the wall. "It's barely eight-thirty."

"There was an accident involving a *moto-taxi* in the early hours. The driver and his passenger both had multiple injuries."

His specialty was sports medicine, but obviously he handled regular ortho surgeries as well. "Are they okay?"

"The passenger will make it, but the driver…" He shook his head.

"Oh, no. My mom said that motorcyclists here have a dangerous life, but I'm sure that's true everywhere."

"It is very true here." He pushed through the door and took his cane, leaning on it for a minute. "Do you mind if we grab a coffee? Peter and Lara aren't due in until noon, and I have a long day ahead of me."

"You don't have to babysit me, if you need to go grab a catnap."

"Cat…nap?"

Oh! Of course he wouldn't know that phrase. "A light sleep? *Soneca?*"

"But why a cat?"

"I don't know. The cat we had when I was growing up slept a lot, and her sleep wasn't exactly light."

He smiled, and started walking, using his cane on every fourth step or so. "It's the same with mine."

He had a cat?

She blinked. Somehow she didn't picture him as a cat person, although she wasn't sure why. But the image of him baby-talking to a sulky feline made her giggle. She quickly swallowed it when he gave her a sideways look.

"Something is funny?"

"No. I was just surprised you have a cat."

"Yes. Me too. I… Let's say I inherited her from someone."

"Your parents?" Her childhood cat had died not long after her mom passed away. The second loss had hit her hard, since her mom had loved Tabby fiercely.

"No. Not my parents."

The gritted words sounded pained, although he hadn't increased his reliance on his cane. Oh. A girl-friend. Or a wife.

"I'm sorry. I shouldn't have asked."

"It's okay. My fiancée considered Rachel her cat. But when we broke up…well, let's just say there were allergies involved. So the cat stayed with me."

Allergies were involved in the breakup? No, that didn't make sense. Her eyes widened. The girlfriend had either cheated or found someone else soon after they broke off their relationship. Someone who was allergic to cats.

That's a whole lot of speculating, Amy.

But the curt way he spoke about it said the split hadn't been exactly amicable. "Well, I'm glad you didn't take the kitty to a shelter."

"There are very few shelters here. But I still wouldn't have. Rachel was originally a street cat, but has adapted very well to life inside my apartment."

She could imagine why. A shot of warmth pulsed through her.

And Roque had evidently adapted very well to life with a cat. Somehow the idea of Roque squatting down to pick up some terrified, emaciated cat and comforting her made a wave of emotion well up inside of her. She'd always been a sucker for a man who was kind to animals. And to name his cat Rachel?

That was probably the doing of the fiancée as well. "How did she get her name?"

"There was a certain American program that my fiancée liked. It revolved around a café."

She'd binge-watched it with her mom. "That's a classic. Have you seen it?"

"I couldn't much avoid it." There went that tension in his jaw again. And there went her stomach.

Thankfully they arrived at the hospital's coffee shop, a trendy looking café that would rival the one in the TV show. "That looks great."

"What do you want?"

"I can get it."

"It's on the hospital."

It was? She didn't remember coffee breaks being covered. "A skinny vanilla latte, please."

She could see the wheels in his head turning as he puzzled through the words, so she tried again. "A latte with nonfat milk?"

"Ah…skinny. Nonfat milk, I see."

"What is it in Brazil?"

"*Leite desnatada*…literally de-creamed milk."

She laughed. "That makes sense."

Roque went to the counter and placed their orders, while she found a seat in the far corner. With cozy upholstered armchairs flanking a wood-topped table, the place had the feeling of a living room, where friends met to talk.

Not that she and Roque were friends, or ever would be anything more than acquaintances. He was in charge of...yes, babysitting her—until she, Lara and Peter were done with this three months. And with how slow this second day was going it might seem like forever by the end of her stay.

Dropping into her seat with a sigh, she studied her surroundings. The coffee shop overlooked the lower level of the hospital, where people were busy coming and going, including a group of medical students in white lab coats. Someone was in front of them, explaining the accoutrements of the hospital. There was another couple seated at a neighboring table. By the tiny touches and long, sultry looks, they were a pair. The sight made her heart cramp.

Amy's last relationship had left her wary of investing anything of value—like her heart. And she certainly wasn't going to start something she couldn't finish while she was in São Paulo.

Which is why she'd thought about just having a quick, casual bout of sex.

Bout? She made it sound like an illness, not something sexy and fun.

Roque came back to the table with an espresso cup, a shot glass with some kind of clear liquid and her taller latte. *"Café com leite desnatada e baunilha."* There were also two wrapped pieces of biscotti on the plate.

Wow, he could even make coffee sound sensual. She touched a finger to the shot glass. "What is this?"

"Seltzer water. It clears the palate and helps the flavor of the coffee come through."

Okay, she'd definitely heard of seltzer water, but had never actually seen anyone use it for that.

He passed her drink over, along with the wrapped biscotti, and sat in one of the other seats, leaning his cane against the wall behind him.

"Sometimes you use that and sometimes you don't," she said, mentally kicking herself for bringing it up again.

"My leg gets tired and cramps up. After the break in my femur was repaired, the leg developed an infection, so I lost some of the muscle. It doesn't bother me all that much, but it's either use the cane or fall on my face from time to time."

"Sorry, I don't know why I keep asking about it. It's none of my business."

"You're curious. It's natural." One side of his mouth tilted at a crazy angle. "Believe me. I will not have a problem with telling you if you step over a line."

Like the question about his fiancée that kept buzzing around her head like a pesky mosquito? What kind of woman would Roque be attracted to? Oh, Lord, she was not about to ask about her. She didn't want to know anything about their relationship, or why it had failed. She was pretty sure he would pull her up short if she even mentioned it.

She took a sip of her coffee and focused on the flavor instead. It was mellow with low rich tones that blended perfectly with the milk and vanilla. "Oh, this is good."

Maybe it was the presentation—the glass showing the color to perfection…and that thick layer of foam on the top. Whatever it was, it tasted so much better than what she could buy in coffee shops back home. Or maybe it was just the fact that she was actually drinking coffee in Brazil. Brazil! It had been one of her dreams for a very long time.

"You have something…" One of his long fingers touched the left side of his upper lip. *"Espuma."*

Sponge? Oh! Foam—from the milk. She touched her tongue to the area and swept it back and forth a couple of times. "Gone?"

His gaze slowly tracked back up, and he took a visible swallow. Their eyes met. Held. They stayed that way for a long, long minute before he said, "Yes. It is gone." His voice had an odd timbre to it, sounding almost…wistful.

No. Not wistful. He didn't seem like the type of man to engage in…well, fluff.

He did have a cat, though, which she hadn't expected, either.

Roque unwrapped his biscotti and took a bite, watching her as she took another sip. This time she was a little more careful with the frothy top layer. "Do you have more surgeries today?"

"Later. I need to check in on my *moto* patient and the Achilles patient first. You're welcome to tag along if you'd like." He drank the rest of the contents of his demitasse cup.

One of his patients today had died, from what he'd implied. He had to be emotionally exhausted. Not wanting to add anything onto him, she shook her head. "I think I'll do a little exploring of the hospital, if that's okay. I can meet you at noon, when Lara and Peter arrive. Where do you want to meet?"

"How about right here." He glanced at his watch. "I'll see my patients, and then I might have that kitty-nap you talked about."

She smiled. And for the first time it felt real and unselfconscious. He was trying to use new words and not worrying about whether they were right or wrong, so maybe she should get off her high horse and be a little more adventurous. She blinked. In the language department, of course.

"I think you mean *cat*nap."

"Kitty-nap does not mean the same thing?"

"No, it doesn't mean anything, really. And I do think you should take some time to rest. You look…" Tired. That's what she'd been going to say. Not gorgeous. Not dreamy. Or any of the other crazy adjectives that were now crawling around the dark spaces of her skull.

"I look…?"

He tilted his head and regarded her as if maybe reading her mind. *Ack!* Time to think of something really unflattering.

"Kind of wrung-out."

His head stayed tilted, but now a frown appeared

between his brows. He didn't understand what she meant.

"It means very tired. Exhausted."

"Ah, yes. I do feel a little tired." His glance dropped back to her lips before he suddenly climbed to his feet. "You will be okay on your own?"

Maybe she should have felt insulted that he would ask her that. But she was in a different culture and she knew it. And actually, she appreciated his concern.

And the fact that he'd just been looking at her mouth again? She wasn't going to check for foam. Not this time. Because it would just dig her in deeper. She needed to be by herself for a little while so she could regain her composure, which was being tested to the limit right now.

"I'll be fine, thank you. I have an uncle in São Paulo. I'd like to see if I can find him. I'm hoping he's still at the old address I have for him."

"Would you like help tracking him down?"

She would actually. She had no idea how to go about it, other than go to his last known address. But to just show up at the door? "Maybe. When you have time. I'm more worried about the language barrier than anything."

"I do not think it will be much of a barrier. But I will be happy to go with you, if you'd like."

She hadn't expected that. But the relief that went through her was so great that it was a struggle not to let it show. "Yes. I would like that. Thank you so much!"

He gathered their cups and saucers and started to

turn toward the counter when he took a wrong step and very nearly tumbled. Her latte glass fell and shattered on the tile floor below.

"Maldito!"

Compassion poured through her, pushing aside her relief and everything else. "It's okay, hand me the other things and I'll get it." She took them out of his hands and went down on her haunches.

He made no move to kneel down to help pick up the big shards of glass, and she realized he either couldn't or he was worried that he might not be able to get up without help. And for someone like Roque, that thought was probably unbearable. He'd said he used his cane when his leg got tired. Well, if he was exhausted, that affected muscle was probably giving him fits.

The barista came over with a broom and dustpan. She murmured to let her get it and in short order had everything swept and tidy once again, taking the rest of their plates and cups and carrying everything over to the bar.

"I'm sorry."

"You don't have to be, Roque. I could have just as easily dropped them myself."

"But you didn't."

She touched his hand. "We've all been there."

"Have you?" This time there was a touch of anger in his voice. He thought she was patronizing him. But she wasn't. Yes, he had a permanent disability, but that didn't make him any less valuable than the next person. Hadn't she almost tripped over her dress at the welcoming party? More than once?

"Yes. I've dropped things for no good reason. Fallen while jogging. Slipped in the shower. All kinds of things. You're human." She forced a smile, maybe to keep the moisture that had gathered at the back of her eyeballs from moving toward the front. "Even if you don't want to believe it."

In a move that shocked her, his hand turned, capturing hers in his warm grip for several long seconds. Her heart picked up its pace until it was almost pounding in her ears.

"Of being human, I have no doubts. But thank you."

"You're very welcome. Now go get some rest. I'll see you at noon."

He let go and gave a quick nod, reaching for his cane. "I will. If you have any questions, just stop and ask someone. Our staff is always happy to help."

She'd noticed that from the time she'd arrived. But not just the hospital. Brazilians in general were a very friendly people. "I will, thank you."

With that, Roque turned and started to make his way across the coffee shop. Only this time, instead of every four or five steps, his cane hit the floor each time he bore weight on his left leg. It really was hurting him.

Damn, maybe she really should suggest he get some PT done. Or at least a deep tissue massage to give that damaged muscle a way to recuperate some energy.

What was the worst he could say?

That she'd crossed over that invisible line.

Even if he knew she could offer him some relief?

She had a feeling it wasn't just about the pain, or whatever else he was experiencing. It was about his pride. Something that Amy was all too aware of. She could remember people wanting to help her after her mom passed away and waving them off like it was no big deal. Like people lost their moms every single day. Even as she felt like she was dying inside.

So maybe she would just have to somehow make him think it was his idea.

Really? She didn't think the man was going to come over to her and say, *Hey, could you bring those magic hands over here?*

Ha! No, he wouldn't say it in those words. At all. Because it sounded like too much of a come-on.

Besides, he'd already tried the physical therapy route, he'd said.

Yes, maybe he had. But how long ago was that? There were always new ways of doing things. Probably ways he hadn't tried, depending on how long ago the injury had occurred.

Well, that was something she could think about later. When she had a little space to breathe. Being around him was a lot more disconcerting than it should be, and Amy had no idea why.

But maybe she'd better sit down and try to figure out what it was about him that was putting her off balance, before she spent too many sleepless nights.

Because the sooner she understood why he was affecting her the way he did, the better it would be for her. And for him.

CHAPTER FOUR

Roque punched his pillow one more time, then dropped back onto it, propping his hands behind his head. He still couldn't figure out why he'd offered to go to Amy's uncle's house with her.

He'd analyzed every possible "why" over the last two days and had marked them off one by one: first explanation, she didn't know the language. Oh, yes, she did. Enough to understand almost everything that was said to her. Second possibility, he worried about her going out alone in some areas of the city. This was true to some extent, except they had the summer lecture program every year, and he had never felt the need to babysit anyone that came through the program. Third, those damned pink briefs that had been hanging out of the suitcase at her apartment. He leaped quickly over that possibility and headed straight for reason number four: there was an uncertainty about her that pulled at his gut. And this was the heart of the matter and something that had kept him up until well after midnight tonight, despite his killer of a day.

Maybe she would decide not to go and let him off the hook. Or maybe she would go without him.

He shut his eyes. Despite the awkward awareness that refused to die, and as much as he might regret offering—and even after all his tossing and turning, he wasn't sure he did—he did want to help her. At least in this one thing.

There. That was the solution. It was one outing. One good deed out of several years' worth of participating in this program. And anyway, she was nothing like the physical therapist that had made a pass at him in those early years of therapy. As long as she didn't offer to treat him, he was fine.

With that settled, Roque finally rested fully against his pillow, realizing for the first time how tense he'd been. He mentally visited each muscle group, limb by limb, and consciously forced them to relax.

He sucked in a deep breath and blew it out, allowing the darkness of the room to seep into him, doing his best to will his subconscious to do the same. Maybe then he could finally get a few hours of sleep, before the new day found him.

Three days down, eighty-seven days to go.

Oh, Lord. That was a lot of days. Amy rotated her neck and tried to work the odd kink out of it. At least things hadn't been too bad yesterday after Roque had met up with the rest of their little group.

She came in through the double doors at the front of the hospital and showed her ID to the guard stationed by the gate.

At his nod, she passed through it, heading toward the elevators and seeing several people were already there.

Oh! Krysta was waving her over. And there was Flávia. She reached them. "I think I'm having a case of déjà vu. Only I wasn't this tired at the welcome party."

"We were just talking about how fast-paced everything is here in São Paulo."

"Did you already do your seminars?" Krysta and Flávia were scheduled to speak on their respective areas. "I haven't even looked at the lineup yet."

"No." Both women answered at once and they laughed. Krysta glanced at the elevator panel that sat out front. "Which floor are you headed to?"

"Fourth. I'm meeting Roque Cardoza."

"Is he the one you were sitting by at the party?"

"Yep. He's in charge of me for the next couple of weeks. I have to do anything he says, evidently."

Both women's heads swiveled toward her, and she realized they'd taken that the wrong way. "I mean related to the job."

"Com certeza. Só o trabalho." Flávia's voice had a touch of mirth in it. "It's not like he's hard to look at. If that's your thing."

A flame seemed to lick up Amy's face and ignite her cheeks. "You guys… I don't think of him like that at all. Besides, he's really *not* all that good-looking."

Liar.

Ping!

"Looks like that's your elevator," Flávia said. "And here's mine. See you both soon."

Seconds later Amy slid into the elevator, just as Roque showed up behind her, his cane draped over his arm today. When she glanced up, she caught a half smile on his lips. Oh, no. Surely he hadn't heard what they'd been talking about. Her face sizzled in mortification. "How are you?"

"I guess it depends on what part of me you're talking about?"

He had! He'd overheard them. "You… Were you standing behind us?"

"Only long enough to hear how not attractive you find me."

If she thought her face had been hot before, it was now an inferno. One she wished would consume her and turn her into a pile of ash.

But there was no way she would be that lucky. "Sorry. I didn't know what else to say." And thank heavens she hadn't sat there and gushed over him or worse.

"I'm glad, actually, that you don't think of me like that, because it could complicate things while you're here. It's much better to stick to the business at hand."

Something she was having a difficult time doing, although she wasn't sure why.

"Of course. I wouldn't want it any other way."

"So, the team is already upstairs waiting on us."

The rest of the ride was spent talking about cases and how her physical therapy would be used over the next several weeks. A little thrill of excitement went through her that had nothing to do with Roque, this time. At least, she hoped it didn't.

"I actually have an old friend who will be at the hospital shortly," he said. "He is going to have his mandible rebuilt after cancer surgery. He'll be looking to do physical therapy afterward, and I'd like you to handle the case."

"Me?" The elevator doors opened.

"Yes. He's had a hard go of it, and our physical therapy staff is stretched thin after a couple of therapists transferred to another hospital. His wife is English, and he has an excellent grasp of the language."

He'd mentioned kind of inheriting her because of how busy things were in the PT department.

"I'll help however I can, of course." She thought for a second. "How much of his jaw was removed?"

"Enough to make it a challenge to reconstruct it. But Krysta Simpson is more than up to the challenge, from what I understand. Our own Dr. Francisco Carvalho will be working with her on this—you'll probably meet him at some point in time. There was a bit of a glitch, but hopefully that's been ironed out."

"Glitch?"

"One of our senior oncologists wanted to take over the case, but that was pretty quickly squashed by all involved, as well as by the hospital administrator. Paulista isn't without its own share of…how do you put it? Drama?"

Flávia's comment about a snake that walked on two legs came back to her. But she wasn't sure of the man's name, so it probably wouldn't be good to ask. "Anything I should steer clear of?"

"I wouldn't think so…but if for some reason a doctor you don't know stops by once the patient starts doing physical therapy, I would appreciate a quick text or call. It's not that he'll do anything wrong, I just don't want Enzo put through anything more than he's already endured."

"Of course, I completely understand."

He nodded off toward the waiting area. "There they are, shall we?"

Today, Roque's steps were firm and sure, and her thoughts of trying to talk him into a massage or a little additional PT flew out the window. Maybe it really was only when he was tired. But watching him carefully, she thought she saw a hint of a limp, still, but it was small enough that she could have been mistaken.

He glanced back. "Coming?"

Lordy. She'd been standing staring at him as he walked. She hurried to catch up, then greeted Peter and Lara, and set out to put her mind completely on work.

She didn't think he was all that good-looking?

It shouldn't have stung, but after being up half the night thinking about her, Roque's head kept replaying the words she'd said to her friends. And hell if it didn't bother him. Maybe because he thought the woman was gorgeous with a capital G. And her smile…

Damn.

Maybe he just didn't "do it for her," or worse,

maybe it was his leg. His ex had certainly changed her tune as soon as she found out he'd never play *futebol* again. She hadn't been able to get out of that hospital room quickly enough, even though she'd said it was because she needed to go and get some clean clothes, so she could stay in the room with him. Only she hadn't stayed. She'd come back for a few more visits. But once he got home, she said she wanted to give him space to recover.

She evidently needed her space as well...for something else entirely. Because not long afterward she'd broken it off, saying she was sorry but she'd fallen in love with someone else—that it had happened before he was injured. She wouldn't tell him who it was.

But then the tabloids had picked up the story and shouted the news to the world: Halee Fonseca, queen of Brazil's telenovelas, had dumped former Chutegol player Roque Cardoza. She was in love with another player. And the "who" would have been laughable if it hadn't been Roque's best friend on the team.

It had been a crushing blow. But who could blame her? She was famous and must have wanted an equally famous spouse. The pair were happily married now with two children. And Carlos had moved up to Roque's spot on the team and was still successfully playing ball.

He shook his head clear of those thoughts. He hadn't thought about Halee in years and wasn't sure what had brought her back to mind. Maybe Amy's comment. One thing he knew, even if his ex came back and wanted to get back together, he'd turn her down. He was well and truly over her.

And if Amy came calling? Would he turn her down as well?

She wouldn't. He'd heard her himself. She didn't think he was all that attractive.

But if she did?

Caramba! She doesn't. Just leave it there, Cardoza!

"Roque?"

Amy had asked a question. One that he'd totally missed. "I'm sorry. Say it again?"

"I asked if your Achilles' tendon patient will come to Paulista for his physical therapy. I'd like to at least watch and see how things differ between here and the States."

"I think you'll find it doesn't differ all that much, which is part of the reason for the yearly lecture series. We study rehabilitation methods from all over the world, as I'm sure you have as well. We adapt the methods to work in our particular situation, but you'll find we're kind of an *amálgama* of all of the world's top hospitals."

And now he sounded defensive…or worse, arrogant, which wasn't what he meant at all. It had to have come from missing sleep last night. All he knew were that his muscles were tightening up all over again. Not a good thing for his damaged leg.

Peter hadn't said much of anything, and Lara's head was tilted as if puzzling through something, maybe sensing a little tension.

A little? Roque had been on edge ever since he stepped on that dress. Which reminded him. His mom had called this morning, saying the repairs on Amy's dress were done. She'd been determined to bring it to the hospital, even though he'd asked her just to drop it by the house. He was too hard to catch there, she'd said. Besides, she wanted to meet this woman whose dress he had.

Why was she so interested? And exactly why was he so uptight about that happening?

Was he afraid she would say something that would embarrass him? Well, his mom *had* dragged out his naked baby pictures and put them up on the big-screen television he'd bought her a year ago, thinking it was hilarious. Not so hilarious was the fact that she still wanted him married. With children. She hadn't exactly hounded him about it, but she brought it up enough to make him roll his eyes. And she'd hated Halee, so he guessed everything had worked out the way it was supposed to.

"I'm sure, which is part of the reason I wanted to come here so badly. It's one thing to read about surgical techniques. It's another thing to see them in person. Just like the beaches here in Brazil." Amy sighed. "I should have planned in some vacation time. But I didn't. So I'll have to squeeze a beach visit in during my working stay somehow."

Peter smiled. "My wife would slay me if I hadn't included her in some vacation time. Which beach are you thinking about?"

"Guarujá actually. It's only fifty miles away from the city and it sounds really beautiful."

"No." The word was out before Roque could stop himself. Everyone stared at him.

"Did I pronounce it wrong?" she asked.

Caramba. No, she hadn't pronounced it wrong. It sounded warm and husky coming out in those low tones of hers. That wasn't the problem. The problem was him…and that particular place.

"Guarujá is beautiful, but it has a reputation, especially this time of year." He suddenly knew what he was going to do. He was going to take his one good deed and make it two. Maybe then he wouldn't feel so awkward about intruding on her reunion with her uncle. He just needed to figure out how to suggest it.

Now she was frowning. "Reputation? It's a nice area, from what I read."

"It is, but…" He thought for a second. "There are quite a few wealthy individuals who live there, and that creates problems, just like it does everywhere. Guarujá can draw those who want to take from them."

Her face cleared. "Point taken. So where would you suggest?"

He glanced at Lara and Peter, deciding he didn't want either of them here for what he was about to suggest. "Would you two mind going on ahead? I left a list of patients I'd like you to look over at the nurses' desk."

Maybe he was wrong, but they both looked a bit relieved to be sent off. He hoped no one was getting the wrong idea about their relationship. Hell, *he* didn't want to get the wrong idea, so he needed to go about this carefully.

"If we can find out if your address is correct for your uncle, maybe we can combine that visit with a trip to Guarujá. How does that sound?"

Innocent enough. Even to his own ears. All he had to do was keep it that way.

"Are you sure? I hate to take any more of your time. You already had to make a trip to my apartment."

Yes, and the glimpse of those damned lacy undergarments still hadn't faded from his memory. Maybe he just needed to replace that memory with others that were less…volatile.

"I don't mind, unless you'd rather go with Lara and Peter."

She tilted her head as if thinking for a second or two. "Actually, your idea is a good one, and neither Lara nor Peter can help with translating for me. I really do appreciate your offering to help with that. Thank you."

"It's not a problem. We'll coordinate times and try to do it on my next scheduled day off."

It had been ages since he'd heard the crash of ocean waves or let the salty breeze flick along his limbs— things he'd learned to love as a child growing up in Rio's Barra da Tijuca. He'd missed making weekly treks to the beach.

That had to be why he was suddenly looking forward to the thought of spending the day with her. Maybe a little too much. But it was too late to retract the offer now. And he found he didn't want to. Besides, it wasn't like anything would happen. She wasn't even attracted to him from what he'd overheard her saying.

"Can you surf in Guarujá? I'd really love to try surfing in Brazil one day," Amy said, eyes shining in a way that made his gut shift sideways.

"Do you surf?" He tried to keep the surprise out of his voice. Of course she did. She was from Florida.

"A little. A friend taught me a few years ago, so I like to at least watch."

The image of Amy in a white bikini paddling out into the surf next to him flickered on a screen in his head. He blinked it away. He would not be paddling out with anyone, much less Amy, who was here for less than three months.

She was so different from Halee, who'd hated the ocean. The only way his ex had tolerated any bodies of water was if she was cruising down them on a yacht. They were such opposites he sometimes didn't know what they'd even seen in each other. Then again, he'd been a different person before the accident. Arrogant and far too sure of himself and his own immortality. A split-second collision on the field had taken care of that forever.

It seemed a lot of things had changed over the years. Including the type of woman he now found attractive?

His gaze collided with hers for a moment, before she smiled. "A day on the beach does sound fun."

It did actually. Roque couldn't remember the last

time he took a day just to enjoy one of São Paulo's famous beaches. It had been a year or two.

"Great." It would also be nice to see his country through the eyes of a tourist. And hopefully it would help her as well. He took his phone out and scrolled through his work agenda. He didn't tend to take very many days off, so there were surgeries scattered through almost every day for the next several weeks, but he finally found an opening. "How about three weeks from Friday? I'll drive us out, rather than taking the bus."

"Should I bring a suit?" Amy asked.

"That's up to you, if you want to go in." Hell, he really hoped Amy would decide against that. He didn't need to go from imagining her wearing skimpy underthings to actually seeing her in swimwear, skimpy or not, although he had no idea why he was so leery of it. There were beautiful women everywhere in his country.

Just then the elevator doors opened. He glanced up and almost groaned aloud. It was his mom. And she was carrying a dry cleaner's bag. Inside of it, the teal color of Amy's long dress was clearly visible.

Amy also turned to look and her face quickly turned pink. Yep. Not the best scenario. And worse, his mother was striding toward them like a miniature powerhouse.

"I could have picked it up," Amy murmured to him.

"Yes, I told her that as well. But my *mamãe* does not always listen."

"*Roquinho, graças a Deus.* You are hard to locate in this place."

Roquinho? Really, Mother?

The diminutive form of his name meant Little Roque, and was one of her favorite ways to address him. It could be cute on occasion, but today wasn't one of those times.

"You could have had me paged. Or texted me."

"Oh, yes. I keep forgetting."

Her eyes zeroed in on Amy with a precision that would have made a surgeon proud. Any surgeon, except him. It brought back memories of their conversation about him meeting someone. The muscles in his gut tensed.

"This is her? The woman whose dress you almost ruined? Oh, the Fates…"

The way she said that made him close his eyes for a second or two. "Yes. Amy, this is my mother, Claudia Cardoza. Mom, this is Amy Woodell. She's here for the lecture series."

"Oh, yes, I know all about that."

Why did every word that came out of her mouth sound like she was concocting something? Something he knew he wouldn't like.

His mother handed him the dress and went up to Amy and put her hands on her shoulders, before pulling her close to deliver a resounding kiss on the cheek in true São Paulo fashion. In Rio it was customary to plant a kiss on both cheeks rather than just one, but in Brazil, people learned to adapt to where they were.

"It is very nice to kiss you, Amy."

Roque cringed at the misused English word. Especially since he'd had a thought or two about that recently himself.

"You mean nice to *meet* her, Mom."

His mom laughed and shrugged. While her English wasn't the best, her strong desire to be hospitable overrode her embarrassment over mistakes. Most people found it charming.

So did he. Usually.

Amy spoke up. "Thank you for fixing my dress, Senhora Cardoza."

She said it in slow Portuguese that was perfect, if a little formal. His mom's eyes went wide and she threw him a nod that had a world of meaning to it.

Diabos! His mom's dislike of Halee had shown in her attitude and actions. And one of the biggest problems with his mother was that her emotions flashed across her face like a strobe light in a pitch-black room. She liked Amy. And, looking back, he could see how she had probably been right about his former fiancée, but that didn't mean she was right now. It was one of the reasons he'd never introduced her to any of his dates, although none of those had been anything more than casual dinners.

He liked his life the way it was. No entanglements. No demands on his time. A night here and there he could afford, but a lifetime of commitment? Nope. Not again. He'd been ready to marry Halee, until the accident happened and she dumped him. Maybe the next woman wouldn't have dumped him, but...

Gato escaldado tem medo de água fria.

Once bitten twice shy—wasn't that how they said it in English? In this case he liked the Portuguese version better.

"Roquinho said your, er, strap break? He step on it. Make it rip."

Amy smiled and replied in English. "It was an accident. Not a big deal. And thank you for fixing it. I would like to pay you for it."

His mom waved her hands. "No. No payment."

"But…"

"It is enough that Roque ask me for favor. He almost never ask. And now I ask favor in return. You come to dinner?"

"Dinner?"

"Yes. It would please me. Roque say your mother is from Brazil?"

"I, um…" Amy threw him a glance. "I would like that—if it is okay with Roque."

"Of course it is."

Great. His mom was suddenly making what should have been a small favor into something big and putting words in his mouth.

He fixed her with a look and responded in Portuguese, keeping his tone low. "Mamãe. Don't embarrass her."

All she did was smile and pat his cheek, making him roll his eyes, suddenly very glad that he'd sent Lara and Peter to the nurse's desk.

"Find out a time that is good for her. She needs to see something besides this hospital. She will meet your father as well."

Why the hell was that even necessary? She didn't need to meet his father. Or any other family members, for that matter. But this was one argument he wanted to have in private.

"I will ask, but no promises."

Amy's quick grin came and went. So she hadn't missed the exchange, despite it being in Portuguese. Perfect. So not only was he going to help her find her uncle and go to a beach with her. Now she would be dining at his mother's house. A house with that big-screen television and plenty of baby pictures.

But the last thing he wanted to do was talk about why that wasn't a good idea. Or have someone bring up how he'd very nearly defrocked her in front of two hundred people. Or why he'd had a vivid dream last night in which she hadn't quite caught the dress before it slid to her feet—revealing her wearing lacy pink briefs and nothing else. He'd woken up in a puddle of sweat and need that he couldn't quite shake.

So, no. The less he thought about that night at the gala or her apartment—or the consequences of them—the better for everyone involved. So he kissed his mom and thanked her and said they needed to get back to work. She took the hint, but the smile she sent Amy said that she wasn't about to forget about this meeting. Or the dinner invitation.

All he could do was give an inward groan and hope that his mom let the subject of Amy and her dress drop.

Dress drop. Damn. There it was again.

He tightened his grip on the dress's hanger and determined that this was one subject he was not going to revisit. Or at least he would set that as his current goal, and hope against hope that he could kick that ball right past the goalkeeper and into the net.

CHAPTER FIVE

"AMY WOODELL—THIS is Enzo Dos Santos and his wife, Lizbet."

Roque's dark eyes were on her as he made the introductions. More than three weeks had passed since his mom had appeared with her dress and the dinner invitation—which was scheduled to happen this evening after work.

The team had really started to sync, and Amy wasn't looking forward to being relegated to the physical therapy end of things, although she knew that was what had been planned all along.

Maybe *relegated* wasn't the right word for it, since Roque had told her about Enzo from the beginning. It seemed kind of funny to be meeting another person in his inner circle. First his mom—who'd given her a searching look that Amy hadn't quite been able to forget—and now his former coach. The man whose physical therapy she would be helping with once he had healed enough from his surgery.

"Nice to meet you both," she murmured.

Enzo's wife came forward and shook her hand,

saying how grateful she was that Amy would be helping her husband recover. "Roque speaks very highly of you."

He did? Amy glowed with pride to think that perhaps Roque had enjoyed working with her as much as she had enjoyed working with him. And tonight she had dinner with his parents and tomorrow they were supposed to go on what Roque had called their field trip.

A phone call to a man named Abel Rodrigo had turned out to indeed be her uncle. Unfortunately, the visit they'd planned to make to him before going to the beach was going to have to be postponed, since her uncle was currently out of town on business. Maybe it was for the best, since she was already stressed about dining with Roque's parents and spending tomorrow at the beach with him.

Something that put her in an uneasy state of excitement, every time she thought about it. A whole day alone with him. Just her and Roque. Most of the last three weeks had been spent with the team, which she'd been glad of. At least, that's what she kept telling herself. Even though there'd been those odd moments when she sensed him looking at her. And she'd certainly glanced at him. More than once.

Lord. She needed to stop this.

Dragging her mind back to the patient, she forced herself to concentrate on what they were saying.

There was a kindness to Lizbet's manner that warmed Amy's heart. Despite that, there was something else—a spark of sadness, maybe?—in her eyes.

Who could blame her? She and her husband had just gone through a terrible ordeal, one that wasn't over yet. Mr. Dos Santos owned one of the most famous football clubs in Rio. The same team Roque had once played for. He said they'd been friends for a very long time and it was obvious he cared for Enzo very much.

The man had almost lost his life to cancer. He'd certainly lost a good portion of his jaw. And now he was recovering from still more surgery. His lower mandible had been completely rebuilt. Enzo's jaws were immobilized at the moment, to allow the repairs to heal, so he had a whiteboard and marker to help him communicate. He was busy writing something and showing it to his wife.

She licked her lips, hesitating. "I, er, I don't know quite how to say this, but that doctor who tried to take over the surgery came to see Enzo again yesterday, under the guise of wanting to make sure he had everything he needed. Enzo doesn't care for him and would prefer he didn't have anything to do with his treatment."

Surely he wasn't talking about Dr. Carvalho. He was an excellent doctor from what she'd heard. "Which doctor was that?"

She handed the whiteboard back to her husband. "He introduced himself once, but he was kind of aggravating. He seems very concerned about Dr. Carvalho's involvement for no reason I can work out. After Enzo's recent difficulties…" Her voice trailed away. "I just don't want anything to set us back on a bad track. Things have been better since we've been in Brazil."

Enzo wrote something on his board and held it up.

She's worried. Felt I was depressed.

Amy could very well imagine he was. The man had been through a lot.

"I know who you're talking about," Roque said. "I'll see to it that he doesn't come see you again."

Wow. Roque could actually have another doctor banned from visiting a patient? Well, since Enzo was also his friend, it stood to reason that he would fight for him.

Was this who Roque meant when he said he wanted to be contacted if any doctor she didn't recognize tried to see Enzo? She was going to ask once they left the room.

Roque turned to her. "Amy, you've looked at Enzo's chart—do you want to give them an idea of how you'll go about physical therapy?"

"Sure." She went over the steps in her head. "First thing will be to pass your swallow test, which I don't anticipate you having any trouble doing."

Enzo nodded, writing something on his board. When he turned it toward her, the words were so unexpected they made her laugh.

If I don't cry, you're not doing your job.

"Well, I don't think I've ever had a patient that *wanted* me to make them cry before. But I assure you,

you'll at least feel like crying at some point. I'll work you hard, but as long as you know my motivation is to meet our agreed-upon goals, then we'll do fine." She touched his hand. "I promise, I have the best of intentions and want us to work as a team."

The man relaxed back against his pillows, nodding and giving her a weak thumbs-up sign.

She couldn't imagine how hard it was for this strong vibrant man to be laid up unable to work. Was that how Roque had felt after his injury?

She had no idea. What she did know, though, was that she was going to do her very best to get Enzo back on his feet and working again.

Roque smiled at his friends and said they'd let Enzo get some rest. She glanced at her phone. Almost four o'clock. They were supposed to be at Roque's parents' house at six.

A shiver went through her that she tried to suppress before he noticed it.

Walking through the door, she sucked down a quick breath and asked the first question that popped to her head. "Who was the doctor you were talking about? The one they don't want involved in Enzo's treatment? Do I need to know his name?"

He looked at her, dark eyes inscrutable, a lock of hair tumbling over his forehead before he dragged it back in place with a flick of his fingers. "Let's head to my office."

Walking down a hallway, she felt her belly tighten. In the time she'd been in Brazil she'd never been back to Roque's office. There'd never been any reason to.

But it wasn't like he wanted to blurt a name out in the open where someone might overhear them. He reached a door with a placard listing his name and credentials. Pushing through it and motioning her inside, he closed it behind them. "Have a seat."

His voice had suddenly gone formal and cool. Or maybe that her imagination. Had she been wrong to ask him who the doctor was? But it wasn't blind curiosity. She wanted to be on guard if someone tried to upset her patient during physical therapy.

Her legs were suddenly a bit wobbly and she was glad to sit. Roque didn't go behind his desk; instead he leaned a hip on it. "Silvio Delgado."

"Sorry?"

"That's the doctor's name. I don't want him anywhere near Enzo. He tried to take the case from Dr. Simpson. Let's just say he was prevented from doing so."

"By you?"

"In part, but also by Dr. Carvalho and the administration. I won't go into the reasons for Delgado not being allowed near him. We'll just leave it at the fact that our patient doesn't like or trust him."

Our patient.

Had he actually said that? A feeling of warmth crashed over her, coursing through her veins and making her heart beat a little bit faster.

"I understand. Can you tell me what he looks like?"

One side of Roque's mouth went up in that devastating grin of his, making her mouth go completely dry.

"Let's just say you'll know who he is before you actually see him."

Why? Did he smell bad? Was he loud?

Ah, that was it. He was probably insufferable.

She was more and more sure that this was the snake that Flávia had been talking about during the welcome party. She'd meant to ask her who it was, but then figured it didn't really have anything to do with her, so she just forgot about it. Until now.

"Okay."

She relaxed back into the leather chair, amazed at how comfortable it was. Actually, his whole office had a welcoming feel to it, which surprised her. She hadn't thought of Roque as a welcoming kind of guy, although that image was slowly shifting the more she got to know him. He was kind of dark with an intense, mesmerizing charm that she didn't quite understand. But she also caught glimpses of warmth in those dark eyes. Like a cup of cocoa that you wanted to savor for as long as possible.

And…making comparisons like that was not very smart. Even though he looked like heaven on earth perched over her like that.

"Okay, so I'll alert you if he shows up."

"Yes. Do." He paused. "And we need to talk about tonight. I don't want you to feel pressured into going."

"I don't, but if we need to postpone it I understand."

"No, I just wanted to give you a—how do you say it?—an out."

She sat up. "I'm not looking for an out. Unless you'd rather I not come."

"My *mamãe* can be rather direct with her requests."

"Kind of like her son?" He'd been pretty direct about not wanting her to go to the beach on her own.

There went that grin again. "You think I'm direct?"

"Aren't you?"

"Maybe." He tilted his head. "But only when speaking from one doctor to another."

He'd evidently misunderstood what she was talking about. "I'm not a doctor."

"No. But I have a feeling you will be. Someday. Why did you never pursue your doctorate in physical therapy?"

That was a hard question. Her mom had been on her own for a very long time, and had helped Amy as much as she could during her years in college. Amy hadn't thought it fair that she continue her studies on her mom's dime.

"It's complicated. But I'm thinking of going back to school to get it once I get home. There are just never enough hours in a day."

"I know that feeling. Okay. So, tonight is set. And about tomorrow. Are you still wishing to go?"

Wishing? Probably more than she should.

"I am, if it's okay with you. Although I really don't mind going by myself, if you have too many things you need to take care of."

"No. I said I would take you, and I try to always keep my word."

Making it sound like he wasn't looking forward to it at all. And how did she feel about going with him without the side trip to her uncle's house?

Excited. And that scared her. Weeks were starting to fly by, and that wild, sexy fling she'd envisioned having with some man while she was here hadn't happened. There wasn't even a single prospect. By the time she finished work each day, she was too tired to feel lonely. And going to a bar by herself looking for a likely prospect seemed kind of pitiful and not very safe. Here or in the United States. There was always Krysta and Flávia, except she'd heard the venom specialist was traveling back and forth to the Atlantic Forest region of Brazil, and she'd only seen Krysta in passing, although she had suggested the pair of them meet up for a dinner or a shopping trip sometime.

"Do you want to surf or swim tomorrow?"

He'd said taking a suit was up to her, but she'd already decided against it. And there was a tension in his voice that said she'd made the right choice.

"I think I'd just like to sightsee this time, if that's okay." She was already in a state about going with him. She didn't need to throw a bathing suit and water into the mix. And although water could conceal a whole lot of what happened below its surface, if she were going to have that fling, she'd rather it be in complete privacy.

Was she actually considering Roque for the position?

No, of course not, although Roque hadn't mentioned a girlfriend, and the blonde from the soiree had never reappeared.

"That's fine. We can see more that way. We'll just walk on the sand."

She smiled. A walk on the beach with him sounded very, very nice. Too nice, in fact. "I don't want to fill your car with the stuff."

"It's seen worse." He shifted his cane, pushing it a little to the left. "How do you feel speaking in Portuguese when it's just you and me?"

Just you and me.

Her toes tingled at the sound of that, the sensation spreading up her calves and tickling her thighs. She loved hearing him speak in his native tongue. Maybe a little too much. "I—I'm not the best at it, but I can try."

Great. Now she was stammering, even in English.

"I think it would be an asset for your work. You said you live in South Florida. Isn't there a large community of Brazilians there?"

There was. She'd had a couple of patients who were Brazilians actually, and Amy had practiced tae kwon do at her local *dojang* with a Brazilian instructor. Marcos had sent a couple of people injured at tournaments to physical therapy and had offered to "hire" her if she ever needed a little extra work. She'd gotten the feeling that the interest went beyond pupil/ instructor relationship, but she hadn't wanted things to get messy and ruin their professional relationship.

And she'd been pretty wary of getting involved with men back then.

Maybe she should remember that decision and treat her relationship with Roque the same way. If she were smart, she'd call off the beach trip. And dinner with his folks. Except she wanted to go to both. More than she should. But she was only here in Brazil for a couple more months, so how messy could it get in that period of time?

Pretty damned messy, if she wasn't careful.

But right now it wasn't, and he wanted to start speaking in Portuguese.

She swallowed.

"You're right. There is a large population of Brazilians there. So I probably should practice."

"We can start by using the language on our beach trip, and I will correct you when you make a mistake. How's that? It will also make you look less like a tourist if we're not speaking English."

Ah, now she got the reason for it. It would make them less of a target for thieves while at Guarujá. "That makes sense."

It would be awkward, since she "knew" Roque in English. Speaking Portuguese with him would seem intimate, even though she knew he didn't mean it that way.

And she knew her mom in two languages, so how was that any different? Maybe it wasn't, except Amy had never been required to respond in Portuguese. She'd just needed to understand what was said.

"I see worry on your face. Don't be scared. I think

it will become easier with practice. And you'll find I am a very forgiving coach."

She bit her lip as the tingling spread to places far higher than her calves.

The image of him "coaching" her in hoarse tones as they practiced things other than Portuguese trickled through her subconscious, becoming a torrent as each mental picture became more explicit than the last.

Oh, God. Time to move this conversation to something else.

"Speaking of coaches. Do you miss playing football?"

Ugh! "Something else" did *not* mean reminding him of a time in his life that was probably painful.

"Or shouldn't I ask?"

"It's okay." His fingers, as if on automatic pilot, found his cane and fingered the handle. "Yes, I miss some things about it. But not others. I miss having a leg that is whole more than I miss the game."

Whole? Did he really think that?

"Your leg *is* whole. It's just a different kind of whole. It's a part of what makes you…you."

"A different kind of whole? I'm not sure I agree with that. I live in this body, I know what it feels."

From her Google search—and yes, she was ashamed to admit that she'd done more of her share of reading up on him—he'd been very good at what he did. Had been one of his team's top players, in fact.

"It's just your normal. People are not cookie cutter

shapes. Everyone has their own strengths and weaknesses."

"Cookie cutter."

"It means people are not exactly alike."

He smiled, and the act warmed any chilliness that had gathered in his expression. "No. People are not just alike. And that is a good thing, I think."

"Yes, it is." Roque was like no one she'd ever met.

His hand had moved away from his cane and was now gripping the edge of his desk beside his left thigh.

A very strong-looking thigh.

She struggled to think of something to say that would stop her train of thought, which was starting to barrel into dangerous territory. "I heard Peter mention missing his wife and kids today."

"It is natural. You don't have someone at home that you miss?"

The sad thing was, she didn't. She had no serious relationship; she wasn't even dating. And although she had friends at the hospital and at the rehab center, she didn't hang out with them as much as she might expect. Many of them were married with families and, like Peter, all they wanted to do was get home to them. More and more, she'd been thinking of what Roque had said about getting her doctorate. She'd put it off as something to do later. But what if later never came and she looked back with regret. Maybe it was a time to make a promise to herself.

"No one special, but that's okay. Especially since

I'm going to apply for the doctorate program as soon as I get home."

And just like that, the decision she'd been toying with for some time was made.

The hand that had been gripping his desk relaxed a little. Was he worried that she might be interested in him…in staying because of him?

The brakes on that train screeched as she applied them hard, the engine struggling to stop, the boxcars she'd added over the last couple of weeks piling up behind it.

"I'm glad you are. The Achilles' tendon patient liked what you had to say. And it would give you opportunities to teach at universities."

She'd thought the same thing. If she ever got to a place that she didn't have the strength she needed to manipulate patients the way they needed to be, it would give her options. And although she hadn't been intimately involved with that first patient's surgery she'd observed at Paulista, she had been at his appointments and observed his rehab. She was due to go again in a few days as a matter of fact.

"Yes, that's what I thought as well." She tilted her head. "When is Mr. Dos Santos going to start physical therapy?"

"In a couple of weeks. The repairs are stable and he's due for his swallow test tomorrow."

The day they'd be at the beach. "You don't want to be here for him? I'll understand if we have to put off our trip."

"His wife will be there, and I'll check on him when

we get back. I think the last thing Enzo wants are for twenty people to be gathered around to watch him. He's a pretty determined guy. I don't doubt he'll pass with flying colors, which is a good thing with where his mind has been lately. I know. I've been there."

Was he talking about what Enzo had written about his depression? Well, Roque had had a right to be depressed, if so. He'd been a brilliant young soccer player, and in the blink of an eye everything he'd worked so hard for had been taken from him.

"Sometimes things work out the way they should. You do brilliant work here at the hospital." She nodded at his left leg. "Would you be at Paulista if you hadn't been injured?"

"Probably not. I'm old enough now that my career would be pretty much over, and I'd probably be coaching or stuck at a desk job somewhere." He sighed. "That doesn't mean the road from there to here was easy. It took ten long years of school to become a doctor."

"No. I'm sure it wasn't. But where are you more needed at this point in your life?"

He laughed. "You have a way of turning things around to look at their best side."

"The dangers of being a physical therapist. We're trained to be positive and optimistic. It's a good way to motivate our patients."

"I think those characteristics come naturally to you."

Did they? She didn't always feel all that optimistic. She just needed to be "up" for her patients. Needed to be a motivator when they came in feeling life would never be the same, ever again.

The exact way Roque had probably felt when told his career as a football player was over. "Thanks, but I'm not sure that's true. It's just part of my job description. You mentioned being a coach. That never appealed to you?"

"No. I thought about it once or twice, but didn't see myself doing that. Not with my old team, anyway."

"It would have been too hard to watch them play while you felt sidelined?" The way he'd said the words gave her pause.

"That would have been hard, yes, but my reasons were more…personal."

Personal? He and the team's owner seemed to get along great; he'd even confided in Roque about that other oncologist, Dr. Delgardo. So she didn't see that "personal" reason arising there. But if he wanted her to know, he would tell her, so that was her signal to leave it alone.

Oh! Roque had been engaged to an actress, according to her search. Who was now married to a player on his former team. Of course he wouldn't want to see her day in and day out. That made perfect sense.

Her heart cramped. Surely it was better to know what a person was like before getting married to them. She could certainly thank her lucky stars now that her boyfriend had dumped her *before* marriage rather than after. Although she'd been gutted at the time.

"Things have a way of showing you a person's

true colors." In case he didn't know that expression, she added, "Of seeing them for who they really are. Like your accident. When your soccer days came to an end, it revealed who you really are."

"Interesting." His smile was slow and unbearably sexy. "And who am I...really?"

The ground had suddenly gotten shaky under her feet. Why had she said that? "You're a man who cares about his patients and his friends, and who likes to keep his word."

There! That was the least personal thing she could think of to say. And they were both true.

He got to his feet. "But you could say that about almost every doctor here at Paulista."

"But we're not talking about every doctor." She was suddenly having a hard time catching her breath. "We're talking about you."

Thinking he was ready to shoo her out of his office, she climbed to her feet as well. Big mistake. Because it set her right in front of him. Close enough to catch the warm musky scent of his aftershave. To see the slight dusting of stubble across his chin. And those lips that seemed to capture her attention time and time again...

Roque made no effort to move away. "So we were. So let's talk about you. Do you want to know how I see *you*?"

She wasn't sure she did, but it was as if her mouth was controlled by forces outside of her body. "Yes."

He touched a finger to her jawline. "I see a woman in a teal dress that's an inch or two too long for her.

A woman who didn't let that stop her from coming to the party." He'd switched to Portuguese, and she stood there transfixed by his touch and his voice as he continued. "I saw bits and pieces of you in that patient file you included in your application to the program. And the real you made me very glad I said yes to you being in the program."

He dropped his hand, but continued to meet her eyes. "You want what's best for your patients and those around you."

"I'm not as saintly as you make me sound."

"Aren't you?" His gaze trailed down her neck. "You're like a marble sculpture that stands in front of a church."

If he could read her thoughts right now, he might change his mind. Her pulse pounded in her head, mouth going dry as she stared back at him. "Sculptures aren't real. I assure you, I am flesh and blood. Just like you."

"Are you?" One hand slid into her hair and cupped her nape, his thumb just behind the tender skin of her ear. But that wasn't what made her take another step in his direction. That came from somewhere inside of her, from the part that wanted to know what it would be like to be kissed by him, to feel herself pressed against him. She could damn herself later, but for right now...

He looked into her eyes, maybe seeing the jumble of emotions boiling just under the surface. Then his head started a slow descent, until it was just her and him. And his lips on hers.

CHAPTER SIX

ROQUE HAD NEVER felt anything so sweet. Or so unde-
niably sexy. The second his mouth touched those silky
soft lips of hers, Amy's arms wound around his neck.

And it was heaven.

She'd said she was no saint. But neither was he.
He'd proven that time and time again when one date
didn't lead to another. But right here, right now, there
was nowhere else he'd rather be.

His tongue eased into her mouth and found a moist
heat that set his body on fire. One arm circled her
back, and he leaned his weight against his desk for
stability. The last thing he wanted to do right now
was fall. Or lose contact with her. And damn if she
somehow didn't wind up between his splayed legs
and pressed against the part of him that had dreamed
of this happening ever since he stepped on her dress
a month ago.

And now here he was.

Right where he shouldn't be, for so many reasons.

She was a visitor at his hospital. And she was only
here for three months.

Maybe it was the latter point that kept him in place.

Amy made a sound in her throat, her hips inching forward and back in a way she probably wasn't even aware of. But he was. He felt every little movement. A vision of his desk and her on it came to mind. That image lingered, toying with different angles and positions.

But before he could even think about turning them so that she was against the desk instead of him, the phone on his hip buzzed, the noise breaking into the silent struggle that was going on between them.

Amy froze for a second. Then she jerked back, her arms releasing their hold on him.

She kept moving until she was against the chair, and no doubt if that hadn't been there she would have kept going until she was out the door. One of her hands grabbed the armrest and the other pressed against her mouth.

Hell, what had he been thinking? He hadn't been.

When she finally spoke, she said, "I am so sorry. I don't know what… I have no idea why…"

He knew why. All too well. And it wasn't her fault, it was his. "Don't. I let things get out of hand. There's no excuse I can give."

"I was a willing participant. You would have known quickly enough if I hadn't been."

That made him laugh, despite the regret that was coursing through him at his behavior. "Really? What would you have done?"

"Put you on the ground."

"Ah, that's right. You know tae kwon do."

"I do. I have a first-degree black belt in it."

His eyes widened. "That shouldn't surprise me."

"But it does? Well, you can thank my mom. She's the one who insisted that I go for lessons. She wanted me to be able to defend myself."

"It sounds like you can."

Roque glanced at his watch, surprised to see it was almost five. "About dinner..."

"Let me guess. You don't want me to go now."

Something passed through her eyes. Like she was expecting him to cancel on her.

"No, I was going to ask if you needed to go home to change first, because we'll be cutting it close, if so."

What looked like relief passed through her eyes. "So you still want me to come?"

"Is there a reason I shouldn't?"

She smiled. "Evidently not. You're very good at compartmentalizing, you know that?"

"At what?"

"Putting everything into separate boxes in your mind."

He was actually. Partly the result of his accident and what had happened with Halee, and partly because of his job. "This is one thing I will not hide away in a box. That way I can make sure it won't happen again."

"I can help with that. Remember that whole 'on the ground' thing?" She let go of the arm of the chair as if having regained her composure.

His smile widened, relieved that she wasn't going to blow this all out of proportion.

"You would use some of your moves on me?" And just like that, Roque was back in a different frame of mind, going over that kiss blow by blow.

"You don't want to find out."

The problem was… He did. But if he was going to get through this dinner intact, he was going to have to keep his head. Because his mother was very, very shrewd. And the last thing he needed was for her to guess what he and Amy had been doing in this office.

Otherwise she'd be on the phone with her priest and reserving the church.

That wasn't going to happen.

If he could just remember that Amy was here for just a few months and that she had her heart set on earning her doctorate in the States, he would be fine.

He didn't want another relationship. And the last thing he wanted was to keep anyone from their dreams.

Claudia and Andre Cardoza welcomed her into the cookout area of their little getaway house with the same warmth his mom had displayed at the hospital.

"Thank you so much for inviting me."

They'd opted to host the meal outside of the crush of São Paulo, instead of at the family home. Roque said it was because his dad—a police officer—liked to get away from town on the weekends, whenever he could.

"We are glad Roque brought you." Andre was the

spitting image of his son, although his dark hair was peppered with gray. With a skewer loaded with some type of meat in one hand and a brick grill behind him, he looked totally in his element.

Unlike Roque, who seemed ill at ease. Well, that made two of them. She'd actually been surprised that he wanted her to come, and maybe it would have been easier if they'd canceled their plans, but Amy had truly liked Claudia and would have hated for her to go to the trouble of fixing her a meal only to have her not show up.

His mom brought her a bottle of water. "Please help yourself to anything. Dinner won't be long. Roque, why don't you show her around."

"Okay."

He grabbed a water for himself and motioned her to follow him. The walled-in compound was alive with flowers and greenery, and there were several hammocks scattered throughout the space. A clay-tiled building was to the left, and must be where they slept when they weren't outside. It was kind of like a cabin they might have back home in Florida. Without the sand.

"What's the Portuguese word for this kind of place again?"

"It's a *chácara*. Kind of like a country home. Only not."

He could say that again. When she thought of a country home, she thought of a white stucco home with a wraparound porch. This was more like a campground. One they had all to themselves. It was charming, and under other circumstances she might have found it heavenly.

Except she was hyperaware of every move Roque made. Of his broad shoulders and narrow waist and the way he had felt against her.

He'd been attracted to her, that much was obvious. She'd felt the very real evidence of that.

And despite her talk about compartmentalizing, it was not going to be easy to lock that particular memory into a box and keep it there.

But somehow she was going to have to do just that.

A fling? With Roque?

Just hours earlier, she'd entertained that exact thought. Until she realized just how deadly his kiss was to her senses.

"How long have your parents owned this?"

"Actually, this was passed down to them by my grandparents, who built it many years ago."

A pond nestled against one corner of the property, the greenery behind it camouflaging the protective wall that kept intruders out. "Does it have electricity?"

"It does now. It didn't originally." He grinned. "They also added plumbing a few years ago."

"I bet that makes life a lot more comfortable."

He motioned to one of the chairs that flanked the body of water. "When I was a kid, I didn't seem to think about what this place lacked. I just liked being with family."

Since the only family Amy had had around had been her mom and dad—her grandparents had passed away before she was born—it was a little hard to imagine family get-togethers that involved more than just the three of them. She sank into one of the wrought-iron chairs with a sigh. "It's beautiful. Serene."

And suddenly she was glad she'd come. This place might be the perfect bridge to transport her from her heightened emotional state to a place that was more tranquil. At least she could hope. The pond boasted a small rock waterfall that had to be powered by a pump, although she couldn't see it.

"Yes. My father's job is very difficult. This helps him put things into perspective. To realize that life is more than fighting drug lords in *favelas*."

Some of the slums of Brazil were known for being controlled by different gangs, going as far as limiting who entered and left the community. "I can't imagine how hard that must be."

"I grew up knowing that my father could go to work one day and never make it home. I think that's why the Chácara do Cardoza is so important to him. He's had offers on the property, but he always turns them down."

"You'll inherit this someday, then."

"I imagine."

There was something in his voice. "You don't want it?"

"At one time, I would have said no. But that was a long time ago." He stretched his leg in front of him, propping his cane against his thigh.

"Is it bothering you?"

"No."

The answer was curt, like it was whenever she asked about his leg. He didn't like talking about it. She could understand that. No one liked to admit to having a weakness.

"Sorry."

He tipped his head back so that it leaned against the high back of the chair, then turned to look at her. "It is I who am sorry. My leg is tired from the day, but it will be fine tomorrow."

For their trip to the beach. They would have a lot of walking, from what he'd said. But it would be better for his muscles than standing in one spot doing surgeries like he probably did day in and day out. She'd been tempted to back out of their trip, but she also didn't want Roque to know how much that kiss had affected her.

"What should I bring?"

"To the beach?" He paused. "Probably the same things you would take in Florida. Sunscreen, maybe a hat. Shoes that are easy to walk in and remove sand from."

"Okay. Do you want me to meet you somewhere?"

"I think it would be better if I picked you up in front of the Fonte Cristalina. Say at nine o'clock in the morning?"

It was already past eight, but Amy was in no hurry to get back to her apartment. Maybe because she knew that once that happened, she was going to dissect every single second of her time in his office and figure out how what had started out as a completely professional conversation had gone so totally off the rails.

"That sounds like a plan."

A half hour later, Amy was sitting outside at a large farmhouse-style table laughing at stories that Andre shared about some of his most embarrassing moments as a police officer. She was pretty sure he'd also experienced some awful moments as well. A couple of times Claudia had reached across and squeezed her hand, smiling at her and asking if Amy wanted this or that and encouraging her to eat another bite of the delicious grilled meat that was so common in Brazil.

"I'm very…*satisfeita*." One of her mother's favorite words surfaced without warning, and she swallowed hard, hoping no one realized she was choked with grief—a grief she thought she'd worked through.

Roque peered at her through the growing shadows. "Are you okay?"

"Yes. Just enjoying the evening."

And she was, much to her surprise. A little too much, maybe. That's probably where that little burst of emotion had come from. Thinking about how her mom would have loved sharing this moment with her.

But they'd had plenty of other happy times. And she treasured each of them.

Roque glanced at his watch. "Well, I know you and Dad are spending the night here, but I need to get Amy back to her apartment. It's been a long day."

Claudia stood up and came around and kissed her

son on the cheek and then turned to Amy and hugged her tight. *"Venha de novo, ta?"*

"I will. Thank you so much." As much as she appreciated Claudia's encouragement to return to visit, she very much doubted she would ever see Roque's parents again.

Hopefully her smile hid any sadness she might feel over that fact. But the reality was, these three months would soon be little more than a tiny moment in time. So she committed as much of this place and their faces as she could to memory.

And maybe one day she would be able to draw those memories back up and remember them with a smile that was a little more genuine than the one currently plastered to her face.

At least she hoped so.

CHAPTER SEVEN

WHY ON EARTH had she told him to meet her in front of her apartment complex? Or agreed to come with him at all? Was she crazy? She was already affected by him in ways she didn't want to think about, and now she was going to spend the day with him. Alone.

She'd gotten outside ten minutes early so he wouldn't have to wait, and in that short period of time several people had come out, commenting on her hat and the straw bag containing her sunscreen. She'd been able to repeat that she was going to the beach. One woman had asked if she wanted company! Which had gotten super awkward when she said she'd been invited by the doctor she was working with.

But it might have been more awkward if there were suddenly five people cramming into Roque's car.

Finally he arrived, and she jumped in and slammed her door, giving him the biggest brightest smile she could manage, hoping that he wouldn't guess how nervous she was. "Ready? Let's go."

He glanced at her with a frown. "What's the big rush?"

"Well, the explanations have been a little difficult."

"Why?"

The single word summed it up brilliantly. Why was it a problem? She was the one who was fumbling around and making it a bigger deal than it was. Somehow dinner with Roque's parents had been easier than this beach outing was proving to be, and she wasn't sure why. Maybe it was that whole thing of him wanting to speak Portuguese when they were alone. So far, she was not following that course, since the words pouring from her mouth were all in English.

"I don't know. I think it just feels…" She couldn't come up with the right word to save her life.

"After yesterday, do you mean?"

"Yes." As usual, he'd hit the nail on the head. If she could somehow stop overanalyzing every aspect of what had happened in his office, maybe she could put it all behind her.

"No one knows about that except us. So our outing will only appear strange to others, if we make it that way."

Which is exactly what she'd done. Maybe because she couldn't just hide her feelings the way others might. Even Roque kept his emotions tucked well out of sight. Except for yesterday.

But had that been due to an overflow of feelings? Or simply because they were a man and woman who were attracted to each other physically?

"You're right, of course. There's no reason to feel guilty. I'm just one of those people who ends up getting caught red-handed if I do something wrong."

"Well, our hands are not red, because no one saw us."

Amy laughed. "That's one way of putting it." She loved the way he used expressions with confidence even if he didn't quite understand the meaning.

With that he started the car and pulled away from the curb. "Are you looking forward to seeing Guarujá? If you brought a towel, we can sit on the beach for a while."

"Sounds great. Have you ever been to Caraguatatuba? Apparently there's a great surfing beach there? Do you know it?"

"Massaguaçu. The surf is not always consistent, but it can get busy at peak times of the year. If you decide to go surfing there, take a buddy."

It's not like she'd be in Brazil long enough to do that or had anyone to do it with. "I'll keep that in mind."

His fingers tightened on the wheel, and he turned to look at her. "Seriously. The riptides can be deadly."

"I won't go alone. I promise."

"Good."

An hour and a half later, they were in Guarujá, and Amy couldn't hold back a gasp. It was almost intimidating, with row after row of pristine condominiums. Nothing like the Chácara do Cardoza from last night.

Traffic was heavy, but not as bad as at the center of São Paulo, which many times saw bumper-to-bumper traffic and motorcycles that whizzed frantically between the rows of cars.

"Are you okay?"

"Yes, just didn't expect it to look like this honestly. There must be thousands of people living here."

Roque smiled. "Hundreds of thousands. And I was right."

"Right? About what?"

"I do like seeing this place through the eyes of a tourist."

So he hadn't brought anyone here during previous years' lecture programs? If what he said was true, it appeared not.

She couldn't stop a smile as a wave of warmth poured over her. "I'll try not to disappoint you."

"You have not disappointed, Amy. Believe me."

Something about the way he said that sent a shiver over her.

He's not talking about that kiss, Amy.

More likely he was talking about how she did her job at the hospital.

Roque found a paid parking garage and slid his car into the first available spot, taking his ticket and paying the attendant.

Scooping her beach bag from the back seat, she crossed the strap of her purse over her chest and kept the wicker tote containing her beach gear in her hand.

"Do you want me to carry something?"

She glanced at his hands, noting he'd brought nothing with him. "I'm good. It's not heavy. I just have a towel and sunscreen in there." She dropped her sunglasses over her nose to help cut the glare from the sun, which was already warm.

Skirting one of the large apartment blocks, they

arrived on a long sandy strip that led down to the water. On it was a sea of red striped umbrellas that stretched as far as the eye could see. "Wow, they're all dressed up for company, aren't they?"

"It's pretty impressive, I agree." He glanced at one of the nearby buildings. "Why don't you keep going, and I'll catch up with you in a minute."

She looked over at where his attention had gone, but saw nothing, so she did as he'd asked and started across the sand. She then took off her shoes and stuffed them into her bag, enjoying the warmth beneath her bare feet.

Less than a minute later, she felt a slight tug on her bag. The hair raised on the back of her neck when she sensed someone directly behind her.

Roque had been right.

When the bump happened again, she instinctively whirled around, hooking her foot around the calf of the pickpocket and yanked as hard as she could, sending him flying to the ground.

Only at the deep "oomph" did she realize her mistake.

Roque lay sprawled across the sand, his cane about three feet to his right. "Oh, God, I'm sorry. I thought someone was trying to steal something from my bag."

He propped himself up with his hands on the sand. "I guess you really can defend yourself."

"Of course I can. I already told you I know tae kwon do." She frowned. "Wait. What do you mean, I can defend myself? Were you *trying* get a reaction from me?"

"I thought I'd see how aware you were of your surroundings." He reached for his cane. "Very, evidently."

"It was pure instinct. Are you hurt? Your leg?"

Pushing off with his cane, he shook his head and tried to get to his feet, only to have his walking aid sink into the soft sand, leaving him stranded on the ground. "My pride is the only casualty, it seems."

She reached down to help him up, and he let her, managing to heft himself to his feet. "This feels like reversed roles. I did the same for you, when your dress was ripped and you couldn't get out of my car. Remember?"

Only too well. "Yes, well, at least you didn't step on my dress on purpose. Unlike me, who purposely tripped you."

He squeezed her hand for a minute before releasing it, leaning against her as he tried to get his cane situated. "But I did reach into your bag on purpose, just now, so you did the right thing."

He took a step, and the color suddenly drained from his face. He stopped in place.

"You *are* hurt. I am so, so sorry!"

"It's nothing." He reached down to massage his left thigh. "Just a muscle cramp. I get them sometimes when the nerves misfire."

She turned and faced him. This was her chance. "I can help with that."

"No, you can't."

There was a darkness to his voice that was at odds

with the reality of the situation. She actually could help. If he'd let her.

She took a deep breath and let it out in a controlled hiss, trying to keep herself from taking his refusal personally. "I can't make your injury go away, but I can help with the pain you have right now."

"I've tried it."

She tilted her head. "And it didn't help at all? I find that hard to believe. I can do a deep tissue massage that—"

"Absolutely not."

This time, she let the anger come to the forefront. "Are you kidding me? You said you liked how I treated Bobby Sellers, said it showed I could think outside of the box, and now you're acting like I have nothing to offer."

She'd lived through this hot and cold nonsense before and wasn't about to put up with it from him.

"I did not say that."

"Not in so many words, but you implied it. Please let me try. If it doesn't help, you've lost nothing. But if it does…"

"You won't always be here, Amy, so it's better if I don't get used to any—"

"Damn it! You're the one who told me Paulista is an amalgamation of all the best hospitals in the world. There are other therapists you could go to if it turns out this works. I let your mother fix my dress. Let me try to help your leg."

"What would you do?"

He leaned on the cane with both hands. It must

really hurt. She'd never seen him this vulnerable before. "I'll use essential oils in a carrier oil and massage them into your skin. The heat generated from my hands will help the oils absorb."

"And if it doesn't help? Will you then stop suggesting I seek therapy?"

She blinked. He was going to let her try? She'd somehow expected a bigger fight than that. While a part of her was relieved, another part was worried that maybe he knew something she didn't. Something that would prove her wrong. "Are you sure it's just a muscle cramp? Could you have landed wrong and damaged something else?" She'd hooked his right leg, not the injured one, but anything could have happened as he went down.

"It's not dislocated or broken, if that's what you mean. I recognize this pain. It's just muscle."

"Can you make it back to the car?"

"I can finish our tour." But when he tried to take another step, he winced and stopped again.

"No, you can't. Give me your cane."

"I don't think—"

She jerked it from beneath his hands and hooked it over her beach bag.

"What the hell, Amy?"

She moved to his affected side. "Put your arm around me."

"No."

"What's wrong, Roque? Scared? Of little ole me?"

"I am not scared."

He might not be, but she was now wondering about

the wisdom of asking him to touch her, even as an offer of help.

Surprisingly, he put his arm around her waist while she jammed her shoulder under his arm, and the second he did, a sense of rightness came over her, the warm solidness of his body fitting perfectly against hers. The side of her breast nestled against his chest in a way that made her nipples tighten at the slightest hint of friction. She held perfectly still and willed it away. It didn't work.

Oh, no. Not what she wanted. At all.

She hesitated, tearing her mind apart for some other way to get him to the car and coming up blank. Maybe this was why he hadn't wanted her helping him. Because he knew how he made her feel.

Not the time to be thinking about any of this, Amy.

"Let's go. Lean on me as we walk."

Slowly they made their way back to the sidewalk and soon all thoughts of how he made her body react vanished. Roque didn't make a sound, but when she glanced up at his face, his mouth was bracketed with white lines of pain. Why had she swept his leg out from under him?

Because she'd honestly thought someone was trying to steal something from her bag, and pure instinct had taken over. He said the pain was muscular. Well, she would know as soon as she laid her hands on his skin. Either the muscles would be knotted and hard or she'd realize something else was wrong.

Lord, she hoped he was right. She didn't think he'd

like having to postpone all his surgeries because of something as stupid as a case of mistaken identity.

Well, they would worry about that when the time came.

"Do you have your international driver's license?"

"Yes, do you need me to drive?"

He leaned more of his weight on her and another warning shimmy went through her stomach, bringing back all the uneasy sensations she thought she'd banished. Evidently not.

His skin was warm against her. So alive. So—

"Maybe. If you can drive a manual transmission."

He's hurt, Amy, why are you even thinking along these lines?

She responded carefully. "My car at home is actually a stick shift. We don't have quite this much traffic, though, except for when the snowbirds come to town."

"Snowbirds?"

"It's what we call people from the north when they come to Florida to get away from their winter weather."

"Country homes? Like what my parents have?"

She smiled. "Not quite, but maybe the same idea."

Fifteen minutes later, they made it to his car, and Amy helped him get inside, lifting his injured leg and sliding it onto the floor gently. The muscles of his calf were firm, no hint of atrophy from babying his leg. She drew in a deep breath. This was a man who would not baby anything. So if he was letting her do this…

He said something she didn't quite catch before muttering, "I feel like a...an...*idiota*."

That word came through in any language. "Stop it. And get ready to hang on." She then sent him a smile that she hoped was full of mischief. If she could distract him, maybe that would interfere with his body's pain receptors. She'd heard of it working.

"Maybe I should drive."

"If what I'm seeing on your face is any indication of your pain levels, then putting you behind the wheel would be even more dangerous than my mad car skills."

He leaned his head against the headrest. "I do not even want to know what 'mad car skills' means."

"Probably just as well. Okay, here we go."

She stowed her gear in the back and then climbed into the driver's seat, adjusting it to her shorter stature. Roque handed her the keys.

Getting the car started, she managed to back out of the slot and drive up the ramp that led out of the parking garage. "Anything I need to do?" Besides take note of every move the man made?

"No. I already included a tip when I paid."

"Do you have a GPS? If not, you'll have to give me some instructions on how to get to your place." One of her biggest failings was that if she wasn't driving, she didn't pay attention to the route when she was a passenger. She'd tried to correct that trait time and time again, but she either got caught up in the conversation or the scenery.

"I'll put it on my phone. You'll just basically take

the Immigrantes Highway all the way back to São Paulo."

"Sorry. That means nothing to me."

"Here." He pushed a button and a voice came out of the phone. It was in Portuguese, so it took a moment or two for Amy to adjust to the computer-generated speech. "Don't worry, I'll help. My leg feels better now that it's not having to support my weight."

Now that her insistence had gotten her what she wanted, she was starting to wonder how smart she'd been in making that offer. Except she was the one who'd caused his pain. The least she could do was try to fix it.

Her heart clenched and she knew she was in trouble with this man. Not that she was going to let herself fall in love with him. She'd meant it when she said she was going back to start her doctoral studies. She couldn't do that in Brazil.

And Roque's life was here. In Brazil. Wrapped up in his work and the life he was living. Just because she liked the way his body felt against hers changed nothing.

The fact that she did meant she'd have to be even more careful. That kiss had sent her senses spiraling toward treacherous territory. If his phone hadn't buzzed…

Yes. That phone. A lifesaver for sure.

There was no room in her life for the long leather sofa she'd seen in his office. And as she'd left the office, her eyes had somehow caught and taken note of the fact that there was a lock on the door.

All they'd have to do was turn the little latch and—
Ridiculous. She needed to stop this!

The GPS said something and she forced her mind back to her driving and getting them home. "Do you live in the same part of town as I do?"

"About five miles before you get there. It's a red-tiled building."

"Tell me when we're getting close, so I can start looking."

For the next twenty minutes or so, he sat in silence, eyes closed tight. She wasn't sure if he'd fallen asleep or if he was in so much pain that he was just trying to cope.

Suddenly he straightened up, glancing at her. "Not much farther."

"On this road?"

"Yes, two blocks ahead on your right. Condomínio Apollo. Just pull into the lower level garage. The numbers are painted on the spaces. I'm 601."

She found his building, and shifting the vehicle into a lower gear, she managed the sharp curving turn that led into what looked like a maze. But the numbers were laid out in order and she found his spot down another line of spaces to the left. Fortunately, most of the tenants were at work so she could navigate fairly easily. Otherwise she might have had to make a couple of three-point turns.

She glanced at him. "Any better at all?"

"I guess we'll find out." His jaw was tight, but that might be from anticipated pain rather than actual current pain.

"I'll come around and help." She put his keys in the pocket of her sundress, retrieved her purse and beach bag, in case she needed to catch a taxi back to her own apartment, and went around to the passenger side door. Opening it, she said, "Give me your hands."

"Let me have my cane, and I'll see if I can manage."

Without a word she got his walking stick, but instead of handing it to him she draped it over her arm. "Take. My. Hands."

"Amy…"

She got down on her haunches next to the lowslung car and looked him in the eye. "Trust me, Roque. Please. The less strain you put on those muscles right now, the more likely we'll be able to massage the knots out of them."

"Merde."

The swear word was so soft she almost missed it. Her heart ached for him in a way that it didn't for most of the cases she'd worked on. She'd learned early on that if she could harden that traitorous organ it was better for her patients, because she had to push them to help them heal. And it was often painful. She'd had strong, strapping men cry in her presence and had to promise she'd tell no one.

She stood and took his hands in hers and gave them a gentle squeeze. "I want to help. I promise. But I can't do that unless we get you into the apartment." She thought for a second. "Unless you have a wheelchair, or maybe a walker in there somewhere."

"No. No wheelchair. Let's just do it."

She helped him swing his legs around until they were both on the ground. "Okay, whenever you're ready. Grab my wrists."

She moved her hands lower until they wrapped around his forearm and waited for him to do the same. "It'll be stronger this way. I'll be less likely to drop you." She said the words with a smile only to hear him swear again. A little louder this time.

"On the count of three. *Um...dois...tres!*"

That did it. He was out of the car, although he was holding most of his weight on his right leg.

It was no better evidently.

"Okay, we're going to do like we did before. Lean your weight on me." She sensed an argument forming and cut him off. "We can work on the cane once we get into the house."

They made their way to the elevator, and she let him push the button. Sixth floor. "How many floors is this building?"

"Six."

Okay, so he was on the top floor. Once the elevator reached number six, and the doors opened, she realized there were only two doors up here. So these apartments had to be huge. The floor she lived on had six residences on it. "Are your keys on the same ring as your car keys?"

"Yes." The words came out in a short burst of air that told her his strength was flagging.

She quickly fished them out of her pocket and held one of the keys up. He nodded and reached for it, opening the door so fast that she almost lost her balance. She caught herself just in time. It would have been great to say *trust me* and then have them both collapse into the apartment.

She got him as far as the couch and lowered him onto it before saying, "Wait here. I'll be right back."

CHAPTER EIGHT

ROQUE HAD TENSED when she'd joked about him having a wheelchair in his apartment. He didn't. Not anymore. What he did still have was a walker. It was hidden inside a closet in his spare bedroom. He could barely look at his old nemesis without myriad emotions clutching at his gut and threatening to rob the strength from his legs.

He'd gone from a young man who could dance his way through a clump of football players on his way to making one goal after another, to a man who could barely put one foot in front of the other—even with the help of that walker. A man who'd aged twenty years overnight.

He'd always meant to donate it, but he didn't like looking at it, much less try to drag it down to his car.

His body had failed him once, and it looked like it was failing him again.

As much as he tried to suppress it, a hole of fear opened up inside him. What if, despite what he'd said, it wasn't just his muscle? What if the fall onto his ass had knocked something loose, or torn a muscle that he couldn't afford to lose?

His cat appeared from the kitchen and came over and hopped into his lap. He picked her up and set her beside him. "Sorry, girl. I'll feed you as soon as I can get back up."

Amy reappeared with a trash can and he tensed. "I'm not going to vomit, if that's what you're worried about."

"Of course not. I took the liner out of it and it's clean. I'm going to put some hot towels in there, but I need to know where your dryer is because I'm going to rotate moist heat with dry." She stopped. "Aw... is that Rachel?"

"Yes."

Amy came over and tickled the cat's head, trailing her fingers over Rachel's thick fur. "Hi, there. I've heard about you. Lucky girl, I don't have allergies." Her head suddenly came up and she glanced away from him. "Dryer?"

"I don't have a dryer, but I do have a heating pad."

"Where?"

He nodded toward his bedroom door. "In the closet in my spare bedroom on the top shelf."

Moving toward where he'd indicated, she slid through the bedroom door, reappearing two minutes later. "Okay, so you do have something."

When he looked up, he saw she was holding the heating pad in one hand, and the walker in the other.

"No. Put that away. Right now."

His voice was forceful enough that Rachel hopped

off the couch, giving him a baleful glance as she stalked away. But the last thing he wanted to see was a reminder of how weak he'd once been. How utterly helpless he'd felt. Especially when faced with a woman who'd had to help him walk to his own damned car.

Amy set the walker down with a frown. "It's not for forever, it's just to give your leg muscles a break tonight."

"Not tonight. Not ever."

She stared him down for several minutes before leaving the walker where it was and coming over with the heating pad. "Okay, we'll talk about it later."

No, they wouldn't. But damn, she was as stubborn as he was. An unwilling smile came to the surface, despite his best efforts to keep it down. "I wouldn't count on that."

All she did was laugh—a knowing little laugh that said she was going to get her way. Some way or another. Maybe she normally did, since she was the power person in her little physical therapy realm. But she was in his world now. And here, he was used to calling the shots.

Only he was pretty sure that Amy wasn't easily intimidated.

"Let me get set up. It'll just take a few minutes, but in the meantime, I'll plug this in and get some heat going to those muscles. Take off your pants."

Shock rolled through him. There was no way in hell. That was almost as bad as her suggestion to use a walker.

"Not happening. You can do whatever it is you want to do through them."

"No. I can't. Not only can't I, but I won't. I have a towel here." She pulled something out of her beach bag. A huge pink towel with a picture of cats.

"What is that?"

"It's an *Aristocats* towel. You know—like the movie? You can drape it over your lap, since you seem to be so, er, modest." She said it with a twitch of her lips.

Modest. Sure. He could show her exactly how modest he was. Because despite the pain in his leg and the pain she was in his backside right now, there was a very real possibility that at some point that towel might reveal a muscle problem of an entirely different kind.

"I'll help you take them off, then." Her smile was teasing. Coaxing. And something shifted inside of him. Something he didn't want to examine. And he certainly didn't want her to catch a glimpse of it in his expression. He had to get rid of her for a minute or two, even if it meant taking his damn pants off.

"Fine. Go in the other room, and I'll get them off myself." He would do it if it killed him.

"Okey dokey." She tossed the cat towel in his lap and picked up the trash can and stack of towels and carried it into the kitchen. "Yell when you're ready. Or when you decide you need some help."

He'd just unbuttoned his jeans when she popped her head back into the room. Was she kidding him? "What?"

"I think Rachel is hungry. What does she eat?"

"There are cans in the pantry and her dish is on the floor beside the dishwasher."

This time she stayed gone, while he did his best to shimmy out of the snug garment, sweat beading his lip when he had to put too much weight on his injured leg.

Diabos. What if he had to have surgery on it? Again. Worse, what if he could no longer *perform* surgeries? Or perform at all.

After his accident, it had been two years before he'd gotten the nerve up to actually try to have sex with someone. Some of that was because of Halee's betrayal, but some of it was also due to his *body's* betrayal.

Well, there was certainly no sign of that kind of trouble tonight. In fact…

He yanked his right foot out of the leg of the jeans and used it to push them off his other leg. He picked up the towel that sported a white cat with a big pink bow around her neck and a smaller one on top of her head.

Caramba! He draped the ridiculous thing over his legs, wondering why he hadn't asked her to leave one of his plain white towels instead. Because they weren't as big as this one was, of course.

A few minutes later, she came back in with the trash can. Curls of steam came out of the top of it.

He frowned. "Exactly how hot are those towels?"

"Pretty hot."

He glanced at her. Several strands of hair had escaped her ponytail, spiraling down her collarbone. And with her standing there in a white sundress that sported tiny little holes all over it, Roque was struck with the thought that the towels weren't the only thing in this room that were hot. Amy was, too. Even the pain in his leg couldn't erase what she did to him. And then there were her feet.

Bare feet.

"What happened to your shoes?"

"They're in my beach bag."

Thinking back, he didn't think she'd put them back on as she helped him walk back to the car. The pavement had to be blistering hot, but she'd said nothing. And she'd driven his car barefooted. Had come up in the elevator like that and padded across his wood floors.

And that was the impetus he needed to do what she asked. If she could do what was necessary for him, he was going to cooperate with whatever she wanted him to do.

That immediately sent another flurry of thoughts spinning through his head that had no business being there.

"Will the moisture hurt your couch? If so, we'll move this operation to your floor. Or…your bed."

Um…no. Not the bed.

"It won't hurt the couch. And the back folds down to make a bed." The black leather was pretty forgiving.

"That's perfect. How does it work?"

"There's a button on the side of it." He leaned forward so the back wouldn't go sailing down with him on it.

She cranked it down. "Okay. Is the pain in front or in back?"

Even as she said it, a little twinge happened that he needed to suppress—that had to do with a pain of another kind. "It's actually on the outside of my thigh, where the scar is."

"Let's have you lie on your stomach, then, like we would if this were a massage table."

His stomach. Good choice. He relaxed slightly. "I want the towel wrapped around my waist, then."

"Your wish is my command."

And that was a phrase he didn't even want to consider. Because what he suddenly wished for, he couldn't have. Like kisses. The kind they'd shared in his office.

Between the two of them, they somehow got him covered and in position. Then there was a quick sting as she draped one of the hot towels over his left leg and then another on top of that. Then she set the timer on her phone and pulled a vial out of her purse.

He gave it a wary look. Had she gotten some kind of herbal potion from Flávia Maura? "What is that?"

"Relax. It's just a blend of essential oils that I carry around for muscle pain. It has wintergreen, peppermint, lemongrass and a few other things in it. I'm going to mix it with some olive oil I found in your pantry. It will act as a natural analgesic and will help lubricate the skin as I work it." She paused. "Unless you want to take a muscle relaxer. If you have some."

He did somewhere, but he tried to avoid taking them, having had a problem weaning himself off narcotic painkillers after the accident. It had made him leery of taking much of anything. "I'd rather not unless I have to."

"That's what I thought."

She took the towels off and traded them for another two. "Once these cool, I'm going to massage your muscles, using the oils."

Massage his muscles. Great. Well, there was one muscle that he was glad she couldn't see.

Five minutes later her hands were on him. And as soon as her touch hit his skin the pain in his leg became so much background noise. It was there, but it was not what his primary focus was. Her hands squeezed and rubbed and worked in strong capable strokes that had his eyes closing. Only to jerk back apart when she got to the seized area.

"Diabos!"

"Hurt?"

"Yes."

"Good."

His head cranked around to look at her only to have her smile. "I can feel the balled-up muscles, but needed you to tell me I was in the right spot."

"Oh, you're in the right spot, all right."

He gritted his teeth and willed the pain away, forgetting about almost everything else. But still she kept working, kneading, using the base of her palm to push against the tightness in his leg. Fifteen minutes later he realized the pain was ebbing, so slowly he wasn't aware of when it had actually started retreating, but it was fifty percent better. Then sixty. Then seventy-five. And that he could live with.

"Thank you. I think it worked."

"Just give me a few minutes longer. I think I can get the rest of it."

True to her word, when her hands finally went still, her fingers paused to trace the furrow of his scar, sending a shudder through him. She'd taken almost every bit of his pain away. And added a pain from a completely different source.

"Amy, thank you."

Her hand moved away, and he immediately wanted it back.

"You're welcome."

He cautiously rolled over and sat up, keeping the towel in place, and felt no flare in his leg. When he looked at her, though, her cheeks were flushed in a way that might have been exertion, but it also might be…

She'd traced his scar, her fingers soft and sure, and had felt totally different from what she had done moments earlier. It had hit him on an emotional level that was new to him. He normally did not like women lingering over that mark.

She was still kneeling on the rug in front of the sofa, but when she went to grab one of the towels on the floor, he stopped her with a hand to her wrist. Then, unable to resist, he stroked a finger along her cheek. "Leave all of the stuff, and I'll get it in the morning."

"How are you feeling?" She peered up at him with eyes that almost sparkled. And he found he liked it. Wanted to be the reason for that look.

"Better. I can't believe a simple massage had that much of an effect."

In reality, there'd been nothing simple about that massage. Or the effect it had had on him.

"I told you it would work. Do you believe me now?"

"I believe…*you*. I once had another physical therapist, though, who…" Not finishing his sentence, he stood, hauling her to her feet, her hands warming his and sending an answering heat straight to the area he'd been trying to ignore. He stared down at her face, watching as her teeth found her lower lip and pressed deep into the soft skin.

Damn. He should have stayed down on the couch, because now that he was standing, all he wanted to do was…

Kiss her.

He cupped her face, and she tilted it as if waiting. For him. "Hell, Amy. What was in those oils again?"

"Nothing dangerous."

That's where she was wrong. Because something powerful was coursing through his veins, taking control of his thoughts. And if he was reading her expression correctly, she was feeling its effects, too.

"Hey." His thumbs stroked along her jawline, the soft skin creating an addiction that he didn't want to fight. "If I kissed you—in this ridiculous towel—what would you do?"

A dimple played peekaboo in her cheek. "Maybe you should try it and find out."

Her smile said this was one time that she wasn't going to put him on the ground with a sweep of her leg.

So Roque lowered his head and slid his mouth against hers.

The second he touched her lips, Amy melted inside. She'd enjoyed the last fifteen minutes of that massage far too much. His muscles were firm beneath his skin, not flaccid the way she would expect them to be. He felt like an athlete. Even though he was no longer one.

His lips were firm as well, moving over hers in a way that sparked tiny fires of need all along her nerve endings. God, she couldn't believe this was happening. It was like he'd somehow read her thoughts and was thanking her for making him feel better.

Only this didn't feel like it was done out of duty. Or gratitude. It felt like he wanted her as much as she wanted him.

A fling. Wasn't that what she'd envisioned having with some stranger? Hadn't she seen it as a way to jump-start her life and send her in a new direction?

Well, who needed a stranger when she had the perfect man right here in her arms. Someone she knew... trusted. Someone who was safe. Someone whose skin she'd already touched and wanted to touch again. In a completely different way.

She didn't need commitment. Didn't want it. Not the way she'd wanted it in the past, only to be disappointed when the man she'd cared about had suddenly pulled away without so much as an excuse or a goodbye. That had hurt. Enough to not want to repeat that experience.

But she didn't need promises of a future from this particular man.

Amy settled in to enjoy, wanting nothing more than to be swept to bed and revel in his lovemaking.

Only he wasn't going to be able to sweep her up in his arms. And that was okay. She didn't need shows of strength. She just needed him, and what he could do for her.

Her hands slid up his arms, loving the way his muscles corded beneath her touch, her fingers continuing their upward journey, before tunneling into the warm hair just above the collar of his polo shirt.

Roque's head tilted, deepening the kiss, his palms skimming down the back of her dress, before pulling away slightly. He fingered the fabric. "What's the name of this?" he asked as he bunched the skirt in his hands, the cool air in his apartment caressing the backs of her thighs in a way that made her squirm against him. "I haven't been able to stop thinking about it all day."

"About what?" Her mind glazed over, having a hard time thinking beyond what she felt at the front of his towel.

He smiled against her mouth. "This material with its tiny little holes. It looks so sweet and innocent, but there's a warm sexy side to it that makes me want to explore each and every inch of it."

Thank God that bubbling awareness hadn't been completely one-sided. She'd been more and more conscious of it as the day went by. At least until she'd kicked his feet out from under him.

"Eyelet. I don't know what it is in Portuguese."

"Mmm... I don't, either." His lips ran over her jawline and down her throat, the heat from his mouth almost unbearable. And when he reached the sweetheart neckline of the dress, he brushed along the dips and curves, making her moan. Still keeping the fabric behind her gathered up, he used the fingers of his other hand to find the zipper at the back of her dress, easing it down until he reached her waist. Then he traveled back up, finding the strap of her bra and tugging it slightly. "So you do have one on. This time."

So he had noticed that first day that she wasn't wearing one. Her senses went up in flames.

She didn't want him laying her down on the couch, since she'd worked on him there. This was one time when she really didn't want to mix business with pleasure. Plus, Rachel had come out a couple of times, trying to get their attention, and Amy would rather not have to share Roque with her right now.

Maybe he read her thoughts, because he gave her mouth a hard kiss. "I'm thinking I'd like to be somewhere else. Somewhere a little more private."

Relief swamped through her.

"I was just thinking that myself," she murmured.

Letting her dress go, he took her hand and pulled her along with him until he reached the back of the apartment, going through a door, which he nudged shut behind them. She took a second to take in her surroundings.

A huge bed, clad in a plain brown quilted spread, sat in the center of the room, large wooden posts making it both masculine and inviting at the same time.

Or maybe that was Roque.

Reaching the bottom of her dress, he hauled it up and over her head, until she stood there wearing only her underwear and her bra, both pink. He fingered the waistline of the lacy briefs. "Are these…?"

She tilted her head. "Are they what?"

"The same underwear that were hanging out of your suitcase that first day?"

Her face flamed to life, remembering the circumstances of that visit. "Yes, they were." Had she subconsciously worn them today, thinking this was where they were going to wind up?

No, there's no way she could have planned any of this.

"They've haunted me for weeks."

She laughed. "And here I was hoping you hadn't noticed them."

He reached down as if he were going to scoop her up in his arms, but she stopped him by stepping out of reach.

"What's wrong?"

A lot of conflicting emotions chased across his face, making her realize he'd misunderstood why she'd moved away. "I don't want you lifting me. Or doing anything that might make that leg act up again. That would make me very unhappy, in more ways than one." She glanced at the bed and then went over and pulled the spread down to the halfway point. "Why don't you lie down?"

"I am not some invalid, Amy."

"Oh, believe me, I know that." To hide the quick ache in her heart his words had caused, she forced a laugh and reached for his towel, whisking it away. He stood there in boxer briefs that gave very clear evidence of what he was feeling. "There. That's more like it."

"You are impossible." But he said it with a smile that chased the ache away. "But there's something else I need. In the nightstand."

Going over to it, she opened the top drawer and found a package of condoms. He was right. They did need something. She'd almost forgotten about protection. Tossing them on the bed, she grinned at him.

"Anything else?"

He nodded. "Yes. If I promise not to do any kind of gymnastics, will you let me take an active role?"

"How active?" She needed to tread carefully.

Coming over to stand in front of her, he gripped her hips and hauled her against him. "Enough to get the job done. For both of us." His gaze turned serious. "Don't put me back in that walker, even in my head. I've been there, and I didn't much like it."

She hadn't been trying to do that, but could see how he might feel a little insecure right now, since she'd been in a place of power as she'd worked on him. Something in her wanted to press the point, but an inner voice warned her that this was one battle she didn't want to win. Because in winning, she would lose.

"An invalid is not what I think of when I look at you. But no gymnastics."

"Not this time."

He didn't try to pick her up again; instead, keeping his hands on her hips, he walked her backward until the backs of her thighs hit the mattress. Then he gave her a soft push and down she went, bouncing a time or two on the soft surface. It felt luxurious and heady, and exactly what she'd been thinking of when she'd imagined being with someone.

The bed was high enough that she could picture him doing all kinds of things to her, and that was enough to make her squirm.

Maybe he sensed it, because he stood over her for a minute and then reached for the pink lace at her hips and peeled it down her thighs. She straightened her legs so he wouldn't have to bend getting them down her calves and then they were off.

"Meu Deus. Você é a mulher mais linda do mundo."

She wasn't the most beautiful woman in the world, but it was nice to hear him say the words. And to hear that her dress had turned him on. And right now she couldn't imagine being any more turned on than she was at this moment.

When he acted like he was going to bend over to kiss her, though, she planted her bare foot on his stomach. "Stay as straight as you can."

"Bossy. So very bossy. But okay. I'll stay all the way up here and just do…this."

He used a leg to part her knees, then wrapped his hands around her thighs and dragged her to the edge of the bed. Then he was right there. Up close and personal.

"Better?" he asked.

"Yes." Her body was on fire.

"But first—" he motioned to an area beside her arm "—I'm going to need that packet."

Oh! That's right. She opened the cardboard box and retrieved one, ripping it open and tossing it to him. He caught it with ease, and set it over her navel. Then he reached down and pulled his shirt over his head and stepped out of his briefs, while Amy unhooked her bra and flung it toward the end of the bed, where it ended up getting caught on one of the bedposts.

He sheathed himself. "Sit up, *querida.*"

She did what he asked and realized almost immediately why when he cupped her breasts, stroking the nipples between his fingers and squeezing.

"Ah…" Her arms went behind her to support herself, arching her back and pushing herself into his touch.

"What you do to me…"

His voice had roughened, tones lowering until they were deep-edged with need. Or at least she hoped it was.

Then he reached to cup her bottom and entered her with a quick thrust that stretched her…filled her. Her eyes might have rolled back in her head—she wasn't quite sure. All she knew was that this was like no encounter she'd ever had before. There was normally a lot of foreplay and give and take, but Roque wasn't interested in her doing anything evidently.

She'd been ready to sit and ride him to completion to save his leg from any pain. But what she saw on his face wasn't pain. It was need. Lust. A bunch of things mixed up together that she didn't understand.

What she did know was that she wanted him. Wanted this. Didn't want it to stop.

Except it would, because she was slipping closer and closer to the edge of a cliff, and once off, there would be no going back.

She didn't care, though. Only knew that as he continued to push into her body and then retreat that she was about as close to heaven as she was ever likely to get.

Tipping her face up, he kissed her as he continued to move, wrapping both arms around her back, using his tongue in ways that put every one of her nerve endings on high alert.

"I've wanted this. Almost since you arrived."

That made two of them. "Me too."

She wanted to say more, but the words wouldn't form, wouldn't come, and she was afraid if she said them she might mutter something that she couldn't take back, so she clamped her teeth together. Then she felt him there, seeking entrance, and she pried them back apart. The second his tongue entered her mouth, it was almost too much, and her hands went to the back of his head to hold him there, even as her legs circled his back and pulled him in closer.

"Amy... I'm not going to be able to..."

One of his hands slid between their bodies, seeking something. Finding it. Squeezing and sliding his thumb over that sensitized nub of flesh.

"Go, Roque. Oh, go!" The words came out in a frantic rush that he must have recognized, because he thrust into her at a speed that drove the air from her lungs, even as the edge of that cliff rushed forward and collided with her, sending her over the edge in an instant. Her body spasmed around him as he continued to surge inside of her, giving gritted mutterings that slid past her ear and escaped into the air around them.

Still he thrust into her, taking a minute or two before he slowed, letting her sink back to the bed, where she lay nerveless and still.

He reached under her and held her tight against him as if knowing what was coming. "No. Not yet."

She echoed those words in her head, knowing once that happened, once they came apart, she was going to be left to try to pick up the shattered pieces of her composure. And she was going to be faced with the reality of what they'd done.

She'd gotten her fling.

But she was very afraid she might have gotten something more than she bargained for—something that wouldn't be easy to put behind her.

All she knew was that she was going to have to try.

CHAPTER NINE

THERE WAS AN elephant in the room that someone didn't want to talk about. And it wasn't him. Worse, his mom told him that she'd sent Amy a card inviting her to a party she was having, but that she hadn't yet RSVP'd. She wanted Roque to "ask" her to come—meaning, coax her into coming.

He was going to do nothing of the sort, although the phone call prompted him to do what he'd been putting off for the last two weeks, as he'd watched Amy frantically work alongside of the other members of the team and then drop just as quickly off the radar. As if she was avoiding being alone with him.

As if?

No, there was no question about what she was doing.

But today, he was headed down to the physical therapy department, where Amy was having her first session with Enzo. He intended to be there when it ended and have his say. Even though he wasn't entirely sure what that was.

All he knew was that he hadn't liked the way

things had ended in his apartment. She'd slid out the door almost before he'd caught his breath.

The elevator doors opened and a large open room stood in front of him.

It was a beehive of activity with patients posted in different stations working on whatever task their therapist had given them.

There. He spotted Enzo.

The man gave him a quick wave. He'd passed his swallow test a couple of weeks ago with flying colors, but Roque didn't expect anything different from his old coach. He walked toward Enzo, noticing that while Amy was also there, she didn't quite meet his eyes when she looked at him.

Addressing Enzo, he asked, "How's it going?"

"She hasn't made me cry yet."

His words came out a little garbled because of the changes they'd made to his jaw, but at least he could talk. He was doing speech therapy as well and they were all hopeful that there was no nerve damage. Krysta didn't think there was. She'd been meticulous in her resection of everything. That muscle memory was just going to have to kick back in at some point.

And he was sure it would. It was just a matter of practice and reopening those neural pathways.

"Don't worry, she's still got a month and a half to work on you—there's still plenty of time."

However, Roque had decided he couldn't put off his discussion with Amy any longer.

They'd done nothing morally wrong, but her attitude told him that *she* believed they'd made a mistake. And on some level, so did he. He just couldn't put his finger on why.

This was a temporary assignment for her. And, actually, for him as well. So logically that should make it easier to resolve. But so far, it hadn't.

She really had helped his leg. The day after she'd worked on it he'd only felt a tiny twinge of discomfort that had worked itself out as the day went on. So when he'd told her physical therapy could no longer help him, he'd been wrong. It had been a knee-jerk reaction to what had happened long before she came on the scene.

"I'm feeling better," Enzo managed to get out.

Roque put his hand on his friend's shoulder. "I'm so glad. It must feel good to be at the last part of your journey." He remembered when he was almost done with medical school. The elation and fear he'd felt as he faced the future ahead of him.

Enzo was probably feeling some of that as well.

"He's worked hard today. Hard enough that I'm ready to let him off the hook. At least until next week." Amy smiled, but it was aimed at Enzo rather than him. "Make sure you do those exercises I gave you. They'll really help get your range of motion back again."

Enzo nodded and hopped off the table. They said their goodbyes, and Roque's friend headed for the double doors that connected the physical therapy area with the rest of the hospital.

Once he was gone, Roque turned back to face her. "Do you have another patient right now?"

"No, that was my last one for the day."

"Good. Do you think we can find someplace to talk?"

Her eyes closed for a second before opening. "About what?"

A muscle tightened in his jaw. "I think you know what this is about."

"Yes, I think I do." She sighed and this time looked at him. "Let's take a walk."

She started, then stopped. "How's your leg?"

"It's fine. And yes, before you ask, I am more than capable of walking."

"I didn't mean that."

He wasn't sure why he'd snapped at her. Maybe it was just that he missed some of that quick back-and-forth *jogo de palavras* they'd had before. There was no hint of that teasing manner now. Everything was stilted and formal. Professional. Just like he'd wanted. Right?

"I'm sorry. Let's go to the *pátio*."

Behind the hospital there was a small private garden area with benches where patients or relatives could get out and enjoy the sun or sit under the shade of one of the trees. It reminded him a little of his parents' *chácara* with its greenery. It was also fairly private, with little chance of anyone overhearing them.

They got out to the courtyard and slowly made their way down the bricked path. "I don't actually think I've been out here yet. It's beautiful."

"It is. I came out here a lot when I was a medical student."

She glanced at him. "I didn't realize you did your studies at Paulista."

"I did. I felt like I needed a change of scenery from Rio."

"Your parents moved here to be near you?"

"My mom's family is from São Paulo, so she had no problem relocating. To a Brazilian—as you probably know—family is everything."

He wasn't quite sure how the conversation had turned in this direction, but it beat the chilly silence he'd tried to ignore for the last couple of weeks. And she'd seemed to relax into the conversation.

"I was always surprised my mom didn't move back to Brazil after my dad died."

"To be near your uncle, you mean?"

Maybe if he brought her thoughts back to her reasons for coming to Brazil, they could both move past the awkwardness of what had happened.

"Yes. She said she and my uncle hadn't spoken in years, though. He disagreed with her marrying so young and so quickly and moving to the States."

Amy hadn't told her uncle about her mother's death. It wasn't the kind of news she'd wanted to break to him over the phone, especially when the man was traveling on business.

Roque wanted to keep her talking, not only because it might help them regain their footing, but also because he genuinely wanted to know. She'd come here because of her mom, to learn a little more about her roots, so maybe he could help her flesh some of that out.

"Did your mom grow up where your uncle lives now?"

"I don't know. She didn't talk much about her life in Brazil. As far as I know, she only came back to Brazil once to visit. When I was a baby. My uncle evidently refused to see her."

"I bet he regrets that now."

"I think maybe he does. At least he didn't refuse to see me." She sighed. "I think the problem was that my mom didn't give him time to process what was happening between her and my dad. My dad worked for one of the major car manufacturers, which has a plant here in São Paulo. He and my mom met on one of his business trips and fell in love. Three weeks later, they were married and heading to Florida. I was born a year after that."

"That was quick."

Amy smiled. "That was my mom. She lived in the moment and gave herself fully to it, not looking back. Maybe that's part of the reason why once she left Brazil, she was loath to come back."

That thought skated through his head for a minute. So once Amy left Brazil would she do the same and never come back?

That sent a pang through him. But it also might mean that if Amy lived in the moment, she would be able to put what had happened between them in the past and not look back at it.

"Do you think you'll come back to visit?"

"I think that depends on how things with my uncle go."

Roque's leg was starting to get tired, so he found a bench and motioned her to it. Sliding onto the seat, he stretched his leg out in front of him to ease the ache.

"So it is bothering you—I thought so."

"Not much. It just gets tired."

"There are some machines back at the—"

He tensed. "I don't want to talk about the machines. I want to talk about what happened back at the apartment."

Her chin went up and she looked him in the eye. "What about it?"

Well, he could name a whole lot of things, but since he'd brought it up, he needed to get to the crux of the issue and confront it. "Things have been awkward. And I'd like to get past that, if we can."

"I don't know if I can, Roque."

The enormity of those words was a punch to the gut. But before he could formulate a response, she went on. "I've never had sex…well, outside of a dating relationship, and certainly never with a patient. It was unprofessional and I—"

So that's what this was about.

"Let's get one thing straight. I am not your patient."

Her shoulders sagged. "I thought maybe you would wonder if I got involved with—" her hand made a little flourish in the air "—I don't know, people like Enzo or other patients."

Roque turned to look her in the eye. "After my injury, I had a physical therapist in Rio who wanted more from me. She tried to draw out my treatment even after I stopped making progress. Believe me, if I even sensed you were like that, you would be out of the program in a heartbeat." He nudged her shoulder. "You didn't take advantage of me. I wanted what happened as much as you did. We were two people who came together for one night, just like so many others before us."

She smiled. "You have no idea how much better that makes me feel. Well, since we're sharing confidences, I had toyed with the possibility of having a fling with a handsome Brazilian."

"A fling?" His brows went up. "You mean like a *caso*?"

"I don't know what that word means. Like an affair?"

He nodded. "Except neither of us is—" he tried to think of the word "—linked with someone."

"No, we're not. So you're right. I think maybe I made too much of it. Like I said, I was worried about how you might view what we did."

"I view it as completely unimportant."

Something shifted in her eyes, a quick flicker of hurt that made him pause. He'd expected relief, not this...uncertainty. He'd sensed a lack of confidence in her once or twice before. Only this time it wasn't related to her work. It was related to him. "Is that not the right word?"

Her arms wrapped around her waist. "It's exactly the right word."

Except she was no longer looking at him. "Maybe 'inconsequential' would have been a better choice?"

Nothing changed in her face. "Those are both good words to describe it."

An uneasiness gathered in his chest. He wasn't

sure where it came from or why her reaction mattered. It shouldn't. He was happy with his life the way it was. No entanglements. No commitments. No one to worry about where he might wind up ten years down the road.

Seeing her holding that walker in his living room had sent acid swirling in his gut. It was like a foreshadowing of what his future might hold. Maybe it was even the reason he'd never brought himself to get rid of the thing.

He did not want to be treated like an invalid. Not by Amy. Not by anyone. It had been ridiculous to feel that way with her. And yet he had—had suddenly felt like he had something to prove, despite her words to the contrary. There was no changing it.

He pushed forward toward his original goal in bringing her out here. "So things between us are good?"

"Yes, Roque, they're good. We should just put it behind us."

And yet the stiltedness was back in her speech. He'd said something wrong, and he had no idea what it was. But he really did want to try to undo it.

So he said something crazy. So crazy he had no idea where the words had come from. "My mom told me she invited you to her party. She very much would like for you to come. And so would I."

Dammit. What the hell are you doing?

"I don't know…"

"It's nothing formal, so there'd no chance that I could step on your dress this time."

She smiled. Finally, and her expression transformed in an instant. "I stepped on it a couple of times myself that night, if you remember. I was very glad my tae kwon do instructor wasn't there to see me."

Mentioning the invitation was the right thing to do. He wasn't sure how or why, but it had clicked something in that beautiful face of hers. "I think he would have been pretty proud of the way you took me down at the beach."

She laughed. "I finally got to see how it works outside of a classroom setting."

"It was quite effective." He paused, then went back to his question. "So you'll come to the house?"

"If you're sure they don't mind. I thought maybe your mom was just being polite."

"Believe me, she wouldn't have invited you if she didn't want you there."

"When is it again?" She got to her feet.

"On the eighteenth."

"I think it depends on whether the head of the department wants me to work or not. He's a pretty intimidating guy."

He got to his feet as well, and it took him a second to realize she was talking about him. He laughed. "Not so intimidating. And no. I'm giving us that night off."

"Okay, it sounds great. Thank you."

Things might not be exactly back to where they were before this had happened. But at least they were on cordial footing again. Hopefully he could keep it that way. At least for the rest of her stay.

* * *

Amy picked up a dress off the rack, before putting it back with a sigh. She needed to hurry. Her uncle was finally back from his trip and she was planning on taking a cab to his house as soon as she finished here.

Maybe she should skip shopping and just wear the eyelet sundress she'd worn to the beach again.

No. That dress was going to be permanently retired. She couldn't look at it without remembering Roque's long fingers worrying one of the holes and trying to figure out what kind of fabric it was.

Although their work relationship was better now, there were still flashes from that conversation in the garden that came back to bite her.

Her stomach twisted.

Roque viewed their night together as "unimportant." And it was. He'd been technically right. But still, to hear those words coming from this particular man's mouth had sent shock crashing through her. Changing the term to *inconsequential* had just made it worse.

That's the damn definition of a fling, Amy. Isn't that what you said you wanted? It was one night. Not six months.

She shuffled through more dresses, getting more and more irritated with herself.

Why did you even agree to go to his parents' party?

Because of something she'd seen in his face. Something that said it wasn't as unimportant as he'd said.

And she liked his parents. She really hadn't had a chance to talk with many people outside of the hospital program. This was a chance to get to know life, as her mom had once known it. At least that was what she told herself. And, in reality, she hadn't seen Roque as much in the last week or two as she had in the first half of the program while shadowing him. And she missed it. Missed being invited to watch surgeries, being asked about her opinion on cases. She even missed seeing Peter and Lara, who were still in the orthopedics department.

Roque still technically oversaw her, but as the program was set up to do, she had been passed over to the physical therapy side of things. Enzo's PT sessions were going amazingly well, and periodically Roque had come down to watch. She now found herself watching to see if he would come through that door, which she hated, but it was like her eyes were instilled with a homing device that kept trying to track him down.

At the end of the month, they would all say their goodbyes at the sendoff party, and she would get on a plane and fly back home.

Home?

For the first time in her life Florida didn't quite feel like home anymore. But her life was there. Her career. Her future doctorate work would be done there. She couldn't just uproot herself and come live in Brazil. She barely knew anyone except for Roque, Krysta and Flávia and a few other people at the hospital. And most of those would be leaving when the summer program was over.

Amy shook off those thoughts and picked up another casual dress, although Roque said jeans would be fine. Most Brazilians loved their denim and wore it for a lot of different occasions.

Actually, maybe she would wear jeans. She had a pair that were dark and slim-fitting and showed off her figure. She hoped, anyway.

Why?

Maybe she really did have something to prove. To herself, if nothing else. She'd had her fling—she kept using that term, although could one night technically be considered a fling? She had no idea, since she'd never had one before. But there was still something in her that wasn't satisfied—that wanted more.

But never mind that. She needed to decide on an outfit, and quickly. She was supposed to be at her uncle's house in an hour. It looked like jeans it was. So giving the salesperson an apologetic smile, she headed out the door, looking for the nearest taxi stand.

CHAPTER TEN

THE DAY OF the party arrived and Amy found she was almost as nervous getting ready for this event as she'd been over the cookout at the *chácara*. So much had happened between then and now. She'd visited a beach with Roque, had had sex with him at his apartment. And had visited an uncle she'd never met.

She and Abel had laughed and cried over memories of her mom, and he'd expressed a lifetime of regret over having turned her away all those years ago when she came to visit. He'd promised he and his wife would come visit her in the States once she got back.

The calendar seemed to suddenly be tripping over itself, the dates cascading past like a waterfall. But she wasn't going to think about that. Not tonight.

She tugged on her slim-fitting dark-washed jeans, pulling out a pair of heeled boots to go with them. She then dropped a slinky green top over her head, cinching it at the waist with the same silver-linked belt she'd worn for the welcome party. That soiree seemed like a lifetime ago.

Pulling her hair back in a sleek ponytail and brushing on a coat of mascara and some gloss on her lips, she declared herself ready.

Roque had offered to come get her, but she'd opted to take a taxi instead. Maybe for the same reason she'd packed away that eyelet dress.

Forty-five minutes later, she arrived, walking up the driveway to the sound of laughter. She suddenly wondered just how big of a party this was, and the urge to turn around and run after her taxi welled up inside of her before she shoved it away.

She'd told them she would be here, and there would be questions if she didn't show. Ringing the buzzer at the gate, she leaned down expecting a voice to come over the intercom system. Instead, the door opened and Roque's mom flew down the walkway, clicking open the gate. She gave Amy a kiss on the cheek, which by now she was accustomed to.

"É bom vê-lo novamente!"

The enthusiasm in the woman's voice erased any doubts she might have had about coming. *"Obrigada pelo convite."*

Roque had been right on that front. Exchanging pleasantries in Portuguese had become a lot easier as the weeks marched by. Her tongue no longer tripped over half of the words. She still spoke to Roque in English, however. Somehow it seemed more important to get the words right when addressing him. She still hadn't quite figured out why. Only that it mattered in a way she didn't understand.

If he minded her speaking in English, he didn't let on. He just kept responding in kind, while tossing in a smattering of Portuguese words when he was unsure of something.

Like "unimportant"?

"Come in, come in. Andre is hoping to be home before dinner. He had an emergency call come in a few minutes ago."

With all these people here, it looked like it was sink or swim as far as Portuguese went.

But it was only dinner. She could last an hour or two before her mind went numb from trying to find words.

She followed Claudia into the house and found a charming array of blue and white tile and clean textiles. It was completely different from their *chácara*, but not in a bad way. The space was spotless, and the scents... Her mouth watered.

"Is there anything I can help with?"

"You can keep my son from causing trouble." Claudia said it with a mischievous smile that made her stomach flip.

What kind of trouble?

She didn't know, but as if summoned the man was suddenly walking toward her in black jeans and a white shirt, his sleeves rolled up to reveal tanned arms. Arms that she had seen and felt and...

Ack! No. No thinking about what she had seen of the man. She was pretty sure his mom would not approve of the images racing through her head.

His cane was nowhere to be seen. Wait. No, there it was. By the front door. He evidently was feeling okay.

"You came." He smiled, taking one of her hands and squeezing it.

A warm buzz of electricity traveled up her arm and burst into pinpoints of heat throughout her body. Yep. It was still there. That awareness that had been there since the very first moment when he'd stepped on her dress. She'd learned so much about him since that time. Had seen a few of his insecurities and had witnessed his incredible, resilient strength.

"I told you I would."

"I know, but when you said you'd take a taxi I had doubts. I am glad you're here."

She didn't tell him she'd very nearly crawled back in that taxi and left. The sincerity in his voice made her glad she'd stayed. As did the fingers that were still gripping hers.

He wanted her here. Unlike when she'd first applied to come, when he admitted he'd very nearly said no.

So much had changed since their first meeting all those weeks ago.

The pinpricks grew in size, attacking her belly... her chest...

Her heart.

She swallowed.

Oh, don't, Amy. Don't. Do not!

It was too late. All the mental lectures in the world were not going to change anything. She was in love with the man.

A giggle came out before she could stop it as a realization struck her. She was a little more like her mom than she thought. But what had taken Cecília Rodrigo Woodell little more than a moment to admit—that she loved someone—had taken Amy nearly three months. And it had been accompanied by a whole lot of denial and fear.

"What's funny?"

"Nothing."

It was true. Oh, *God*, it was true. The man who'd said sex with her had been unimportant and inconsequential…

No, he'd said the words but had been unsure if he'd chosen them correctly. She was ascribing meanings to him that weren't necessarily there. And he'd said he was glad she was here. That had to count for something, right?

Realizing he was still staring at her as if she had two heads, she tried to find a subject that was straightforward—that would conceal the huge shift that had just happened inside of her. "What is your mom cooking?"

"Feijoada."

"I thought it smelled familiar. My mom used to fix that on special occasions. It was a lot of work, but it was so, so good."

"Well, my mom has three great loves in this life. My dad, sewing and cooking. Not necessarily in that order."

She grinned, not so sure why she was suddenly feeling so giddy.

It was supposed to be a fling—a one-night stand. Not true love.

Maybe it wasn't. Maybe she was mistaken. It could be the country itself that she was in love with. As in she would love to stay here.

But she couldn't. Her life was back home.

So where did that leave them? Nowhere. She had no real idea how Roque even felt about her.

Taking her hand, he towed her into the living room. He was at ease in this environment. And as he introduced her to aunts and uncles and three or four cousins, she spotted something on a tall shelving unit in the corner. As Roque continued talking to his relatives, she tugged her hand free, making her way over to the case, where trophies and ribbons and newspaper articles were encased in ornate frames.

She read the name on a couple of the awards and realized these were Roque's. All of them. From his football days. In one framed photograph, a very young-looking Roque stood with Enzo Dos Santos, who introduced him as Chutegol's newest player.

She glanced at Roque to find him watching her. He didn't look quite so carefree anymore as he made his way toward her. And that hitch in his step was a constant reminder of what had changed in his life.

He grimaced. "She treats it like a shrine. Refuses to throw it out. Any of it."

Amy's eyes widened. "You don't seriously want her to, do you? This is part of your life history. Your journey to where you are now."

"It's not relevant anymore. I'm not a fan of hanging on to things that are in the past. Or of saying long goodbyes to things I can't retrieve. I'd rather the cut be swift and final."

The almost brutal words jogged something inside of her. She tried to connect them with something, but couldn't find where to put them.

Just then Roque's mom called them to the dinner table.

She sat next to the orthopedist while seven other people gathered around the meal. In front of them were long wooden trays loaded with different types of meat and sausages. Rice and beans were in deep, black cauldron-like bowls. There were orange slices and shredded sautéed greens. And it looked like home. Like her mom. She blinked moisture from her eyes.

"Andre isn't back, but that's the life of a *polícia*. He'll understand if we start without him."

Claudia stood and served everyone, rather than passing bowls around the table like they might do in the States. When she got to Amy, she said, "Can I put a little of each on your plate, or is there something you don't like?"

"I think I will love all of it."

Including your son.

Soon they were all served and dug into their food. As she suspected, it was luscious and succulent and she was pretty sure she would have to waddle her way out of the house by the time it was all over. Claudia was a wonderful hostess, engaging everyone and making each person feel special.

Including Amy.

She'd half suspected the woman to try to match-make or make a sideways comment, but she never did. She just smiled and kept everyone's plates and glasses filled.

Maybe it was the wine, but as she looked around the table, she was suddenly glad she'd gone to see her uncle, hoped someday she could meet her cousins as well and have a little of what Roque's family seemed to have. They were full of happiness and hope and just plain love of life.

When Claudia tried to fill her glass again, she shook her head. "Thank you, but I am very, very full. It was all so delicious."

"Mamãe, would you excuse us? I want to give Amy a tour of the house."

"Of course." His mom lifted her glass and smiled over the top of it. "I'll make sure to call you if your father comes home."

He showed her the grounds and the various rooms of the house, taking her up the stairs, showing her the guest bedrooms before walking into his child-hood room. Once she was inside, he closed the door and leaned back against it while she looked around. Only in here there were no trophies or pictures of his various accomplishments in football. Instead, there were clippings of various medical cases he had helped with. Pictures of him graduating from medical school.

"*This* is my life. Not the football stuff. I want to live in the present, not cling to the past."

Amy turned to face him. He was speaking in rid-dles today, and she wasn't quite sure what any of it meant. But when he pushed away from the door and walked toward her, Amy's mouth went dry. He had the same look in his eye that he'd had the day they made love.

"Did I tell you how beautiful you look tonight?"

"No. But then I didn't tell you how handsome you look, either. But you do."

"I thought you didn't find me all that attractive."

"I lied."

He laughed, then reached for her hand and slowly reeled her in. "I've had a hard time taking my eyes off you all night."

Splaying her hands against his chest, she tipped her head back to look at that firm jaw, the slightest dusting of stubble across his chin making her want to slide her fingers across the scruff, let it tickle her cheek, her neck… Her lips parted as the thoughts continued.

"I didn't really want to give you a tour of the house, you know. I wanted to get you alone."

"You did?" She smiled. "I never would have guessed."

"I think that is yet another lie."

"Maybe." Happiness shimmered in her belly, making its rounds as it captured more and more of her doubts and locked them away. "Why did you want to get me alone?"

"So I could do this." His kiss took her by surprise. It wasn't the hard, desperate kisses from their night together. No, this was the slow brushing of lips. The touch and release that repeated over and over until she was breathless for more. He whispered her name, drawing it out in a low murmur that set her heart on fire, made her hope he actually felt something for her, despite what he'd told her in the courtyard at the hospital.

"I want to come to your house, after this. Say yes. Please." His hand came up and cupped her breast, thumb finding her nipple with a precision that made her breath catch. "Afterward I want to talk."

Talk. If his behavior right now was any indication of what he wanted to say to her, it couldn't be bad. Right? Because right now the man was burning red hot and setting her on fire right along with him.

"Yes. And I have something I want to tell you, too. I think I—"

A long pained scream from below shattered the intimacy in an instant.

"It's Mom."

He let her go and opened the door, hurrying down the stairs and leaving her to follow. When she got to the bottom Claudia was in Roque's arms sobbing uncontrollably, her choppy speech too broken up for her to follow.

And then Roque's eyes came up, and in them was a kind of pain she'd never seen before.

"My father has been shot."

CHAPTER ELEVEN

ROQUE DIDN'T CALL her like he'd said he would when he'd dropped her off at her house on his way to the hospital. And as the hours grew longer she became more and more concerned. She'd offered to go with him, but he thanked her and said he needed to be with his family right now, effectively shutting her out.

She didn't think he meant to; he was just in a hurry. Completely understandable. He was worried.

Well, so was she. She cared about his parents, too. Maybe more than she should.

And she'd been almost convinced he cared about her, too, after the way he talked to her in the bedroom.

She finally gave up waiting and tried to call his cell phone, but it went straight to voice mail after one ring. She didn't leave a message. There was no need. He would know what she wanted. She decided to just go up there instead. She could at least show him support, even if he had to stay by his father's bedside.

Or was it too late? Had he died, and they were all trying to come to terms with it? Seeing Claudia broken and weeping in her son's arms had torn her heart in two. She'd felt helpless, unsure what to do.

She still did.

And that look in Roque's eyes...

She saw it every time she blinked. The despair. The horror.

Calling a taxi, she went to the elevator, glancing at Lara's door and remembering the day of the party and how her eyes had widened when she saw Roque standing in the corridor with her. How embarrassed she'd been.

It seemed like forever ago. And now it was almost over. The goodbye party was rushing toward them at breakneck speed, and once that happened she would have one more day before she boarded a flight taking her back to the States.

And she hadn't told Roque how she felt. She'd started to in the bedroom just before he got the news about his father. And she certainly couldn't do it now.

The taxi ride took a mere ten minutes, but it seemed like hours. The closer they got, the more uneasy she became. If he'd wanted her there, he wouldn't have taken the time to drop her off at the house; he would have just gone straight to the hospital.

Unimportant. Inconsequential.

He'd never taken those words back.

Roque had been a star footballer. He was probably used to adulation and women throwing themselves at him.

Do you really think he could fall for someone like you?

The insecurities she'd felt when she first came to

Brazil surfaced all over again: What did she think she was doing here?

But the taxi had pulled up outside of the hospital, so it was too late to turn around. So swallowing, she got out of the vehicle and paid the driver before slowly walking toward the entrance of the hospital.

She spotted Roque immediately; he was sitting in one of the chairs facing the glassed-in entrance to the emergency room, his head between his hands. No one else was around him.

Oh, God. Had his father died? He was a police officer, one of the most dangerous jobs in all of Brazil. She hesitated by the door, trying to decide whether or not she should intrude. Then his head came up and he speared her with a look. He looked neither angry nor glad. He just looked…empty.

She slowly made her way over, clasping her hands together. She sat, leaving one chair in between them, just in case he really didn't want her there.

He sucked in a deep breath and blew it out. "I saw that you called."

Amy had assumed he was busy with his father or trying to comfort his mother. But maybe he just hadn't wanted to talk to her. "I didn't leave a message. I figured you had other things to think about." She hesitated. "How is he?"

"He's in surgery. They don't know if he's going to make it or not." He swore softly. "He went into one of the *favelas* to make an arrest and there was a shoot-out. A bullet nicked his femoral artery. He almost bled out at the scene. His heart stopped on the ride over."

"I'm so sorry. Your mom…?"

He looked away. "She's in the chapel, praying."

And Roque was not. He was out here. Alone.

The people who were at the house were nowhere to be seen. Maybe they were in the chapel with his mom.

She wanted to touch his hand, but the space between them seemed too great, and not just in terms of physical space. There was something distant in his attitude. Maybe it was just fear and worry.

"What can I do?"

"Nothing. If he lives, he'll have a long recovery ahead of him. That has to take priority for me." He turned to look at her. "I've asked to be replaced for the rest of the lecture series, so you'll be working with someone else for the remainder of your stay. I probably won't be at the sendoff party. Or see you before you leave. I'm sorry about that."

He was sorry that he wouldn't be there to see her leave? But not about the fact that she *was* leaving? That he might never see her again?

She was being selfish. The man's father might die, for God's sake. She could always talk to him on the phone before she left.

And maybe it would go straight to voice mail like it had tonight.

What had he said back at the house?

His voice ran through her head as if he were reciting the words all over again: *"I'm not a fan of hanging on to things that are in the past. Or of saying long goodbyes to things I can't retrieve. I'd rather the cut be swift and final."*

He hadn't offered to keep her updated on how his dad was doing, while she was here or once she left Brazil.

Her stomach cramped with grief.

She wasn't going to sit by the phone and wait, though. Not this time. Evidently ghosting could occur while the person was sitting right beside you.

She stood. "I understand. You need to be here with your dad. Please tell your mom that I'm thinking about her and hope Andre will be okay."

"Thank you."

Amy looked at him for a long time, committing the lines and planes of his face to memory. Then in a soft voice she said, "Goodbye, Roque."

And with that, she turned and walked away.

She was right. He didn't contact her—although she had heard that his father pulled through his surgery. Nor had he come to see the final days of Enzo's physical therapy treatments. And he was nowhere to be seen at the party, which was now in full swing.

These festivities didn't seem as new or full of hope as the welcome party had. Amy could see Francisco Carvalho chatting quietly to Krysta, his face full of sadness. And her friend told her that Flávia had been bitten by a venomous snake not long ago and had almost died. Thankfully she'd made an almost miraculous recovery. Amy hoped there were enough miracles floating around to touch Roque's dad in his long rehabilitation. She still wished Roque well. Despite a heart that was swollen and heavy. Of all the people to fall in love with.

All she could do was go home and do her best to forget him. Pack him away like that white eyelet dress of hers.

She could throw herself into her doctoral studies where she had no time to think about anything except school. Roque was right about one thing: letting go of the past. She'd held on to her parents' home for far too long, treating it almost like a shrine, the way Roque's mom did with his football memorabilia. She loved her mom and dad and they would always be with her, but she needed to make a fresh start. Maybe even in another part of the country.

This time she could do things right and not hold on to what she couldn't have. So, taking one last look around the swanky decor with its loud music and sad goodbyes, she looked for the nearest exit and showed herself out.

Roque's dad was finally out of the woods after three grueling weeks of advances and setbacks. He was going to have to go through cardiac rehab to strengthen the damaged muscle in his heart, and it would take months before he could go back to work, and that might not even happen if he couldn't recover enough of his strength. But he was nearing retirement age and was thinking about just handing in his badge and drawing his pension. It was certainly what his mom wanted.

And what did Roque want?

He knew he hadn't been exactly welcoming when Amy came to the hospital, but his thoughts had been so chaotic he hadn't had time to think. His dad's surgery had made him realize how uncertain life was. How painful endings could be. As he'd sat in the waiting room his thoughts had turned to Amy right about the time her call came through.

When Roque's own injury had sidelined him, he'd tried his damnedest to hold on to his old life, convincing himself that he was going to play football again. It had taken the reality of using a walker for months, and a visit from Enzo Dos Santos, to make him realize he needed to let go.

Which is what he'd needed to do with Amy. She had her whole life ahead of her. Her whole career. He told her he knew she was going to get her doctorate one day, and she said she was planning to start working on it when she got home. She couldn't do that if he was sitting there clinging to her, like he'd clung to his football dreams.

He'd had no business sleeping with her. Or anything else. It had been rash and irresponsible, and if he'd followed through with what he'd been about to tell her in his childhood bedroom, he could have derailed her life. It had been on the tip of his tongue to ask her to stay in Brazil. With him.

He realized as he was sitting at his mother's dinner table that he loved the woman. In a way that he couldn't say of any other woman. Not even Halee.

And as his mom sat in the chapel of the hospital, begging her husband to stay with her, begging God to keep him there by any means necessary, he knew he couldn't do the same with Amy. He wasn't going to ask some deity to make her stay, wasn't going to make promises he couldn't keep.

He was going to let her go. *Because* he loved her. Because he wanted her life to be as rich and full as it could be. His life before his accident had been selfish and self-serving. He thought he'd grown past all of that. Until he realized he'd be going back to his old ways if he asked her to stay.

There was a knock at his office door. He grunted at whoever it was to come in, only to meet his mom's chiding face.

"Roquinho, is this how you greet your mother?"

"I'm sorry. Is Papai okay?"

"He is in rehab and doesn't want me there. He can't stand for me to see him weak. What he doesn't know is that he's the strongest man I've ever met." She leaned over his desk, her hands planted on its surface. "And I thought you were just like him. But now I am not so sure."

He barely kept himself from rolling his eyes. He knew exactly where she was headed with this. "She's going to continue her education, Mamãe. I'm not going to keep her from her dreams."

"Did you *ask* her what her dreams were?"

"I already know what they are."

"So you didn't. And when you were hiding in your bedroom with her? Why did you not ask her then?"

He couldn't hold back a laugh. "How did you know where we were?"

"I know where all young men want to go with a pretty woman. One they're in love with." She dropped into the chair in front of his desk. "Don't try to deny it."

He gritted his teeth and forced his way through. He did not want to talk right now. Not about Amy. Not about anything. He wanted to work.

"It changes nothing."

She leaned forward. "Why not ask her?"

"I already told you. I know what she wants." He picked up a pencil and twirled it between his fingers. "Asking her to give that up would be selfish."

"Why would you ask her to give it up? A...what did you say? Doctorate? It takes how long to get?"

"I don't know. Three years. Why?"

She blinked. "Oh, Roquinho. Don't you see? Three years is not such a long time."

"I don't see how any of this—"

She held up her hand. "She left Brazil to pursue her dream, yes? So why can you not leave Brazil... to pursue *her*?"

He sat back in his chair, the creaky wheels in his head starting to turn again. For someone who was not even a surgeon, his mom had cut clean through to the heart of the matter. Why couldn't he go to the States to be with her, while she worked on her degree? With his credentials, he could probably do something while he was there, maybe even research how to get his certification in the States. But that wasn't what was important; it was something that could be decided afterward. Once they both got what they wanted: Amy her degree and a fulfilling career. And maybe Roque…could somehow, in some weird twist of the universe, get Amy.

If she would even have him after the way he'd brushed her off.

All he could do was try. The question was, was he willing to?

Yes.

He came around the desk and took his mom's wise face in his hands, giving her a hard kiss on the cheek. "Have I ever told you how glad I am that you're my mother?"

"I think you just did."

She stood up and hugged him tightly. When she let him go, he saw tears in her eyes.

"Now, go. And tell her I would like to work on another of her dresses. This time it will be white with layers and layers of lace."

"I'll tell her. I promise."

CHAPTER TWELVE

AMY SAT IN her first day of classes, trying to concentrate on what the professor was saying. But even two months post-Roque, her thoughts still returned toward him. And it made her furious.

He doesn't love you, Amy. Get over it.

He would have made some effort to contact her if he felt anything at all. She'd been so, so sure that he cared when he kissed her that last time in his bedroom. But she'd given him every opportunity to say something. And instead there was only silence. A silence which continued even now.

Class was dismissed, and she headed out to the parking lot, slinging her book bag over her shoulder. Getting her degree seemed so worthless right now. *Right now* being the operative words. Once she stopped daydreaming about a certain Brazilian orthopedic surgeon and stopped seeing him at every turn, like at that lamppost over there.

She rolled her eyes, until she realized she'd never actually seen him teleported from her head to a physical location. Looking again, thinking she'd just mistaken someone else for him, she stopped dead in her tracks when she realized she wasn't mistaken. And he hadn't teleported.

He was here. In Florida, looking just as outrageously gorgeous as he had in Brazil.

Then he smiled. And, just like always, something inside of her somersaulted.

What was he doing here? Was he at a conference?

Maybe—but that didn't answer the question. Why was he *here*? At the university where she just happened to be studying.

He pushed away from the post and walked toward her, his cane nowhere to be seen.

"Is…is your dad okay?"

"He's still in rehab. And retiring from the force, which makes my mother very happy."

"I'm so glad." And she was. She knew Andre had survived his surgery, but the last news she'd heard after that was that it was still touch and go.

She had been in contact with Krysta and Flávia, and it seemed she wasn't the only one who'd had man trouble while in Brazil. She'd been too busy with her own love life to realize that her two friends were also sliding down the same slippery slope she'd been stuck on.

She hoped they both got their happy endings, but as for her, she'd been so sure she wouldn't be one of them…

Except Roque was here.

"Let's try that again, shall we?" The smile was still in place. "Hello, Amy."

"Hi."

Good going—you couldn't think of anything more profound than that?

"You look good. You've started on your studies obviously." He nodded at her bag.

"I have." Why wasn't he telling her why he was here? Was he trying to torture her? Had she left something behind in Brazil?

Ha! She had. But it wasn't something you could pack in a bag and carry through customs.

"Can we walk?" The last word stuck in her throat. She remembered the last time she'd suggested they do that. It had been to say that sleeping together had been a mistake. And it evidently had been. But try as she might, she couldn't make herself regret the short amount of time they'd spent together. She'd hold it with her for the rest of her life, just like that shrine Roque's mom had made out of his football artifacts. Because he was wrong. Some things shouldn't be tossed away as if they never existed.

He fell into step beside her, that little hitch of his still in evidence. But she loved it. Still loved everything about him.

"I don't know where to start. Other than to say I was wrong."

"Wrong?"

"Wrong to not call you. Wrong to not try to work out some kind of alternate solution for a very real problem."

She stopped, her heart flipping around in her chest. "What problem is that?"

"The fact that I live in Brazil, and you live in Florida." He smiled. "It took my mom to make me realize that it's not such a big problem at all."

Was he kidding? This wasn't just a matter of physical distance. He'd been like a water spigot. On one second and off the next.

"But you were hot, then cold, and now... I'm very confused." Her mind was still stuck somewhere behind her and was pedaling as fast as it could to catch up. "I thought you weren't a fan of long goodbyes."

"I'm not. But I was mistaken in thinking this had to be goodbye at all."

And just like that, the spigot was on again. She wasn't sure she'd be able to survive if he suddenly turned it back off. She needed to be sure. Very sure.

"Are you saying you don't want it to be?"

His fingers bracketed her face, and her eyes shut at the exquisiteness of feeling his skin on hers once again. "No. I don't want it to be."

"But how can you be sure? You were so distant at the hospital."

He gave a pained laugh. "Part of it was the shock of the shooting, but part of it was the realization that your future was half a world away from mine. I was trying to do the right thing and let you walk out of my life."

"Try? You were very good at it, from what I remember."

"I know. And you don't know how many times I've regretted it. Am I too late?"

No, he wasn't. And hearing his explanation made

all the missing pieces fall into place. She finally understood why he'd seemed so distant. So completely unmoved by her presence. She'd done quite a bit of pretending herself over the course of her time in Brazil. Suddenly she knew what she was going to do. He'd sacrificed something. Maybe it was time for her to do the same.

"I can drop out of the program. I only just started and—"

"No. You're not going to do that. I want you to finish."

She reveled in his words, his touch…his very presence. In those talented hands that were bringing hope back to life. "I don't want you to feel you have to wait for me, though."

"My grasp of English is not always good, but I think if we change out one little word, it will make more sense. I'm not going to wait *for* you, Amy. I'm going to wait *with* you. Here in Florida." He stopped for a second. "I love you. I was wrong not to say the words earlier, to let you go the way I did. Once I realized the truth, there was still my visa to get and flights to be arranged. What I had to say couldn't be said over the phone, which is why I didn't call you."

He kissed her cheek. "I'm hoping maybe you feel a little something for me, too."

There were a couple more things she needed to understand, although she was pretty sure she already knew the answers.

"You called our time together unimportant."

"Yes. I knew that I'd chosen the wrong word. Because it wasn't unimportant. It turned out to be the most important thing I'd ever done in my life. More important than my football days. More important than my medical career. I found love, when I thought I never would again."

She shut her eyes, and when she reopened them, he was still there, the imprint of his lips still fresh on her face. "You crazy, gorgeous surgeon, I do love you. You had to realize."

"I thought I had. But when my dad was shot, I realized I didn't want you giving everything up for me. But you don't have to."

She thought for a moment. But that still left… "I don't want you giving everything up for me, either."

"That is a bridge we can cross in three years. When you walk down the aisle of the university and hold your degree in your hands."

He was really going to do it. He was moving here. For her. Because of her. With her. There were all kinds of prepositions she could substitute that would each end with her being with the man she loved.

"Paulista let you leave?"

"They did not have a choice. I was coming, whether they liked it or not. But the administrator assured me that I would have a job waiting if I ever decided to come back."

If he ever. "You mean you might stay here? For good?"

"It's a possibility. I actually contacted a nearby hospital and asked what the process would be to have my medical license transferred over. They want me to come in for talks. But I didn't want to commit unless I know where your heart is."

"That's the easiest question of all, Roque. My heart is wherever you are. I love you."

He leaned over and kissed her, this time on the lips, right there in the parking lot of the university. The world around them was still turning, but she felt like this moment was suspended in time. When he finally raised his head, he said, "Before I forget. My mom has a message for you."

"She does?"

"She wants you to know that she has dreams of her own. Of working on another of your dresses. Only this one would be all white and would see me waiting for you at the end of another kind of aisle."

He reached in his pocket and fished out a little velvet container. But when he started to go down on one knee, she stopped him. "Your leg."

"My leg will survive. Let me do this." He knelt in front of her and snapped open the lid of the box. Inside was a gorgeous ring, a center diamond flanked by two glowing emeralds. "Amy Woodell, will you marry me? Both here and in Brazil?"

"Yes. Oh, yes! I'll marry you wherever you want."

"We can have the ring resized, but I wanted to bring it." He plucked it from its velvet bed and slid it onto her finger. It fit almost perfectly. "I love it." She couldn't stop looking at it, almost too afraid to believe this was happening.

"Amy?"

"Yes?" She shifted her attention back where he was still kneeling in front of her.

"When you're done admiring that, I may have overestimated the abilities of my leg."

She stared at him, then realized what he meant and burst out laughing. Laughter she tried her best to suppress. It was no good. In between chuckles, she managed to get out, "Here. Let me help."

She hauled him to his feet, and soon all thoughts of laughter were swept away by the power of Roque's kiss.

And by the very strength of his love.

EPILOGUE

AMY WAS NOT the bride. Not this time, anyway.

That had happened six months earlier, and Claudia had indeed made her dress.

But she *was* one of the bridesmaids at this particular ceremony, as was Flávia. Her two lecture series friends had also gotten their happy endings, and she was thrilled for them both.

Krysta and Francisco stood in an intimate circle of their family and closest friends and repeated the vows they'd written to each other, their voices ringing with happiness and conviction.

Roque gripped her hand tightly, leaning slightly on his cane today. But it was okay. They'd each learned to provide support to the other when it was needed the most.

Krysta's wedding was much different from her own, but it was still beautiful, their love for each other permeating the air around them.

She glanced to her right and caught sight of Flávia holding her baby against her chest, her husband's arm around her shoulders. No one had realized the venom specialist was pregnant during the last part of their stay in Brazil, not even the man standing next to her.

Those days spent together at Paulista seemed like an eternity ago. But the hospital's pull on them was still strong, the bonds forged during their time together proving to be unbreakable. Unlike Roque's words, she didn't want to say goodbye to that past, since it had played a role in the future they were carving out together.

And whether they decided to come back to Brazil after she earned her degree or stay in the States, she knew it wouldn't matter one way or the other as long as they were together.

Evidently the other two couples felt the same way, because standing in a simple garden in a small Brazilian town near where Francisco's family lived, the friends were bearing witness to a love they'd all found.

The officiating minister lifted his right hand and pronounced Krysta and Francisco husband and wife. And when he invited the bride and groom to kiss, it wasn't the only kiss that was had in that tiny garden.

And it wouldn't be the only kiss in the days to come. For Brazil had woven a tapestry of love and friendship in their lives that would endure long after they said their goodbyes and left for different parts of the world.

Because that was what love did.

It endured. For always.

* * * * *

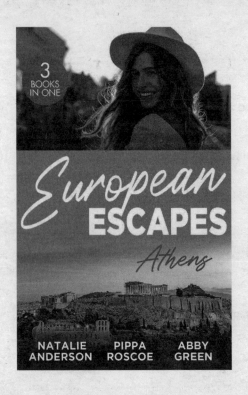

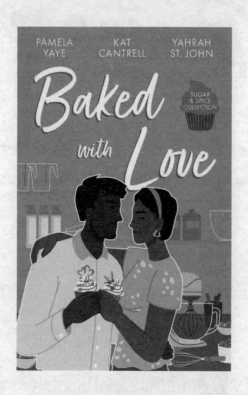

LET'S TALK
Romance

For exclusive extracts, competitions and special offers, find us online:

f MillsandBoon

X @MillsandBoon

⊙ @MillsandBoonUK

♪ @MillsandBoonUK

Get in touch on 01413 063 232